ALSO BY DANIEL WATERS

*Generation Dead*

*Kiss of Life*

# PASSING STRANGE

## DANIEL WATERS

SIMON AND SCHUSTER

A **pulse** book

First published in Great Britain in 2010 by Simon and Schuster UK Ltd
1st Floor, 222 Gray's Inn Road, London, WC1X 8HB
A CBS COMPANY

Originally published in the USA by Hyperion Books for Children,
an imprint of Disney Book Group, New York, 2010

Text copyright © by Daniel Waters 2010

1 3 5 7 9 10 8 6 4 2

Simon Pulse, and colophon are registered trademarks of
Simon & Schuster UK Ltd.

A CIP catalogue record for this book is available from the British Library

ISBN: 978-1-84738-960-2

This book is a work of fiction. Names, characters, places and
incidents are either the product of the author's imagination or are
used fictitiously. Any resemblance to actual people living
or dead, events or locales is entirely coincidental.

Printed by CPI Cox & Wyman, Reading RG1 8EX

*For my parents, Jeff and Elaine*

# PASSING STRANGE

# CHAPTER ONE

I DON'T WANT TO DIE, I thought. Not again.

I was on my knees. The man with the gun was saying something, but my head was a nest of buzzing wasps, their wings vibrating against the inside of my skull. White light filled my eyes, and the pitch of the man's screaming rose to match the humming in my brain.

We can be killed. "Reterminated." My friend Evan was reterminated not all that long ago.

No one knows why we started coming back, or why only teens have a chance of returning. There are theories of course— mold spores, bovine growth hormones in the food, you name it—but no real answers. Conventional wisdom states that suicides don't come back, but I'm unliving proof that isn't the case.

When I was alive I wanted to be dead, and so I committed suicide. Now that I was dead, all I wanted was to feel alive again.

I guess the irony struck me in a funny way. Maybe I laughed, I don't know. Laughing takes effort for my people. I must have moved, though, because the shrill man shot me. Bullet Number Three. I'd already been shot in the back and in the face. I couldn't feel the new shot, not as pain, anyhow, but as a vague dull pressure that was there and then it wasn't. I actually saw the bullet pass out of my body high on the chest, just below my collarbone.

A spray of dark fluid hit the asphalt, and for a crazy moment I thought of my little sister, Kaitlyn, blowing grape juice through her sippy straw. The wasps in my head scattered, as though they were escaping through the hole the bullet had made in my body. I started to think again. How did it come to this?

We—the Sons (and Daughter) of Romero—Takayuki, Popeye, and Tayshawn—and I—had been setting up an art installation on the lawn of St. Jude's Cathedral when the police arrived. Popeye had this grand idea that was going to be his greatest "artwork" yet. We were going to put some raggy-looking figures—the meek, the poor, the zombies—on the lawn of St. Jude's, a little ways away from the manger scene. The zombie figures would be these forlorn, wretched-looking creatures, all tattered and bent, and they'd be in darkness, away from the bright lights and warm colors of the manger. One of them, its neck bent, would be looking over at the manger, at the kings and animals and the Holy Family. It was supposed to represent a couple of things, in Popeye's mind—the dissociation we zombies feel from religion, and the longing many of us have to rejoin that community.

I've kind of felt that way myself for a long time—I was brought up Catholic—so it made sense for me to participate. I wasn't sure why my friend Takayuki helped, though. Tak's feelings are more extreme. He doesn't think we've been rejected by a church or a religion. Tak thinks we've been rejected by God.

"I told you not to move!" the policeman yelled, his words coherent, now. I couldn't see him through the light he was shining in my face, but I imagined that the gun was shaking in his hands. Adrenaline and fear would be twin rivers raging in his bloodstream. "Put your hands on your head!"

The commands seemed contradictory, but I did my best to comply. I'd covered my face with my hands, acting on some primal survival instinct that kicked in and urged me to hide my true nature from the world. I dropped my hands and raised my chin, letting the white light bathe my ruined face. I didn't take any satisfaction in the policeman's horrified gasp. My friend Tak—he has a section of his cheek missing, so when he brushes his long hair back you can see his teeth and everything; it's pretty gross—loved to get a rise out of the beating hearts with his visible zombie-isms. Not me. I liked to get a rise out of them in other ways. I'm quite attractive for a dead girl.

*Was* attractive, anyhow. When I exposed my face, the cop flinched like he was looking at still-quivering roadkill.

I think I was hit by the very first bullet the cops fired—and they fired quite a few. Why they singled me out as Zombie Enemy Number One is a mystery, especially when you have scary old Tak and Popeye all in leather, like extras from *The Matrix*, and you've got George—poor George, the most zombified of all zombies—trundling down the hill right *at* them.

Regardless, it was me that got it first. That one I could almost feel: a short slap in the face, much like the one my mother gave me when I told her who I was in love with.

Some slap. I went over backward and wrecked most of Popeye's diorama as I went down.

Time stopped for a moment when I hit the ground. I saw Popeye moving off to my right; I thought I could see another pair of bullets suspended above me, frozen in mid-flight, but then I blinked and they were gone. I guess the world really was going all Matrix-y! I realized what had happened and what was still happening, and the first thing I did?

I touched my face.

What a vain little tramp I am.

The bullet had struck my cheek about an inch and a half below my eye. I pushed against my cheekbone and there was a sickening moment where my face gave, and it was like pressing against a rubber bag filled with sand or broken shells. I could hear my bones rasp against each other as I pushed, and I jerked my hand back after finding the hole the bullet made with the tip of my index finger. My fingers were wet with a bluish fluid. Zombie blood, I guess. Yuck.

So much for leaving a pretty corpse.

I can't say if the police followed appropriate procedure or not. I know they're supposed to identify themselves first, which they did (as though the wailing sirens and flashing lights weren't enough of a clue), but beyond that it seems like their response to us was a little . . . excessive. I don't really think that the Winford police are trigger-happy gunmen eager to draw down on shoplifters and jaywalkers, but who knows what training they've received with regard to the living dead? Maybe zombies show up next to rabid dogs and multiple murderers in their policing manuals, and maybe it isn't considered deadly force if the target is already dead.

More than anything else, I think they were just scared.

I stared at my bluish fingers for a long moment. Tak was yelling to me from somewhere, and I saw Tayshawn running away, but it was hard to see because my left eye wasn't sitting right anymore, so when I started running again I did so without looking back. I went about ten yards and got hit again, high on my back. There was a spray of bluish fluid. The impact, and the shock of seeing part of my body *outside* my body, made me lose my balance, and I pitched forward on my face.

I took my time getting up, and to be honest there was a moment where I thought it would be a lot easier—and a lot better—if I just let the stupid cops catch me and that would be the end of it. But then time sort of slowed down again and I started thinking about all the people who depended on me— Phoebe, Tommy, Adam, Sylvia, Colette, Tak and the boys, my parents, Katy—I didn't think about anyone else. The thing about depression is, all you can think about is the pain. The pain grows and pulses and becomes so large, it blots out any thoughts of friends or family. Eventually it can grow so large, it even blots out your self.

But now, in that moment, I was thinking of the people I

knew and loved. I was thinking how sad they'd be if I was retermed.

The death of a loved one is one of the few things that can create a pain similar to depression in the non-depressed. I didn't want anyone to be sad—I *don't* want anyone to be sad—and then I realized how sad I'd be, if *everyone* was sad. The worst, absolute worst, thing about coming back from death was when my father asked me why. *Why, Karen, why did you do it?* And when I tried to put it into words, it sounded like the most awful, most self-serving answer ever—because in a way, it was.

So I kept going. I didn't get up, because I didn't want to get shot again. Getting shot wasn't pleasant at all. I crawled as fast as I could for this big thick tree that had a short hedge around it. I stood up when I reached the tree, then started running. I had to run with my hand on my face because the shattered pieces were grating against each other. I ran in an almost straight line, trying to keep the tree between me and the police, who'd stopped shooting. Probably because they were busy with poor George.

I made it off the church property and into the residential section beyond, where rows of old white New England homes stood. A dog barked at me. A screen door slammed. I ran through a yard that had plastic toddler toys strewn about like the remnants of Popeye's art installation, then slid through a gap in the hedge and into the empty street beyond.

Where this policeman, the one with the bright lights and itchy trigger finger, was waiting for me.

I really didn't want to die again.

A headshot would do it. That was the one thing all those movies predicted correctly. "Shoot it in the head."

I drew air into my lungs, even though I don't have to. My eyes were wide open. The first time I died I'd been unconscious, drifting away from the shores of life on an ocean of pain and sleeping pills. If I had to die again, I wanted to see it coming.

But the cop lowered his gun. It was hard to see in the glare of his headlights and with one eye not sitting properly, but I could tell that he was whispering to himself. He might have even made the sign of the cross.

But that could be my imagination, I thought, because who would make the sign of the cross while holding a gun?

It was so quiet now that the hornets were gone and the sirens were off.

He walked toward me, gun lowered but still at his side. The policeman was about my father's age; a square, stocky man with a mustache and tired eyes. The hands holding the gun that shot me *were* shaking, after all. I could hear him breathing from twenty feet away. He looked horrified, sick to his stomach.

"I used to be pretty," I said.

My words had a strange effect on him. If he'd been a sworn enemy of zombies, he probably would have put the next bullet into my brainpan—*shoot it in the head, shoot it in the head*—and that would be the end of me.

But he didn't shoot.

"Get up," he said, voice as shaky as his hands. His eyes looked moist.

Still on my knees, I waited. Was he looking for an excuse?

Something that would let him feel justified about his actions when he lay down to sleep at night, or when he was back at the station, regaling everyone with tales of his anti-zombie heroism?

Maybe he could sense what I was thinking, because his voice was whisper soft. "Get up," he said. "Please."

I rose, my movements slow and deliberate. I risked putting my hand over my damaged eye socket, because the world didn't look the way it was supposed to when it wasn't covered. With my good eye I searched the policeman's face for intent, not certain what I would find there. Disgust? Pity? Contempt?

"Go on," he said, waving across the street with his gun hand. "Get out of here."

I decided that he looked more sad than anything.

Maybe he knew a zombie, I thought. Maybe his wife's cousin's friend's sister was a zombie.

Or maybe he'd just come to the realization that the thing that he'd just fired a bullet into wasn't a thing at all, but a *person*. A dead person, but a person nonetheless.

I felt a little unsteady on my feet, but I also felt something I hadn't felt in a long time. I felt energized, as if the slugs that had hit me had triggered some inner wellspring of power within.

"Thank you," I said, facing him. I brought my free hand across my body and covered the hole his bullet had made. I don't know if I was trying to alleviate his guilt or encourage it.

He didn't say anything, just gave me the slightest tilt of his chin. A muscle in his jaw flexed, and he swallowed rapidly, his Adam's apple bobbing up and down the length of his throat.

I became aware of every gesture of his life, every physiological nuance. In the deep rasp of his breathing, the rise and fall of his chest, I was acutely aware of how alive he was.

He didn't look right at me, but he didn't turn away, either.

I crossed the street. Sirens kicked in from another part of the city, and I figured that the blaring whine signified that the other cops were on their way to the station with George and whomever else they'd caught. Melissa maybe—she's a zombie who had taken sanctuary in the church. She'd had the misfortune of coming out just before the shooting started.

I guess not everyone could be as lucky as me.

So much was going through my head. Why had this happened? Why did they start shooting? Why didn't they just let us surrender?

I quickened my pace but still chose my steps with care.

There was nowhere else to go, so I walked home.

# CHAPTER TWO

I
T WAS A LONG WALK FROM
Winford to Oakvale, especially
after being shot three times. It
was weird, too, because I didn't feel anything. There wasn't
any pain—physical pain, anyhow—from the two wounds in
my body or the even more gruesome one in my face. The flow
of blue fluid seemed to have stopped, but I wasn't sure that
was a good thing. I was moving very slowly, too, which was
scaring me, because most days I can beat a slow trad in a foot-
race. I started to think really bad thoughts, and I couldn't help
but wonder if each step I took would be my last. We aren't
even supposed to be up and walking around; maybe there were
methods other than headshots to shut us off.

I took my time once I reached the Oxoboxo woods. I knew
I should have gone straight to the Haunted House to warn my
friends, but I was too scared. My friends think I'm this incredibly brave person for all of the odd things I do, but it's all

show. *All* show. I'm one of the most cowardly people to walk the earth; most certainly the most cowardly person to walk the earth twice. For the things that count I'm just a scared little girl. The police could have been over there right then, rounding up all of my friends or worse, and what was I doing? Hiding. Cowering in the brush, afraid to be seen. Always hiding, that's little Miss Karen DeSonne.

I watched the sun rise from the relative safety of the trees. There were shorter routes I could have taken home but I wasn't prepared to see living people just yet. At one point I stumbled and tried willing my body to get up, but it just wasn't listening.

I don't want to die again, I thought. I'm sorry. Over and over. The sentiment was becoming my mantra. I might even have been saying it out loud while crawling along the frozen ground toward my house.

*I don't want to die again I'm sorry I don't want to die again I'm sorry I don't want to die . . .*

And then I was there, on my own private doorstep at the back of my house.

Dad had a door installed there so I could come and go as I pleased without disturbing anyone above. Sort of like a doggy door for his dead daughter. I'm quite nocturnal. I think Mom would just as soon have barred all the doors and windows to keep me out, but Dad does what he can to improve my quality of "life." One of the first things that he twigged to was how restless I'd get at night when everyone in the world is supposed to be asleep. We talked about it a little and he thought it might be better for me if I made use of the small hours, and I told him about my friends and the Haunted House and everything, and he must have thought it was a good thing for me to spend my time with others like me. "You need friends," I think is what he actually said.

Sometimes he'd drop little pieces of regret like that into our conversations, because I know that what he was saying was that I'd needed friends, past tense, as in "when I was alive." As though my lack of friends was his fault or his responsibility.

One of the worst things about killing yourself and coming back is seeing how everyone around you assumes responsibility for your selfish act. "If only I'd said, if only I'd done . . ." *I* wasn't even really responsible for it at the end; how could they be? I mean, obviously I had some kind of sickness, some mental imbalance. How could they know?

I think that's why my mom avoids me now—the guilt. It makes people angry and it makes people cold. That part of it *is* my fault.

I saw that the back porch light was on. Right after I'd started spending my nights and early mornings at the Haunted House, I'd start noticing all of these little signs that, dead or not, someone was still worried about me. Someone still cared. Lights that had been doused when I left the house were turned on. Magazines and books were moved from coffee table to couch. A milk-stained glass would appear in the sink.

Mom doesn't drink milk.

I let myself in and dragged myself into my basement abode. Phoebe tells me that my room is musty (it is a basement, after all), and for her to say anything at all, it must be really bad. The room probably smells because it flooded a few years ago and never really dried out properly. My room is dank. Dank and rank. And it stank. I call it the tomb.

I sat down at the vanity opposite my bed and looked at myself in the mirror. You would have thought I'd have other concerns at that moment—concerns about my friends and my family, concerns that I wasn't the only one shot and pursued by angry authorities, but no.

I was concerned with what I looked like.

The damage was much worse than I'd even imagined. It was as if I were looking at myself through a broken mirror, but it wasn't the mirror that was broken. It was me.

Half of my face was pushed in, the white skin of my cheek all mottled and stained dark blue from the weird zombie blood. I suppose there'd have been swelling if I were alive, but instead my face seemed deflated, and all sorts of strange things happened with the muscles in my face when I frowned. Atop my newly hideous face sat a platinum blond fright wig that looked as if it had been used to sweep the forest floor.

I don't know how long I sat there, staring at myself. Pretty long, I guess.

Eventually I remembered I'd been shot three times, that the wreck of my face wasn't the only damage. I reached for the third button on my blouse—the first two weren't buttoned, naturally—and then decided to just rip the shirt open, popping half the buttons off as I did.

Why not? It wasn't like I'd be wearing it again, anyhow, with it full of bullet holes.

I was full of bullet holes, too. Swiss cheese.

A round hole, the same color as my bra, was above my left breast. There was a second hole, this one an exit wound, higher up and further to the left, just under my clavicle. I turned in the mirror and saw where the bullet had gone in. There was no exit wound for the bullet that hit my face, meaning it was still rattling around somewhere inside me.

I put my index finger over the first hole. Adam's life had bled out of a hole very similar to that one. I thought it looked as if it had gone through at an upward angle, which I took to mean that whoever fired it was trying to kill me with a head-shot. Nice. I looked a thousand times worse than Tak, and a couple dozen times scarier than George. Worse even than poor Sylvia.

Sylvia, I thought, somewhat guiltily. Here I was fretting and moaning about my shattered face, and that poor girl had been taken apart—literally—and was supposedly being put back together, Dumpty-esque, by all the king's horses and all the king's men. Well, by Alish and Angela Hunter, anyhow, and the other witch doctors at the Hunter Foundation. I didn't think I'd be around when the Hunters released her in a few weeks. Assuming, of course, that they had any real intention of releasing her at all.

I heard the floorboards—my ceiling—creaking as some-one—my father, most likely—began to shuffle around the kitchen. Before his morning coffee my father walked not unlike a zombie, whereas my mother was swift from the moment she sprang out of bed.

And then I heard the *thump thump thump* of tiny feet, and panicked.

Every morning upon waking, Kaitlyn runs down the hall and the two flights of stairs that separate our bedrooms to come see me in my cellar lair. It drove my mother crazy, I'm sure. On the rare occasions I'd come upstairs before she left for work, I'd see Mom bustling about, her movements clipped, her mouth a thin line. Dad was usually a bit more generous; he would at least say good morning, and might even make some small talk if the caffeine had kicked in. But Kaitlyn—Kaitlyn was consistent in the morning.

Kaitlyn's thumping was getting closer—she would be at the cellar door soon.

I couldn't let her see me like this.

My quarters didn't offer much in the way of hiding places; the only option I had was the closet beneath the stairs, which was usually filled with Christmas ornaments and decorations, but now held only the empty boxes and bins they spent the other eleven months of the year packed away in. I ran to the closet just as I heard the cellar door swing open, and I went inside, hoping that the boxes I was forced to lean against didn't rustle too much as I slowly drew the closet door closed.

"Caring? Caring?" My sister's high, sweet voice drifted down to my hiding place, and I prayed she wouldn't come downstairs. I loved the way she said my name; I felt like every time she said it my heart broke and then healed stronger than before.

"Caring?" I heard her step, cautious now, on the creaky stairs above my head. At least I didn't have to worry about my breathing giving me away.

I heard her come down the rest of the stairs. If she were to find me in the closet, face ruined, shirt ripped and buttonless, lying on boxes in the dark . . . I couldn't imagine how her tiny growing mind would recover from the trauma. I held on to the doorknob and pulled back so her tiny hands wouldn't be able to turn it.

But it could be just as bad if she tried to turn it and couldn't, because then she'd probably run upstairs and tell Dad, and then they'd both come down and . . .

I guess what I'm trying to say is that I was even more frightened of my sister seeing me in my ruined state than I was of actually being in that ruined state.

Kaitlyn. I could hear the soft scratch of her footy pajamas on the thin, padless carpeting of my bedroom.

I had a very clear image of her just then, as though I could see right through the wall. Her long blond hair would be sleep-tangled and static-y on one side, her lips pouty with concentration. Her footy pajamas were white, with a pattern of round, Hello Kitty!-esque panda bears. Katy likes the ones that are upside down the most, because she says that when she's wearing the pajamas they look right side up to her.

I knew that Katy liked to go into my room when I wasn't home, which, if my mother ever found out, would bring me to the point of eviction and would surely mean some form of minor punishment for Katy, who has been warned not to go down there. Mom probably sees it as the equivalent of letting Katy play in a crypt, one that has worse things dwelling within than spiders and the occasional bat or rat.

But Katy braves whatever threats that have been offered, and I know this because there's evidence of her visits. The blankets of my bed pulled back, the satin pillow on the floor, a drawer open. Once for three days running there was a new stuffed animal propped up on my pillows, and when I asked her about it, she said that she was worried I'd be lonely in the cellar by myself.

"Caring's still not home!" she called. I couldn't make out the muffled reply that answered her, but it was probably a command for her to leave my room. My tomb.

I heard her steps recede slightly, and then a hollow clunk, and I knew that she'd taken the seat that I'd just vacated in front of the vanity. I pressed my ear to the door and heard the rough whisk of my brush through her hair. A box shifted beneath me, and the brushing stopped.

"Caring?"

I pretended to have rigor mortis. I was totally motionless. A moment later there was another clunk followed by the sound of Kaitlyn's feet scraping along the carpet, then thudding on the stairs. I was relieved she'd gone but also worried that I might have scared her.

She *is* gone, I sighed. I still practice breathing and facial exercises. Shallow breaths, deep breaths, three stage breaths. Popeye makes fun of me when he catches me doing it—"What, you aren't relaxed enough?" he'll say. But the breathing does something for me. I don't know what, exactly, but I think it's good to fill my body with the things it used to need to operate, like air. Maybe I'm hoping my body will remember.

After my nice long sigh I listened to my sister's voice greeting my father. His response was a low rumble, the male version of Charlie Brown teacher-speak, but her voice was loud and sharp as she told him again that I wasn't home. Sometime later I heard them leave the house, he on his way to work, she on her way to day care.

I heard the door slam shut behind him and felt an enormous sense of relief. But I also felt something else, something I haven't felt since I died.

I felt tired.

The feeling covered me like a shroud. It was as if whatever spark had kept me going all these post-death months was suddenly extinguished. I took one step, and it felt like I was dragging a train behind me. I sat down on my bed, my arms and legs heavy, wondering if the bullet that had smashed my face was still somewhere in my head, worming around. Maybe I was on the slow path to retermination, my number up a second time. I felt like maybe the bullets had gotten me and that it was time to lie down and let go.

I lay back on the bed and rested my head on the square silk pillow.

I closed my eyes.

But I'm not ready this time, I thought.

And then, nothing.

* * *

I fell asleep. I mean I *really* fell asleep, with dreams and everything! My psychology teacher told me we only dream in black and white. I've always disputed that idea. My first dream as a zombie was definitely in color, bright vibrant color. I was standing on a beach, looking out at the most sparkling blue water I'd ever seen. The sun was just beginning to rise, its rays dappling the waves with shining light. I stared at the water while the wind was blowing back my hair and pulling at my clothes, and I lifted my arms, half expecting to be scooped up and carried into the sky like a kite.

I heard someone behind me whisper my name, and turned around. There, at the edge of a thick band of vibrant tropical foliage, came Mal, shouldering his way through some Jurassic-looking fronds. He was smiling. Mal was smiling!

The moment his foot stepped onto the white sand beach, other zombies began to appear from the "forest primeval," walking through the brush and onto the sand. Colette, Adam, Popeye—people I recognized from the Wall, the room in the Haunted House where we hung photos and notes from zombies all over America. There were also people I'd never seen before. Melissa, who I saw first as a shock of red hair and a white Greek comedy mask. She dropped the mask when our eyes met, and she was so beautiful it made me want to cry.

Tommy was there, and Sylvia, and Kevin, and just about everyone I know. Tayshawn. Jacinta. They all kept walking toward the sea. Some of them touched me as they passed, lightly, on the hands or the cheek. When I turned around some had just begun to walk into the water; I remember Cooper

Wilson breaking into a run, splashing around and flopping face-first into the light surf. It was so beautiful watching all of us together.

Soon, everyone but me was in the water, and most of my friends were already *under* the water. I was the only one left on the beach, but I didn't mind. I was having fun, like a new mother watching toddlers splash around a kiddie pool.

And then they started coming out of the water. I think Tommy might have been the first.

But he wasn't a zombie anymore. No one that came out of the water was a zombie anymore. I remember seeing Popeye and noticing that all the awful things he'd done to his body had healed. I saw someone I didn't recognize and then realized it was George—but George restored! He was actually really cute!

Everyone walked by me and headed back into the forest or jungle or whatever it was until I was the only one on the beach, and I thought, well, here I go. I'm going into the water so I can be healed and whole and won't that be wonderful, and I took one step and thought I could feel wet sand squishing through my toes, and when I looked up again there you were.

The one I love.

You were so beautiful and strong and clean-looking, the water glistening in your hair. The sight of you stopped me in my tracks.

I haven't laid eyes on you since I killed myself. I never got the chance to tell you the things I wanted to say. In what passes for "life," I had no idea how you would react to me.

But in my dream you were smiling. And you spread your arms.

I looked at you and you started to speak and then I woke up.

# CHAPTER THREE

**M**AYBE I SHOULD HAVE BEEN happy—everything in the dream had been so nice, and just the idea that I *could* dream was nice—but instead I was very, very sad.

Once again I didn't get the chance to say all the things I needed to say. Once again I'd been so close to you, and now you were gone.

A moment later, I realized that I was lying on my bed with my shirt ripped open and my black bra exposed. I got another blouse from my closet, and while buttoning it up I started sifting through the dream, looking for meaning. I'm not as witchy as the Weird Sisters, maybe, but I've always believed in signs and portents. And what else could the first zombie dream be but a cryptic message to be deciphered?

I felt like crying. I'd have *been* crying if my stupid body worked the way it was supposed to.

I tried to remember as much as I could about the dream, about the parts of the dream that weren't you. I thought about the ocean water, how incredibly blue it was, as if it were being lit from below as well as above. How it healed everyone who had stepped into it, and how I didn't get the chance, but of course as soon as I thought that, I thought about you and how you stepped out of that healing water, and I wasn't sure but it might have been a you I'd never seen before—you as you might be today, three years older than you were when I died. But then I wondered how that could be; since then I haven't seen you anywhere but in my mind's eye.

I happened to walk by my vanity at that moment and glanced at myself in the mirror. That's a testament to the ability of dreams to transport you from all your worldly cares—I'd completely forgotten that my face was a shattered ruin.

But that isn't what I saw in the mirror. What I saw was my eyes, which had gone from diamond clear to a brilliant blue, like two sapphires filled with sunlight.

"Like two sapphires filled with sunlight."

Do you remember when you said that to me?

I remember everything about that day. We'd ridden our bicycles to the edge of the woods of a forest very much like the one where I spend most of my time now, the Oxoboxo. We took off our shoes and socks and followed the grassy path that led into the forest and the lake.

We were holding hands, and walking, and talking, and everything we said seemed to be silly and important at the same time. I remember one of us saying—and it really is hard for me to remember who said what because we were so simpatico, so in tune with one another's thoughts—something about how different the woods would be if the skunks were as plentiful as the squirrels, and there seemed to be great wisdom in this observation, even though we were both laughing.

We'd been friends for so long—sort of like Adam and Phoebe, in a way—it was so natural to be together, whispering, laughing. And then hand in hand went to arm in arm, and then we were walking more slowly and you moved your arm around my waist. We were walking toward the lake—a different lake, a different state—and the sun had just begun to set, and the old cliché about a handful of coins being scattered across the surface of the water, glinting in the sun, came to mind. We'd stopped talking, but then we sort of laughed at our silence and sat down on a rock outcropping that overlooked the shore. We were serious but lighthearted, too. There was a sailboat tacking in the light wind that seemed determined to entwine our hair. Sitting beside you, I compared our late-summer tans—yours far deeper, the color of fresh honey—and you pressed your thigh against mine to prove it. School would begin in a few days, and I was scared. I didn't want it to begin, but mostly I just didn't want the summer to end.

"Don't worry," you said. "We can do this. We'll be fine." And I believed you. You alone knew me. You were the only one who knew what I was like, about the blue fog of depression that could sometimes drop between me and the rest of the world. You couldn't make the fog disappear—no one could—but you could always find me when I was lost within.

We hadn't looked at each other in some time, I realized. We'd looked at our dusty legs and our tans and bare feet, but not at each other. I turned toward you then, and you said my eyes were sapphires filled with sunlight, and then I knew. I could see it in your eyes. I could see it; it was more than just sunlight, and it was like I could see myself, reflected. I leaned forward, or maybe you did, and our lips brushed, and we pulled back, together, as though to make sure it was okay, and it was. And then I was pressing my lips to yours and our mouths opened, and I couldn't imagine that what we had would ever go away.

But it did. It went away as if it had never been there at all.

We'd stayed at the lake until the sun had gone down, and I was terrified as we walked back through the forest in the darkness. We were only a mile or two in, and I clung to you the whole way, shrieking every time some unseen animal scampered through the underbrush. But we made it out to where our bicycles and our shoes lay, and we were unharmed, if not unchanged. We embraced once we were there, safe, and we kissed once again before we rode home.

Somehow, the sunlight all drained away.

We were together for almost the rest of the summer, but the closer we came to the start of school, the more scared I became. I wouldn't let you come near me once school began, and when you called me at night I'd try to convince you that we'd made a mistake.

I think—I know—that I was also trying to convince myself. Then one day at lunch I made it clear to you that you needed to give me space. And you were finally convinced.

Before long, you were with someone new.

And I know why. Now I know why, although then I was nothing but devastated, in the grip of a devastation so complete that I couldn't think clearly. I was so stupid, a coward. We'd been friends for so long, and for things to change . . . What would people think? What would people say? I realize now that it must have been just as hard for you to go through what we did.

Harder, maybe. You stayed alive.

I blinked, and my blue eyes were gone. Maybe they'd never been there after all. But as I looked more closely at my reflection I noticed other changes that didn't go away when I blinked or turned my head.

My face wasn't as lopsided as it had been—as though the bones that had been shattered had started to knit back together. The bullet hole looked like it had begun to close up, but when I brought my fingers to my cheeks I could feel a bump just below the skin where the hole was. I pushed lightly and—this is another gross part, I'm sorry—I could see a flat gray lump, like a small pebble. Somehow the bullet had worked its way up to the surface of my skin.

I leaned over the sink and pressed at the edges, squeezing slightly. A few seconds later I could feel part of the bullet protruding from my cheek, and then I brushed it and it clattered onto the basin with a small tinkling sound.

The bullet was so small. I pinched it between my thumb

and forefinger, then flicked it across my room.

The hole in my face looked smaller, even after pressing the bullet out. It was no bigger than a nostril. I probed around the wound gently with my fingertips, and though there was still a slight sensation of looseness between my bones, the sickening movement beneath the surface of my skin was gone. The hole was centered on my cheekbone, which the night before had felt like small shards of pottery in a thick plastic bag. Today the bone felt solid, with maybe a slightly tenuous anchor to the rest of my face, but solid, nonetheless.

I was healing.

My body was repairing itself, and at an incredible rate. This was no hallucination. I had the slug to prove it.

I stared at my reflection—vanity, vanity. I imagined—was I imagining it?—that there was a slight itchy sensation under my skin, as though my cells were reattaching themselves to each other.

Zombies don't heal. Tak's cheek never healed. Tommy still has an open wound where he'd been shot with an arrow. The burns that Melissa received after her death have never gone away. Why was I healing? The type of wound didn't factor into things, either—when Adam wears a T-shirt, you can see a raised bump on his chest from the bullet that killed him. I'd read hundreds of e-mails and posts that zombie kids have sent to Tommy's site, mysocalledundeath.com, and I've never once heard anyone mention that they had the ability to heal.

I wanted to call my dead friends and ask them if they had experienced this, but I was scared. I've always been one of the "fast" zombies—I can move and talk in a way that lets me pass for human—and I've always been conscious that my ability might make others feel bad. Traditionally biotic people hated me because I was dead; what if differently biotic people started to hate me because I was, well, coming alive?

I went upstairs and turned on the television and surfed over to CNN. I still had no idea what made the police react so violently. There was some talk-show type thing on, so I went into the kitchen and took a handful of spices out of the spice rack. I went back to the couch, unscrewed the caps, and sniffed them one at a time. The cumin and the coriander I could smell, but not the nutmeg. Is there something about nutmeg that is scent-invisible to zombies, or is this a Karen-specific thing? Anyhow, my advice to zombiekind everywhere is to keep practicing your sense of smell. I'm convinced it's one of the keys to life.

Eventually there was a news update that had a brief segment on zombie murders. They ran the clips on the lawyer who we supposedly killed—Gus Guttridge. There were very grainy clips of the Guttridge home and some "zombies" removing lumpy forms that viewers were supposed to think were the corpses of the Guttridge family. One of the "zombies" looked a lot like Tak, if you didn't know that Tak hitches on his left side and not his right like the big faker in the video is doing. One of the other fakes does this weird arms-out-in-front walk, along with not bending his knees at all. The faces are completely frozen, and I can only guess that they're masks, the kind of thing that people who assume we all look alike would wear if they were going to pretend to be us.

The newscaster, looking grave, ha-ha, said that one living impaired person was taken into custody, and others were wanted for questioning. I guess they didn't think they should mention that the cops fired about a hundred bullets at us.

As mad as I was over the coverage, or rather the lack of coverage, I was happy that the report only mentioned one zombie in custody. Poor George. I was very sorry that they'd caught him, but I was also glad that the other Sons of Romero (or, as I think of them, the Beastie Boys) managed to get away. I hoped that they weren't as, well, hole-y as I was.

I touched my face again. Already the hole seemed a little smaller than it had been a few minutes ago. My friends don't heal; all of the Sons of Romero, except Tayshawn, bear some scar, some visible reminder that they are no longer among the living. George has wounds that no living person could endure. Tak's cheek and skinless knuckles mark him as dead, and Popeye creates "bodifications"—new wounds and scars he thinks of as artistic statements—that further distance him from the living.

I switched off the television and stared at my reflection in the flat black glass. The televisual replay of my near-redeath experience—or maybe my nap!—reminded me that I wasn't without responsibilities.

I was supposed to work that night. Nearly get reterminated one day; the next, start worrying that you're going to miss your shift at the mall. I thought about calling in sick—which was hilarious—but decided to text Tamara instead, to see if maybe she could switch shifts with me.

My father bought me a cell phone about six months after I died. He paid for it and paid the monthly bill up until last month, when I started working. We didn't make a big deal about it or anything. I'd gotten him to open up an account for me at a local bank, so I could use an ATM card instead of having to walk in all the time and try to pass as human. It was tough enough doing it at the mall every shift—I don't know if I would have gotten away with it if Wild Thingz! wasn't an alternative store. Anyhow, one day I handed my father two twenties and told him it was for the cell-phone bill that month. He took the money without saying anything, but I think he was pleased.

When I was done texting Tamara, I called my favorite breather. She said hello on the first ring, her voice a stuttering whisper as she said my name in the form of a question.

"Hi, Phoebe," I replied, whispering, myself. "Can you talk?"

"I think so," she said. "I'm on the bus. With Adam." Even through the "cellusphere," I could hear the little hitch in her voice when she spoke again—not a zombie hitch, which is caused by having to concentrate on moving the air through your body and getting your tongue in the right position, but a human hitch. You know—an emotional one.

"Karen," she said, "I'm so happy to hear your voice!" She was, too. It warmed my dead bones, it really did.

"Awww," I said. She and Adam are so cute. I'm more than a little jealous. They are they first two people I kissed since dying.

"Phoebe, I wanted you to know I'm all right. Just peachy."

"Karen, where are you? Are you really all right? Tak said you'd been killed! He was over at Adam's, and he took him . . ."

"Phoebe . . ."

"Out to the Oxoboxo, and he wanted Adam with him, and this morning on the news they said you killed . . ."

"Phoebe."

"That horrible lawyer, the one that got Martinsburg free. And his whole family! Karen, I know it can't . . ."

"Phoebe!" It was like talking to Margi, really, but with more logic and a softer voice. "Slow down! All will be revealed. But start with Tak, please. He's okay?"

"He's fine. Well, not fine, really. He'd been shot a couple times. And he went . . ."

And she told me where he went. I was going to ask a series of clarifying questions: what do you mean, what are you saying, what what what. But for some reason, a chill—a metaphorical one, of course—ran down my spine. The "cellusphere" was probably the least secure of all methods of communication, ever.

"Phoebe," I said. "Forget I asked. We'll talk about that stuff later, okay? Is there anything else you can tell me that's public knowledge?"

There was a pause, but gawd bless her, Phoebe knew exactly what I was getting at.

"They've got George," she said, carefully. "The police Tasered him, and it seems to have . . . shut him off. He's not . . . animate."

I don't remember what I said then, or if I said anything, but I did remember George heading off down the hill in front of St. Jude's, toward the police, drawing both their fire and their ire. Doing so gave the rest of us just a little bit wider of a window to escape.

Poor George. My hole-y heart was breaking.

Eventually I said something about how sad that was. Then I said something like, "Wow, a lot happened while I was watching TV last night."

Phoebe caught on, such a smart girl. "We really need to talk, Karen. It seems like ages since I've seen you."

"I know what you mean! But I had to call in sick to school. I just haven't been feeling myself lately."

Phoebe laughed. It was good to hear her laugh, even if our conversation was a little forced. I wondered if she'd be laughing if she knew I'd just plucked a bullet out of my face.

"Actually," she said, "you might not want to go to school. Technically you aren't allowed to go anymore."

"Adam's still going, isn't he?"

"Yes. But we're trying to keep it quiet. So far, Principal Kim has let him, even though she could probably get in big trouble. Should we meet at the mall?"

"Probably not the mall," I said. "How about I let you know?"

"Okay," Phoebe said, and I could tell from her tone she thought I was hiding something from her. "I'll get Margi to drive us over."

I hoped she wouldn't ask me if I was working, in case

someone really was listening in on the call. Kind of dumb, really, because you'd think if "they," whoever "they" are, were bugging my phones, they would also be able to figure out that I've been passing as a human and working in the mall at Wild Thingz! for the past three weeks.

"Okay, then." I paused, not because I'm a slowpoke but because I didn't really want to hang up. "See you later."

"Karen?" she said, that hitch back in her voice. "I . . . I'll see you."

Phoebe has such magnetism. *Such* an attractive quality. I didn't want to let her go, not after what I'd just gone through.

But I had to.

"Okay, sweetie," I said. "'Bye."

I'm a little in love with her, I guess. But so is everyone else.

# CHAPTER FOUR

I WENT BACK TO WORK ONLY one night after being shot full of lead. Who says American teens aren't as dedicated a workforce as generations past? (Or should that be "generations passed," yuk yuk). By way of clever disguise, I placed a small Band-Aid over the bullet hole in my cheek.

I was trying to pass everything off as my personal vision of "normal," despite what had happened. Dad called, like he always does on his way home, and I offered to get something in the oven like I always do, and he said that's okay, Karen, the way he always does—I always offer, even though I know my mother has placed a taboo on me preparing food of any sort. She doesn't want me touching the oven, microwave, or coffee-maker, either, for fear that I'll contaminate them with my deadly death germs. She's never told me this directly, of course—she'd have to speak to me for that to happen. But I get the idea that she doesn't even want me in the kitchen.

Dad always calls me on my cell, now, even though there's a perfectly good wall-mounted cordless phone just inside the kitchen door.

"I have to work tonight," I said.

"I remembered," he said, sounding weary. Sometimes work made him that way, sometimes having a living dead daughter did. "Karen, were you home last night?"

"Home is where my heart is," I said, Creative Truth-dodging 101. "Why?"

"Some pretty disturbing things happened," he said, "involving differently biotic people."

He's so cute; he still can't say "zombie" around me without getting all embarrassed. He summarized the evening's events for me: alleged murders, a videotape, desecration of a church(!), shots fired.

"Oh my gosh," I said. "Those poor people!" I didn't indicate whether or not I meant the Guttridges or the differently biotic people. Instead I asked Dad who the zombies were.

"They weren't positively identified," he said. "I didn't see the video, but on the radio they said that the killers, and this one zombie that was arrested, were pretty, ah, 'zombified.' Like with visible wounds and such."

"And such?"

He cleared his throat, the sound like a roll of static on my cell phone. "Like with parts missing."

"Oh my."

"I've heard rumors that others have been rounded up

across the state," he said. "Some released to legal guardians, some not."

Rumors. Stories not making the local or national news.

"Maybe work isn't such a good idea tonight, Karen."

It was touching that he could still feel concern for me. I'd have loved to say, "Sure, you're right, Dad. I'm going to stay with you and the moms and little Katy and we can have popcorn and play Parcheesi and it'll all be just swell!" but of course I couldn't. That nagging feeling of responsibility kept creeping in. Responsibility to my job, to the undead everywhere who'd one day learn from my example, but mostly just responsibility to myself.

"I think work is a better idea than ever, Dad," I said, but humble-like. I didn't want to oversell it.

"You've been banned from school, too," he said. "Your principal called."

That sort of took me by surprise. "Um, yeah. I couldn't get on the bus." Advanced Truth Obfuscation 201: not a lie exactly. I *couldn't* get on the bus, being too shot up. I could almost hear the gears of his brain turning during our connection.

"Karen," he said, "what are you trying to prove with the passing thing?"

That was a pretty complex question. I could have played tennis with him—what was he trying to prove by allowing me to do the passing thing? But instead I chose to respond with rarely applied knowledge from an almost forgotten class in Karen's Syllabus of Human Interactions: I used Intro to Unguarded Moments.

"Good question, Dad. The easy answer is that I just want to be like everyone else."

He waited.

"But it wouldn't be the true answer, at least not for me. I'm sure there are tons of zombies who would give that answer and it would be one hundred percent correct—most people want to fit in, to be like everybody else. Not me. I want to *seem* like everybody else."

"Explain that to me, please."

"I didn't know this when I first took the job, Dad. I just thought it was cool that I was tricking everybody. It was sort of exciting. For a while it felt like fitting in. But then I realized that it was even better than fitting in. I'm hiding in plain sight. I may seem like everybody else, but I'm really, really different. And I like that."

He sighed. "That makes sense. Sort of."

I could have told him more, like how passing was the opposite of my "persona" at school, wearing the too-short Catholic-school-girl shorts and patent leathers every day—the difference between purposely calling attention to myself versus purposely not calling attention to myself.

"I know, it's hard to explain. But I'm trying to not be 'the dead girl.' I'm trying to just be 'me.'"

"At work."

"At work."

"Karen, I think things could get very hostile for you if people find out."

"It's pretty hostile for me already, Dad. I might as well do something. This could be useful to other zombies some day. It's useful for me right now."

I could hear him thinking again.

"Come on, Dad," I said. "Fight the power."

So much for not overselling. But he laughed. He'd been a Reagan-era punk, after all.

"Okay. What time do you need to be there? Six?"

"Yep."

"Okay. I'll see you later, Karen."

"Bye, Dad."

I could still hear him thinking after I clicked my phone closed. He was wondering if he trusted me too much. He wondered if too much trust led to my suicide the first time around, and even though counseling and conversation has indicated repeatedly that it was not trust—or lack of love, conscience, etc.—that led to that act, you can't always explain your feelings.

Anyhow, I went to work with a tiny bandage on my cheek to cover up the bullet hole. Dad didn't notice it when he picked me up, but Katy saw it right away.

"Caring's got a boo-boo," she said, in a matter-of-fact voice, after a very exuberant hug. Did I mention how cute she is?

Dad stopped whatever he was doing—sorting bills or some such—and turned to me, the question clear on his face.

"I did it walking in the woods," I explained. "Low branch. It's just a scratch."

The bandage was the first thing Tamara commented on

when I got to work. She got a different story.

"Pimple that got out of hand," I said. What a liar! One of the best things about being dead is not having acne!

I went into the back room to sign in. My boss, Craig, who usually starts giving orders the moment you walk in, looked up from his paperwork and asked me what I did to my face.

"Cut myself shaving," I said. And then I said, "Sir," because we have that flirty antagonistic thing going on.

He shook his head, his pierced lip curling. "Restock the Z display."

So I started restocking the Z display. People came in, people talked to me, I talked to people. No one pointed and yelled "There she is! That murdering zombie!" No one noticed me at all, except for the hornier young men, and they only notice *parts* of me. Even when one of those parts happens to be my face, they aren't looking for a zombie. Just a pretty girl. So I smile at them, pretending to be just that. And I get away with it. Even though the night before I had more lead in me than 50 Cent, I got away with it.

Which was weird enough. Even weirder, that very first shift after getting lead poisoning, I saw Pete Martinsburg. He came into the store, stood right in front of the Z display, and asked me—me!—if I could help him out with something.

Pete Martinsburg. Watching him, I was certain, absolutely certain, that the figure I'd seen in the blurry videotape pretending to be Takayuki was none other than our pal, Peter Martinsburg. The way he walked, the way he carried himself, the arrogant thrust of his chin. The videotape "Tak" was broad across the chest, with the same musculature as Pete. I didn't need telepathic powers to know it was him. If anyone had killed Guttridge, it had been him, the lawyer's own client.

It was hard not to appreciate the twisted symmetry in Pete being the one to masquerade, to "pass," as my good friend Tak Smiley. If there was such a thing as poetic injustice, this was it.

Seeing him was like getting struck by a lightning bolt. Isn't that how Frankenstein got his start? Getting zapped by lightning? I claim ole Frank as the original zombie. Unless it was Lazarus. But as for me, seeing Pete was an epiphany. For the first time in my second life, I felt like I had a purpose.

I put on my sultry smile and asked him if he thought I could give him the kind of help he needed.

His response couldn't be any more clichéd; it was total Leisure Suit Larry territory. He did this slow scan of my body, starting low and taking a long, long time to get to my eyes. I suppose my flesh would have crawled and I'd have turned red if I still had humanisms like the blush response.

"Yeah," he said, making his voice all gruff. "Yeah, I think you can." I felt like I was an alt in The Sims or something.

It's not fair for me to complain, though. I went at him like a dizzy airhead blonde, and he responded in kind. I giggled and cut my eyes away, and when I looked back it was from under lowered lashes. I could almost hear his heart beating faster.

"I meant with the merchandise." I'd clasped my hands behind me and put my shoulders back, swaying a little. His eyes didn't stay on mine for long.

"Oh, I know what you meant," he said. The boy had confidence, I'll give him that. And he was still very handsome, even with the souvenir Tak gave him: a thick pink-red line that ran from his cheekbone to his lower jaw. "Why don't you tell me about these products here?" He indicated the revolving display of Slydellco products.

"The Z line?"

"Sounds like a subway. Yeah, this Z stuff." He took the tester bottle of the men's body spray, misted the air beside him, and sniffed. When he looked back at me, his eyes were on mine again, and for a second I thought: he's on to me; he knows. I even wondered if I'd forgotten to put my contact lenses in before going to my shift. But of course I had; Tamara and Craig would certainly have commented if I hadn't. And I was wearing a Band-Aid on my cheek—that meant I was human, right? But the way Peter Martinsburg was staring at me—almost through me—I thought he knew. I bluffed my way through, anyway.

"So this is supposed to make corpses smell better?"

"The Z line was specially formulated for living impaired people," I said. "That's the men's body spray. We have one for women, too. There are also skin products. There's a foundation that makes the skin look less gray. The 'eye de-shadow' is popular; it removes the dark circles living impaired people sometimes . . ."

"Smells like burning leaves," he said, not really interested. "What do you think of all of this stuff?"

"What do *I* think about it?" I kept my expression as blank as possible—I didn't think he'd be as interested in me if he

43

thought I thought about anything.

"Yeah. About all of it. Do you ever wait on any corpsicles?"

I pretended to stifle a giggle behind my hand. "Yes. We get a few. Well, we used to. After last night I don't think we'll see any for a while."

He laughed, and I could see a hint of pride in his expression. He was Fake Tak, there's no question about it. "If Williams gets his way, they'll be all over the place."

"Williams," I said, trying to look like I was thinking and that thinking took major effort. "Is that the football zombie?"

"Yeah, that's right," Pete said, looking at me like I deserved a doggy treat or a pat on the head. "He's gone down to Washington to try to get rights for the living dead. Martin Luther Zombie King, that's Williams."

I frowned, pouting my lower lip.

"Do you like waiting on them?"

"Zombies, you mean?"

"Cadavers, corpses, meat puppets. Yeah, zombies."

I leaned in a little, dropping my voice to a whisper. "I usually get Tamara to wait on them," I said. "They scare me, honestly."

He nodded like I'd just passed some purity test.

"Hey, don't get me wrong," he said. "I'm all for making the worm burgers smell better. I just think a flamethrower would do a better job than this spray bottle."

I feigned a shocked but amused look. "You're soooo bad!" I said, tapping him on the arm, letting my hand linger. He smiled, proud of his muscles. He has a right to be, I guess.

"Don't I know you?"

And here's where I wondered if a change of clothes, eye color, and hair were really going to succeed in giving me a whole new public identity. I was glad I didn't have to regulate my breathing, as I stared back at him evenly and, I think, provocatively.

He knew me, all right. I asked him to kill me, once.

He'd followed me into the woods one day after school, and I knew even then that his intentions were less than honorable. He caught up with me on the path going toward the Oxoboxo and said he was going to kill me. I didn't run away, or scream, or fight, or anything, I just said, "Go ahead." I'd even told him how to do it.

Maybe I thought he'd lose his nerve and take off, have a major life epiphany, and change his evil-doing ways. Maybe I thought he'd kill me, but have the same epiphany when he saw what a terrible thing he'd just done.

Or maybe I *hoped* he'd kill me, because I still had feelings like that, feelings that are both impulsive but also so deep inside me, so always-there that I forget about them.

I don't know what I was thinking when I told him to do it; all I know is that he would have if Mal and Takayuki hadn't showed up when they did (and I still don't know *why* they did—it wasn't like they came out to meet me every day after school or anything. Chalk it up to my secret telepathetic powers). They were so cute, scampering up the woodland path!

Tak caught up with him on the night Pete killed Adam, but I don't think Tak's attack on Pete had anything to do with that—Tak always said he didn't care if the living wanted to do his recruiting for him. I think it was all about me.

45

I feel guilty—if I did something other than ask Pete to kill me; talk to him, hug him, clobber him, anything—then maybe Evan and Adam would still be alive, and maybe we wouldn't be on the run.

But here was a chance for atonement cloaked in the flesh of Pete Martinsburg.

"Don't I know you?" he'd asked.

The look I gave him, putting my hands on my hips, would have caused most living boys to faint from lack of oxygen to the brain.

"You'd remember if you did, don't you think?"

He held my stare, a slow grin appearing on his lips as he licked them. "Yeah, I guess I would. *Can* I know you? Better, I mean?"

"Sure. Call me." I said. I took a pen out of my shirt pocket and started writing my cell phone number out for him.

"What's your name?" he said.

"Christie Smith," I said. Christie Smith was the name of Tommy's new girlfriend, but it was the only name I could think of. I'm not a very creative person, I guess. Thank God Wild Thingz! lets its employees wear piercings and tattoos instead of name tags.

I handed him the scrap of paper, a receipt for some gum from the mall drugstore. Zombies don't chew gum, do they? See how tricky I can be? "Here you are, Peter."

He took the paper, his eyes narrowing with suspicion.

"How do you . . ."

"I knew who you were as soon as you walked in," I told him. "We get the newspapers in Winford, too, you know."

I had him on the ropes with that statement—I guess he was probably wondering why I was interested, him being a murderer and all. In fact, he looked a little pissed off, like the control he thought he'd held during our conversation had suddenly been yanked out from under him. I did a risky thing, then. I reached out and traced the tip of my finger down the length of his scar.

"You missed, that's all," I said. "You won't next time."

He looked like he might hit me. Or kiss me. Or both.

"But I knew who you were before that," I said, my finger lingering on his chin, just below his lips. "You creamed a wide receiver I was dating last year. Gave him a concussion and everything."

He laughed, the "compliment" regarding his former gridiron feat waving away whatever complex bundle of emotions he was trying to process.

"No kidding? Well, I'm real sorry about that."

"Don't be. He was a wimp."

Not a jerk, or a creep, or a dull lad. A wimp, as though to say, You, Peter Martinsburg, are a strong man. And I need a strong man.

I gave his cheek another pat.

"Call me," I said.

He nodded, and then I watched him leave the store. He didn't look back.

Living boys are so easy.

Except he didn't call me, at least not right away.

I guess the obvious question to ask is Waitaminute—this

is a guy who stalked you into the woods, looked you dead in the eye, and told you he was going to murder you. Do you honestly expect me to believe that he didn't recognize you?

Yes.

I looked a lot different working at Wild Thingz! than I did when I went to school with Martinsburg, for one thing. My eyes were blue, thanks to the contact lenses my father had bought me; my hair was darker, thanks to the coloring I'd put in it; and my skin was less white, thanks to *Night Shades*, a skin product from the Z line, "for that healthy, living skin glow!" I wasn't wearing a skirt about four inches too short for the dress code (and no one at Oakvale High ever talked to me about my violating the code; too scared I guess) and I wasn't wearing a filmy white shirt, so I didn't have any of the easily recognizable attributes of my day-to-day appearance.

I didn't have my Karen DeSonne costume on when I went to work, in other words.

But I think it was more than that. I think Pete has trouble seeing girls as individuals. I *know* he has a problem seeing zombies as individuals. He'd identify Tommy, maybe, because he's got something personal for him, but if you lined up Cooper and Evan and Kevin, all he would see is "zombie." Likewise, put Colette, Sylvia, Jacinta and me, minus my uniform (but with normal clothes on), together, all he would see is "zombie." Maybe girl zombie, maybe not. It's like how you can have your groceries bagged by the same guy every day, but won't recognize him if you see him on the tennis court or at the library.

Pete might not be able to see the real me, but I could see

right through him. He was part of the conspiracy that forced my people underground.

Of course I had no proof, nothing I could pass on to right-thinking breathers who would bring the truth to a world that might not want to handle it.

I was certain that I could get that proof. But then weeks went by and he hadn't called.

# CHAPTER FIVE

THE ARIZONA CAMPUS was a pretty cool place, Pete thought. Except for all the gorgons. If it wasn't for the gorgons, he really might like staying here at the compound.

Oakvale, Connecticut, might be infested with zombies, but the One Life compound was overrun with ugly girls. Ugly, overweight, and just plain unpleasant girls. Gorgons.

One of them was coming his way, her bare arms and legs the color and texture of a canned ham. Most of these girls were from the Midwest, it seemed, where they'd apparently never learned that the sun can burn. Especially in Arizona.

"Hi, Pete," she called, lifting a pudgy arm in a shy wave. Pete bit back his disgust and returned the wave. He didn't want it getting back to the Reverend that he was unfriendly. He knew he was the Reverend's favorite—the gorgons knew it too, which was why they were all so interested in him. Well, that and his awesome physique, which was now accentuated by a nice, even base tan. The gorgon giggled and kept walking, leaving Pete to bronze.

He closed his eyes, letting the sun bake him. That was something he'd missed after spending the summer with "Dad" in Cali; the rich hue he'd developed began to leach away as soon as he got back to Oakvale. He'd started to worry that he'd fade so much he'd look like one of the crypt things crawling around Oakvale like maggots on roadkill. The deadheads. The meat puppets.

The demons. The Reverend wanted him to call them "demons."

He heard giggling, and cracked an eyelid to see a beastly figure standing over him, her hands folded behind her lumpy body as she watched him soak up the rays. Pete propped himself up on his elbows in a sort of half crunch, so that the gorgon could get an eyeful of the definition on his abs.

"Hi, Pete," she said in a small, hiccuping voice. It wasn't really that there were *lots* of gorgons at the compound; actually there were way more men. Almost all the adults were male, as were a full three quarters of the teens and kids. But as for the girls his age, they were all gorgons. Every last one of them. Overweight or spaghetti thin, without a healthy complexion among them.

There wasn't anyone like that Christie he'd met at the freak store—*that* was for sure. She'd even made that little acne bandage on her cheek look sexy.

"What can I do for you?" he said, wondering if the

perfection of his glistening body had stunned the gorgon into silence. She was practically drooling on him.

"The Reverend wants to see you," she said, all breathless. For a moment he almost thought it was one of the worm burgers standing there. Maybe they'd shrivel in the sunlight, like a slug.

"Oh, he does, does he?" Pete said. "I guess I better put some clothes on."

She giggled, hiding her mouth behind her hand. She was fat, he thought, but she'd almost be passable if it wasn't for her hair, which hung around her face in a slack curtain. Maybe the Reverend ought to give a few lessons in proper hygiene along with all the fire and brimstone. Cleanliness and Godliness and all that stuff.

Pete asked the girl to hand him his towel, hoping that doing so wouldn't trigger a massive coronary.

Pete might be the favorite son, but he still had to live in the crowded dormitory with all the Youth. That's what the Reverend called the teens that lived at the compound. Youth. Kids under twelve were the Children, and twelve to seventeen were the Youth. Pete hated living with the Youth. The dorm—a big open room, with beds lined up in two rows like a military hospital—smelled like an old sweat sock filled with Parmesan cheese. And the kids—if the girls were all gorgons, the boys were all creeps. Furtive, sniveling specimens, many of whom had run away from home. The kid in the next bed— who looked like he was a year or two older than Pete—cried himself to sleep every night, and half the little bastards in the room snored.

Pete didn't have any friends on the campus, although everyone wanted to be his friend. It was like having a room full of Thornapples, that runty never-shuts-up kid who tried out for the Badgers back home. So poor was the quality of kids at the dorm that it actually made Pete nostalgic for TC. Dumb, lumbering TC—at least that kid could hang in a scrap. At least he peed standing up. The rest of them—ugh.

Pete avoided conversation as he headed to the showers outside the main room. They were gang showers, and they were surprisingly filthy despite the fact that no one other than him seemed to consider regular bathing a priority. Pete showered at least three times a day; once in the morning after his run, once in the evening, and once after his noon tanning session. In the three weeks he'd been there he'd only gotten one sporting event going, a lame game of touch football with a dozen nonathletes who had spindly arms and legs and only played because they wanted him to like them. He blocked a kid too hard after just a few minutes of playing and ended up dislocating the kid's shoulder. Sports—unless you counted time spent on the firing range—were given as much priority as bathing here.

Pete hung his towel on a hook, brought his bucket of soap and shampoo to the center spigot, and turned the handle. He'd have liked to have a nice cool spray to refresh him after his time in the sun, but the showers only offered one temperature. Hot. Hot like the fires of hell that Pete would no doubt be hearing about in his meeting with the Rev.

He'd just lathered up his chest when Dorman walked into the showers, a faded and threadbare Spider-Man beach towel tied loosely around his skinny waist. Pete gritted his teeth, because he knew that the kid was in there so he could get a look at Pete in the buff, the creepy little perv. "Hey," Pete called. He wanted the kid to know he was onto his sick game. Dorman muttered a greeting. Wearing only his flip-flops, he wouldn't meet Pete's eyes as he walked to a different spigot at the end of the room.

Pete looked over at him. The kid had a spine like a question mark. The skin on his back was covered with bumps. Backne, Pete thought. Real attractive. He hoped Dorman used soap, because he always smelled like day-old bread. Dorman turned to get his head wet, and cut his eyes away, embarrassed, when he saw that Pete was looking at him.

Yeah, caught you looking, didn't I, you freak, Pete thought.

"I'm going to see the Rev," he said, liking the way his voice echoed in the tiled room. No one else dared to call the Right Reverend Nathan Mathers anything less than "the Reverend." Half the time kids walked away, praying, when they heard Pete refer to him as the "Rev."

"I jutht met with him," Dorman said. He had a slight lisp, just enough to make Pete want to smash his face in. "I'm going away again. Back home."

"That's good, right?" Pete forgot where the kid was from. Some southern backwater where he had it pretty easy because *everybody* hated zombies there.

"Yes," Dorman said. *Yeth*. What a freak. A skinny, fleshless creep. There was absolutely no muscle tone on his skeletal frame.

"What are you going home for?" Pete asked, leaning his head back into the spray. The temperature might be off, but at least they had good water pressure.

"I'm not supposed to talk about it," he said.

Pete laughed. "No? We're pals, aren't we, Dorman?" he said.

"I'm thupposed to go hunting," he said, blushing under Pete's stare. He didn't say it like he was bragging, though, which caught Pete's attention. He almost sounded like it was something shameful.

All of the kids in the dorm bragged about killing zombies, and Pete could tell that most of them were full of crap. The kid that cried at night claimed to have personally "sent six demons back to hell," and a few of the other bed wetters made their encounters with zombiekind sound like dire ninja battles, complete with Norris-esque roundhouse kicking and lethal karate chops that launched zombie heads from zombie shoulders. Pete didn't believe any of them.

"Really? So you're going out to reterm yourself some deadheads, huh?"

He looked at Pete then, and it was like the water coming out of the showerhead had dropped a few degrees in temperature.

"Yes," Dorman said. "Yes. I like hunting the dead." The kid wasn't lisping anymore, Pete noticed.

Dorman's eyes were as empty as any zombie's Pete had ever

seen. And his skin as gray. If it wasn't for the fluidity of his movement and his speech, Dorman could be one of the demons he pretended to hunt.

"I like hunting them," he said. His voice didn't seem to resonate the same way Pete's did in the room. "I really do."

The shower washed away a thin sheen of soap suds, revealing four blue-black lines, hash marks, etched into the sallow gray flesh of his shoulder.

A dreamy, beatific look blossomed on Dorman's face as he looked up at the sputtering nozzle and started humming a tuneless song to himself.

Once clean and out of the shower, away from the weirdo in the flip-flops, Pete dressed quickly for his meeting with the Reverend. When he got to the long corridor that led to the office, Pete stepped up his pace.

The Reverend's desk was in the corner of the room, his back to a large open window that made him hard to see clearly in the wash of sunlight that streamed through. A large ink drawing of an angel treading on a thick serpent was on the wall to the right of the desk. The angel's expression was impassive as he poised to stab the serpent with a long thin spear.

"Peter," the Reverend said. "Please sit. Are you well?"

"I'm fine, sir." Pete took a chair in front of the big desk.

"Your time here is at an end, Peter," he said. "You're going home. For now."

"What?" Pete said, his voice almost a cry as he half came out of his seat. "I just got here! What do you mean I'm going home?"

"Peter," the Reverend said, his voice stern. "Your emotions."

Pete slumped back, fighting his frustration. In the three weeks he'd been on campus, he'd met personally with the Reverend six times, and each time the Reverend spoke at length on the necessity of mastering one's emotions. Pete inhaled deeply before speaking.

"I don't love the idea of going back, sir. I'm not happy in Oakvale, living with my mother's jerk of a husband, and . . ."

"Peter," the Reverend said, the features of his face all but obliterated in the light streaming from the high window.

"You don't write like you've mastered your emotions," Pete replied, too quickly.

The Reverend looked at him over his steepled fingers for a long moment before replying.

"Explain what you mean by that statement," the Reverend said, the outline of his robes and his dark eyes the only things visible in the wash of light.

Pete's nerve faltered, and his reply was weak and stammering. He thought he sounded like Dorman. Something about looking into Reverend Mathers's eyes, which were dark and penetrating, made him acutely aware that being in his presence was a rare gift.

"Well," he began, "I just meant that . . . that your feelings are pretty clear when it comes to the undead scourge."

"And how would you describe my 'feelings?'" His eyes flashed with a baleful fire as he said the final word. Pete glanced quickly at the snake-destroying angel, but found no help there; its bland expression suggested that the divine being had mastered its emotions at the dawn of creation.

"You . . . you write very . . . *passionately* . . . about the real meaning of the zom . . . of the undead scourge, and what should be done about it."

"Which is?"

"'The undead need to be driven out of the material plane,'" Pete said, "'by force and by fire. And the way behind them must be sealed by prayer and righteousness.'"

If the Reverend was pleased by Pete's ability to quote word for word from his works, he didn't show it. He unlaced his fingers and leaned forward on his desk, rendering the deep lines of his face visible as he spoke.

"You are confusing *displaying* emotion with *creating* emotion," he said. "I write the way I do in *The Undead Plague* not to purge myself of any 'feelings,' but to cause *others* to feel."

He paused for a moment, then leaned back and let the light streaming from the window obliterate his features. "You also confuse 'feeling' with 'fact.' The undead are a certain sign of the apocalypse. The Bible is incontrovertible on that matter, and feelings have nothing to do with it. This is why we must do everything in our power to get our message across, as our society is so steeped in sin that they permit abominations to walk among them, to *mingle* with them, rather than obey the Lord's commands and do what they should be doing. Which is destroying the abominations."

He kept fading in and out of the light; the effect was almost hypnotic.

"If I employ emotionally charged language with my readers, it is only because I am concerned for their lives and their immortal souls. Unfortunately, people have a tendency to respond more rapidly and more appropriately when frightened or angry than they do if shown care or concern. Fear and hate are stronger motivators than love. And, you'll find that people respond more to feeling than fact."

He leaned forward again, the features of his face once again solidifying out of the curtain of light.

"That is why I write the way I do."

His eyes seemed to be boring into Pete's head.

"Am I making myself clear on this point, Peter?"

"Yes," Pete said. "Yes, sir."

"Good." The Reverend did not look overly pleased, because even pleasure was considered an emotion that should be suppressed. "As to why it's time for you to return home to Oakvale. As you know, the undead have been driven underground by the actions of you and Mr. Davidson. It is now illegal in the state of Connecticut to be undead in public and unaccompanied by a legal guardian. We believe that the Oakvale undead are in hiding, and that they never left the town. One was reterminated in Winford the night of yours and Mr. Davidson's excursion. Another has been given sanctuary by the local Catholic church."

Pete thought he detected a slight twitch of the lip, a slight sneer, on the Reverend's face as he imparted this last bit of information.

"And then there's the leader of the demons, Tommy

Williams. He has gone to Washington where he seeks to trick the American government into believing that he and his rotting kind are an oppressed people, deserving succor instead of destruction."

"Shouldn't I go to Washington?" Pete said. "If that's where Williams is." He hadn't been to Washington since an eighth-grade field trip.

The Reverend shook his head. "No. We have other plans for the Williams demon. I want you to go back to your hometown. You have unfinished business there."

"Unfinished business" made him think of the girl from Wild Thingz!, Christie. Maybe it wouldn't be such a bad thing to go home again. There were a few scores he wanted to settle.

"What do you want me to do?"

"I want you to find them," the Reverend said, allowing a controlled smile to grace his lips. "The ones that got away. I want you to find them and dig them out of their holes."

# CHAPTER SIX

**S**EEING PHOEBE, ADAM, and Margi a few days after being shot full of holes (a.k.a. the Swiss Cheese Incident) was one of the happiest days I've had since returning from death. I was all James Bond-y about it; I had Margi drive to a super-secret location on Oxoboxo Cross Road to pick me up, and then I had her drive to the parking lot of a local fast food restaurant. I was crazy paranoid by this time, of course, seeing white vans everywhere, imagining *Men in Black*–type, anti-zombie goons looking high and low for me.

"Are you sure nobody saw Adam get in your car?" This was after the hugging and kissing and teary stuff. They were of course wicked glad to see me, but I guarantee I was even more wicked glad to see them. It's unbelievably nice to have people that care about me.

"Nobody saw me," Adam said. I thought he was speaking

really, really well now, with fewer of the pauses that made speech so difficult for him in the early days of his return. And moving! He's getting back that big guy grace he had pre-death. Not many people know this, but Adam is quite a good dancer.

"Look," he said. "I'm even . . . wearing . . . Johnny's coat."

"A clever disguise," I said. "What about your other brother? The jerk? Or your stepfather?"

"Jimmy was out. And the STD—Joe—he's okay."

We passed an actual white van going the other way on one of the back roads, but it was a minivan kind of thing with a ski rack. When I looked back I could see a mounted DVD player playing *Wall-E* to two car-seated children. "Are you sure he's okay?"

"Karen," Adam said, in that patient, steady way he has. "He's . . . okay. Are you . . . okay?"

I sighed. "I'm great. I'm really, really great. I feel like I've got so much to tell you."

"Speaking of disguises, I like the new look, Karen," the ever fashion-conscious Margi said. "Trying to go incognito?"

I told her I was. "Absolutely. Getting shot changes your perspective on the world. You know?"

That wasn't the only thing that was changing my perspective. Toward the end of my shift, after my encounter with Pete, I peeked under the Band-Aid on my cheek. The hole was gone. I pressed my cheek where the hole had been, but very lightly—I was half afraid that my face would collapse inward like a poked mushroom. Then what would I have done?

*Boss, I have to go home early. My face broke.* My skin was a little squishy and maybe a bit discolored and pinkish, but nothing really noticeable. It almost looked like I had a tiny blemish or a freckle.

"I love your eyes. Did you have blue eyes when you were alive?"

Adam, bless his heart, grumbled that he liked my zombie eyes better.

"I did, Margi," I said, "but these are contacts. And when I was alive my hair wasn't this dark. It was blond, though—sort of between this color and the, um, zombie platinum."

"You look great," Margi said. "If I died would I get your figure?"

I laughed; she didn't.

"Karen," Phoebe said, touching my arm. We were in the backseat. "What happened?"

I told them almost everything. I mentioned getting shot, for example, but didn't tell them about being hit in the cheek. I told them that I was fine, but I didn't tell them I could heal. They knew about me passing at my mall job, but I didn't tell them that I wasn't quitting anytime soon. I told them about my theory that Pete Martinsburg had something to do with the Guttridge "deaths," but I didn't tell them that I'd seen and talked to him.

I was afraid they'd want to get all involved if I told them my plans to get to the heart of the Guttridge case; form a su-per-secret crime club, and soon we'd be piling into the Mystery Machine so we could be those lovable meddling kids who ruin the bad guys' day. But from what I remember of those stories, Scooby-Doo never took three slugs from a policeman's gun, and Nancy Drew never scratched her way out of a coffin after a case went south. This wasn't fun and games. This was life and death.

And I thought of my "conversation" with Pete. I don't think Nancy Drew would have fully approved of my, um, methods. Karen DeSonne, girl detective, would go it alone.

We went through the drive-thru so Margi and Phoebe could get coffee. Addicts! The coffee smelled great, though, and the aroma filled the entire car.

"Have any of you gotten to see Melissa?" I said.

The girls looked ashamed, the poor dears. I wonder if their parents, their teachers—heck, even their friends—understood how stressful it was for them to have zombie friends, never mind zombie friends who were getting arrested, shot, Tasered, destroyed, etc. The stress of watching someone you love being persecuted is enough to drive a teen to drink or become seriously depressed.

"I called her," Phoebe said after a moment of silence. "At St. Jude's. It took a while for me to get through because the priest there, Father Fitzpatrick, has been swamped with reporters and media types. But he put her on and I told her that we loved her and that we were thinking about her."

Phoebe. You've got to love her. I certainly do.

"Father Fitzpatrick thanked me," she said. "He said that Melissa drew a big smiley face on her whiteboard, and that my call meant a lot to her. To both of them."

"That's great," I told them.

"She's the . . . only other . . . one of us . . . I know of who is still in town," Adam said. Like I said, his speech is so much better. There were pauses, but nothing like when he first died.

"Well, that makes two of you," I said. "Like Margi said, I'm going incognito."

"You aren't going back to school?" Phoebe said, and she had that militant streak in her eyes again. I think she had visions of me and Adam doing the whole social-protest thing, the demand-equal-education trip, but that's not for me.

"Nope. Besides, Phoebe," I said, all wide-eyed and fake innocent, "isn't that illegal now?" I could see Adam scrunching low in the shotgun seat, trying to hide his smile.

"So you're quitting Wild Thingz! too?"

Quick as a bunny, smart as a fox. "Um, no."

"Karen," Phoebe said. I wonder if she knows how cute she sounds when she gets all den mother-y. "What do you think will happen if you get caught?"

"Well, Phoebe," I said. "I suppose they would destroy me."

My flippant remark was met with a silence as cold and silent as a tombstone. Adam cleared his throat.

"I'm serious, Karen!" Phoebe said. She might have been choking up a little. "I'm worried about you. Hasn't there been enough tragedy already?"

I took her hand in mine. "Phoebe, sweetie. We're fighting for our lives. There's going to be more tragedy before we're through. A lot more."

She was trying not to cry as she squeezed my hands. "Why? Why do you have to do it?"

Phoebe knows that I killed myself. I could have told her that I'm fully aware that what I did was the most grievous sin a person could commit, and that clearing my people of the crimes they were accused of would go a long way toward helping me feel as if I've atoned for that sin, but I didn't.

I could have told her that when I took my own life I left someone behind, someone very special to me, and there was something inside me that made me want to do something good on this earth before I could see that special someone again. But I didn't.

"A couple reasons. But I can't tell you what they are, Phoebe."

And I couldn't! If I told them that passing at the mall might give me an edge in exposing Martinsburg and his role in the frame-up of our people, they'd never stand for it. And if I told them what I had done—that I'd actually *flirted* with him—you can believe that they'd never let me out of their sights again. In fact they'd probably tie me up, throw me in the trunk, and drop me off at the Hunter Foundation for intensive study. They knew Pete. They knew that he was a threat. They knew what he was already responsible for. Including them would have put them directly into the line of fire.

"You're breaking the law," Phoebe said. "Like you said. It is no longer legal for a zombie to be without a legal guardian in public."

I could have pointed out that Adam was breaking the same

law, but I didn't think that would help anything. She was grasping at straws, and she knew it. Instead, I tried a joke, which probably helped even less.

"I'm committing a crime against nature just walking around. What's the difference?"

She sighed and looked out the window. A living family of four was exiting their SUV, the father gently lifting a little boy from his car seat. They were all smiles as they headed toward the restaurant, the girl skipping ahead. The silence in Margi's car grew.

"Speaking of illegal," Margi said, eventually. "Do they really not know that you're a zombie at Wild Thingz!?"

"They really don't know. I've got them completely hoodwinked."

"Are you sure? That seems sort of implausible."

Margi really is the cutest thing in the world. I can't watch her drink coffee and not wish with all my might that I was alive enough to enjoy it the way she does. She holds the cup in both hands, forming a cradle with her black-and-pink-nailed fingers, and she sort of hunches over it with an expression of total reverence on her face, like she's honoring the Spirit of the Bean or something. And she always inhales the steam and scent before she leans farther to take a sip.

Ahh, life!

"Gee, being a zombie doesn't make a whole lot of sense, either, Margi. But I'm going with it."

She laughed, maybe for Phoebe's benefit, then sipped. Cute as a button.

"Aren't you afraid the police might still be after you?" Phoebe asked.

"Nah. They're looking for Tak and the Sons of Romero."

I wasn't really sure about that last point. But three cheers for optimism, right?

"Hey," I said. "What about our fair-haired boy? How's Tommy?"

Phoebe told me that his travels had gone well and that he was in Washington, D.C., at the moment trying to rally support for a sort of undead bill of rights. Being undead had not yet been criminalized at the nation's capital, and zombies were arriving there "in droves."

"You mean 'hordes,' don't you? Isn't a group of zombies a horde? Like a flock of sheep or a murder of crows?"

"A gaggle . . . of geese," Adam said from the front. I think he was trying to help me lighten the mood. "A google . . . of giraffes."

"You made that one up," I said.

"Tommy's taking a huge risk," Phoebe said, ignoring our banter. "But he thinks it's worth the risk. Or will be, if he succeeds."

Maybe she was trying to tell me she understood what I had to do, even if she didn't agree with it. Or maybe she was trying to convince herself; I wasn't sure.

That fire was in her eyes again, that grim, steely resolve. I don't know why it still surprised me. One of the first times I ever saw Phoebe, she was wrestling with one of those football players while they attacked Tommy in the woods.

But I think I could understand how she felt. In their own individual ways, all of her dead friends were risking their lives.

We all got together again a week or so before Christmas, keeping an appointment we'd made with the Hunters to check in on Sylvia. When we'd last seen Sylvia, she was going through some horrific "augmentation" process that was supposed to leave her restored, but instead seemed to have her—literally— in pieces, like an unassembled doll. We went to the Hunter Foundation expecting the worst, but were pleasantly surprised when Sylvia herself met us at the door, looking better than ever. Looking, in fact, almost human.

"Happy . . . birthday." She greeted us under the watch-ful yet angelic gazes of Angela and Alish. "Sorry. I've been . . . OD'ing . . . on Christmas . . . specials . . . all week."

I think we were actually stunned into silence by her happy return, watching her move, walk and talk far better than she ever had as a pre-augmentation zombie. We were so used to negative outcomes that I don't think any of us—myself, Margi, Phoebe, or Adam—had even dreamed that she would be bet-ter off after the procedure. Margi offered her a bed at her house, as she once had with Colette, but Sylvia said that she was going to stay on at the Foundation and help the Hunters with their studies.

"This is . . . my chance . . . to make a difference," she said. "Like . . . Tommy."

Like Tommy. Like Colette, like DeCayce. Even like Tak, in his own way. Leaving her I was all the more determined that I, too, would make a difference by proving that my friends weren't murderers.

I had Margi drop me off at the edge of the Oxoboxo woods, against the protests of my friends. It was late, it was dangerous, etc. I told them not to worry and that I was probably safer in the woods than I was at my family's home, even, because who knew how long it would be before breathers started banging down doors and dragging zombies out into the street?

This really didn't help my case any, but Margi pulled over and let me out.

"Kisses, kisses," I said, stepping out onto the shoulder. Snow-covered leaves crackled beneath my feet.

"Be careful, Karen," Phoebe said.

"Don't you worry," I told her. "Because I'm not. Worried, I mean."

Hugs, hugs. I turned to watch Margi waving as she swung the car around, and also Adam and Phoebe in the back seat, Adam bending his head low to kiss Phoebe. It was just a quick kiss, a stolen peck taken when you thought the eyes of the world were on something else. But what I saw was the kiss that brought us—me and the one I loved—together. Something about the way he kissed her so brought back that moment.

The beautiful couple, boy and girl, in a close embrace, about to kiss.

One kiss to grant life, one kiss to take it away.

All our kisses were stolen moments like theirs. All our

kisses were secrets: they were secrets that I couldn't reveal to the waking world. I was too afraid to make those secrets public, and the one I love waited for me and waited for me, but my fear overcame me and we said good-bye. I tried to move on, but the blue fog washed over me, and all I had to cling to were my secrets.

My secrets weren't enough to protect me, though, and the blue fog filled me.

And I took my own life.

I watched my friends kissing. They weren't supposed to be together, either, I thought. Living girl and dead boy. They aren't supposed to be together, but they're facing the world, hand in hand. Looking at them filled me with shame.

And then I turned away.

I told Phoebe that I wasn't worried, which wasn't truthful, but I've had a lot of practice at pretending something other than what I really am.

I pretended I wasn't depressed. I pretended I wasn't in love—look where that got me. I pretended lots of other things, too, and now I'm pretending I'm alive.

Why do I pretend to be all these things I'm not? I guess at base level it's because I'm a coward. I was afraid of my sadness, and I was afraid to profess my love. I didn't want to be different, I just wanted to be like everyone else. Even the Karen that everyone knows in Oakvale, the provocative Karen, the risk taker in a short skirt, is really just another mask, a false front. And now I'm trapped—what if Phoebe found about who I really am? I can't risk losing her. I can't risk losing any of them.

It was flattering for people to think that I was a normal, healthy girl, back when I wasn't really healthy or what passes for normal. But that feeling was nothing compared to the feeling I get when living people think I'm alive.

I'd had some moments at school where I seemed to be crossing a line, the life-death line, but my real chance at passing came when my father decided that he needed a new cell phone (how mundane), and announced that he was going to the spectacular and thrilling Winford Mall to get one. And then he did a very strange thing. Instead of putting on his coat, picking up my sister Katy, and wishing me good night as he proceeded with jangling keys to the front door, he spoke words that were like a magic spell to me.

"Come on, girls."

"Girls," as in, plural. The shock must have shown in my face, because when my father looked at me, he reddened a bit, but I wasn't sure if he was embarrassed at the obvious effect his invitation had on me, or that he had, for one sweet moment, forgotten that I'd killed myself.

You see, my parents didn't go anywhere with me—not to the homes of relatives or friends, not to the beach, not to the grocery store. They didn't restrict my comings and goings from their house, and they didn't shun me at home, but they didn't want to be seen out in public with me, either. Sort of like normal people who don't want others knowing them as the owners of a dog that misbehaves in public.

I'm not blaming them—I killed myself, after all. I'm fortunate that they took me in. Not all of us deadheads are so lucky.

For the most part my parents saw me as a child who they felt responsible for, but didn't particularly love or care for anymore. I expect that theirs is a pretty common reaction among parents whose child has done something so horrible, so unforgivable, so offensive to their sense of self and their world that they've effectively cut that child from their hearts with precise incisions.

My Dad, though, I don't think he'd ever been able to cut me out of his heart completely. Or maybe I grew back, like a tumor. There were moments, like the moment of shock that hung between us after his invitation, where I thought he wanted to hug me. And I wanted him to hug me, I really did. But he didn't, not then.

Katy's reaction was far less ambivalent and was a welcome break from the awkwardness between us.

"Yaaaaaaaay, Caring coming!" she said, the little sweetie. Scary how well little kids can pick up on things.

I saw the slight smile on my father's face, and I was happy. No hugs, but I was happy.

Katy was born about nine months after my death; it didn't take a math whiz to figure that one out, but I don't have a shred of resentment for my little replacement. She's an improvement over me in every way.

"I'll be right up," I said, running for my basement abode. "Or down, then . . . up. Whatever." Two minutes later I was upstairs and looking presentable in a fashionably wrinkled black denim jacket and low-heeled black boots. I even put in my contacts.

My friends tell me my eyes look like diamonds, but they just look kind of colorless and glassy to me. They disturbed my Dad, though, so he'd bought me nice blue nonprescription contact lenses. They were pretty close to the color my eyes had been before I died. I felt sort of silly wearing them, but secret-agentish cool, too. Even so, I hoped none of my dead friends saw me wearing them.

"Okay," Dad said. He blinked when he saw my eyes. Anthony DeSonne always seemed to be on the verge of saying something when he looked at me, but whatever it was remained a mystery. Did he disapprove of my clothing? Did he think I looked nice? Did seeing me with blue eyes allow him to believe, if only for a few seconds, that I'd never taken my own life?

Sometimes it's better to let the mystery remain.

"Let's go," he said.

During the short trip to the Winford mall, Katy managed to convince our father to let me take her to the toy store while he ran his errands. I listened to Katy's argument—which bordered on but never crossed into whining—without comment. To offer to take Katy myself would be to cross that unspoken line that demarcated my place within the home. For that reason I was thrilled when Dad, after the slightest hesitation, said that it was fine by him.

"That is," he said, as though he were bound by the

same unspoken line of decorum that restrained me, "if Karen wants to."

"I'd love to," I said, too quickly, no doubt.

So we split up at the wide neon maw of the mall entrance, my father off in search of the newest cellular technology, Katy with her tiny soft hand in my own.

"I can feel how warm your hand is," I told her, giving her hand a gentle squeeze. "I really can." Katy beamed up at me with her eyes. Her naturally blue eyes.

"I think blue eyes go better with this coat, don't you, Katy?" I said as soon as our Dad was around the corner in the half deserted mall.

Katy shrugged.

"I like your real eyes," she said. "Nobody else has eyes like you do, Caring."

I looked at my sister and saw how smooth and supple her skin was, how subtly pink, how rosy her cheeks. I felt like a ghost beside her, she was so filled with life.

We walked around the birch tree that rose up from the first level of the mall, looking for the unseen birds that we could hear chirping away. I was still staring at the eye-level branches when Katy gave my arm a sudden tug.

"Caring! Caring!" she said. "I want to go there!"

She was pointing at the Wild Thingz! store, which had a window display of Halloween items left unsold after the holiday: masks, haunted houses, spiders as big and hairy as house cats, a rubbery painted leg that looked gnawed at the knee—all marked down fifty percent. "Prices slashed" the sign proclaimed, in a blood-spattered font.

"You like all that scary stuff?" I said, surprised. A month before, Katy had burst into tears at the thought of wearing a fuzzy costume that would make her look like her favorite television puppet, and now she wanted to go rushing into a store filled with ghoul masks, dark cloaks, and spiderwebs.

Katy gave a solemn nod.

"You aren't afraid?"

"No such thing as momers," Katy said, with true conviction. "Momers" was Katy-speak for monsters.

"Well," I said, "if you say so."

We walked into the store, where Katy began playing with the hacked leg. I had a brief moment of panic, wondering just how I could translate the story to our father on the way home if Katy blurted out that she'd been playing with body parts. Scanning the wall of concert T-shirts, I was thankful that Katy couldn't read.

"Squish, squish," Katy was saying as she used the heel of the severed leg to stomp on the fat plush spiders that had spilled to the floor from a bin on the lower shelf.

"Awww, poor spider," I said. I noticed a rack of Skip Slydell's "Zombie Power!" T-shirts beside a display of zombie hygiene products, the top shelf of which was a large black bottle of Z, the body spray "for the active undead male." There was a separate line of Lady Z products, which differed mainly from their male counterparts in that they were in smaller, curvier bottles.

Kaitlyn's next words made me laugh out loud in a way that

I didn't even have to think about, like I do most of the time when I'm trying to laugh.

"He's a bad spider, Caring. I have to squish him."

Still laughing, I left Katy to her squishing and drifted over to look at the other products on the display. There was a perfume called Endless, in a slender purple-lacquered bottle. I chanced a spritz on my wrist from the sample bottle. The scent had a hint of incense beneath a floral base.

"Isn't that just the best?" a way perky voice called out, nearly making me drop the bottle.

"Hey, I'm sorry, I didn't mean to scare you," the perky girl said.

Scare me, I thought. Funny.

It was a revelation that I could be startled, actually. We—the dead, I mean—aren't exactly famous for our reaction time; most of my reflexes are no longer reflexive. You could tap my knee with a hammer all day and not get a movement, unless I wanted you to.

I saw a girl who looked like a taller, slighter version of Margi, except her hair spikes were purple over brown, and she'd shaved one side of her hair down to her skull. She had a wide silver ring through her nose, and an ascending column of silver studs curving along her ear. She was wearing a black T-shirt from the Zombie Power! line, which had the words "Open Graves, Open Minds . . ." across the chest in a Day-Glo green script. I had one just like it in my dresser at home.

"No worries," I said, turning away, but not before I saw a

Celtic braid tattooed on the inside of her arm. I set the bottle back on the shelf and rubbed my own arm through my denim jacket.

"What do you think?" the girl said. "Different, huh? I think it's the new patchouli, I really do. I wear it all the time. I bought the Z for my boyfriend, Jason."

Katy was still squishing spiders. The clerk didn't seem to mind.

"You date a zombie?" I asked.

"Naw," the clerk said, smiling in a way I thought conveyed a trace of disappointment. "We don't have any zombies at Winford High; they all go to Oakvale. Mostly it's trad kids that buy the colognes, anyway. We don't sell much of the skin stuff. But a zombie once came in here to buy some Z, and he was with a trad girl. It was great!"

"Great?" I said, now looking at the girl. I didn't see a name badge.

"Yeah," she said. "I mean, that was really brave of him, you know? And her, too. I *so* love your hair. How do you get that blond-y, silvery color?"

"It's . . . natural," I said. I was hitching in my speech a bit, something I only do when I'm emotional. Most zombies have trouble speaking at a normal pace, but big-mouth me usually speaks without pauses.

I guess I *was* a little emotional. My hair is even blonder than when I was alive, but the blond is all natural. Or all unnatural, if you prefer, since it happened when I died.

She reached out toward me, toward my hair, hesitating a

moment for a sign from me that it was okay. I told her it was with a flicker of my eyes. My bright blue eyes.

She let the long threads run through her fingers. "It's so soft," she said, "God, I'd die to have hair like this. It's just the best."

Irony! She doesn't know, I thought. She really doesn't know I'm dead.

"Thanks. I like the purple, too. And how you made it look wet. Very cool . . . What did you say your name was?"

"Tamara," the girl said. "But not Tammy. I hate Tammy."

"I'm Karen. That's my sister, Katy, destroying all your spiders."

Tamara turned back, laughing. "She can't hurt anything; they're stuffed," she said. She held out her hand at an angle, and each finger had a ring of some sort, some at the knuckle. "Nice to meet you, Karen."

I hesitated a moment before taking her hand, hoping that if I could concentrate on fur and sandy beaches and oven-fresh apple pie, Tamara wouldn't notice how cold my skin was.

"Nice to meet you too, Tamara not Tammy," I said. Really corny.

Tamara's grip was vigorous; there was a strength in her wiry, gangling frame, hidden like the spark of unlife is hidden somewhere within me. If she thought I was clammy or cold, she didn't say so.

My sudden self-consciousness made her look around. There were few people in the store, and a pair of teenage boys by the CD rack were looking at us and whispering to each other. The blond one with the bomber jacket smiled and nodded in our direction.

At me. He was smiling at *me*.

My God, I thought. I'm actually *passing*.

Tamara also saw the boys. She turned back to me with a wry, knowing smile on her face.

"Hey," Tamara said, finally releasing me, "I just thought of a great idea."

"I like . . . great ideas," I said, hitching again. It felt so good to be mistaken for alive!

"How about you apply for a job here? We just started looking for Christmas help."

"A job?" I said. Nothing could have been further from my mind.

"Sure. You'd fit right in. Then your sister could come back and squish Grinches or goth Frostys."

"Is there really such thing as a goth Frosty?"

"If there is, we'll carry it. Come on, it'll be fun. Besides," she said, her voice dropping to the whisper of conspiracy, "I get a twenty-five dollar gift certificate for every employee I recruit as long as they stay through Black Friday."

I laughed. "A whole twenty-five dollars? You could buy Jason a bottle of Z for Christmas."

Tamara pointed a sharp-nailed finger at me, her silver-knuckled thumb upraised.

"Now yer thinkin'," she said. "Come on, let's go fill out the application."

\* \* \*

Katy was asleep before we were halfway home. My father's gaze drifted to the rearview when he heard the soft squawk of a snore from the backseat.

"Thanks for letting me come tonight, Dad," I said.

"Sure," he said, looking at me with what seemed like real affection. His face was almost the same shade as mine in the greenish light from the dashboard. "Katy loves being with you."

"I know. I love being with her, too."

"We should do this more often," he said. "You coming out with us, I mean. Out places."

"I'd like that," I told him. I wasn't trying to be all cool or anything, just careful—because if I flipped out with Margi-esque enthusiasm, he might get all weird, and that would be the end of his wanting to be seen in public with me.

"We could go out more, to most places," he looked back at the road, and sighed. "You know what I mean."

"I know what you mean."

He turned the car stereo on. He had one of his Santana discs in the CD player and he let it play, turning it low so it wouldn't disturb Katy.

"Dad?"

"Yes?"

"I was offered a job at the mall tonight. At Wild Thingz!"

"Really?" he said. "Just like that?"

"Just like that."

He shook his head, laughing. "You always were full of surprises, Karen," he told me.

And I waited for it; I could almost hear it at the pause at the end of his words, a memory lingering just out of reach. What I waited for was for him to call me "honey," or "sweetie," as in "You were always full of surprises, Karen honey," which is the way he used to talk to me. Back when I was alive. I waited, but the words never came.

I'm a firm believer in epiphanies. I wasn't always, certainly not when I was depressed. A life of depression is a life without epiphanies. When most people think of the term "epiphany," they think of a moment of great personal insight, but the word often has spiritual significance. I'd like to think that my father had an epiphany in the car that night.

He didn't say it, but when he turned away from the road for a moment to look at me, I could see that the affection was still there in his eyes, and that it might actually be blossoming into more. Four years was a long time to some, but I hadn't aged a day, and for the love of my parents I could wait an eternity.

"I'd really like . . . to take the job," I told him.

"Absolutely," my Dad said. "I think it's about time you go to work."

"Really?"

"Really."

I wanted to hug him, to lean over the seat and kiss his cheek just like a real girl would do. Of course I didn't. I still had part of the story to tell.

"But, Dad?"

"Yes, Karen?"

"I don't think they realize I'm dead."

He didn't answer right away, and I assumed he was considering how to phrase his reversed position in a way that would be the least psychologically damaging to me. I was already placing a lot of faith in the tiny gleam of affection I'd seen in his eyes, wasn't I? The next light turned green as we approached, as did the next, and finally he spoke.

"Well," he said, "I won't tell them if you don't."

And then he did a beautiful thing, my Dad did. He winked at me.

# CHAPTER SEVEN

THINGS AT HOME IMPROVED, strangely, in the days that followed the Guttridge "murders." The new state rules regarding zombies—the curfew, the banning from schools, the requirement to be staying with a legal guardian—created a feeling of solidarity at home. Even with Mom, who was much kinder to me, although Dad must have told her about all the various ways I was breaking the law.

I think she was reaching out to me in her own way. Christmas at the DeSonne household almost felt like a real Christmas for me, even though I wasn't invited to attend church with my parents. Maybe if they weren't such sporadic attendees—they were lapsed to the point where they only set foot in the church for Christmas, Easter, funerals, and weddings—they would have risked bringing me along, but in truth I wasn't so disappointed that I couldn't go. Since my suicide I've been scared of setting foot in a church.

Katy threw a minor tantrum, saying that she wanted to stay with me, when in reality we all knew that she wanted to stay with her new toys. New dolls and a house for them to live in, stuffed animals, DVDs, an electronic keyboard, games, sneakers—she'd gotten a pretty good haul. My parents included me this year and supplemented my usual mall gift certificates with a present I could actually unwrap: a book.

"We'll play when you get back home, Katy," I told her, once she'd settled down a bit.

"Those are my dolls," she said, sniffling. If I wasn't a zombie I would have been struggling to hold my laughter inside.

"Oh, I know they are," I said, nodding gravely. "I'll wait for you to get home."

She stuck out a pouty lip. "You can play wif them if you want," she said. "Just one."

"We'll be back in a couple hours," my father said, his tone apologetic as my mother waved from the car. "If you could just keep an eye on the turkey, I'd appreciate it." He was leaning in close to me because he knew that Mom didn't like me around their food.

"Okay, Dad." I said. I stood in the doorway and watched them drive away. The sun was shining and I had to squint my eyes against the reflection of the light on the snow.

I wasn't sad. Not really. I sat on the sofa with my new book on my lap and looked at the colored lights around the tree blinking on and off. I'd bought my mother a jacket, my father a retro punk T-shirt, and my sister a trio of stuffed bears. I could smell the pine. I could smell the turkey cooking in the next room. I opened my new book and I could feel the pages beneath my fingertips.

When they came home, Mom rushed into the kitchen to check on the food, Katy rushed to the tree to check her toys, and Dad just rushed.

"How was church?" I asked.

"Long," was his reply.

I watched Katy play. Eventually she asked me if I wanted to help her bring her dolls to her room so we could play with them there.

"Why don't we stay here and play?" I said to my sister, knowing that Mom didn't like me in her room. "It's so pretty by the tree." It was a reflexive suggestion on my part; I didn't know that my mother was watching us from the doorway, wiping her hands dry with a dish towel.

Mom smiled at me. I know this doesn't seem like much, but it meant the world to me. I was so used to the tight expression she wore when she saw me with Kaitlyn, so used to her manufacturing some silly errand for me to do just to keep us apart. But this time she smiled and sat on the couch in the living room while Kaitlyn and I played dolls, looking at the newspaper, then a magazine, and then her library book. She was supervising but not policing, I guess.

Kaitlyn had four dolls, two blond Barbies, a brunette, and another that had a few strands of crinkly blond hair attached to the taupe plastic dome of her head. This one was Señorita, and it was Katy's favorite, even after the haircut. As usual, Katy asked me to be a Barbie named Anne, one of the blondes.

"This dolly is a zombie dolly," Kaitlyn said, handing me bikini-clad Anne.

"She's very pretty," I told her.

"She's the dead one," Katy said, "so she's the prettiest."

"You think so, Katy? The other girls are pretty, too." I tried not to look up at my Mom.

"Anne is the prettiest one. But nobody likes her."

"Because she's the prettiest?"

"No," Katy said, using a microscopic plastic brush on Señorita's remaining strands. "Because she's dead."

I glanced at my mother then, but she was pretending not to hear our conversation. She turned a page after wetting her index finger.

"Anne is sad," Katy continued, "but she's still very, very pretty. And she likes to dance."

"Well," I said, standing Anne up on the toes of her impossibly arched feet. "Maybe the other girls will try to like her if she's really nice and friendly."

I twirled Anne slowly on the carpet, and then pushed one of her legs in the air and back down again, humming a slow but happy tune. Katy had Señorita and the other blonde join in the dance by hopping them up and down six inches off the floor, as though the carpet was a dolly trampoline.

"They're friends now," Katy announced. "We need to decorate their house for them."

See how easy it could be for zombies and trads to get along? I looked at my mother. She turned another page. Quick reader.

"When I grow up, I want to be a zombie, too," Kaitlyn said.

My mother either didn't hear or was pretending that she hadn't heard.

"No, Kaitlyn," I said. "You don't want to be a zombie. It's much more fun to be alive."

Isn't it funny, the look a child can give you to let you know just how insane they think you are? Kaitlyn gave me one of those looks just then.

"Someday you'll be alive again, too, Caring," she said, her tone matter-of-fact. She started brushing zombie Barbie's hair with the pixie-sized brush, and that was her final word on the subject.

An hour or so later dinner was ready.

"Would you like to sit at the table?" my mother asked me. Behind her I saw my father nearly drop his glass of wine.

"I'd love to," I said, and I sat with them, watching them eat.

Katy started yawning around seven thirty, and my father picked her up to take her to bed, but not before she wriggled out of his arms to plant a kiss on my cheek. She Godzilla-stomped her way to my mother and kissed her, too. It wouldn't have surprised me to see my mother turn away from Katy's kisses, as though the zombie virus could be passed by kissing, but she didn't. Katy gave her a big wet one on her cheek, and Mom responded with a flurry of little pecks and a smooch on the lips that made Katy giggle.

"She loves you," Mom said when Dad had disappeared down the hall with his warm bundle. She'd looked almost proud when she'd kissed Kaitlyn, as if she were proving something not only to me and Dad, but to herself.

"I love her," I said. "She's . . ." I paused. I was about to say, "She's the only good thing that came out of my dying," but I checked myself, not knowing how Mom would react. I made the pause seem like a typical zombie pause rather than one of self-censorship.

"A great kid."

Mom nodded and went back to her book. When Dad came out of Katy's room twenty minutes later, I wished them both good night and went downstairs into my cave, a big smile on my face.

But it wasn't all healing, psychic and otherwise, that was taking place at the DeSonne household. I'd Tivo'd the Guttridge footage and must have watched it a thousand times over the course of the holiday season. I was searching for clues, of course, and clues began to appear.

Not only were "the zombies'" walks all wrong, but the carpets they were carrying didn't look like they had bodies in them. They didn't bulge enough and there didn't seem to be enough weight on the "zombies" shoulders. And then another weird thing I noticed: In one brief clip, two "zombies" were facing each other at either end of the carpet they were carrying across the Guttridge's back lawn. Other clips of the house showed the front steps and a sliding door that led to a high deck, which meant that there were multiple cameras and the footage had been edited together.

One day my father came into the living room while I was watching the footage.

"Something bothers me about those clips," he said.

I tried to be nonchalant, even though I'd just paused the screen on the most distinct image of Fake Tak, who was much wider across the shoulders and chest than real Tak, who is tall and lanky. Fake Tak looked like a football player. Fake Tak looked like Pete Martinsburg.

"Oh, really?"

"Yeah. I've watched it a few times now. The whole time I was thinking, those look like movie zombies, really low-budget movie zombies. And they're built like men, not kids. Except for maybe that guy you've frozen on."

Sometimes I really wanted to hug my Dad. I probably should have hugged him then; I don't even think he would have minded. But you never know. "Yeah, you're right," I said.

"There's a story out now that Guttridge was under investigation by the IRS."

"Oh?" Like I said, my Dad was a Reagan-era punk. It makes him more attuned to the idea of governmental conspiracy and cover-up. "I hadn't heard that."

"And then there's the evidence having gone missing. Very strange, in light of there being a newly formed unit of the FBI to deal specifically with crimes involving zombies."

"The Undead Crimes Unit," I said, and then I told him about having met agents Alholowicz and Gray in Undead

Studies class. It was just like every cop show you've ever seen, with Iceman Gray acting all bad-coppy while his overweight partner, Alholowicz, shirttails flapping out of his suit-from-Sears pants, did his best to be all buddy-buddy. They came in to grill us about stuff that happened at the Winford cemetery, and they already thought Takayuki was responsible for that crime and probably a dozen others. I went all dumb blonde and asked them if Takayuki was the chicken you could get on sticks at Sakura in the mall food court.

They were less than pleased with me.

Dad slipped a couple gears when I told him about the grilling. At first he was a little miffed that I hadn't told him about it before, but we haven't really had the sort of relationship where I come home and blather on about my school day. He never asked, and I never offered. I never told him about the Undead Studies class, even. I just went. I think for us dead kids, parental permission was sort of optional anyhow; there was a space for a signature on the information slip, but I went ahead and filled in his name—the fact that I forged his signature probably would have ticked him off, but me taking the class would have had no impact on him whatsoever. I just didn't want to discuss it at the time.

"You spoke to federal agents without us even getting a phone call?" he said, really spun up.

"Dad," I said, "they aren't required to tell you anything. We're dead. We're not citizens. In the eyes of our country, we're non-persons."

I could see it really getting to him, so I laid it on thick. "We can't get insurance. We can't vote, we can't get married. There isn't much we *can* do."

Now Dad was getting agitated. He'd somehow compartmentalized the things that the undead dealt with on a daily basis—the inability to get licenses of any sort, the inability to leave the country legally, the inability to even be seen in certain public arenas—but the idea that the feds could detain his little dead girl without even a courtesy call was somehow too much for him to bear.

I was worried that Dad was going to start making a battery of calls to congressmen, state reps, et al., which wouldn't work with my plans to be an undercover agent, so I started talking to him about the Undead Studies class. I guess I wanted him to know that not every institution out there was bent on subjugating the undead. I mean, there was the fact that Oakvale High School, under the leadership of Principal Kim, opened their doors to zombies—that alone was pretty rare, right? Yes, recent events banned zombie children from attending school, but at least we'd been allowed to go for a little while.

It's as if he and my mother assumed that the world no longer had any consequences for me. Who cares if I got an A on my math test (or, more likely, a C)? It wasn't as if I was going to college. Who cares if I dated? It wasn't as if I was going to get married. I was just marking time, and the time I was marking had already expired in their eyes.

But the idea of trads and zombies discussing the social impact of the Undead in America was interesting to him, and I have to admit, the more I talked about it, the more wistful I became about the class. I didn't join because I thought we were going to solve the world's problems, like Tommy and some of the others did. I joined because I thought it would be a hoot and because some of the other people who were joining looked interesting. And I guess it was expected of me.

But if I hadn't joined that class I wouldn't have any living friends. No Margi, no then-living Adam, no super-cute Thornton J. Harrowwood III, either. No Phoebe. That alone would be a reason to do it all again.

# CHAPTER EIGHT

I DIDN'T KILL MYSELF BECAUSE of unrequited love. I killed myself because I was depressed. People can argue the chicken-or-egg aspects of depression all they want; is depression triggered by life's trials and tribulations, or do life's trials and tribulations lead to depression? In my mind there's no argument, no discussion. The blue fog existed before I did; it could come without warning, and when it did it annihilated everything. Maybe life could trigger it, but it was going to be there one way or the other.

But I didn't kill myself because the one I loved didn't love me. I don't have any blame to assign. I killed myself because I'm sick.

Because the one I loved *did* love me. But I couldn't let anyone find out.

\* \* \*

He called me while I was walking around the mall, on a break. Christmas had come and gone and we were into a new year. I didn't recognize the number, but I answered anyway. What can I say? I'm a lonely girl.

"Hello?"

"Hey," he said. "What are you doing?"

Not "How are you, this is Pete" or "You might not remember me, but . . ." I knew it was him the moment he spoke. That sort of self-assurance is hard to mistake.

"Hi, Pete," I said. "I didn't think you were going to call."

His voice was a low, dark presence through the tiny cellphone speaker.

"Now why wouldn't I call you?" he said.

"I don't know." Because they upped your meds? Because you are an insane, murderous freak?

"Can I come see you?" No footsie, no flirting, right to the point. Just straight ahead and damn the torpedoes—that was my experience with Pete.

"I'm at work," I replied, all giggly, but trying not to overdo it.

"So quit."

"I can't quit, Pete!"

"Why not?"

*Um, well, I . . .*

"I'm saving to get a place of my own," I said, actually stammering. "Well, with a roommate or two. I need this job."

"I want to take you for a drive."

"A drive?"

95

"Yeah, a drive. I got a new car this summer and I want to see how you look in it."

Bold, bold. "I can't just leave."

"You live with your parents now?"

"'Fraid so."

"What time do you get out?"

"Four o'clock. When Tamara gets here."

"I'll see you then. Better call Tamara and tell her not to be late. Meet me out front."

I simulated a sigh, like I was weighing this as a major life decision.

"What?" he said.

"Nothing. Okay, four o'clock." Then, "I'd really like to see you, Pete."

"Great. Later."

And that was how I began dating Pete Martinsburg.

Of course, I wasn't really *dating* him dating him. I was spying on him.

After Pete hung up I was feeling a little excited but also a little blue, as in blue-foggy blue. I went into the back room to open some freight. The box cutters that we use are six-inch-long metal rectangles, about an inch wide, that are coated with yellow rubber. You push at the back of the rectangle to unsheathe the blade, which is the corner of a razor held in place by a metal band. Opening my very first box, which turned out to be full of zombie skin products, I accidentally slashed right across the underside of my forearm about halfway between my elbow and my wrist. The cut was long and deep, and in the twenty seconds I stood there staring at it with what I'm sure was a stunned look on my face, it began to well up with blackish-green fluid.

I *think* it was an accident.

I wasn't going to let a lethal cut spoil my date with Pete. I went into the bathroom, washed away the zombie blood (so much like caterpillar guts—good thing I'm pretty on the outside, because I'm nothing but gross on the inside) as best I could, and then used half a dozen bandages to try and press the edges of my skin together. I took my sleeves down and hoped for the best.

The whole point was that I was going to Solve the Mystery. I was going to Uncover Evidence. I was going to Blow the Lid off the Great Anti-Zombie Conspiracy. I was going to help bring Pete Martinsburg and his coconspirators to justice.

But things, as they tend to do, got out of hand.

Craig let me leave my shift fifteen minutes early. Ten of those minutes I spent in the bathroom trying to look alive. I'd already called my father to let him know that he didn't need to pick me up because I was going out with friends. If I were alive, there would have been about three dozen follow-up questions—the who, what, where, when, and why of it all. Instead he told me to be careful, and to have fun.

Pete was waiting for me outside, leaning against a gleaming red sports car that was parked at the curb right by the front entrance. There was sand and salt and snow all over the roads, but his car was sparkly clean, the low purr of the engine like that of a just-fed cat. It was close to dusk but he was still wearing sunglasses, and I could see my reflection in their silver-mirrored surface.

"I left it running for you," he said, "so you'd be warm."

"Nice," I said, indicating the car but still looking at him.

"C'mon," he said.

He opened the door for me, just like a gentleman, and let his hand linger on the small of my back as he guided me expertly into his car.

"It still smells new," I said, running my hand along the seat. I caught traces of cologne on top of the scent of leather.

"I like things to be clean," he said, watching my legs as I tucked the hem of my skirt out of the doorway so he could seal me inside. I don't blame him—we can all agree I have great legs.

He got in and drove off. Casually, as if he enjoyed the feel of the machine, and not like some knuckleheads do with their first four-wheel toy, peeling out and leaving an inch-thick streak of rubber on the pavement. He turned the radio on but didn't blare the music as one of those commercial alternative bands with three words in their name came on. They were singing about something that seemed vaguely related to the life I'd left behind. We drove like that for awhile, not saying anything until he asked me if I was warm enough, his hand already on the temperature control.

Such a funny question! Warm enough for what? Well, sure, I'm warm enough!

Karen's rules of flirting, Number seventeen: In order to

appear both mysterious and exciting, avoid direct answers to the questions your target asks. Instead, answer ones the target hasn't asked.

"It's so nice in here," I said, trailing the fingertips of my left hand along my shoulder strap and stroking the armrest with my right.

"Yeah," he said, glancing over at me. And when I say "glancing at me" I actually mean my face—not my chest or my legs. I suppose I should be making him out to be the totally loathsome creep I know him to be, but in the interest of truth in advertising and full disclosure, I can't do that. He was forward, sure, and maybe just a little aggressive, but in a way that was flattering and not stalker-y or gorilla-like at all. I know the difference; I've been with a lot of gorillas. He repulsed me, obviously, but not because of the way he was acting.

"So," I said, "where are we going?"

"Does it matter?"

"Not really."

We were both pros at this, I could tell. It was sort of like a complicated dance where your partner knows all of your moves.

A car cut him off on the highway and he didn't even get angry. The other times I'd watched him—in school, or that time in the woods—you could almost see the anger, like a snake slithering beneath his skin. With me in the car he was calm, relaxed.

"I thought we'd go to Lake Oxoboxo. Have you ever been there?"

"Yes," I said, and debated adding "many times," which would have made him think I was, um, promiscuous. The lake—like secluded lakes all over the country—is our town's make-out spot.

"I like it there," he said, managing to make it sound like it was the lakeside ambiance he craved and not the opportunity to paw me in the backseat. "You said you went to school at Winford?"

"Yes," I said, and I wondered if I should steer him away from the lake—not because I was afraid he was going to try to jump my bones (although the odds of that did seem likely), but because most of my friends were hiding inside of it.

"You guys always beat us in football," he said. "Except this year."

"I haven't been to any games since I quit school," I told him.

"Were you a cheerleader?"

"Nope, not me."

"Huh," he said, glancing at me. "I'm still trying to figure out where I've seen you before."

"One of the games, probably," I told him. "I used to go."

We arrived at the lake. Pete pulled into a small dirt lot near the boat launch, next to a few snow-dusted picnic tables in front of the beach.

"You weren't Gino Manetti's girlfriend, were you?" he asked.

I shook my head, trying not to panic. What if he knew all

the other players, studied their stats or whatever. "No. I used to go out with Jordan." There were hundreds of Jordans in Winford, right?

"Huh. We beat Winford this year, though. Last game I'll ever play."

Pete kept the engine running, killing his headlights. The frozen lake was a luminescent blue in the darkness; the moon swallowed up by the clouds. I felt like I was stepping out onto that ice, with my next question.

"That's the game that zombie played in, isn't it?"

Pete nodded. He was looking out at the lake, not at me. "Tommy Williams played one series of downs," he said. "What a hero."

"You didn't have to, like, shower with him, did you?"

This was me being all spy-girl. I wasn't actually commenting on Tommy's hygiene; he's quite clean and uses the full line of Z products. Pete thought it was funny, anyhow.

"No. Thank God."

"I'd hate to have one of them in the shower. In the locker room. Ick."

"They snuck him out the door when the game was still going on, afraid people would attack him or something. People threw rotten fruit at us during the game."

"I saw. That was pretty terrible."

He looked at me with a weird smile on his face, as though he suspected that *I'd* been one of the fruit hurlers.

"Williams is in D.C. right now," he said. "Trying to get government aid for zombies. There's talk about him organizing a protest march or a rally or something like that, and people are actually coming out of the woodwork to support him."

He drummed his fingers on the steering wheel.

"All because of my bad aim," he said. Then, "You want to take a walk?"

"Sure."

We exited his car, and I pretended to hug myself against the cold. Pete was wearing a thick ski jacket, and I was wearing a heavy coat, hat, and gloves. I looked like a proper little snow bunny, except that my breath wasn't visible when I exhaled the way it would be if I were a, um, breather.

"I grew up in this town," Pete said, as we walked down to the short dock. "Back before there were any zombies."

He didn't just say zombies, though. He made the term a little more colorful.

"Your school was one of the first to enroll dead kids, wasn't it?" As if I didn't know. That was why my parents had moved to Oakvale one summer after our first move to a remote town in Maine.

"Yeah. And then they started that stupid zombie-love class, which was like leaving out a piece of raw meat and waiting for the flies. Corpsicles from all over started coming to Oakvale."

I was trying to think of something to say when he abruptly changed subjects.

"So," he said. "What's your deal?"

"My deal?"

"Yeah. How come you dropped out of school?"

I shrugged. "Oh, I don't know."

"Grades?"

I licked my lips. "Let's say discipline problems."

"Yeah?"

"Yes. I'm very undisciplined."

I was dancing again. He was obviously intrigued by my discipline problems, but I didn't want to have to create some elaborate story about how I was a candidate for reform school or anything.

Not that I didn't have the material. I could have just told him about the months that led up to my suicide.

"So you were aiming at him?" I said. I figured he wouldn't have brought it up in the first place if he didn't want to talk about it. "The zombie?"

He stood on the edge of the dock, looking out over the lake. If he thought my segue was strange, he didn't react.

"He was trying to get it on with a living girl. How repugnant is that?"

"Pretty repugnant," I said, thinking how different his version of the story was from the one I'd heard.

"More zombies were coming. When I saw that I shot Layman instead of the zombie, I lost my head. He used to be one of my best friends. Layman, I mean."

"I didn't know that."

"Yeah. But he pretty much chose being friends with the walking corpses instead of me. Still, I wasn't happy about shooting him, you know?"

We left the dock and walked along the short beach toward the woods, the frosted sand crunching under our feet.

It must have been freezing but Pete was too cool to show that temperature could affect him.

"After I shot him I just took off through the woods. TC—he's this guy I used to hang out with—we got separated. I was attacked by a bunch of zombies. A freakin' horde—seven or eight of them, at least. Some of them had knives. This one guy had really long hair and only half a face."

He pointed to his scar. I thought it was weird that I could heal bullet holes but he'd have that scar forever.

"He gave me this."

"Oh," I said, hoping that my eyes looked wet and sympathetic. Tak never talked about his rendezvous, but I'd always had the impression that he was alone when he caught up to Pete in the woods. Neither George or Popeye was staying at the Haunted House then, and Tayshawn hadn't allied himself with Tak yet. But being attacked by a ravenous horde of zombies sounds more impressive, doesn't it?

"He said they were going to kill me. And they tried like hell, but I managed to overpower the one that cut me."

*Yeah, right.*

"It gave me enough time to get away. Corpsicles aren't very fast."

I looked at the tree line, pretending to be terrified.

"You don't think there are any zombies there now, do you? In the woods?"

"Nah. Not with all the new laws, and with the police looking for them. They'll arrest any corpsicle that doesn't have a legal guardian. I figure they've all burrowed back into their graves. Or someone else's grave, whatever."

"Really?" I said, trying to shudder. "Really, that's what you think?"

"Yeah. But I'm going to find them. I'm going to find them and burn them out of their holes."

The vehemence and conviction in his voice was frightening, but it also got me very angry. I might be a good little actress, but those were my friends he was talking about.

"Is that why you came back to Oakvale?"

"Yeah. And I've got something else planned. Something the Reverend is going to love."

"What?"

Maybe I sounded too eager, because he looked at me, smiling. Smiling like a wolf, I thought. "How do I know I can trust you?"

I looked up at him. "You can trust me." I whispered. I left my lips slightly parted.

"Sure," he said, laughing. He put his arm around my shoulder. "You're shivering. Let's get out of here."

He drove me home—or a few streets away from home, because I told him my father couldn't know I was with him—without making a move or anything, which seems ludicrous, considering how hot I am. He asked me if I was okay walking the rest of the way, and when I said I was, he nodded, and for a moment I thought he was just going to drive off, but then he asked if we could get together tomorrow night.

And I said yes.

# CHAPTER NINE

THIS MIGHT BE THE hottest chick that I've ever been with, Pete thought.

Perfect skin, perfect figure. Maybe it only took a few weeks among the gorgons, to cement the idea in his head that Christie was something special, but he thought it was more than that. She was even hotter than his sisters' friends, the ones he used to go with in California, there was a little something different in the way she walked.

She was funny, too, whereas most of the girls he knew were brain-dead.

"You smell nice," he'd told her when she climbed, oh-so-slowly, like a cat, into his car.

"Thanks," she said. "It's Lady Z."

"Lady Z? That zombie stuff?"

The way she'd looked at him, her blue eyes seemingly sparkling from within, was like a caffeine spike to the blood.

"You don't like that zombie stuff, I take it?"

"Not a big fan, no."

"Do you still like me?" she'd said.

"Oh, yeah."

And he did. Hot, smart but not smart-assed, and natural. That was something that was different about her than most of the girls from school; she was very natural, very real. Without pretense.

But mostly, she was hot. It had taken a great deal of effort not to put the moves on her the other night.

He chuckled to himself. If the Reverend only knew how good he was getting at so-called "emotional mastery"!

She was so hot he wanted to show her off, so he took her over to his old haunt, the fast food restaurant where all his friends used to hang out. The parking lot was full of cars, and there was a loose group of teens, six or seven of them, having loud fun beside a pair of humming muscle cars.

Pete watched the guys watching Christie as she got out of his car.

"Friends of yours?" she said. She knew they were watching her, but she didn't seem bothered or threatened by it. He liked that.

"Maybe," he said. "Used to be."

They went inside and he ordered three cheeseburgers, large fries, and a soda. He asked Christie what she wanted and she said a hot fudge sundae.

"Ice cream?" he asked, getting his wallet out of his jacket. "On a night like this?"

"I like sweet things."

Oh, man, Pete thought.

He took the tray and led her to a corner booth, taking the seat facing the wall so she could see and be seen.

"So," he said, unwrapping the first cheeseburger, "tell me all about Christie."

She laughed, and he took a big bite of his burger.

"Not much to tell. I'm seventeen, I live with my parents and little sister. I quit school to go work and have fun."

"Bold move," Pete said after swallowing. He drew on his straw. "Did you grow up here?"

She shook her head, and he watched the light catch in her hair. "No, we're from Iowa. We moved here a couple years ago."

"You and all the zombies," he said. "Iowa, huh?"

"Iowa."

She seemed to be watching him eat very closely, but not like she was grossed out by him or anything. More like she was interested. Pete knew a girl like that in California; she was always bringing him cookies and all sorts of other junk that she'd made for him to eat. She wasn't one of the more attractive girls that hung around, so he figured she was trying to make up for it by feeding him or something.

Pete was a very fastidious eater, unlike some of the guys he played football with who sounded more like grunting swine when they ate than like human beings. TC especially. Pete polished off the first burger and watched Christie watching him chew.

"How's your sundae?" he asked, unwrapping his second burger. She hadn't even taken a bite yet; the soft-serve vanilla was still a gently swirled mound, as pristine and smooth as her skin.

"Oh, it's great!" she said. She looked down at the sundae for a long moment, as if contemplating what the dessert could do to her figure. He liked that. The sundae was packed with calories, and a girl should be concerned with how many she ate.

She took the slightest nip of hot fudge off the tip of the sundae, then licked the spoon. He liked that even more.

"What about you, Pete?" she said. "Why'd it take you so long to call me?"

"I've been away."

Another nip of the sundae. "Mmm-hmm."

"I was. I've got tell you, I hate cold weather. Hate it. I had the chance to go out to Arizona and . . ."

Christie looked up at the door with something like shock, and when Pete turned he saw a lumbering form making a bee-line for him.

Speak of the devil, he thought. Stavis's face was florid beneath a Dallas Cowboys stocking cap.

"Pete," he called, his voice loud. "Pete, man!"

Pete turned back to Christie. "Friend of mine," he said, trying to put her at ease. She didn't look like she enjoyed having their conversation disrupted.

"Pete," TC said, tagging Pete on the shoulder with a blow that would have sent a less solid companion sprawling. "Pete, why the hell didn't you call me? How long have you been back?"

"Hey, TC," Pete said. He may have been gritting his teeth.

"I saw your car in the lot. How long have you been back, man?"

"A little while," Pete said. "TC, this is Christie. Christie, TC."

"Oh, hey," TC said. Pete watched his friend take Christie in, his eyes never rising above her neck. Class act.

"Hi," Christie said, sliding along the bench to make room. Pete knew that she knew where TC's attention was focused, but she didn't seem to mind.

TC slid in beside her, managing to press himself against her despite the vast amount of room she'd left him. Christie's eyes met Pete's, and she smiled as though to tell him she didn't mind his friend's boorish behavior.

"So how's life in the seminary?" TC said, helping himself to a cluster of french fries.

"It isn't a seminary, dumbass," Pete replied, watching TC bring the cluster to his fleshy lips with his fat fingers. "It's a retreat center."

"Yeah, like a religious place, right?"

"Like," Pete said. He glanced at Christie to see how she was fielding this new info about him. She looked intrigued.

"What's it like? Pretty dull, I bet." Another bunch of fries went into his mouth.

"Are you enjoying those?" Pete said.

"Huh? Oh, yeah."

Shaking his head, Pete turned to him to speak directly to Christie.

"I was living at the One Life Retreat Center in Arizona, which is part of One Life Ministries, an organization started by the Reverend Nathan Mathers. Do you know who he is?"

If life were a cartoon, there would have been a large black question mark hanging in the air over TC's thick head. He answered before Christie could speak.

"He's the guy that writes those books about zombies, right? I saw him on TV once," he said, as though to banish the idea that he might actually have read one of those books.

"That's right. *And the Graves Gave Up Their Dead* and *Cloaked in Human Flesh*, among others. The Reverend has a school program there."

"Dag," TC, incredulous, said. "I thought you got off with just community service and counseling."

"What? What do you mean?"

"Well, being there is, like, punishment, right? It's like a reform school, isn't it? A religious reform school?"

Pete laughed.

"No, dummy, it isn't like that at all. I wanted to be there." He winked at Christie, who really did seem intrigued at this point. He leaned in across the table and whispered to her.

"He teaches us how to kill zombies," he whispered.

"Seriously?" TC said, eyes widening, a fry almost escaping from the corner of his mouth.

Pete, laughing, punched him with a raised knuckle to the sternum. TC coughed and swore.

"Not exactly," Pete said, as TC inconspicuously rubbed his new bruise. "But pretty close. You might like it there, TC."

"I don't know. I'm not exactly the churchgoing type. And there's no football."

"You can't play football with the Badgers anymore, either, you idiot. And it isn't about forcing everybody into church every day, anyway. His ministry is more about helping you understand yourself and the way you relate to other people. The idea being that by understanding yourself you'd be more inclined to want to understand the divine."

"Really?" Christie asked.

"Yeah. It works," he said. "I went to church for the first time since I was a little kid."

"No kidding," TC said, dubious.

"Too soon to tell, but I might have even gotten something out of it, too."

TC grinned. "That mean you can't hang out with me anymore?"

"Nah," Pete answered. "I just don't want to."

TC's laughter was nervous, and Pete waited a beat before joining in with him.

"I'm just kidding, man. Maybe you can visit me out in A-Z, though. You might like it." He looked at me. "You, too, Christie. There aren't nearly enough women at One Life for my liking." Gorgons aplenty, he thought, but no women.

"Oh," she said with a practiced nonchalance. "Is that what would make you happy? More women?"

"It's a start."

"Church, and no girls? You really pitch a strong case, Pete," TC said.

"Hey," Pete said, feinting with another raised-knuckle punch, making TC flinch. "At least it's warm."

"Okay. Sold," TC answered, probably just not wanting to get hit again. "So, are we going to hang now that you're back?"

"I'm only back for a few more days," Pete said, trying to see if the news disappointed Christie. "But yeah, we'll get together."

"We should kick Lame Man's ass while you're here," TC said around a mouthful of fries that had cooled, untouched, in their cardboard carton.

"Layman's still around?" Pete said. "I thought the zombies were confined to their houses or something."

"Yeah, but the maggot farm is still going to school, if you believe it. I thought it was against the law or something, but nobody seems to want to do anything about Layman."

Agitated, he started choking on his wad of fries, and it took a few minutes of violent coughing for him to regain his wind.

"We've got something planned for him," TC said, his face bright red from his near-death experience. "You want in?"

"Nope. You're on your own with that one. I do anything to him, and I could end up in prison. You better watch it, too. You almost got dragged in as an accessory."

TC waved the concern away with his greasy mitt of a hand. "Whatever. He's got it coming."

"They've all got it coming. Which reminds me—you haven't seen any of his other corpse buddies around, have you?"

"It's like they vanished, man. I haven't seen a zombie since before Christmas, other than Lame Man. It's been great."

"Hmm. None of them, huh? Where do you think they went?"

Christie shivered. Pete wondered if all this zombie talk was scaring her.

"Underground. Like worms." Here he wiggled his fat fingers, still glistening with fry grease. "Back to their graves. Hey, did you see the footage of what happened to your lawyer?"

"I saw it," Pete said, the corner of his lip twitching.

"One of them was the guy that cut you, wasn't it?"

Another twitch, just short of a smirk.

"Yeah."

"Bet you'd like to get back at that guy, huh?"

"I don't think about it anymore," Pete said.

"Don't worry, Pete. We'll get him, too."

Pete didn't answer right away.

"Glad we could catch up, TC. But maybe you can let me get back to talking with Christie here, okay?"

"Huh? Oh. Oh sure, yeah. Listen, I'll . . ."

"I'll call you, TC."

TC blinked. "Okay. Yeah."

"Nice meeting you," Christie said, waving at his back as he walked away.

Pete lifted his hands like "what are you gonna do?"

"Sorry," he said. "No manners."

"He was pretty happy to see you," Christie said. "If he had a tail it would have been wagging."

"TC's a moron. But he's a loyal moron."

"Like a dog."

"Yeah, just like a dog."

"Do you think he's serious about getting back at Layman?" she said, shaving a layer of vanilla off the sundae with the edge of her plastic spoon. "That's the kid that you . . ."

Pete nodded. "Yeah. He's the kid I zombified. But TC won't do anything without me around to lead him."

"But you don't want to get back at them? The zombies, I mean?"

"Oh, I didn't say that. I've got something really special planned for Layman and his creepy girlfriend."

Christie leaned in toward him, smiling.

"And just what would that be?"

Pete laughed, watching her as she brought the spoon to her pink lips.

"I can't tell you. If I get caught, you could get arrested as an accessory."

"Is that all I am to you?" she said, pretending to pout. "An accessory?"

He regarded her closely. "You really should come out to Arizona with me."

"Oh. So you were serious about that."

He looked at her, thinking it over. Young girl, attractive, lousy relationship with her parents, dropout, directionless—if she wasn't perfect for One Life Ministries he didn't know who was.

"Yeah, Christie," he said. "You should come with me."

"It sounds kind of interesting."

"It is. It really is. Life changing."

He looked down the remains of his meal: the half eaten burger, the few fries that had escaped TC's greedy fingers.

"I'm done. Let's blow."

"Okay."

Christie asked him not to drive to her house but to let her off at the edge of her neighborhood. She said that her father was a violent man, and said it in a way that implied regular, repeated violence to her, as well as the prospect of similar treatment for him, and once again Pete thought that she needed to go out west with him. He liked her, which was something he couldn't say about any of the other girls he'd been with.

None of them, at least, since Julie.

The interior of his car was warm. The heat seemed to be coming off of him as much as it did from the vents on the dash.

She turned to him.

He leaned forward and kissed her.

# CHAPTER TEN

I WALKED HOME THROUGH the woods. The neighborhood where I'd had Pete drop me off wasn't the one I lived in. The whole way home I couldn't stop thinking, *I just made out with Pete Martinsburg.*

It was gross in so many ways. I guess it's a good thing that zombies can't throw up.

After his initial kiss, which kind of took me by surprise, I resisted, and of course that only got him going even more. He was that type; the type who believed that no was just a more challenging stage of yes.

Toward the end—and although in my head it seemed like an eternity, it really didn't last long—I managed to give him the impression that I was enjoying it. I guess I can act. And then he sat back like the conquering hero, like he's such a good kisser and a stud that he broke down all my resistance. I'm sure that when he came up for air he thought I was the one left wanting more.

I wondered what it was like for him. Were my lips cold, less responsive than a living girl's? I tried to think of beaches, of kittens, of warm fuzzy sweaters—but did he feel how cool I was when he touched my skin? Did he notice that sometimes I forgot to breathe, or did he think passion was making me breathless?

*Ick.*

Walking home through the woods, the places where he'd touched me felt like they'd been splashed with acid. Of course I couldn't taste anymore—except sometimes strawberries when I ate a whole bunch of them—but I had this weird sensation in my mouth, akin to the feeling you'd get from biting on tinfoil. That's how attracted I was to Pete Martinsburg.

This was going to be harder than I thought.

But now I had even more reason to play girl detective, more than just getting to the bottom of his previous crimes. He was planning to do something to Phoebe and Adam, and whatever it was, it was something I couldn't allow to happen. I couldn't tell them just yet, though. Not until I could prove that he framed my friends for the Guttridge murders. Until I could do that, zombies would never be free. My people would remain underground.

The house was quiet and everyone asleep when I finally made it home. I crept upstairs to look in on Katy, hoping that there weren't any monsters walking around in her dreams.

The next day, my father asked me if I wanted to go for a spin. Mom and Katy were out shopping.

"Sure," I said.

"Okay," he said, tossing me the keys. "You drive."

And it was just like falling off a log. Or like riding a bicycle, whichever. Actually I think we dead folk would have a tougher time with the bicycle.

I used to be a good driver. My reflexes were a bit slower now, but I managed.

I thought maybe we were going to have a deep conversation, but we didn't talk much at all. He mentioned work and I mentioned work, and we sort of pretended I was normal.

When we were headed home, a squirrel ran out in front of the car, and I was quick enough to hit the brakes and avoid squishing his furry little head. Maybe a little too quick; the road was icy, but luckily we didn't shimmy or swerve.

Dad frowned at me. "Next time, kill the squirrel."

"I couldn't do that!" I told him.

"Better him than us."

I smiled.

"Squirrels don't come back," I told him.

Dad turned red. He really was forgetting I was anything but normal.

"Damn shame," he said before the silence could grow too thick.

When we got home he told me he thought it would be okay if I took the car out every so often.

"Are you sure?" I said. "That's illegal in about half a dozen ways."

He shrugged. "Fight the power."

I asked him if Mom was okay with it.

"I think she will be," he said, without elaboration. "Just give it some time."

He pushed the front door open. It wasn't often I entered our house through the front door. Upstairs we could hear Katy shouting with joy and running down the hall to welcome us.

"She'll come around," he said.

Time, I had. Or so I thought.

The first time my father let me take the car out, it wasn't so I could go to work, but so I could go visit a friend. Other than Adam and Secret Agent K. DeSonne, Melissa was the only zombie in the Winford/Oakvale area that wasn't underground. The poor girl had come out on the lawn in front of St. Jude's just before we got shot to pieces, and likely would have been shot herself had the priest there, Father Fitzpatrick, not thrown himself across her body. That story should be told: a human—a trad, a bleeder, a beating heart—threw himself in harm's way to protect a girl who was already dead. People should know about that type of love.

Melissa wasn't in on the plan that night. I mean she wasn't part of the group that was setting up the art installation, a Son of Romero. I think she just came outside because she was curious about what we were doing. And about George. Call me crazy, but I detected a certain chemistry between those two when we had an open house for the Hunters over at our old crib. She wears a mask to cover her scars, and George's face is so zomboid the only expression he wears is "scary," so how could I tell?

Well, Auntie Karen knows. I can sense these things.

Oh, poor George. Poor Melissa, to have to see what they did to him.

Father Fitzpatrick refused to turn Melissa over to the cops, even though lots of people in his own church weren't happy with him, just like they weren't happy that he performed the funeral service for Evan Talbot. Eventually the police who arrested George issued a statement that they didn't believe that Melissa was involved in the crimes against the Guttridges, and the case cooled as a media story. I guess whoever is pulling the strings figured it was a huge mistake to go toe-to-toe with a Catholic priest. I think they didn't want the attention, or for the details of what happened to Melissa at Dickinson House to get out. It wasn't enough that the poor girl had to endure being a zombie; now she had to live with the disfigurement that she received when bioists torched her home and retermed almost all of her friends. The flames took away her ability to speak, and she hides her face behind masks. Her hair was all burned off, and she wears a red wig. But that story, in short, would be too likely to generate sympathy for our cause. So they froze it out.

St. Jude's Mission is in the heart of Winford, in the basement of the squat gray building that served as the rectory for the cathedral next door.

I'd never been inside the cathedral before, the steeple of which towered far above any of the other buildings in the town. I parked the car on the street and stared up at the stone Christ high above, His arms wide and welcoming. An elderly couple had just begun the trek up the lengthy flight of steps that led to the massive wooden doors. They were hunched and leaning on each other for support, wearing heavy wool coats that they'd cinched to keep the chill out. The man had a battered gray hat covering his head. They looked adorable.

There wasn't any trace of the artwork that Popeye had done; rumor had it that Father Fitzpatrick insisted that both our scene and the manger, bullet holes and all, be left up throughout the holidays, as a reminder of the crime he felt had been committed against us, but a well-meaning (perhaps) parishioner cleaned up the ruin of splintered wood and toppled figures.

I locked the car, crossed the street, and followed a short walkway lined with tall arborvitae. The rectory door was unlocked, and I stepped inside, nearly crashing into a figure in black who was moving swiftly toward me.

"Pardon me," the figure said. If I had to breathe I would have been holding my breath just then.

I looked up and saw that the man, a priest, was trying to get his collar into place. I recognized him immediately; it was Father Fitzpatrick.

"I nearly bowled you over," he said. "I'm so sorry; I'm late for my turn in the confessional, as usual."

Confession. The thought of the elderly couple taking their turns in the confessional made me smile. "Father forgive me, for I have sinned," Grandpa would say. "I just don't *like* Gertie's lasagna."

"No worries," I said, "seeing how you're in such a hurry to save souls."

His laugh was rich and sincere, laugh lines deepened around his eyes as he rocked back and forth. "Absolutely," he said, regaining his composure. I could still see the light of mirth dancing in his eyes as he peered into my face with sudden interest. My wonderings about my trad facade as he scrutinized me disappeared with his next statement.

"We've met," he said, and he lifted his hand to his chin as he thought about where or when that event might have occurred. I shrugged as though to convey that I didn't recall our meeting.

"Karen," he said. "Karen DeSonne. We met at the funeral of your friend. The Talbot boy. The contact lenses threw me."

"You have a good memory . . . for faces," I said. (I paused because, for some reason, his authority or his knowledge that I wasn't alive threw me.)

"Yes," he said, smiling. "Are you here for Melissa?"

"Yes, Father," I said.

"Excellent." He beamed at me for a moment before checking his watch. "I've got to go. Miss Riley is in the basement; the stairs are at the end of the hall. I think she'll be pleased to have a visitor. I'm off to save some souls, as you say. Good-bye, Karen."

"Good-bye," I said, watching him hurry down the steps and then jog down the walkway.

I started down the dim hallway, passing beneath a huge portrait of Mary. There was a ghostly amber halo around Mary's blue-veiled head, and the artist had imbued her expression with a lifelike peacefulness and compassion, but I felt only anxiety as I passed beneath her loving gaze. There was a statue of a bearded saint on a pedestal at the end of the corridor, the green paint flaking off his robes in scales. I wasn't sure that I liked the way he was staring at me. I also didn't like the way the heels of my boots sounded in the hollow hallway, and I made an extra effort to keep silent as I descended the stairs to the basement, which was dark except for dim red exit signs on either end.

"Melissa?" I said, my voice echoing. Dark as it was, my dead eyes could see everything. The rectory basement was basically one long open room, with sofas and beds, bookshelves, and a large round table ringed by metal folding chairs. There was a television cabinet in one corner, a monstrous relic of another era. It stood on a braided rug, and a few battered recliners gathered around it like faithful dogs awaiting command. The room must have been styled by the same decorator and yard-sale aficionado that worked his threadbare "magic" on the encounter room of the Hunter Foundation.

"Melissa?" I repeated. She was across the room, sitting on an old couch. I could see the pale green flash of her eyes from within the white mask that she wore, the lone spot of color in the room save for the feeble glow of the exit signs. "Melissa, can I come talk to you?"

The white mask—different than the one she'd worn to class—lowered and raised in a nod. The mouth of this mask curled slightly upward in a smile. Melissa reached up and clicked on a floor lamp standing beside the couch. As I made my way around the random groupings of furnishings and support poles I saw that Melissa was holding a whiteboard that was a little larger than a spiral notebook. She began writing on it with a green marker. When she was finished she held it up for me to see.

She'd written Hi Karen in tall streaky letters, the curves in the e and the r giving her a little trouble.

"Hi, yourself," I said, sitting on her sofa. I greeted most of my friends, dead or alive, with a hug, but there was something standoffish in the way she sat, as though she were constantly trying to pull her limbs into her body, that made me think a hug would not be welcome—no matter how it was needed.

The light from the floor lamp cast shadows in the eyeholes of the mask, so now even Melissa's green eyes were hidden from my view.

"My friend Mal used to stay here," I said. "And a girl name Sylvia. We talked about her at the Hunter Foundation. Colette and Kevin, too. You know them from class."

I guess it was a little awkward. I realized that I was talking to her as though she were about six years old and couldn't remember anything prior to the event on the church lawn. She just nodded at me, the red corona of her hair bobbing with the gentle motion. She probably thought I was an idiot.

"Are you okay?" I asked. What else could I say? "You know, relatively speaking?"

Melissa erased my name and wrote something new on her board.

OK she'd written.

"That's good. Really good. I'm sure you're lonely here and all. I'm lonely, too. I live . . . I stay with my parents and my sister, but there aren't any dead people around anymore, you know? I guess it isn't the same kind of lonely, but . . . I'm babbling, aren't I?"

Melissa gave one slow nod of her head. She erased her board but didn't write anything.

Melissa tapped her pad twice before writing. The words took a little longer, and she stopped at different points to cross words out.

Its XXXX okay here. Father Fitzgerald is awesome. I XXXX miss XXXX Cooper.

Then

He wouldn't come w/ me when I left the Foundation, and we had a fight. I get XXX lonely.

She waited until I had read the whole page, before erasing and writing some more.

"You didn't want to stay at the Foundation?" I asked.

Melissa shook her head with a little more vigor this time.

"How come?"

Melissa took a few moments before writing.

Its haunted is what she wrote. She underlined the word haunted three times.

"Haunted?" I asked. Without the benefit of inflection or expression, it was difficult to tell what she was thinking. I guess that's how the trads felt most of the time when talking to us. "As in, ghosts and stuff?"

Melissa nodded again.

"Have you been able to get out much?"

Squeak, squeak, write, write.

I'd ♥ 2 get out, she wrote. The ♥ was underlined. Fr. Fitz thinks too dangerous.

"He's probably right," I said, which kicked off another flurry of erasing and writing. I looked around the room. There was another portrait of Mary, a smaller version of the one upstairs on the wall behind them, and this time her beatific gaze was trained on a portrait of Jesus done in the same style a few feet away.

But U R Out?????

She'd capitalized the O in "Out," which was funny, because I wasn't Out, capital O, at all, was I? I was In. I was passing. But how could this poor dead, scarred girl feel about that?

I didn't know. But I decided to tell her the truth. Part of it, anyhow.

"I'm passing, Melissa," I told her. "As a human. I mean, a traditionally biotic person."

Erase, squeak, squeak.

Passing?

"People don't know I'm dead. I don't know if you can tell in this light, but my hair is a little darker."

Erase, squeak, squeak, squeak.

W/A yr eyes?

"Oh," I said. "That. Contact lenses."

She leaned forward, her head tilting to the side.

"You know, Melissa, you don't need to wear that mask with me, if you don't want."

Melissa sat completely still for at least a minute, and I worried that my offer had offended her. The time lag gave me enough time to realize how hypocritical my statement was, considering the mask I wore on a daily basis.

When Melissa finally responded, her reply was brief.

*Thank U*

She made no movement to remove the mask.

"Well," I said, "I've got to get going. I've got a job—if you can believe it. I work at Wild Thingz! in the mall."

Melissa drew an exclamation point that covered her whole board.

I laughed. "Yeah, I know. Pretty crazy, huh? They don't know that I'm a zombie yet, if you can believe it."

*I can believe it,* she'd written.

"Thank you, Melissa," I replied, as Melissa flipped to a new page and started writing again.

*I want 2 not be a zombie someday*

"I know what you mean," I said. I put my hand on Melissa's knee. The masked girl didn't try to shrink away from me.

"Take care, honey," I said. "I'll see you soon, okay?"

Melissa nodded. She wrote *Thank U* on her tablet and then lifted her hand in a wave.

"Soon," I said. I leaned forward and tilted her mask to the side, gently. I thought she might turn away, but she didn't. I kissed her cheek, and her skin made a crackling sound beneath my lips.

She sat back and her mask was back in place, her eyes hidden in its shadows. I said good-bye again and stood up.

I hadn't yet crossed the room when I heard the click of the floor light going off, and I left Melissa in the darkness.

I was going off to pretend I was a real person, selling lame T-shirts and tongue studs to kids who most likely wanted to set fire to the Haunted House and everyone in it, while people like Melissa sat alone in the dark with nothing to think about besides the grim circumstances of their deaths and the even grimmer circumstances of their unlives. It wasn't fair.

A voice in my head told me that my working and having a job was a good thing for dead kids like Melissa, because only by our getting jobs and going to dances and joining football teams would we ever get the opportunity to do anything else in this society. I knew that the sentiment made sense, but I couldn't help but think there was an element of selfishness in it, too. I was going because I *liked* to "pass." I *liked* living people flirting with me, and I liked buying new clothes with the money I made. When I first started passing, I told myself I was doing something radical, that I was contributing to our cause, whatever. I thought I'd be helping. But really I was just hiding.

What I should have been doing was sitting in the dark, trying to teach Melissa how to laugh. How to heal her skin.

I passed under the portrait of Mary, amazed that there was no hint of reproach in the blue painted eyes. I reached the edge of the arborvitae just in time to see the elderly couple step onto the sidewalk from the stone steps. They both smiled at me as they went by. I looked up at the stone Christ and, before I was even aware of doing so, I began to climb the stairs they'd just descended. They looked even happier now than when I first saw them.

I stood in the atrium for a long moment before going in. There were a few people in the pews awaiting their turn. I forced my lungs to draw a deep breath, and I stepped into the church proper.

The roof didn't cave in, flames didn't burst through the floor to engulf me. There was no shortage of people in the world that thought me a damned thing, a damned dead monster, an abomination in the eyes of the very Lord whose image looked down on me from the cross at the front of the cathedral. I took a seat in the back pew beneath a stained-glass image of Jesus holding a lamb, a ring of smiling children gathered at His feet. I looked up at His image and then I took the kneeler down.

What am I doing here? I thought. What?

But I knew. I had a lot to atone for, didn't I?

I'd been to confession twice in my life but not once since my death. The door to the confessional opened, and to my horror none of the three other people in the pews rose to enter next.

Saying their rosaries, I thought. What am I doing here, damned thing that I am?

No heaven for me, I thought, rising from my knees. No heaven for me, no afterlife. Just afterdeath, back here on earth.

I exited the pew with every intention of bolting out of the cathedral as fast as my undead legs could carry me. Instead I walked into the confessional and closed the door. The curtained box smelled like antique wood and incense. The curtain was closed.

"Father, forgive me for I have sinned," I said, and I told myself that the wooden booth was nothing at all like the coffin that my parents had picked out for me. I was pausing in my speech, like when I first came back.

"Go on," Father Fitzpatrick said from behind the curtain. I could tell it was him just from those two little words.

"I . . . I . . ." I began, my zombie speech impediment coming on full bore. "I . . . have . . . not . . . always . . . been . . . truthful." Like that. "With my . . . parents. With . . . with friends."

"Take your time," he said, his voice free from judgment.

"I have been . . . neglectful." I thought about when I'd made the sacrament of confession for the first time, with the rest of my catechism class, how they joked about all the fake sins they manufactured in "the box" so as to somehow minimize the existence of their real sins. "I have . . . I . . . I have . . ."

I could hear the priest sigh on the other side of the divider. "You do not have to worry," he said. "You are here for forgiveness."

"Father, I . . . I don't . . . I . . ."

"Yes?"

"I killed myself," I whispered. "And . . ."

I was shaking, actually shaking, something I didn't think my body was capable of doing any longer. I had more to say, but the words wouldn't come. I was kneeling and shaking, and my hands were clenched together so tightly that my nails bit into my skin. I was shaking because I was there for forgiveness, but I was afraid I would not get forgiveness. How could there be forgiveness for me, who had taken God's gift and thrown it away?

And was that even the worst of my sins?

Just when I thought the priest hadn't heard me, he spoke. He said my name.

"Karen?"

And then I ran as fast my undead legs could carry me, bursting out of the confessional as though I were bursting out of the coffin I was almost buried in. The door slammed against the side of the booth with enough force to split the wood, and the faithful crouching over their beads looked up at me with shock and horror, and I knew that they could see me for what I really was: a monster. An undead monster.

The noise of my exit echoed throughout church. As I passed through the feeble light beneath the stained-glass window I felt my heart beat in my chest three times.

I literally fled from the church, wondering if the stone Christ's arms were open not to embrace me, but to catch me.

# CHAPTER ELEVEN

WHAT THE HELL, PETE thought, punching the button on his cell phone and throwing it to the floor of his car. He'd just left his fifth message for Christie in three days, which is about four more messages than he'd ever left for any girl in his life, after Julie.

His fingers drummed an arrhythmic beat on the steering wheel of his mother's car. He knew Christie wasn't dodging him because she was offended by the way things went the other night. She'd been around. And she'd enjoyed it as much as he had, so why couldn't she answer her damn phone?

Was she playing a game? Was that it? Was this some kind of childish payback for when he went to Arizona? She'd seemed more mature than that.

He turned into the parking lot of the Winford Mall, parked, and went inside. The mall was dead; the only part that had any traffic was the food court, and only because it was lunch time. Pete walked to Wild Thingz! and appeared to be the only person in the store.

Pete hung around the counter for a minute or two before the beady-eyed guy with the piercings came out of the back room, wiping pizza sauce off his chin.

"Hey," Pete said. "Is Christie working today?"

The guy looked irritated, as though he couldn't believe Pete was interrupting his delicious pizza lunch to ask him that.

"I'm not really supposed to discuss employee schedules with the customers."

This guy—Craig, by his name badge, which had a sticker of a comic skull next to his name—had a very hittable face, Pete thought. He considered knocking Craig down and asking him, "How about if I step on your neck, could you tell me then?" Instead he played it cool. Playing it cool wasn't easy, though—he felt a dark tide of anger that had been building since his first unanswered call to Christie a few days ago.

So instead he smiled. He smiled, but what he said wasn't a question.

"But you'll make an exception for me."

He could see the impact of his words—and their tone— on Craig's face as his beady eyes grew wide and he licked his lips.

"We don't have a Christie working here," he said.

The dark tide swelled. "Don't be cute. Slim, blond—probably the only person here that doesn't have any hardware or tattoos on her skin."

"Oh," Craig said. "You mean Karen." Craig said, looking

relieved. Pete saw no point in arguing with him, he just wanted to know where she was.

"You her new boyfriend?" Craig said.

Pete nodded, gratified that she'd talked about him at work.

"She was supposed to work today," Craig told him. "She called in sick. That's why I'm all alone."

Poor baby, Pete thought. He debated leaning on Craig a little harder, because he could probably squeeze Christie's home address out of him.

"She called out two days ago, too. She must be at death's door or something, because she's worked every shift I've ever given her. She's usually the one covering for everyone else."

"Yeah, that's Christie," Pete said, implying a long-time familiarity. He noticed that Craig didn't try and correct him this time. "She must have gone to the doctor, then."

"Probably," Craig said.

Pete knocked on the counter with his knuckles.

"Okay," he said. "Thanks for your help."

He went back to his car, not knowing what to feel. Should he be worried about her? Or pissed that she'd taken the time to call Beady Eyes but not him? He cruised through her neighborhood, scanning mailboxes for "Smith." He didn't find any Smiths, but most of the boxes had no names, just numbers. He looped through each street three times, just to be sure, and then he drove to the school.

If I can't see Christie, he thought, then at least I can get going on the plan.

The buses were already lined up along the curving ramp by the school, forming a vehicular wall that made seeing the school entrance difficult. Pete parked in the student lot and walked up the steps to the faculty lot, where he could get a clearer look at the entrance. There were a few cars parked at the end of the bus lane; parents of the dorkier children, he figured. He stood near one of the cars, smiling at a middle-aged woman who looked at him over the top of her *People* magazine. She smiled back. The humming buses gave the air a pleasant diesel smell; the vapor of their exhaust rose into the crisp air.

Layman used to bring his stepfather's truck into work most of the time, Pete remembered. Back before he died. Probably wasn't doing any driving these days.

Pete frowned at the sound of the end-of-day bell. They used to let the zombies out of class five minutes early so they could shamble on down to the buses without slowing everything down; with Layman being the only corpse left in the school, they probably abolished that policy.

It wasn't long before kids started spilling from the front doors. One of the first ones out was that little shrimp who had gone out for the football team, Thurston or Thornton or whatever his name was. He moved at a swift clip toward Pete. When he drew near, the recognition—and fear—showed on his face.

Pete lifted his index finger to his lips, and winked. The shrimp wasted no time in getting into the car where his mommy sat reading *People*, slamming the door before she could even finish saying "Hi, honey!"

Pete walked a little further up the hill. Kids were coming out in a steady wave now; he saw Harris Morgan and Holly Pelletier and a bunch of his other old "friends" as they fanned out to clamber aboard buses or cross down to the student lot. He saw a bouncing sheaf of pink hair that belonged to Scarypants's pudgy friend. What was TC's nickname for her? Something based on her anatomy, no doubt. Knockers. Pinky McKnockers, that was it. He laughed.

Right behind Pinky came Scarypants herself. Pete almost missed her because she wasn't as gothed out as usual. Her skirt didn't look like it had been previously owned by a turn-of-the-century gypsy, for starters. She was wearing functional, not decorative, boots, and the coat she wore could be purchased at Macy's and didn't have to be special ordered direct from Transylvania.

Her hair, though, was still long and as black as a crow's wing.

Behind her, like a huge lumbering shadow, shambled Adam Layman. Pete realized that he'd been holding the door open for the girls.

Aw, how cute, he thought. What a gentleman. An undead gentleman.

There were enough people walking around now that Pete didn't feel as conspicuous, and Layman and his goth groupies were busy laughing at something the fat pink one said. Pete remembered how slow and ungainly Layman had been during the trial. The big dummy could barely even talk, but now it looked like he was making comments to the girls as they walked onto their bus. Then again, maybe Layman faked the whole thing in the courtroom, trying to pass himself off as a low-functioning zombie to try and garner additional sympathy from the judge.

Pete watched the trio board and the bus pull away, then noticed another hulking oaf leave the school. He'd seen TC's car in the lot, so he decided to join up with him there.

TC saw him waiting. His face lit up like the proverbial Christmas tree.

"Hey, Pete!" he said, breaking into a trot but then slipping on a patch of wet snow and bouncing into a parked car as he tried to regain his balance.

"Easy," Pete said as he walked toward him. "Don't kill yourself."

"Yeah," TC said, his stocking cap askew on his lumpy head. "Suicides don't come back."

Pete forced a laugh. "So they say."

"Hey, what are you doing over here, anyhow? I thought you could get arrested if you came back or something."

"Or something. But thanks for shouting my name across the lot for everyone to hear."

TC looked shamefaced. "Aw, crap. I'm sorry, Pete."

"Forget it," Pete said, punching his shoulder to show there were no hard feelings.

"Hey, how'd your date go the other night? Get any?" TC said, trying to be inconspicuous about rubbing the spot on his arm where Pete had slugged him.

"You know I did," Pete said.

"Sweet. She from around here? She looked sort of familiar."

"How would you know? Your eyes never went higher than her neck." TC started to protest, and Pete feinted throwing another punch at his bruised arm. When he flinched, Pete drilled his other arm with his left, laughing as TC swore.

"I'm just playing with you, man," Pete said. "Can't blame a man for checking out the merchandise."

"She's pretty hot."

"In every way. But listen, I'm not here to talk about my many sexual conquests—neither one of us has the time for all that! But I've been giving a lot of thought to what you said about getting back at Layman."

TC, flattered that Pete actually took something he said seriously, grinned. "Yeah?"

"Yeah. But I want us to be smart about it, you know? I wasn't thinking clearly enough when we first went after Williams."

"That got out of hand. If Layman hadn't showed up . . ."

"Yeah, but he did. But I've thought of something that's going to destroy him. Him and Williams both. It'll be like pounding nails into their empty coffins."

"Williams is in D.C. right now. He was actually on TV the other day, talking about zombie rights or some crap. Can you believe that? He . . ."

"Whatever," Pete said, cutting him off. "I bet you anything he's still in love with Scarypants. What I've got planned is going to derail the whole zombie love train."

"What are we going to do?" TC asked.

Pete looked around as though suddenly suspicious of the kids heading out to their cars. "Later. I'll give you the full plan later. But here's what I want you to do . . ."

TC leaned in close as Pete's voice dropped to a whisper.

"You know where Layman lives?"

"Yeah."

"Did you know his creepy girlfriend lives right next door?"

"Seriously? No, I didn't know that. How do you know that?"

"I've been watching them for a few days now."

"No shit?"

"None. Here's what I need you to do. Cruise by his house a couple times a day, and see what you can see. Pay attention to what cars are in the driveways. Layman's stepfather owns a garage or some crap, so there's always a couple junkers around. Take a notebook and write down the times you go by and what you see. If you can figure out who's driving what, even better."

"Like, you want me to see who is home when, that sort of thing?"

"Exactly," Pete said. TC was grinning like the idiot he was. "The more information you can get, the better. I know that Layman has two older brothers and his mom and stepdad living in his house. Kendall lives with her parents, but I don't think she has any siblings."

"Okay. You want me to go now?"

"See if you can go by around four thirty-five o'clock. I'm going to follow their bus."

"You want me to come with you? If there's nobody home . . ."

Pete shook his head. "No, no. I want to plan this. From what I can see they don't go anywhere but their houses and school. Doing something here would be too dangerous, which leaves us with one option. But I want it to be flawless. I don't want their families around, nothing. Flawless."

"What are we going to do?" TC asked.

"Later," Pete said, knowing full well that "we" weren't going to do anything.

When he was done giving TC his marching orders, he followed bus 3 along its route, managing to position himself two cars back, until it stopped off in front of Layman's house. Phoebe and Adam both disembarked, and Phoebe walked Layman to his door before trekking through the light snow to her house.

To her *empty* house, he thought.

He watched her get a glittering ring of keys out of her bag and unlock her door. Her house was empty, with only a yapping little mutt to greet her, a mutt that Pete could take care of with a quick kick to the head. Her parents were at work; the earliest he'd seen them home was five thirty.

She must have felt someone walking over her grave, because she turned and looked over her shoulder in his direction while opening her door.

Pete turned his head away and joined the flow of traffic as the bus ahead went into gear.

# CHAPTER TWELVE

DYING WAS NOT PLEASANT. Coming back wasn't any better.

I was in the hospital morgue when I returned from my suicide, in a room full of corpses, none of whom would be making the return trip. I was alone.

Really and truly alone. I didn't see any white lights, I didn't hear any warm voices or see an outstretched hand. My faith was pretty clear on what was in store for people like me.

The morgue was locked, but only from the inside. Even so it must have taken me an hour to get the door open. My body wasn't working right; my arms flailed, my hands were bent into hooks. Sounds were coming from my open mouth and I couldn't stop them. I dragged myself into the hall, but when I reached a stairwell, my body didn't remember what it needed to do, so I had to crawl. I'd made it halfway up the flight when a nurse saw me and screamed loud enough to collapse the roof.

I was there for quite a while before they found a doctor brave enough to help me the rest of the way up.

I was given a hospital gown. Someone retrieved my information and called my parents.

"They probably won't come," I heard someone say.

But they did.

Depression isn't something that can be adequately explained to someone who has never felt it before, to someone who thinks it can be cured with a hug, a bouquet of flowers, or a pink teddy bear. Bouts of depression can be triggered by external events—and maybe mine was, when I realized that you and I weren't going to be together—but even this fact, as devastating as it felt at the time, wasn't the reason I took a bottle of sleeping pills and drifted away in my bathtub. The reason was internal, not external—the pain I felt would never, could never go away. This is what I thought and believed. That pain had been with me before you and I fell in and out of love; sometimes I think it was there before I was even born, a dark twin that preceded me into this world. Pain was the only thing in my life I had faith in.

Dying wasn't peaceful, either. Imagine someone setting fire to your throat and your lungs and your chest and then you being too weak to do anything but watch and wait. That's what drowning was like. Nothing romantic about it at all.

Supposedly I'm the only one who has come back from suicide. And now I was the only one that I knew of who was healing. I tried to convince myself that it all must be for a reason.

Did my heart really beat?

I was a wreck after my partial confession.

I barely left my tomb for, like, three days. The blue fog returned, as obliterating as ever. There's no refuge from your problems in death.

When my parents called downstairs to me I wouldn't answer, and pretended I was far away. My father came down to check on me, once, but whatever he saw in my eyes scared him so much that he didn't make a return trip, and no doubt he forbade my mother or sister to go see me. I didn't go to work. I didn't even move. I was worse than sick. I was dead, and feeling it. I guess it was the closest I felt to the time when I killed myself.

Maybe I should have felt overjoyed. Maybe my heart really did beat. Maybe I wasn't just healing or regenerating or anything; maybe I was actually *coming back*. But sometimes *almost* feeling alive is worse than not feeling alive at all. When I was depressed, that's what I felt like, like I was almost alive. And knowing I'd never quite make it the rest of the way.

Three days of having the fog press in on me, surrounding me. I didn't even want to move.

I think I know why the confession triggered the blue-fog response. I *was* trying to atone, after all—I was trying to exonerate myself and my friends for the Guttridge crimes, I was authentically reconnecting with my parents, I was, in my own way, trying to ask God for His forgiveness. All good things. But there was one essential piece—in some ways the most essential piece—that was as yet unaddressed.

The piece I didn't get to confess.

The piece about the one I love.

I've been thinking about us since I saw Adam kiss Phoebe in the back of Margi's car. That kiss brought back the memory of all the times we'd kissed, and how each time it felt like something was slipping out of my grasp, because each time brought us closer to the decision we both knew we had to make. You didn't want to hide anymore, but I couldn't stop. And because of it I've been hiding ever since.

After we said good-bye, we both tried to live our lives as normally as possible. Accent on the "normally." It took you a while, but eventually we started seeing other people. And then I saw my love kissing someone else.

It wasn't the kiss that killed me. I did that all myself. The blue fog took me away. Kisses don't kill; depression does. There aren't any reasons for most young suicides beyond depression, just triggers.

I don't know why I was made this way. I don't know. I may never know. All I know is that when he leaned in and lowered his mouth to yours, his big body blocking all but your eyes, I felt like I was dying, felt it more than when I really did die a few months later. And when your arms went around his neck, it might as well have been your hands around my throat.

I try not to think of those things.

I try to stay positive, you know.

But, Monica, I'm sorry. I'm so, so sorry.

* * *

My confession, obviously, was incomplete, and with it, my atonement and my absolution. I'd been able to confess to suicide but not to the other piece; faced with the totality of my cowardice again, the blue fog came rushing in. I considered laying on train tracks, immolating myself with gasoline, scarring my body so completely that I couldn't heal again.

But on the third day I heard Katy crying, and dragged myself upstairs to see what was wrong.

"Caring!" she shouted as soon as she saw me climb the stairs. She ran to wrap her arms around my legs, almost sending us over backward.

"Karen," my father said. I thought he looked awfully pale, and then I realized that after three days in my basement tomb I was probably a fright to behold.

"Caring, I thought the bad mans got you!" Katy said, cutting him off. For such a peanut she had a mighty grip, and it took me a moment to unwind her long enough to return her hug.

"Oh no, honey," I said, guilt flooding me. "No bad men are going to get me." I hoped I was telling the truth.

"Where were you? Where were you, Caring?"

I looked at her. She was like a tiny version of me, but without the scars and sins. As guilty as I felt about frightening her as I had, I also felt something like warmth blossoming inside me. It was as if her face, troubled and fraught with worry as it was, were like the sun, dissipating the blue fog that surrounded me.

"I was somewhere else," I told her. "But I'm back now."

And I was. There was no other way to explain it. The blue fog was beaten back, and I approached my new purpose in "life" with renewed clarity. I was going to solve the Guttridge murders, but even more, when it was all over I was going to stop hiding. Stop passing.

And I was going to find Monica, and I was going to tell her the things I had to tell her.

Dad took me for a ride after I crawled up from the tomb.

Or rather, I took him for a ride.

"Feel like taking a drive?" he said, tossing me the keys.

"Where to?" I asked, once I was behind the wheel.

"I don't know," he answered. "Anywhere you want to go?"

I thought about it for a minute.

"Yes," I said. I took him to the Haunted House.

There was police tape across the porch and the doorway. I cut through the tape with my fingernails.

"Who lives here?"

"My friends," I said. "Well, they used to."

The front door let loose a nice Haunted House-y creak as I pushed it open.

"So this is where you hang out?" Dad said, peering into the gloom.

"Used to."

"Comfy," he said. He took a seat on the battered futon in the living room. "I called your boss for you. I said you were sick and would be out a few days."

"Thank you."

"Karen," he said. "Are you okay?"

"Um, no, Dad. I'm not okay."

Dad wasn't as easily brushed aside by flippancy as many people I knew.

"Karen," he said. "Are we going to lose you again?"

"We," I said, the word out of my mouth before I could stop it. And once it was out I kept going. "I don't see any *we* here other than you and me, Dad."

"Your mother . . . your mother took your death very personally, Karen. You have to understand that."

"My suicide, you mean." I said. I don't know that I'd ever said the word to him before.

"Yes. Your suicide."

I *know* he's never used the word in front of me before. The word, in our house, was like one of those really awful words that couldn't be said on network television and would get you an instant R rating in the movies. A word with impact. A whispered word. The weird thing is, it hurt me when I said it, but it made me feel better when he said it. I don't know. I guess I took it as another sign that he was starting to come to terms.

"You have to know, Karen," he said, "that your suicide is something that we, your mother and I, are having a very difficult time understanding. Never mind accepting."

He held up his hand before I could speak. "Let me finish. I know, intellectually, that we're not to blame. My brain knows, but I don't know if my heart ever will. I might know that the things you did, before you died, weren't really a reflection on me as a father. I may know that I didn't *cause* you to be suicidal.

But I'll never, ever know if I had been there for you more, had watched and listened and cared more, that things might not have ended when and how they did. If I'd just paid more attention, maybe I'd have seen the signs and gotten you some help."

Watching him cry was not easy, especially since I could tell he was trying as hard as he could to control himself, probably out of some misguided notion that it would heap trauma upon trauma for me to see him cry.

As painful and harrowing as it was, there was a part of me, the part that still wanted to live, that was glad he was crying. My parents had never mourned in front of me.

"I've read stacks of books on suicide since you died," he continued. "Articles, journals, notes." Here he paused to blow his nose. "Time that I probably should have spent reading about zombies. Or time I should have spent just being with you."

He wasn't able to regain his composure for some time after that last revelation. I almost hugged him then, but something held me back, some internal directive that said he really needed to work through all of this stuff before I could give him any type of physical expression of solace.

"I hid the books from your mom for weeks, months, even. Then one day I found one in the magazine bin by the sofa in the living room, and I thought I'd slipped and left it out. But it wasn't one I'd bought. Your mother was doing the same thing I was. We just didn't talk about it."

As sad as that was, I felt a spark of happiness flare up in me. I'd thought my mother had written me off completely. That I was dead to her.

"She . . . she won't touch me, Dad." I didn't have to tell him that the last time I remembered her touching me is when I told her about Monica. It was the first and only time one of my parents hit me.

"We've never talked about it. Your death, I mean," he said. "I'm sorry if this is upsetting you. I think your mom will come around, but it may take time. There's no mechanism inside a parent to deal with their child's suicide, Karen," he said. "Nothing at all. No way to prepare, no way to assimilate it or understand it or deal with it in any way."

"It wasn't Mom's fault, Dad. It was . . ." It was the depression, I wanted to tell him. The blue fog. My voice trailed away as he stood.

"I just hope that you can forgive us."

"Forgive you?" I said. "Forgive *you*?"

I kept saying it. Then we were hugging. I'm not sure who embraced who first, and in the end it doesn't really matter, all I knew was that it felt good to have my Daddy's arms around me again, even if the feeling wasn't quite the same as before I killed myself.


I called Pete. His answers on the phone were curt, monosyllabic. I asked him if he wanted to go out that night. He said he did.

I met him at the top of the street. There was a single red rose on the passenger seat.

"Is that for me?" I said, taking the flower. He nodded, solemnly.

"I was worried about you," he said. The weird thing is I think he really meant it.

"I'm sorry," I said. So maybe I'm a better liar than he is.

"Are you okay? I heard you were sick."

Now that was creepy, because I didn't tell anyone I was sick except for Craig. I didn't want to think about him asking questions about me at work.

"Let me guess," I said. "He wouldn't admit he had a Christie working for him, either."

Pete watched me closely. Thank heaven I only blink at will.

"That's right."

I nodded, smiling. "He lies to every guy that comes in asking for me," I said. "He thinks it isn't good for business."

"A lot of guys come in asking for you?"

"Kind of. Don't be jealous."

"Not the jealous type," he answered. "But your boss is an idiot, because you're probably the only reason anybody comes into that stupid store."

"Pete . . ."

"So where have you been? Are you seeing someone else?"

Good thing he isn't the jealous type, I thought.

"I needed some time away, Pete," I said. "Things are moving kind of quickly for us and I needed to think."

"So have you been thinking?" The scar on his cheek was a vibrant red line; the muscles in his jaw clenched tight.

"Yeah."

"What do you think?"

"I think I need to see you," I told him. "Only you."

I don't know what made me look down at my wrist at that moment, but I noticed that sometime between slashing myself with the box cutter and lying to Pete, the cut had healed. I could see no trace of the wound, and it had been a deep one. It had been deep enough for me to sink the very long fingernail on my index finger all the way in. There was no scar, and I found myself comparing both wrists to see if I could spot a difference. I couldn't.

Pete and I went out that night, and again the two nights after that. Somehow I was able to avoid a dinner date, although Pete wanted to take me to one of the chain restaurants in Winford where all the foods are fried, and even the soft drinks taste like bacon. "No thanks, I'm already dead" would have been a really funny thing to say, but instead I just said I really wasn't hungry.

"You don't have an eating disorder, do you?" he asked at one point during the thrilling first two weeks of our relationship. I think it was the only harsh thing he said to me the entire time we were going out—which makes him unique among people I've dated. The boys I've dated, I mean.

We went to a movie. We drove around—Pete likes driving. We went bowling. I scored a forty-eight, and was so awful that it was probably the closest I came to blowing my cover as a zombie. We went sledding, and it was after the sledding date that he kissed me a second time. I tried to think of a volcano, a roaring fire, the heat of the sun, hoping that I could influence my own temperature. Maybe it worked. Or maybe I was like a rock that lined a campfire, absorbing and reflecting the heat I enclosed. We kissed for some time, and Pete never noticed that he was kissing a corpse.

Me kissing Pete Martinsburg; what could be more revolting? At least my puffy coat made it easy to keep his hands outside.

I had to kiss him to gain his trust, which, when I think about it, makes me feel just awful. And I'd made comments here and there about zombies during our dates, but I wasn't getting anywhere. I had no more information about the Guttridge murders than I had when he first came into my store at the mall, and I didn't know anything about his plans for my friends. I needed to do something—something other than stringing him along and letting him kiss me—fast.

I asked some questions about what his life was like at the One Life.

"I was only there a couple weeks," he said, grinning. "Even though it must have seemed like months for you. It's just like school," he said, "only spirituality is brought into all the subjects. All the classes are the same, except we also have a class in self-mastery."

"Self-mastery?" I asked. "Is that to help you stay celibate?"

He laughed. "No. It's about controlling your emotions. Making them work for you, not against you."

"Oh," I said, nodding like I understood. "So it *is* about helping you stay celibate."

Laughing, he told me a bit more. Foundational to Mathers's teachings, apparently, is this idea that God wants you to have a tight rein on your emotions and that you learn to be disciplined and not reactive when dealing with other people and their concerns. He—Mathers—connects this with a pretty harsh old-school fundamentalism that has no room for undead Americans, who he refers to, among other things, as Satan's plague. I'd read a few of Mathers's books, but I understood them much more after talking to Pete. It is almost as if Mathers's message of total restraint and the elimination of "emotive spikes," to use his term, allows him to plant within his followers a single large emotive spike, one aimed directly at zombies.

Even so, I thought that this bizarro concept of self-mastery sounded like a good idea, I guess because of the implication that someone like me could have used it to combat depression. Most of the examples that Pete gave were about defeating the sudden and frequent rages he experienced, which was a good thing, but he also said he was supposed to use the technique when he experienced an intense feeling of happiness. Not surprisingly, he didn't have an example for that emotion.

It was very strange listening to Pete talk about his time at the One Life campus, because he talked about the classes he was taking in the same way that Adam and Phoebe talk about Adam's karate—in terms of the benefits he derived. Both disciplines seemed to teach students to know themselves better, and by applying that knowledge they were able to change both the way they perceived and they way they were perceived by the world at large. But I could tell that Pete still walked with violence inside him, and I didn't think being with Mathers was going to help him use all that energy in a positive way.

Interesting info, but after that speech, and after yet another gruesome kissing session, I still hadn't solved the great anti-zombie conspiracy. Still, that didn't mean I wasn't getting anywhere.

I was getting somewhere, all right. Where I got was in his bedroom. And then finally, Karen DeSonne, Girl Detective, had a break in the case.

He lives in the basement just like me, although his sitch is a bit different from mine. He's got padded carpeting, the walls are paneling instead of exposed cinder block, and he's got just about every boy toy that you can imagine down there—wide screen television, a Wii and an Xbox, high-end stereo, weight bench, the whole works. He asked me to spot for him on the weight bench, which I guess was his idea of a thrilling date. He's pretty strong. I think he'd be surprised at how strong I was, but I didn't actually need to help him.

He has quick hands, as well, but he didn't seem too upset after I removed them when they went under my shirt and against the skin of my back. I'm pretty sure he was counting to ten—I think I'd be insulted if he wasn't—but he didn't get angry. I guess religious self-mastery classes *did* help with celibacy.

"I just figured why you seem so familiar to me."

We were sitting on his unmade bed. I'd only known Pete for a short while, but the undercurrent of menace that pulsed beneath his skin made it difficult to know what he was thinking (other than: I must get this bra off). If I were a real girl I would have tensed up, afraid that I'd been discovered.

"Why?" I asked, trying to make my voice light and flirty. "Do I kiss like someone you know?"

"A little bit," he said, without emotion. He said it as if he was just being honest, not hurtful, so I wasn't sure how I should react.

"Really?" I replied, straightening a little. "Why don't you tell me all about her."

"Her name was Julie," he said, really, really surprising me, because I'd asked in a snotty tone meant to convince him that I was deeply offended he thought kissing me was like kissing someone else. "I just felt . . . peaceful around her."

I was going to make another comment with an extra dose of snottiness, but he looked away from me.

"She died," he said.

My heart kind of broke for him just then.

I know who he is. What he is. But he looked and sounded so alone in that moment, I couldn't help but feel for him. Even monsters have their scars.

"Oh, poor you," I said, almost meaning it, and I stroked his cheek with my cool hand. "Is she . . . is she a zombie?"

He shook his head. "She didn't come back. This was a few years ago, just after the Dallas Jones thing. We were young."

"I'm so sorry, Pete," I said.

"She was stung by a bee," he said. "She went into anaphylactic shock, and she didn't have her meds with her. She died before anyone could help."

I know who Pete is. I know that he killed Evan and turned

Adam into one of us—and I was certain he was involved in the conspiracy that sent all of us into hiding.

Still, I couldn't help but feel for him. Call me human—crazy, huh? Plus, as a suicide, I can't help but feel stabbing pangs of guilt whenever I hear about the remorse someone feels over a life lost. Julie didn't ask to die, like I did. And unlike mine, Julie's death was not revocable.

The blue fog had led me to commit suicide. Maybe Pete had a crimson fog inside him, one that made him direct his anger and sadness against others, instead of hurting himself.

Pete didn't cry, but his right hand was squeezed into a tight fist.

"She didn't come back."

"Would . . . would you have wanted her to?" I asked him.

There was a moment where I thought I'd asked exactly the wrong question, because the tension in his fist seemed to be traveling up his arm, and I really thought that he was going to punch me. He didn't, but the tension didn't go away when he answered me, his voice just above a whisper.

"I don't know."

I rested my hand on his shoulder. I could feel him vibrate beneath my fingers.

"But she didn't. That's how I know."

"That's how you know what?"

"That's how I know that zombies are evil."

Quite a deductive leap, I thought, but one that someone in a great deal of pain could make without much difficulty. I'd made similar leaps when the depression had me in its grip; both

Pete and I plunged headlong into our own personal abyss. He turned to look into my eyes, but he was looking through me.

"Everyone else was coming back. When I was in California with her, this kid drowned in a surfing accident, and a day-and-a-half later he came back. They hadn't been able to recover his body, so it was a big deal when he finally crawled up on the beach. I remember three kids dying after driving drunk and wrapping their car around a telephone pole, and all three came back, and the newspaper printed before-and-after photos. One of the kids had gone through the windshield, another one lost an arm. Julie told me they'd been the biggest hoods in her school. They all came back, but when she didn't, I knew something was wrong. She was so good—I can't explain it, she was just good. I was a different person when I was with her. Totally different."

I tried my best to look sympathetic.

"She was my first real girlfriend, I guess. I spent two summers with her. The things we did—I felt like I was growing up when I was with her, but I also felt like if we stayed together, we'd stay young."

He smiled, but the smile slipped off his face when I spoke.

"First love," I said. I should have just let him talk, because I think in his mind he was adding "and last."

"Yeah, I guess," he said. "We knew it was a summer thing, so we saw other people during the school year. I saw a lot of girls. A lot of a lot of girls." Emphasis on the lot, as though my "first love" comment might have been a slight on his masculinity, but then he said, "I always thought about her, though."

"She must have been a very special girl."

"She was. She was the best."

I rubbed his back, feeling the rhythm of his breath entering and leaving his body, but then he stood up.

"But she's gone. And all these others came back. I think the Reverend is right about them."

"That they're demons?"

"Yeah. The Reverend says they're trying to infiltrate society, not because they want to join *our* society, but because they want us to join theirs. The society of the dead. He says 'the goal is the soul,' meaning that the zombies aren't looking to destroy us physically without taking our souls first."

"How do they do that?" I was really interested, thinking maybe I'd start up a soul collection.

"Take Williams," he said. "He's the most obvious example. He gets people to think that it's okay for zombies to walk around, that they're just people. Instead of rooting out and destroying the evil, people accept it. He's like a recruiter for Satan."

I frowned. "Don't take this the wrong way, Pete, but isn't that kind of what you did when you killed Adam? You made another zombie, so you increased Satan's army?"

He didn't get mad, he got excited, as if I were his student and I'd stumbled wide-eyed into a teachable moment.

"No! That's just it, I didn't make the zombie at all. Adam prepared the way for the zombie when he gave his soul over to Satan. See, when Adam started hanging around the demons, taking classes with them, accepting them, basically choosing their company over that of real people, he lost his soul. He chose evil over good. So when he died, his soul went straight to hell, and a zombie came back."

"So," I said, wishing that Tayshawn was around—he's seen, like, every horror movie in existence and would probably understand this goofy occult belief better than me—"you're saying that Adam Layman isn't really Adam? He's some sort of demon?"

"Exactly. That's all a zombie is. A demon cloaked in human flesh."

Ewww!

I didn't feel like a demon. I felt like me. Blue-foggy me. It was very hard to sit there with an attentive look on my face and not feel totally humiliated and offended. I mean, really. A demon? No. An imp, maybe. I'd make a good imp. Cloaked in human flesh, indeed!

"So the real goal of the zombies is to take souls?" I asked. I was learning so much. I'm all about self-discovery, as you know.

"That's right."

"Why do you think they killed your lawyer, then?"

He broke out into a grin. A really wide and scary grin, a you-got-me grin, like you'd see on the face of a mischievous little kid with his hand still in the cookie jar.

"Sometimes," he said, "sometimes things aren't what they seem."

He's telling me this? But I told him to go on.

"It's like this. The demons' art is subtle, and the devil has many ways to ensnare a human soul. It would seem like the easiest thing to do is to go out with some right-thinking people and destroy every zombie you find, right? But the media puts it out there that the zombies are the victims, not the aggressors."

I was having a difficult time picturing a zombie who's tied to a stake and set on fire as an aggressor, but whatever. Must be the imp in me. I let him go on.

"The media takes these examples of zombies being destroyed out of context, like they didn't have it coming. They paint sympathetic portraits of them, to humanize them when they're clearly not human. Why do so many parents refuse to let their kids come home after they die? Because they know! They know that those aren't their kids anymore. They know this instinctively, and send the demons from their door."

Which made me think of Colette and a ton of others whose parents sent them away.

"But the media manages to plant the seed in the minds of a large part of the public—the ignorant, sheeplike part—that zombies should be tolerated, or worse, integrated, instead of destroyed. It makes our work a lot harder."

"Our work?" I asked. It was really weird. Watching and listening to Pete as he went from this brokenhearted, sad character into a crazy fanatic in the space of a few minutes.

"The Reverend taught us that the social climate isn't right for the simple expunging of the zombies. First we need to win the battle for hearts and minds."

Expunged. He said *expunged*.

"The way to do that is by turning the demons' tactics against them. Help the general public—the sheep who flock in the middle of the fight between good and evil—see them for what they really are. Not victims, but *victimizers*."

"Well, I guess when they do things like murder your lawyer, they're really helping out, aren't they? But why do you think they did that, if they want to collect souls?"

He laughed. "The story is that Guttridge, in his public stance against the zombies and in defending me, was not someone they could corrupt."

"Why do you say 'the story'?"

"Guttridge isn't dead."

And there it was: a break in the case. I affected a look of utter surprise and incredulous innocence. Pete stopped pacing long enough to see the effect his bombshell had on me, and hopefully I was a good enough actress. I must have been, because his riff was getting a bit cocky, and when he started pacing again there was a little more of the old Pete Martinsburg swagger there.

"Nobody got killed. We faked the whole thing."

"What . . . what do you mean? Who is *we*?"

"We faked it, Christie. The murders, the video, the whole thing. We even had blood samples from the Guttridges that we splashed around."

"No way."

"Did you see the video? It looked real, didn't it? Those carpets were empty. Heavy, but empty. We were in and out of there in an hour, and an hour later the television stations had the video."

"You're kidding me. Who is *we*?"

"One Life Ministries. Guttridge owed One Life big and they came to collect. Something about not being able to pass the bar. I guess there's lots of folks in power and in the media that owe One Life."

I sat there, probably forgetting to breathe. Luckily Pete was in the grip of high fervor and didn't notice.

"One Life has a group of people who the Reverend picks to fight special battles against the demons. I'm one of those people."

I looked suitably impressed.

"So you're telling me that you're one of the zombies in the video?"

"Oh, yeah."

"Which one?"

He smiled, walked to his dresser, and opened the second drawer. He turned around and held something out to me, and when I saw what it was I started back on his bed in fright. For the first time that night, I wasn't faking, because he was holding out a face. Takayuki's face. I hadn't seen Tak since the night we all got shot, and my first thought was the totally irrational "ohmigod, they caught him," as though what was hanging from Pete's extended fist wasn't a latex mask but actually the skinned remnants of my friend.

He tossed the mask into my lap, and I shrieked as the eye-holes rolled up to face me. The hair was long and still retained some luster, like the real Tak's.

"Pretty cool, huh?" Pete said.

I forced myself to look closer and saw that the mask didn't look anything like Tak. The rent in the cheek was almost comical: the exposed rubbery teeth would have been more at home on a werewolf than in a human mouth, and the eyeholes didn't do a great job in bringing out the epicanthic folds of the real Tak's eyes. He had the most beautiful black eyes I've ever seen. The cheeks of the latex, or rubber, or whatever it was, were rough and pitted, and Tak has very nice, smooth skin. The hair was brittle, not at all like the real thing.

I was right. Pete was Tak.

"That's the bastard who gave me this," Pete said, pointing to his scar. "Kind of poetic that I get to be him, huh?"

"Poetry," I said, beaming at Pete like I'd never been more proud of anyone in my life. But of course I was thinking of how and when I could steal the mask.

Here I was wearing a mask daily, and Pete wore a mask to help discredit Tak and all of our kind—in effect, his wearing a mask assured the necessity of my wearing a mask. And then when you consider that Tak's face—his real face, I mean—is a sort of mask because he intentionally uses it to shock and scare . . . well, my poor little off-blond head started to spin.

Not just a break in the case but a full confession. Pete spent the rest of the evening telling me how clever he and his pals in the One Life Ministry were. *They* dug up the graves in Winford Cemetery. *They* were the ones responsible for pet disappearances and animal atrocities in town. They were the ones responsible for the fact that everyone hated and feared us even more than they had before.

It seems impossible that their plan (so far) had succeeded as well as it had, but just a brief glimpse through a history book will reveal countless instances of people intentionally spreading false information about someone who's different from them. It makes you want to question everything.

If I could get that mask into the right hands, then maybe someone could start poking holes in the Guttridge "murder."

I held the Takayuki mask, rubbing the latex with my fingers.

"The Reverend asked me to come back here to do some things," Pete said. I was only half paying attention to him at this point, envisioning a hundred Petes, all wearing masks, roaming around the country causing trouble for zombies.

"Yes?"

"Yeah. He wants me to find out where the rest of the worm burgers are hiding. He thinks they never left town. He's also got me taking photographs and watching people who were close to Williams. His mom is a nurse; she lives over in the trailer park in Oakvale, all alone."

"Really?" I said, suddenly alert.

"Yeah. Then there's the foundation . . . the Reverend thinks that Oakvale is an important domino in the war against the demons."

"And you are one of his generals," I said, pretending to be all impressed.

He laughed. "More like a secret agent. I'm just gathering data." He sat down on his weight bench. "Although there's something else I've been thinking about doing to advance the war, something the Reverend doesn't even know about."

I leaned forward. "You keep hinting. You're such a man of mystery."

He'd already decided he was going to tell me, though. I suppose, in his mind, that after telling me about Julie, other secrets like the Guttridge fraud and whatever his new scheme was were minor secrets. I wondered if telling my friends about Monica would make me feel similarly unburdened.

I didn't have time to think about it. He licked his smiling lips, his dark eyes shining as he told me his plan.

"I'm going to kill Phoebe Kendall," he said.

# CHAPTER THIRTEEN

"**I**'M GOING TO KILL PHOEBE Kendall," he said. "I'm going to kill her and make it look like her corpse boyfriend did the crime."

Even though I'm dead, his words had the power to chill me. I don't know how I managed to act my way through the rest of the night, when what I wanted to was jump up and claw his eyes out. Whatever sympathy he'd generated with his story about Julie evaporated when he said he was going to kill Phoebe.

"It'll be great," he told me. "I'm going to do it so Layman gets the blame. It'll totally cut Williams's legs out from under him, if his big dead pal kills his girlfriend. Whatever gains he's made will be erased; the whole country will believe that the zombies want nothing more than to end lives." He laughed. "They'll probably shut down Oakvale High, too. You can bet they won't be letting any more dead kids walk through the school doors."

"How are you going to get Adam blamed for it?" Inwardly, I winced. I was fortunate that he was so excited about his cunning plan that he didn't notice that I said *Adam* instead of *Layman*.

"I'll make sure he's around when I do the deed. People in town are so anti-undead right now—did you see that bit on the news where a bunch of grade school kids caught a zombie who was out past curfew? All they had were sticks and boards with nails pounded in them."

I had seen the clip, but all I'd noticed was one scared boy being tortured by another group of scared boys.

"So you're going to frame him?"

"Why not?" he said. "It worked before. People will believe anything they hear about zombies right now. The 'living impaired,'" he added, throwing air quotes around the term.

"Great plan," I said, trying to sound enthusiastic. "But what if . . . what if she comes back?" I said.

"Even better. He'll get to see her zombified, and then I'll kill her again. Head shot. If I do this right, zombies won't just be criminalized. They'll be hunted down in their holes and destroyed."

I held the mask in my lap, the rubbery, eyeless face staring up at me in silent accusation. I knew that I should warn Phoebe. Even though Pete elaborated on his plan, saying that he wanted to kill Phoebe while she and Adam were at her house, I knew that she wouldn't be safe until he was caught.

When he let me out at the top of the street, he plucked the mask—my only tangible evidence—from my lap.

"Hey," I said, my disappointment unfeigned. "I thought that was a present."

He laughed. "I'm not done with it, yet," he said. "Me and Scarface still have some work to do. Tonight, actually."

"What type of work?" I said, trying to sound enthusiastic. "What are you planning?"

"Can't tell you, babe," he said. "It could get rough."

His statement would have frozen my blood in my veins were it not already cooled. His grin was overly smug and I could tell that he was puffing himself up to show off, but that only made me more nervous. Who knew the lengths he'd go to impress me?

I told him that I wanted to help him with his "work," especially with his plan against Phoebe.

"Yeah, I might need you for that," he said. His smile was a rubbery as the mask that he'd made of my friend.

I called her early the next morning, before the bus came to pick her and Adam up. We made small talk for a while—or rather, she did, chatting away about Colette and DeCayce and the Skeleton Crew tour, and then about Tommy, who'd had a meeting with Congressman Armstrong, which meant more support for his march. Phoebe would have gone right on talking until the bus came if I hadn't interrupted.

"Phoebe," I said. "I need you and Adam to be really, really careful."

She laughed, not the reaction I hoped for.

"What are you talking about?"

"I'm serious, Phoebe. I can't tell you everything, but you and Adam are in danger. Just please tell me you'll be careful."

"Karen, you're scaring me."

"I know," I said. "I know I am, honey, and I'm sorry. Just please trust me. There are people who aren't happy Adam isn't in hiding."

"Karen, is this about Pete Martinsburg? Thorny said he saw him lurking around the schoolyard the other day."

Phoebe is the only beating heart I know who actually has telepathetic powers. "I can't say any more, Phoebe. I . . ."

"Karen, are you still working at the mall? I think *you're* the one who's in danger. And I . . ."

"Phoebe, I don't want to argue. Just please be careful. Okay?"

The silence on the other end of the phone was broken by a Mesolithic roar.

"The bus is here, Karen. I've got to go."

"I'll see you soon, Phoebe. I've got a lot to tell you. Have a great day at school."

She laughed at my somber tone, God love her. "Okay, Karen. Quit your job. I promise we'll be careful."

And she would. But that might not be enough. I needed help, and I knew only one place to get it.

I walked around the lake for a long time, telling myself I was looking for that perfect spot, one that offered seclusion along with a patch of the thinnest ice. Of course my hesitation had nothing to do with the fact that, under the ice, there was water. I wondered if Colette was hesitant around bodies of water, too. She'd also drowned, but her death was an accident.

Eventually I stripped down to my underwear, folded up the clothes I'd been wearing and put them in the backpack I'd brought. When I was done I hung the bag from a low branch. I was on the wooded side of the lake, far from the beach or the boat launch, and I was relatively certain that no one would come by and poach my clothing while I was under the ice.

I found a big rock, which I heaved up and onto a spot where the ice looked brittle, and luckily it plunged right through. I had to chop at the edge of the hole with a fallen branch, but before long I had a gap big enough to fit through.

I lowered myself in gently, gingerly, as though I could actually feel the coldness of the water and needed to acclimate my body to its freezing chill. I held my breath when I went in all the way; how stupid is that?

One thing I hadn't really counted on—it was really, really dark. Like ink dark. Above the ice it was a typical midwinter day in Connecticut, the landscape a study of whites and grays. The feeble light was insufficient to penetrate the ice, which was quite thick in places. My bare feet touched bottom, and I had to duck my head at first to get it under the frozen shelf. I started to walk, and when I could no longer touch my fingernails on the ice above, I swam. I'd always closed my eyes when swimming anyway.

I went to where I thought the lake would be deepest. There's a legend about a fishing cabin at the center of the lake, one that plunged through the ice when its owner tried to move it from one bank to the other. I liked to imagine Mal and Tak and the others sitting around in the submerged cabin, spinning yarns about the one that got away. I swam until I got tired—bored, really, because I don't get tired—then I let myself sink to the bottom and walk. Every so often I'd bump into something, and sometimes whatever it was would move away, and sometimes it was solid and unyielding. I believe that I ran my palms over the smooth hull of a sunken boat at some point, and the heavy lump I stubbed my toe against may have been a rock, or a treasure chest. The world will never know.

Being aware of my movements but not able to see them was exhilarating and terrifying at the same time. I could imagine I was drifting right into another dimension. Everything was a complete unknown. The only things in existence, the impenetrable water and my consciousness; the only thing that could save or destroy me, my own imagination.

I drifted far from the little hole I'd made in the ice. I didn't hear the voice of God, not unless God was one of the many voices in my head. I wish I had, because then I might not have been so terrified when something looped around my ankle and pulled tight.

I tried to scream, but all I managed to do was to expel the last little pocket of air that had been trapped in my lungs. I thrashed, and the grip on my ankle loosened, then disappeared as another appendage caught me around the waist. I tried to pry it off me, but it only constricted that much harder. Something grabbed my wrist, then enclosed the fist I'd made to fend it off with. It pried my fingers apart one at a time and then I realized it wasn't some mutant freshwater squid or octopus that was manhandling me. It was a human hand.

A zombie hand.

I relaxed, spreading my fingers, which the zombie laced with his own. Even before his grip loosened from my waist and before he brought my hand up to his ruined face, I knew who he was. I knew because I could feel his knucklebones beneath my fingertips in the spaces where the skin was split like the cushions of an old leather couch.

Tak. He'd found me.

The trip back to the hole I'd made in the ice was surprisingly quick, as though I'd traveled twice the distance to get away as I did to return. Tak led the entire journey, tugging me along as if I were a balloon tethered to his hand. He gave me a boost up and out of the hole, then he hauled himself out, planting his scarred hands firmly on the ice, which groaned but did not crack under his weight.

Once we were both out, we just sort of stared at each other a long minute. I watched as frost formed on his skin; his long hair quickly becoming brittle and frozen in place. I started to speak, but instead of words, water burbled up and out of my mouth—it was really gross. He showed me how to expel the water—it wasn't pretty and it wasn't pleasant—and in a few minutes we were able to speak.

"Karen," he said, recovering first. "I'm so . . . glad . . . to . . . see . . . you."

What a sweetie.

"Are you surprised?" I asked. It took me a while to get the words out. He'd had no way of knowing that I survived the St. Jude's massacre.

"Yes and . . . no."

"Did you think I'd bit the dust? Kicked the bucket? Bought the farm? Taken the ol' dirt nap?" I said. I was feeling a little giddy, I guess. "Again?"

He shook his head, his frozen hair rasping against the shoulders of his leather jacket like the bristles of a broom.

"No? It looked pretty grim for poor little Karen."

"I knew."

The thing is, I knew he knew. I don't know why I knew, but I did.

"How is that, Tak?" I said, softly. "How do you always know when I'm in trouble?"

"I just know."

"Telepathetic, are you?"

He didn't answer, just shrugged, dislodging a newly formed mass of slush from the hem of his coat. He was regarding me in a strange manner.

"But Karen," he said, eventually. "You were . . . shot. I know you were . . . shot."

I was going to laugh it off, make jokes about the bullet holes not being visible, but then I realized that *everything* was visible. I mean everything. Here's a little fashion tip from K.

DeSonne: avoid wearing white lingerie while swimming, if you want to keep secrets. Tak was still wearing everything he'd gone into the water with—T-shirt, jeans, studded motorcycle jacket, boots—and I might as well have been naked.

What was even stranger, and I'm sure that Tak noticed this as well, even though he didn't mention it, was that my skin wasn't going all frosty like his. The water was beading up and dripping off me, as though it were warmer than that which covered Tak. Or as if *I* was warmer than Tak.

"Um," I said. I was really, really embarrassed. Tak doesn't do "expression" unless it's for effect, so I don't know if he liked what he saw, but I have a feeling that he did.

"About that," I said, walking to where my bag hung, "let me just get my clothes on first, okay?"

"Sure," he said, and then did me the gentlemanly courtesy of turning his back as I peeled off my wet things, toweled myself dry, and got dressed in the clothes I'd put in my duffel.

Unlike the half story I'd given my (mostly) living friends, I decided to tell Tak everything. I started with what happened at St. Jude's, my narrow escape, about how I seemed to be, well, changing. I told him about the healing, and he found that pretty interesting because the bullet he'd taken in the leg was giving him a lot of trouble. I told him about the wounds, where they were and where they aren't any longer. I even told him about the box-cutter wound I'd given myself. He listened to all of it without so much as raising a frosty eyebrow.

"I don't know why I can do this stuff, Tak," I said. And I didn't, really. Still. The power of positive thinking? A kiwi fruit I ate the week I got shot? Clean living? True confessions? I had no idea.

"Williams thinks it is . . . love," he said, like he was reading my mind. "He thinks it is . . . love that . . . brings you back."

"No one loves me," I said, mostly joking. I was probably thinking about Monica when I said it. Say the L word out loud, and hers was the face that came to mind.

"Everyone . . . loves you," he said. "But maybe . . . it isn't how much . . . you are . . . loved, but . . . how much . . . you love . . . that matters."

I didn't answer with a quip. This was special; this was as close as Tak got to expressing his feelings. And maybe he had something there. I mean I *do* love everybody. Phoebe and Tommy and Tak and Adam, Margi, Melissa, Colette, Angela, Katy, my parents, Alish, George. Everyone. Monica.

"Well, I don't love Pete, even though I'm pretending to," is what I actually said. It just sort of slipped out. Tak's lip curled up on the side near the hole in his cheek, which I'm sure took real effort.

"Pete . . . Martinsburg?" Tak asked.

So I told him the rest. He already knew about me passing, and had tried to talk me out of when I told him. "No good . . . will come . . . of it," he'd said, the grumpy old dead man. But here I was, Nancy Dead Drew, ready to solve the big mystery. I told him how close I was to getting the evidence, that I'd seen it, actually seen the mask that bore Tak's face, and now all I needed to do was get it and find out where Guttridge was hiding, and then I'd have it all and the mystery would be solved.

"Besides," I told him, "I have to see it through. He's threatened to hurt Phoebe. To kill her, actually."

As much as he'd been against me getting a job in the first place, Tak didn't try to talk me out of what I was trying to do, even though he of all people would be aware of how dangerous it was. If I'd had more friends like Tak when I was alive, maybe I would have stayed alive. Friends who can listen are a good antidote against the fog.

"Even if you get . . . the evidence . . . there is . . . a good chance . . . they will destroy you . . . anyway."

Tak carries around a lot of anger, I know. Anger for the living people he feels rejected him. And anger for more celestial beings. I guess that's why Tommy's theory about love and the dead seems plausible to me, because despite everything they—the living—have done to me, I still love them.

"Maybe," I told him. "But I have to take that chance."

I told him about what Tommy was trying to do in going to Washington to lobby to get Prop 77 passed. I told Tak how much better a chance Tommy would have if I could clear zombies of these horrific crimes "against breathing humanity." How Tak can look amused without twitching a muscle, I may never know.

"Do your . . . beating-heart . . . friends know . . . about . . . the danger? Of . . . what . . . you are planning? Adam and . . . the Kendall . . . girl?"

I shook my hair, which still had some life to it. His was

frozen into a blackish-gray helmet.

"Adam isn't a beating heart anymore," I said, a superfluous comment that he ignored.

"Does . . . Williams?"

"Nobody," I said. "Just you."

"Just . . . me."

I told you about Tak's beautiful dark eyes. When he turns their full intensity on you, you have a choice—melt, or turn away. I turned away.

"They would try to stop me," I said.

This was about more than not putting anyone at risk; this was about my atonement. I think he understood. I think Tak has some sins of his own that he'd like to seek forgiveness for, someday.

"And if you don't . . . succeed?" he said. "What do you want . . . me . . . to do?"

"Forget me?"

He wasn't amused. I guess I hadn't really thought about failure as an option.

"I thought about meeting you here every other week or so, but . . ."

He shook his head, coming quickly to the same conclusion I had. There were twenty-one other zombies beneath the ice in this lake, and each visit increased the odds that they would be discovered. The speculation—yet to be tested—was that unregistered zombies without breathing guardians would be destroyed.

"I figured you could sneak away when the lake thawed,"

I said. "But I don't know how you'll know if something happens to me before then. Timing could be critical, with Tommy already . . ."

He cut me off, and I think there was the ghost of a smile on his lips.

"I'll know . . . Karen," he said. "I'll always . . . know."

I wanted to hug him, but he moved away, as though by instinct. If anyone on this planet needs a hug, it's Tak; I was terribly sad when I realized why he moved.

He's in love with me.

Poor Tak. He must know how I feel about him. I was sad, because he knew and turned away.

And truthfully, I felt sad for myself, also.

"I want you to help me, Tak," I said. "I want you to protect Phoebe."

He just stared at me.

"How . . . do you propose . . . I do that?"

"Watch her. Watch her house. He won't try anything at school, and I don't think he'll try to catch her elsewhere; if he does anything it will be at her house. If Pete comes and I'm not there, stop him."

"You are . . . risking . . . her life," he said.

I turned away. For a moment I felt as cold as I should have felt standing by a lake in January.

"I know," I said. "But . . . I think it is all our lives, if I don't . . . stop them. Pete and all his kind."

Tak nodded. He didn't require any more discussion on the subject.

In the end, I didn't tell him everything. I didn't tell him about Monica. Maybe it would have helped him and maybe it would have hurt him, I don't know. The only reason I didn't say anything was because I still wasn't ready.

So much sadness. Before he left, Tak told me about everyone under the lake. The sky was darkening by the time he slipped back into the water. I thought about him and all the others on my way back to my house.

I'm determined for them to be walking among us, dry and safe, by the time that the ice that imprisons and protects them is fully melted.

# CHAPTER FOURTEEN

S HE WAS WEARING THAT
Endless perfume, the one for
dead people. He could smell
it even before she entered his mother's car. It actually smelled
pretty good.

"Where have you been?" she asked, her voice laced with
anger and the scent of cinnamon gum. "You're almost two
hours late."

"I called to tell you I wouldn't be here on time, didn't I?
Your boss wouldn't let you work a few more hours?" He tried
to sound put out, but inwardly he was thrilled that she was
feeling so possessive about him.

"That isn't the point, Pete. I've been waiting . . ."

Pete waved the comment away and put the car in drive.
"You know I had some things to do." He winked at her. "Special
things."

He knew she was angry as soon as he saw her, but her reaction was fiercer than he'd imagined. The growl she made in her throat, almost subvocal, didn't even sound human as she struck him in the face with a half-closed fist. The car had begun to roll forward, and his jerk of the wheel nearly put it on the curb.

"Christie, what the hell?" he said, slamming the car back into park while he tried to hold her at bay. She was clawing at him with both hands, going for his face. She opened up a tear on the arm of his leather jacket. He got a hold of her left hand with his right, but he was still belted in, and the shoulder strap was making it difficult to turn toward her. Her right hand came across with a raking motion that just missed his eyes.

"Christie!" She was strong, too. Unnaturally strong. "Christie, will you stop?"

She slipped his grip and punched him, hard, on the sternum, and was launching herself at him full force. He barely held her back with his forearm. If this kept up he'd have no choice but to hit her.

"You said that you wouldn't go without me! You said . . ."

"Take it easy!" Was she actually trying to *bite* him? He was trying to keep from laughing, despite the ferocity of her attack. "I was only kidding around!"

She froze for just a second, and he grabbed both her wrists. He had terrible leverage, though, and if she pushed off against her door with her legs he'd be in trouble again, especially if she really was trying to bite.

"Easy," he said, trying to be soothing, as if she were a

strange dog jumping all over him. "I was kidding. Just kidding. I got stuck on the phone with the Reverend, that's all."

Christie looked at him, her pretty blue eyes sparkling with fury. Or passion. Or both.

"You were on . . . the phone?"

"Yeah, that's all." He took a risk and let go of her wrists, but kept his hands up in case she went at him again. She was still leaning over him, but after a minute he realized the fight had gone out of her. Moving with caution, he began to caress her shoulders.

"I promised you could be there when I zombified the girl. I keep my promises."

Christie sighed. "Really?"

"Really." Pete kissed her. He never realized how much he'd liked cinnamon gum. She let the kiss happen and then sat back in her seat.

"I guess I . . . overreacted."

Laughing, he eased the car back off the curb. "You guess? I thought you were going to claw my eyes out. It was like I had a rabid badger in the car."

"I'm sorry, Pete."

He looked over at her. She was staring out his windshield with a sort of shocked, dead stare.

"Hey, it's okay," he said, chucking her under the chin. "No blood, no foul."

She was still weirdly expressionless when she turned toward him. Kind of psycho-looking, he thought. He'd dated psycho chicks before and had to admit that he liked the unpredictability and randomness they brought to his life. He liked volatile girls.

"There could have been blood," she said blankly. "And look, I ripped your jacket."

"Don't worry about it," he said. "You must really hate zombies."

"You have no idea."

"Why?"

She blinked.

"What do you mean, why?"

"Why do you hate them? Did a zombie hurt you? Hurt someone you love?"

"In a way," she said, her voice hollow. She sounded sort of like Dorman the zombie killer, back in Arizona. She was starting to creep Pete out a little. "They pretend to be something they aren't. They pretend to be alive, and they aren't. They aren't alive at all."

"No," Pete said, hoping to mollify her and shake her out of this spooky funk. "They aren't."

"You promise I can be with you?" she said, turning her baby blues on him. "When you . . . do it, I mean?"

"Yeah. I promise."

She sat back in her seat. "I don't know, Pete."

"What? What don't you know?"

"I'm worried about you. What if you get caught? I don't think you'll get away with just community service a second time."

"Oh, you heard about that, did you?"

She took her time answering. "Everyone heard about it. It was the talk of the town that you got away with murder."

"Criminal negligence," he said. "My sentence was criminal negligence, not murder. I wasn't convicted of murder."

"I'm sorry. Don't get huffy."

"Huffy? This from the girl that nearly rips my face off."

"Don't be mad at me, Pete. I'm trying to tell you I care about you. I'm worried that you'll get caught. I'm worried that they'll find your lawyer."

"Fat chance," he said. "He's holed up someplace in upstate Maine."

"I don't want you to go to jail, Pete," she said, stroking his cheek with her cool fingertips. "I really like you, Pete."

"I really like you, too," he said. "But I hate zombies even more."

# CHAPTER FIFTEEN

THE ICE CRACKED IN A star-shaped pattern, the lines spreading like thin fingers reaching for the shore. Takayuki had been pounding at the blue-white sheet above him for some moments, using a small-craft anchor he'd found near the deepest part of the lake not far from where the submerged cabin lay. Pieces of ice were chipping off with each blow he struck, and the sound of his hammering was only a faraway tapping to his waterlogged ears. He imagined a stricken submarine, propellers stilled, reactor spent, caught in a crevasse miles away, the suffocating crew pounding on the hull with lengths of pipe.

The ice ceiling gave way all at once, the anchor smashing through like a body flung through a car windshield. Chopping at the edges with the flanges of the anchor and then clearing away the fragments with his free hand, Tak soon had a hole big enough to permit his head through.

He passed the anchor back to Tayshawn and then pulled himself halfway up with his hands, letting the air hit his face.

He opened the lids fractionally and saw that he was coming out to a spectral moonscape, the pale light from above reflecting off the hard white shell covering the lake and the land beyond. He looked around and saw no one, saw nothing living except a pair of birds streaking across his field of vision, their silhouettes blacker than the bruise-colored sky. He'd wanted a nighttime exit just in case there were breathers hanging around. Apparently he'd timed it well, because the moon was directly above, making it feel as though the whole world, and not just he and his friends, was dead.

He slid back down and resumed his work until the head-sized hole was big enough to allow the rest of his body through. Gripping the ice with his hands and pushing off the sandy lake bed with his boots, he managed to haul himself up and out of the hole. Tayshawn came up behind him, and the ice creaked and split beneath his additional weight, at one point separating as Tayshawn's foot plunged through.

His expletive was incomprehensible, as his throat and lungs were filled with water. Tak motioned with a dripping finger to head toward the bank of the lake.

Popeye was the last of the three dead boys to climb out. On his first two attempts, jagged shards of ice came away in his grip, and he thrashed the black water in frustration. His hands flopped on the ice like a speared salmon as he struggled for purchase, a gout of lake water spewing out of his mouth. Tak watched him flounder a moment, noting that his left hand actually was salmonlike—black webbing spread between each finger, and forefinger and thumb, making it look more like a fin than a human hand.

"Don't . . . just . . . watch," Popeye said, gargling out the words as he clung to the crumbling shelf. "Help."

Tak looked at Tayshawn, who was leaning over and trying to drain the rest of the water from his chest. When the liquid discharge slowed to a trickle, he spit out the slushy remainder. He came up grinning, although only the left half of his upper lip worked. The lake water, air-cooled, was already crystallizing in his hair.

"Not . . . funny," Popeye said, thrashing like a cat tossed into a swimming pool.

Tak, never as talkative as Popeye to begin with, was almost afraid to speak. They'd been in the lake for about five weeks, and he was concerned that his friends' vocal chords would pop like guitar strings if they tried to use them too quickly. When they went under, Popeye, a "fast" zombie, could speak with almost no pause whatsoever, and now he sounded like a newlydead.

Tak shook his head but was disturbed by the soft cracklings he heard as he moved. The water clinging to him had begun to ice up the moment he emerged from the lake. Frost could be seeping into his skin, sending white roots deep within him, into his unworking organs. His long hair was all icicles that clattered like wind chimes when he moved.

He planted his boots on either side of the hole and reached down, grabbing Popeye's arms. He leaned back and pulled, yanking Popeye out of the hole like a carrot. He let him go, to keep his own balance, and Popeye splayed and went spinning across the ice, sliding a decent distance away.

Freezer burned he might be, but Tak felt strangely powerful, as though their time under the ice had let them store up energy.

Popeye, perhaps surprised by the release of that energy, stared up at him with his forever unblinking eyes. Then he leaned over and emptied the sludge from the bottom of his lungs as best as he could, the stream of water being followed by a stream of curses when he was done.

"It . . . must . . . be . . . February," he said. "I died . . . in . . . February."

"Dude . . . put . . . on . . . your . . . glasses," Tayshawn said. He was not a fan of the self-proclaimed "bodifications"—skin art more extreme than tattooing or simple piercings—that Popeye had made to himself and some of the other zombies, the more impressionable kids who were always seeking their approval.

Tak started walking across the ice, clenching and unclenching his hands into fists with each step. They'd left nineteen zombies below.

"What's . . . the . . . matter, Shawnie?" Popeye said, thin canals appearing in the clear ice coating his face. He sat up and sheets of ice fell away from his chest, bare beneath his leather jacket. "Hating . . . me . . . cause . . . I'm . . . beautiful?"

"That's . . . it . . . exactly," Tayshawn said. He scrutinized Popeye a moment longer. "Aw . . . no."

"What?" Popeye said as he sat up, withdrawing his sunglasses from the inner pocket of his leather jacket.

"Dude," Tayshawn said, "what did . . . you do . . . to your . . . neck?"

Popeye lifted his left hand, the webbed one, to his throat in an oddly subconscious, human gesture. His fingertips probed a rent in his skin just below and back of his lower jawbone.

"Gills," he said, managing a smile. "I figured with . . . us . . . being underwater . . . and all. You . . . like it?"

"No. And what is . . . up . . . with your . . . hand?"

Popeye held his hand up. The webbing between his index and middle finger had started to tear loose, and he picked at the threads with his normal hand.

Tayshawn shook his head. "How did you . . . do that?"

"With . . . fishing line . . . and a scuba . . . flipper. You can . . . find . . . anything . . . down there," he said, indicating the lake with a nod of his bald head. There was a sharp crack, and the patch of ice Popeye was sitting on gave way.

Tayshawn looked at Tak, rolling his eyes skyward. His right eye stayed in that position until he rubbed at the frosted orb with his fingertips.

"What?" Popeye said, more to Tak than to Tayshawn, as he scrabbled toward the shore. "You don't . . . like . . . it?" He flexed the webbed hand, and the unstitched corner of black rubber poked up over his knuckles. Tak knew that his was the only opinion he cared about, the only person who could dampen Popeye's enthusiasm for his "art," and so he reserved his true judgment.

"Be yourself . . . Popeye," Tak said, looking at the array of fishhooks Popeye had put through his left ear—the lowest, one of those four-pronged jobs Tak's father liked to call a gut-ripper.

He looked away. He hadn't thought of his father in months, since long before they fled the beating hearts by disappearing into Lake Oxoboxo.

"Be . . . yourself," he repeated. "That's all that . . . matters."

Popeye chose to take the remark as a high compliment, and his thin lips twisted into a bloodless, smug grin at Tayshawn, who was too busy coaxing his eye back in place to notice.

"Ever read . . . H . . . P . . . Lovecraft?" he asked Tayshawn, smug. "*At the . . . Mountains of . . . Madness*? *The Dunwich Horror*? I'm a . . . Deep . . . One."

"Yeah, you're . . . a . . . deep . . . one, all right," Tayshawn said, helping Popeye to his feet.

Tak scanned the tree line across the frozen surface of the lake, trying to ignore their chatter. The thing he'd miss most about being underwater wouldn't be the relative safety, but the silence.

"Tayshawn," Popeye said, adopting a pedantic tone, "bodifications will . . . become . . . a primary . . . art . . . form of post . . . living . . . society."

"You're one weird kid, Bug-Eyes," Tayshawn said. "I . . .

don't even . . . know . . . what you are . . . talking about."

"That's . . . why I'm trying . . . to educate . . . you. You . . ."

"Oh, so . . . you're educating . . . me? I . . ."

"You . . ."

"Will you . . . be quiet, please?" Tak said.

It was an odd request for people that had been under the ice for nearly two months, but his companions complied. For a moment, anyway.

"So . . . Tak," Popeye said, eventually. "What . . . are we . . . doing . . . outside?"

Popeye could be clingy and irritating, but he was loyal. All Tak had need to do was beckon him, and he followed. Tayshawn, too.

"Recon," he said, his voice alien. He was aware of moving much more slowly than usual, and without the languid grace that he and his people had when under the water. He wondered if it was the cold or simple disuse that was causing his limbs to seize up. The bullet he'd taken above his knee wasn't helping, either.

They'd left eighteen of the nineteen zombies that had followed him into the water at the submerged cabin, a two-room, post-and-beam structure that had settled at the deepest part of the lake. The cabin was found by the only zombie still underwater that was not inhabiting it—Mal. Mal seemed to climb into a shell after Tommy left, which was a niggling irritation to Tak, who thought a friendship existed between him and the large zombie.

Mal had listened to Tak's plan to go into the lake, without comment, and when he finally moved off of his rock in the forest he did so without any acknowledgment. Tak wasn't even sure that Mal had gone into the water until he swam over to the rest of the zombies who were scouting along the lake bed. He managed, with just a few gestures and hand signals, to convince them to follow him, whereupon he led them all to the cabin, which had some benches, a table and chairs, the remains of some fishing gear nailed onto the walls, and a plethora of fish.

Oddly, Mal left soon after, apparently not needing the psychic comfort the building provided, or the psychic comfort the zombies provided each other. Tak found him one day when he was exploring. Mal had been sitting on the bow of a sunken Chris-Craft, staring up at the ice ceiling the way he used to stare at the stars from the backyard of the Haunted House. He didn't move when Tak approached, and Tak left him undisturbed.

"Uh, Tak?" Popeye said. Tak realized that his companions were staring at him, waiting for him to give instructions of some sort. "Are we . . . going . . . to find . . . George?"

"George is . . . dead, man," Tayshawn said. "I mean . . . really . . . dead. He wasn't . . . moving . . . after they . . . Tased . . . him."

"We've . . . got . . . to find . . . out."

Tak rose to his feet. He couldn't feel the temperature, but he found himself imagining how cold he should feel.

"George is . . . gone," he said. "But Karen has a . . . job . . .

for us." He turned back toward the forest. "Karen needs us."

"Karen, huh?" Tayshawn said.

"To do what?" Popeye said.

"Bodyguarding," Tak replied. "The Kendall girl."

"Whaaaaat?" Popeye said, freezing in his tracks.

"Phoebe?" Tayshawn said, catching up to Tak. Tak had forgotten that he'd been in class with both of the girls. "Why? What's going on?"

"Pete Martinsburg," Tak replied. "He framed us. He . . . is responsible . . . for George. He . . . wants . . . to kill . . . the girl. And frame . . . Layman . . . for the deed."

"What the . . . hell. Are we . . . ever going . . . to be rid . . . of that guy?"

"Why don't we just . . . kill him?" Popeye said, serious.

"We don't . . . kill," Tak said.

"Oh, sure," Popeye said. "But we can risk . . . our necks . . . for a . . . beating heart. Our necks and . . . everyone's . . . under the . . . lake. Does that . . . seem right . . . to you?"

"We don't . . . kill, Popeye," Tak said.

"Yeah. That'll make me feel . . . just great . . . when I'm getting . . . reterminated. When our friends . . . in the lake get . . ."

Tak turned. "If you don't want to . . . help . . . then go."

"I'm staying," Tayshawn said. "Phoebe's a little . . . weird, but . . . she's a good . . . kid. We need more . . . beating hearts . . . like her, not . . . less."

Popeye lifted his webbed hand skyward, popping one of the stitches that secured the rubber to his thumb. "Fine. I'm just . . . saying. We have other . . . responsibilities, is all."

"Yes," Tak said. "We . . . do."

They made it to the edge of the woods by Adam's house, just before the sun began to rise.

# CHAPTER SIXTEEN

"SOME PLACE IN UPSTATE Maine." That's all I had to go on. That, and if I could get it, a latex mask that looked like Tak. Would that be enough to prove that my friends were framed for a murder that hadn't actually happened?

It was a starting point. It was also, unless I could somehow charm Pete into confessing the whole thing to someone other than myself, all that I had.

My first attempt to steal the mask was a dismal failure. I had it all planned out; I was going to break through one of the basement windows that led to Pete's bedroom, make a beeline for the dresser I'd seen him take it from, grab it, and maybe take his iPod and whatever small items I could grab, just to make it look like I was there to steal stuff and not to look for evidence. The first part—the window breaking—went reasonably well, but that was about the only thing that did. How was

I to know that the house was alarmed?

So there I was, standing in Pete's room, rooting through his dresser. I found socks, underwear, a large unopened box of condoms, a gold chain, a bundle of letters and cards in an elastic band, a knife, shirts, jeans, a deck of playing cards with some sports-team logo on the back, an empty vodka nip bottle, and a pair of panties I assumed was a souvenir and not Pete's typical undergarment. No mask, though. Not in the drawer where it had been, not in any of the drawers.

I looked under his bed and found an old pair of cleats. I looked in the closet. There was a red milk crate that held football pads, helmet, and a hockey stick. A couple of porno magazines were wedged behind two stacked shoeboxes, one filled with baseball cards and the other with a pair of shiny leather dress shoes. No mask.

I looked through jacket pockets, under pillows, and behind the headboard. I looked in every drawer in the TV stand and found only video game cartridges and a set of drink coasters made out of cork. He had his own refrigerator and I even looked in there, but there was just a six-pack of Sprite Zero and three cans of beer.

I walked up the stairs, not expecting better luck but not wanting to give up, either. Pete's house was laid out in a very similar fashion to mine—I think most of the residential homes in Oakvale were built by the same developer, because there are only three or four different kinds of houses in Oakvale.

I bypassed the kitchen to look in the family room, which seemed unused. I thought I'd check out the bookshelves, anyway, when I saw a police car pull into the driveway outside.

Good thing I'm a fast little zombie. I didn't even hesitate, I just turned around and ran back through the kitchen and into the dining room, which had a big sliding glass door that led to a large deck. I had a little trouble with the lock, but then I had the door open and was running across the deck. Pete had a large backyard, but luckily it was unfenced and bordered in the back by the Oxoboxo woods.

The yard was slippery with the light crust of snow that had been shined to a gloss by the sun, which sat in a blue, clear sky. My shoes crunched through the crust with each step, giving the police a clear path to follow if they wanted, but it couldn't be helped. I half expected the impact of a bullet to fling me down on my face again, but no bullets came my way.

Maybe the cop went to the front door first and knocked, or maybe he sat in his cruiser while waiting for backup to arrive. Maybe he was too late to see me streaking into the woods, or maybe he thought his first duty was to search the house. I don't know, because I didn't wait to find out. I didn't even look back.

I ran for a while, going on and off the path so that my footprints would be impossible to follow. I hadn't bothered to take anything when I left the Martinsburg home, which was not a good thing. Although I'd given him no impression that I was a thief, or anything other than a fairly blank but interested girl, I thought that maybe the lack of destruction and theft after the break-in would give Pete the idea that it was me snooping around. I was still thinking this hours later when I was at work.

I was in the back room opening the freight when my cell phone rang. It was Pete.

"Hey."

"Hey yourself," I said, trying to activate the telepathetic powers that are by no means reliable. I set my box cutter down gently on the table. I haven't had an "accident" in a few weeks.

"What are you up to?"

"Oh, you know," I said, "the usual."

"You'll never guess what happened."

"I've never been good at guessing."

He chuckled. "Zombies tried to break into my house," he told me. "I'll tell you all about it. Can you be ready in fifteen minutes?"

"Um," I said. This is the way things went with Pete. Half the time I thought I had him completely fooled, buffaloed into thinking that I was a real girl who was crazy about him, and the other half of the time I thought *he* was playing *me*. "Can you make it a couple hours? I'm off at eight."

"Sure. See you then."

Maybe tonight, I thought. I'd gotten through the rest of the Christmas season at the mall without being shot at or over-whelmed by the fog, which are accomplishments in themselves, I guess. I'd worked a metric ton of hours at the store, and at no time was my secret identity compromised. Maybe I was getting overconfident.

Tommy's mother, Faith, came in the store, just in time to overhear Craig yelling at me to go take a break, something he did often (Tamara, on the other hand, got yelled at because the many breaks she took were too long). He said I was trying to get the labor board on him, or something equally goofy, and told me to go get something to eat.

"Hi, Karen!" Mrs. Williams called, and if it was still able to, my stomach would have flipped.

"Oh hi, Mrs. Williams!" I said, taking her arm and leading her toward the door. The last thing I needed was for Tommy's mom to out me as a zombie. "I was just about to take a break! Bye, Craig!"

He gave a half-hearted return to my wave, a confused look on his pierced face. Craig often looked at me as if he knew something wasn't quite right. Then again, Craig looked at almost everyone that way.

"Was he trying to be funny about the food comment?" Faith said before we made it outside, and as we got to the threshold of the store and into the brighter light of the mall, she really got a good look at me—the hair, the clothes, the skin. "Karen! Your eyes are blue!"

I rushed her out of there lickety-split, hoping that Craig hadn't heard her. "Let's go to the food court, okay, Mrs. Williams?"

"Oh my," she said, lowering her voice, even though we were now out of earshot. "You're pretending, aren't you?"

Supersweet, and supersharp, too. I could tell she thought the idea was pretty funny.

I winked at her. I'd gotten pretty good at it so that my lids didn't fuse together before separating. "Shhhhhh."

"How are you getting away with it? Your eyes . . ." she said, lifting her hand to her mouth to keep her mirth inside.

"Magic," I told her. "I keep telling everyone that we're magic, but no one wants to listen."

"They're contacts, aren't they? You have blue contacts."

I shook my head. "Magic."

Giggling, she told me how wonderful I looked and how funny her son would think it was. My passing, I mean. But then she got really serious for a minute and held my hand.

"What you're doing is dangerous," she said.

"*I'm* in danger?" I said, trying to laugh it off. We took seats at one of the wobbly round tables in the food court. Two tables away, a young woman was trying to simultaneously feed two children in a doublewide stroller, and a third small child on the seat beside her. "Isn't Tommy in Washington fighting for zombie rights? *Who's* in danger?"

"I didn't say you were the only one," she said, lightly.

I was going to explain, make assurances, etc.—but I realized I didn't have to. She wasn't going to try and talk me out of what I was doing any more than she tried to talk her son out of doing what he's doing. She was making a statement of fact, that's all, so I agreed with her.

"I worry about Tommy all the time," she said. "But he's on a mission, an important one, and I have to swallow my worry and replace it with hope. He really believes that he has a calling to make the world a better place for the differently biotic. He always had such a strong sense of duty and responsibility."

She was talking about him, but she was also trying to tell me something.

"When I think of the danger he's putting himself into by going on this trip, I just start shaking. He's already so far away, and he's so sad about Phoebe and Adam."

She smiled, and I saw that the tears I'd been fearing were not going to come. Faith was sad, confused, and maybe a little hurt, but these feelings were tempered by the fierce pride she had for her son.

"He's not like you, Karen. He would never be stealthy about things, like you are, or bluff his way through."

"I know," I told her. "That's why we all love him. Because if he were me he wouldn't be tricking people into hiring him. He'd be demanding a job not necessarily because he wanted one, but because one of *us* might want one."

"I'm not trying to criticize you. You know that, right, honey? I'm not saying your way is wrong," she said.

I gave her hand a light squeeze. "Hey," I said. "What would a great leader be if he didn't have his covert ops?"

But I felt better after talking to her, I guess. I felt like I had a real job to do.

We didn't chat long, and I didn't want to, in case Pete showed up early. I worked the rest of my shift and he didn't show up in the store at all.

I thought about calling him, but when I walked out of the mall and into the crisp air, I could see his sleek car gliding my way. He pulled up to the curb and I climbed in.

He leaned over and kissed me, one hand around the back of my neck, holding my head still. The other he placed on my knee.

I felt loathsome. Actually, I'd experienced that feeling with a lot of guys. And I saw a *lot* of guys before and after my brief relationship with Monica.

I didn't want to be gay. I was too scared to be gay. And so when Monica and I started something that was more than a friendship, I tried to keep it quiet. I wouldn't let her hold my hand when we went to the movies. I wouldn't let her kiss me good-bye. And when I saw my name in a heart on the cover of her notebook, we fought. And we kept fighting.

And yet, in my heart, which still beat at the time, I knew I was in love with her. I let the boys hold my hand, and I let them kiss me and more when we said good night, but there was nothing like the spark of electricity that passed between Monica and me when we touched, and there was nothing like the breathless longing I had for her when we were apart. Usually I just felt rotten.

But I was too afraid to do anything else. I thought I'd "come around," that I'd eventually meet a boy who I'd actually feel something for. I told Monica—and myself—that what we were feeling wasn't love. It was just really, really strong friendship, the natural intimacy that grows between people who've been best friends for years. It wasn't love. Of course not. We weren't really gay, we were best friends who let things get a little out of control. Somehow I convinced both of us that all our feelings for each other would go away if we dated boys.

And that's what we did. I dated frequently and widely, while Monica took her time. But when she finally started, it was just with one person. A handsome boy, someone who was a lot like Adam.

I thought Monica was in love, but the relief I should have been feeling wasn't there. Instead I felt dead inside.

And soon I was dead, both inside and out.

Pete's kiss wasn't a long one, but it was like spending an eternity in the fiery pit for me.

"Jesus, you're freezing," he said when he was done. Ironic.

"I went for a walk," I told him. "I got out a little early." I half expected him to have the long knife I'd seen in his drawer, but instead he stroked my cheek with the back of his hand.

"God, you're beautiful," he said. "But so cold."

"Sorry." He was in a good mood. Maybe he was in a good mood because he was considering destroying me, who knows. "What's this about zombies breaking into your house?"

He turned from me and put the car into gear. "Yeah. Somebody broke in. It's got to be zombies. I'm thinking they were trying to kill me like they killed the Guttridges. Wink, wink. Good thing I wasn't home."

"Okay," I said. "Now you've really lost me."

"I'm going to get something to eat. You hungry?"

I shook my head.

"You're never hungry," he replied, and maybe there was accusation there, or maybe it was my overactive imagination again. "How about some coffee?"

"Sure," I said. "But Dunkin' Donuts, okay?"

"Yeah. So anyhow," he said, "that scar-face zombie was seen again this morning."

I was so surprised, I almost blurted out Tak's name. I got as far as saying the T out loud, but then I caught myself and said "Tell me you are kidding."

"No, he really was. The way the radio said it, he came running out of the woods and scared the hell out of a bunch of grade school kids waiting for their bus."

I think my near discovery by the police and my walk through the woods must have frozen my brain, because it took me some time to realize that Pete meant that *he* had gone out and scared those kids. Why his smug grin didn't immediately tip me off, I don't know, but it wasn't until the grin began to be replaced with a look of uncertainty that I realized what he was saying.

"You didn't," I said, eventually, going for that breathless ohmigod inflection that I'd heard brainless girls at school employ. "Little kids, Pete?"

"No harm done, except maybe their moms will have to do an extra load of laundry. I don't think I've ever seen anything as funny as those rugrats falling all over each other to get away. The street was kind of icy, too, which made it even funnier."

"So this is how you spend your mornings?"

"Nah, this was my first time since . . . since my poor, poor lawyer bought the farm. This was definitely the most fun, though. You should have heard them howling."

"Was this *your* idea?" I asked.

"Duke thought it was time we did something to shake things up. My old teammate is getting too much traction in Washington."

By "teammate," he meant Tommy, but that wasn't the part of that sentence I focused on.

*Duke. He said it was Duke's idea. How many Dukes do you know?*

"And it just so happens that someone did break into my house today. Right into my bedroom, but it doesn't look like they took anything. Had to be zombies, right?"

"It probably was, Pete," I said, touching his arm as though I was filled with concern.

He shook his head. "No way could a zombie have gotten out of the house that fast. The cops were there eleven minutes after the alarm on the window was set off. They probably had just enough time to get the window open and climb in before they heard the cops. I don't even think the great Tommy Williams could have cased my house and taken off in eleven minutes. I think it was probably just some crackhead looking for something to pawn."

Relief, sort of. But did he flinch when I touched his arm?

"I thought you said they didn't take anything?"

"They didn't, but probably because they didn't have any time. My guess is that they would have grabbed the Xbox and games, those things are pretty easy to convert to cash. Maybe some stuff from my mom's room, jewelry or whatever."

"Was your mom scared?"

"Oh yeah. Especially when I told the cops that I thought there was some grave dirt on my carpet. They ate that up with a spoon."

"Grave dirt?"

"Yeah. Probably just some loose soil from when the thieves

crawled through the window. The ground was all packed down and a little muddy by the foundation."

"Grave dirt," I said. "Unreal."

"Yeah. Two stories for the price of one. I ought to get out more often."

As bad as I felt for the little kids he'd terrified, the good news was that Pete had given me another opportunity to expose him. If I could get that mask and give it to the right people, everyone would understand that it was Pete who scared the kids, not Tak.

"Anyhow," he said. "What are you doing tonight?"

"I've got no special plans," I said, thinking he was going to ask me out on another date. "Other than being with you."

I could see the words forming in his head even before he said them. I don't know if it was because my conscience could no longer live with all of my lies, if this last statement was the final crack in the wall that held back the blue fog, or if it was what I saw in Pete's eyes, a crazed mixture of love and hate, as he looked at me.

"Good," he said, smiling his insane smile. "Because Phoebe Kendall dies tonight."

# CHAPTER SEVENTEEN

S HE DIDN'T REACT THE WAY he wanted her to.

Pete shook his head. "I can't even believe I'm hearing this," he said. "Here we are on game day, and you want to back out."

"I want *you* to back out, Pete," she said. The way she was looking at him was doing something to his insides.

He didn't like girls who said no. Scarypants had said no to him, and the more he thought about it, the madder he got.

"Why? Nothing's going to happen. She'll die and I'll make FrankenAdam look guilty. No one is going to believe *him*. Look how quickly everyone swallowed the Guttridge 'murder.' Everyone *wants* to believe that the zombies are guilty."

"I'm still afraid she'll come back, Pete. What if she does and she identifies you? Did you think about that?"

"I hope she *does* come back. Then I could kill her twice."

"Pete, I'm serious."

"So am I," Pete told her. "And I'm going to make it so she can't come back, trust me."

She stared back at him, and for the first time since they'd met, Pete thought she looked scared.

"Christie," he said. "Are you in or are you out? Because I can stop the car right here, kiss you good-bye, and call it a day."

"Could you, Pete?" she said. "Kiss me good-bye?"

He looked away, fingers drumming on the wheel. He could and would if he had to. But he didn't *want* to, so he stayed quiet.

Christie let his non-answer slide. "What about Reverend Mathers?" she said. "Does he know you're doing this?"

"He'll appreciate my initiative."

Pete's cell phone rang. He glanced at the number and answered, winking at her.

"You're sure? Okay. Okay."

He hung up. "It's time, Christie. They're all alone."

"How do you . . ."

He lifted his hand. "Ah. Let me instruct you. Every Friday night, Morticia's . . ."

"Morticia?"

He grinned. "Yeah, Morticia Scarypants. That's what we call her."

"Great."

He continued, ignoring her sarcasm. "Every Friday night her parents go out to dinner and a movie. Clockwork. Mr. and Mrs. Typical America. And every Friday night Morticia curls up on the couch with her annoying yap dog and her corpse, and watches a movie from Netflix. Every week."

"You've barely even been in town a month," Christie said.

"Doesn't matter. T.C. just followed her parents over to Winford Landing. He didn't get close enough to see what tickets they bought, but he did see Mr. Scarypants pony up for the megatub of popcorn. I figure we've got about an hour and a half," he said. "Plenty of time."

She shook her head and crossed her arms over her chest like the petals of a flower at nighttime.

"Listen to me for a second," he said. "I want you to do this with me. All you have to do is drive the car. You don't have to go in the house, or do the deed, or any of that. I'll take care of it. I just want you to drive."

"Oh, God . . ."

"I'll be quick. Very quick."

"How? He's going to try and stop you, you know. It isn't like . . ."

Pete laughed. "He won't even know."

"What do you mean, he won't know?"

"Every night, at eight thirty, she walks the dog. Lets the dog do its business. Every night except Friday, which is when she and Frankenstein play house. Then she lets *him* walk the dog while she makes herself a snack. Coffee, usually, even late at night."

The expression she wore was either fascination, admiration, horror, or a combination of all the above.

"How . . . how are you going to do it?"

"Layman brings the dog to the backyard. While he's out there with puppykins, I'm going to run into the kitchen, where little Miss Scarypants herself will be waiting for me, no doubt getting ready to put the cream in her coffee. By the time Layman gets back—and it takes him a long time, never mind the dog— I'll be gone. And so will she."

"Are you . . . are you going to . . . shoot her?"

Pete shook his head. "No. Right inside the kitchen, between the sink and the toaster, is a block of wood with a half-dozen carving knives stuck inside it." He smiled. "I'm sure one of those will do."

"You're going to get caught," she said.

"How? You haven't seen how slow he is."

"She'll fight. What if you can't get the knife? What if she isn't in the kitchen?"

"She'll be there. It's a rendezvous with destiny."

"I'm scared, Pete."

"Don't think that way, Christie. Adam's going to be blamed. Don't even think about it."

"I just don't understand why you want to risk everything over one stupid zombie. You'd risk us going to jail and never seeing each other again over this."

"Christie," he said, pulling into a gas station parking lot. He left the car running. "If we do this, we'll be closer than ever. We'll be bound by blood."

"Pete . . ."

"I've got to know, Christie," he said. "I've got to know right now if you're with me. If not I can let you out right here, and neither one of us can ever look back."

She didn't even seem to be breathing as she wrestled with her answer. The moments dragged on and on for him, but he didn't turn his gaze from her until finally, her voice a soft whisper, she spoke.

"I'm with you, Pete," she said.

"Good," he said, cupping the back of her head with his hand. "You drive."

They got out of the car and crossed in the twin beams of his headlights. He stopped her, and then they embraced, and Pete held her close. The atmosphere seemed charged with electricity; the scent of diesel and asphalt filled Pete's nose, the steady hum of his engine and the electric whir of the gas station signage filled his ears. She'd made fun of the idea, but as Pete held her, he really felt as though they had a rendezvous with destiny, that history was going to be changed irrevocably by his small but decisive actions.

"We'll be closer than ever when tonight is over," he whispered, her hair against his cheek.

When they separated she looked scared. He kissed her mouth, then kissed her cheek and told her it was going to be all right.

She pulled away from the station, and a light snow began to fall. He watched the tiny flakes appearing briefly from the darkness to reflect the glow of the headlights.

He reached under his seat and withdrew a plastic shopping bag.

"What's that?" she asked him.

"Insurance," he said, taking out his zombie face mask. "One way or another, a zombie is getting blamed for this crime."

He pulled the mask on.

"Don't be afraid to drive faster," he said, his voice muffled by the latex as he fanned the long black hair over his shoulders. "The snow isn't sticking yet, and this is a pretty heavy car. The tires are new, too."

"Okay."

"Don't worry," he said, resting his hand on her thigh. "Everything will be fine."

She looked at him as though seeing his mask for the first time. He thought that she couldn't look more filled with horror.

Under his zombie skin, he was smiling.

# CHAPTER EIGHTEEN

"DO WE REALLY . . . NEED . . . three of us for this gig?" Popeye asked. His pacing had cut tunnels into the frosted earth behind the tree line where Tak sat watching the house.

"You do not . . . need to stay," Tak replied. "But . . . whisper . . . if you do."

"They can't hear us. Nobody can . . . hear us . . . except . . . the squirrels and the . . . raccoons," Popeye answered, making no attempt to lower his voice. He walked next to Tak and stretched, his long torso shirtless beneath his jacket. Popeye had removed a section of skin from his lower abdomen, and Tak could see the exposed gray muscles contracting as he completed his stretch.

"Sit," Tak commanded, yanking him down by the hem of his jacket. Popeye lost his footing and fell onto his back. "Nothing reflects . . . light . . . like . . . skin."

Popeye swore. If he had breath he would have lost it. His sunglasses had gone askew, exposing yet another one of his nauseating bodifications, the one that had given him his name.

"What the . . . hell, Tak," he said, sitting up and brushing snow off the sleeves of his jacket with his flipper hand. "The only ones . . . home . . . are Adam and . . . the beating heart. They won't . . . even look out .... the window."

"Layman's mother is . . . next . . . door. She . . . might. Now go . . . away."

Grumbling, Popeye crawled off to irritate Tayshawn, who was sitting about fifty feet away, where he had a decent view of the front and the opposite side of the house. Tak wanted to watch the kitchen door, because it faced the driveway and was the one that the Kendalls used most often.

Peeking into the house, he saw Phoebe rise, then stop half-way across the room and look back over her shoulder to laugh or smile at something Adam must have said to her. Tak wondered what it was that they said to each other, and what sort of future they imagined together.

If they were both dead, like him and Karen, they could be together forever, but they couldn't feel. If they were both alive, beating hearts, then they could feel. They could feel, they could grow older, and they could die. Die and not come back. Which was the better future?

A sparrow flew close and lit on Takayuki's head. He didn't move. As long as the sparrow didn't intend to build a nest there, he thought that it was fine for her to take a short rest.

He watched Phoebe turn off the light from a switch on the

wall, and then she was backlit by the flickering ghost light of a television screen. Adam must be watching from an unseen couch.

He wondered if they held hands. He wondered if Adam put his arm around her shoulders, and, in doing so, if he imagined that he could feel her warmth? And what of her reaction? How was it that she was able to put aside the revulsion that comes naturally to the living when being touched by the dead?

A truck passed by in the street beyond the houses. The bird flapped its wings, taking flight as he watched Phoebe walk back and then disappear. She was a beautiful girl. He couldn't blame Adam for not wanting to follow him and the others under the ice.

He wondered if Adam's condition allowed them to ignore the future and live purely in the present. So few people do, Tak knew. Most young people live in the future, always looking ahead toward the next big change they think will make their lives complete. "Things will be different when . . . I graduate, I get a new boyfriend, I get that job, that promotion, that new car. When my parents finalize their divorce." Others lived entirely in the past, never able to move forward from the way things used to be—which, by definition, means the way things will never be again. Maybe Adam's death brought them face to face with the realization that every moment you spend with another person is a moment that will never come again, and therefore should be treasured and cherished.

But, he thought, what about the future? Phoebe is sixteen or so, an age which gives her a two-year window, three years at the most, to decide if she wants to try to join the other side. Eighteen or nineteen seems to be the oldest a person can return from the dead. What will they do when Phoebe turns eighteen? Will she elect to try and join Adam, or will she miss her chance and allow herself to get older? Will she become a woman while Adam physically remains a boy of sixteen forever? What then?

A squirrel padded out of the brush three feet from where he sat. Seeing him, the squirrel raised its head and regarded him with suspicion, cheeks and nose twitching.

I feel the same way about you, he thought. The squirrel scampered back into the brush.

I should have discussed this with Karen, he thought. Martinsburg's actions could prevent Phoebe and Adam from having to make the toughest decisions further down the road. There could actually be a positive side to Martinsburg's plan succeeding.

There are many things I should have discussed with Karen, he thought.

Like her healing. She'd told him about the bullets and the cut. Why had her wounds gone away while everyone else's—his, Popeye's, Mal's—remained?

Love, he thought. Maybe Williams was right.

The ghost light from the unseen television threw flickering shadows on the walls inside her home. The flickering—and her absence from view—gave the home a forlorn appearance. The cold, empty landscape and the silence contributed to a sense of loss. It was so quiet that Tak could hear an animal—another squirrel or a raccoon, maybe—walking around the side of Layman's house. He could hear cars coming from miles away. Sometimes the wind played tricks on him, and he would think he heard random sounds, noises that sounded close but may have been from a distance: a chime, a baby's cry, a car door.

The quiet was disrupted by the sound of Phoebe's dog barking from inside the house. Tak had never been a fan of smaller dogs—his family owned cats, some of them nearly as big as Phoebe's pet. The dog's routine, at least, was predictable. Once outside in the morning with Mr. Kendall. Once when Adam and Phoebe came home from school, with Phoebe. And again in the evening with Phoebe or Adam, depending on if he was over or not.

The dog yapped again. It must be about that time.

Two mornings ago, the dog had looked in his direction. The wind must have been blowing just right to have brought Tak's scent all the way over to where the dog pranced around on the end of his leash. He looked right at Tak, his ears back and a low growl building in his throat. Mr. Kendall told the dog to stop being silly. Tak didn't shift a muscle throughout.

Inside, Adam rose into view, all but blocking the window. Phoebe rose as well, laying her hands against his chest. A moment later, Adam sat down. Phoebe bent low, as though she were talking to her dog. A moment later she crossed toward the kitchen and out of view, and a moment after that, the door opened and out trotted the little dog, leading Phoebe, who was coatless but sweatered against the nighttime chill.

Her sweater was white, although it had the same bluish cast to it that the snow had in the moonlight, and she was wearing blue jeans and sneakers. When they reached the center of the yard, she stopped, and the dog started pacing, his nose to the ground.

She hugged herself and turned away from the dog each time it looked ready to crouch. Tak didn't often get to observe the living, but he was always fascinated with how fluidly they moved. Karen was the only zombie he knew whose movement even began to approach the traditionally biotic. Trads moved in curves, zombies moved in angles. As though to illustrate his thoughts, Phoebe sighed, and as she turned her head toward the opposite edge of the wood where Tayshawn and, presumably, Popeye were hiding, her long black hair fanned out over her shoulder and curled along her jawline, framing her pretty white face. He was so intent on watching her that he almost didn't see a slant of light from the kitchen appear and disappear as the inner door was opened.

But the shadowy form wasn't Adam coming out. It was someone going in.

Tak stood and started moving as fast as his injured leg allowed. The dog saw him first.

# CHAPTER NINETEEN

THIS COULDN'T HAVE WORKED out any better, Pete thought, his gloved hand going around the handle of the knife. The handle was heavy and the blade whisked against the wood as he unsheathed it from its slot. *Layman probably thinks I'm Scarypants, fresh from letting little Rover have his tinkle.*

He paused just long enough to watch the light gleaming on the heavy beveled blade. Pete had been scarred by a switchblade; it had flicked in and out, and he only felt it as a sudden burning brand on his cheek, a brand that was wet to the touch. The knife he had in his hand would do more than draw on the flesh. This blade could etch; this blade could cut right through to bone.

He looked out the door and saw that Phoebe and her dog were facing the woods. At first he'd been thrown off by the variation in their pattern—Adam usually took the dog out, probably because he couldn't feel the cold. But this was even better— with her outside, he'd have even more time to kill her, and he wouldn't have to worry about escaping from the house while Adam came back with the dog. This way, Adam might not even realize that something was wrong until Pete was long gone.

He had plenty of time. Pete had been one of the fastest kids on the football team, and he hadn't missed a step since his season ended abruptly, along with Adam's life. And he wasn't weighed down with twenty pounds of pads, now, either.

Or a helmet, he thought, straightening his mask. He could be down the steps and across the lawn in the time it took Phoebe's heart to throb out its last three beats.

He could picture Adam going to investigate and putting his big corpse paws on the hefty handle of the knife and then on her cooling body. It would work best if he went a little crazy then, finding her dead and un-resurrected, his shuffling feet turning the snow around her into a bloody slush.

Pete threw the screen door wide and took the stairs in one leap, not even skidding as his sneaker hit the snow. Then the dog started barking and Phoebe screamed, but it took him a moment to realize that she wasn't screaming at him.

He slid to a stop, realizing she'd seen something in the woods beyond. He heard a crash from inside the house, as though a lamp was knocked to the floor—Layman responding to her shrieks. Her back was still to him; she was only ten yards away. He had her. Even living, Adam couldn't reach them in time.

He took one step, and then he saw it loping out of the woods. It held its arms before it as it attempted to run, half dragging its leg behind it.

"Phoebe!" it called, the word seeming to escape from the

hole in the side of its cheek. "Behind . . . you!"

She was paralyzed, Pete realized, even as he was paralyzed at the sight of the thing whose face he wore. The thing who'd cut him. The sight of it, seeming to form out of the very gloom of the forest, drove a sliver of icy fear into Pete's heart. He gripped the weighted handle of the knife. The Reverend expected him to master his emotions. He needed to fight the fear. Fight the fear and move.

I was parked on the shoulder just down the road from Adam's house. I was gripping the steering wheel of Pete's mother's car, and I knew it was time to turn the key in the ignition, but I couldn't move.

My plan had been to wait until he reached the edge of Adam's driveway, count to three, then speed over to Phoebe's house while leaning on the horn. That would give Pete enough time to reach her house, but certainly not enough time to kill her. I'd tell him I saw lights approaching, or that I heard a siren, anything. Maybe I'd just tell him that I got scared. Maybe he'd think I ruined everything or maybe he'd think I'd saved him, but it was the only thing I could think of to foil his plan yet still give me a chance to get the evidence I needed.

I counted to three. Then I counted to ten, and then I stopped counting.

I'd watched him leave the car, watched him steal across the snow-covered lawns, a shadow gliding in the moonlight. I needed to start the car. I needed to start the car and I needed to blare the horn, blast the radio, scream a warning. But I was frozen. My hands were clenched and my fingernails were pressing into my palms.

The blue fog. It was all around me—it was inside me. I could feel it seeping in, flooding into my brain through the blue portals of my contact lenses. I couldn't see. I couldn't breathe.

*But Karen,* a small still voice from inside whispered, *you don't have to breathe anymore.*

The voice wasn't mine. It was Monica's.

My inaction with Monica, my failure to do something as simple as take her hand in public, led me down a winding path to my own death. If I didn't act now, there was a very good chance that Phoebe would die—and it would be my fault.

I placed my hand on the steering wheel, on the horn.

I reached for the key, praying I'd find the strength to turn it.


Her back was still to him. Phoebe couldn't tell what the freak, the real zombie, intended to do. Pete knew he could still kill her, if he could only will his feet to move. He could kill her, and if the freak got blamed for it instead of Adam, that would still be a good thing, wouldn't it? The freak knew he'd never reach her in time, and he shouted a second warning, one made unintelligible by frustration. She dropped the leash, and her dog took off running.

There was the sound of screeching tires and a car horn from the street. Another crash from inside, and then Phoebe turned.

She looked at him and her eyes went wide, almost as if she could see right through his mask, into his eyes and into his soul. Christie was leaning on the horn now.

Pete made his decision, and ran toward the blaring horn.

Christie was standing outside the running car, watching him run.

"Did you kill her?" she yelled.

"Get in the car," Pete yelled back. "Get in the car and drive!" He opened his door and slammed it shut before she was even behind the wheel. "Go! Go!"

She stomped the accelerator to the floor, and the car fishtailed as it ran across the edge of the Kendalls' lawn. Unbuckled, Pete was rocked against the door.

"Did you kill her? Did you?"

"Jesus, watch out! You're heading for that tree!"

The tires squealed beneath them, and Pete thought the vehicle was no longer in contact with the earth.

"Did you?" She was yelling now.

Her eyes were crazed in the radioactive-green glow of the dashboard lights. She looked sickly and unreal, her hands tight on the wheel.

"Slow down. I . . ."

"Did you?"

"There wasn't time!" he shouted, his voice breaking. She was going to drive them right over the guardrail and into the embankment beyond. "Zombies!" He was aware that he sounded hysterical, that he couldn't even form whole sentences. "Zombies!"

At what seemed to be the last second, she pulled the wheel hard. The back end of the car whipped around, and for a moment he thought it was over, that they wouldn't make it; but then as if by magic, the front end cut back and they were pointed in the right direction, all four wheels in contact with dry asphalt.

His breath was coming in gulps. He tore off the mask and threw it over his shoulder into the backseat. He wasn't sure for a moment who was more intent on killing him: the half-face zombie or his girlfriend.

"Zombies," he said, gasping as though breathing were something new. "There were zombies coming out of the woods. A dozen, maybe more."

She didn't answer right away.

"I know," she said, the manic edge now gone from her voice. "That's why I came for you."

She has the strangest look on her face, he thought.

Takayuki knew he had no chance of catching Martinsburg, but that didn't mean he wasn't going to try. Then Layman came through the door just as Tak reached the edge of the driveway, and laid a hit on him that sent him flying. He flew ten feet in the air and slid on his back in the snow until he came to an abrupt stop against the wheel well of one of the many junkers in Layman's driveway.

Tak didn't feel a thing. Nothing but a twinge of memory— his final living memory, when he was launched from his motorcycle while cruising down the Garden State Parkway.

That was kind of fun, he thought. Something in his shoulder crackled as he sat up. Layman was standing over him, his huge hands balled into fists.

Tak looked up at him and showed his teeth.

"Adam! Don't hit him!"

Phoebe ran into view, and again Tak was struck by how fluid her movements were. Adam moved like a big muscle-bound oaf, but one whose limbs were controlled by puppet strings instead of reflexive will.

Adam didn't look convinced. He must have been a terror on the football field, Tak thought.

"There was another one," Phoebe said, putting her hand on Adam's arm, on the bare skin below the cuff of his Oakvale Badgers T-shirt. His skin did not yield at all to the gentle pressure of her fingers, Tak saw, as though Adam were made of lead and not flesh and bone.

"Another . . . one?" Adam said.

"And Gargoyle ran away!" she said. "He got scared."

"What do you . . . mean . . . another . . . one?"

Tak made no attempt to get up. He tried to imagine what a real fight with Adam would have been like, back when they were both alive. Probably short, if he hit me, he thought. But Adam wouldn't know how to fight, really. Not fight dirty, anyhow.

"Another Tak," Phoebe said, distracted, no doubt, by the thought of her dog lost in the cold, dark Oxoboxo woods. "Oh, Adam, did you hear that car? What if Gar ran out in the street?"

"Wait, Phoebe," Adam said. "Gar will . . . be fine." He glared down at Tak. "What . . . are you . . . doing here?"

"Just . . . checking in," Tak said.

"Just checking in?" Phoebe said. "Who was that, then? He looked like you."

Tak tried to read Adam's expressionless expression as Phoebe helped him to his feet. "You . . . think?" he said. "Didn't get . . . a good . . . look at him."

"How did you know he was going to be there?"

"I had no . . . idea. Just good . . . timing."

They didn't believe him. He was glad they hadn't seen what he'd seen just before Adam tried to launch him into orbit. Karen, at the wheel of the car that sped Martinsburg away.

"You're . . . kidding."

"When have you . . . known me . . . to kid?"

"You aren't going to tell us anything, are you?"

"What's . . . to tell?"

Adam and Phoebe exchanged a look, then resumed staring at him, suspicion etched onto their faces. It was Phoebe who softened first.

"Tak, I want to find my dog," she said. "But I have wonderful news. Karen survived the night you went into the lake. She's okay."

"She . . . did?" Tak said, forcing his mouth into an approximation of a smile, and not the one he usually wore to terrify the beating hearts. "Somehow . . . I always . . . knew it."

They heard a sharp bark behind them.

"What . . . the?" Adam said.

Popeye and Tayshawn were walking toward them, Gar curled up comfortably in the crook of Popeye's arm, his furry little body pressed against his bony ribcage.

"Hey, Phoebe . . . Adam," Tayshawn called, waving. Tak lifted his index finger to his lips, kissing his knucklebone.

Tayshawn nodded, almost imperceptibly. "How's life among . . . the living?"

Gargoyle yapped again, and Popeye was almost gentle as he handed him over to Phoebe.

"Aw," he said. "There goes my . . . midnight . . . snack."

Phoebe clutched Gargoyle tighter, but not before the dog's little tongue licked out across Popeye's flippered hand.

"We . . . wondered . . . if you thought . . . it was safe . . . to leave . . . the lake," Tak said, hoping that Popeye didn't run his mouth.

"Um, no," Phoebe answered. "Not yet."

"I . . . wouldn't," Adam said. "How . . . is . . . everyone?" He looked at Popeye's flipper hand, frowning.

"Wet," Popeye said, and forced out a high stream of giggles.

"They're fine," Tayshawn said. "A little . . . bored, maybe, but . . . fine. Everyone's . . . together in this . . . sunken . . . fishing . . . hut. Everybody but . . . Mal. He's still . . . meditating . . . on a . . . rock."

Tayshawn's hair rasped against the cracking leather of his jacket.

"He's . . . waiting . . . for God . . . to speak . . . to him." From the corner of his eye he could see Phoebe shivering. The dog was squirming in her embrace, and he could hear her teeth chattering as she tried to calm it down.

"Adam," he said. "What . . . of . . . George?"

He knew the answer already from his talk with Karen, but it was the question that Adam would expect.

The larger boy shook his head. "He didn't . . . make it. I'm . . . sorry, Tak."

"How's . . . Colette?" Tayshawn said. "And . . . Melissa?"

"Williams," Popeye added, drawing the final syllable of Tommy's name into a long sibilant hiss.

Tak watched Phoebe bend low to release her dog, the leash wrapped securely around her hand. She hesitated a moment and then reached down for something in the snow. Adam was telling Tayshawn and Popeye all about Tommy's efforts in the nation's capital.

Phoebe looked up and her eyes locked onto Tak's. She picked up the knife that his doppelganger had dropped as he fled.

"Tak," she said. "Tak, what happened here?"

The dead boys all turned to her, but no one answered.

"I'll get out here," Christie said, pulling the vehicle over to the side of the road. Pete thought he should offer to take her to her front door after their misadventure, but on the other hand, his heart was still hammering in his chest after the many near-death experiences he'd had with her driving.

"Okay. Hey, before you go," he put his hand on her shoulder as she made to exit. Her blue eyes flashed at him. "You saved my skin back there. You really did."

She reached out, her cold hand laying alongside his scarred cheek. "I want you to give up on hurting Phoebe. Forget about it."

He felt like he should protest, but at the same time he'd been thinking the same thing. Scarypants was a girl not much different than Christie was, and suddenly the thought of killing her seemed insane, regardless of whether or not a zombie was held responsible for the deed.

"We almost . . . lost each other, Pete," she said. "Do you want that to happen?"

Leaning across the seat, he took her in his arms and pressed his mouth against hers. She tasted like the cinnamon gum she was always chewing, but she was so cold, the poor thing. He realized that she must be absolutely terrified. He held her tightly, and when he stopped kissing her he whispered in her ear.

"I couldn't lose you," he said. "Not again. No more schemes."

She moved him back, gently, with her slim, cool hands.

"Really, Pete?" she said. "You mean it?"

"Honest," he said. "I'll finish up taking photos for the Reverend, then get the hell out of Dodge."

She hugged him and kissed his cheek.

"That makes me happy," she said. "I really should get going."

"Christie," he said. "Are you coming with me? To Arizona?"

She reached behind him to get her bag from the backseat.

"I don't know, Pete. I think maybe yes."

They got out of the car and crossed each other in front of the headlight beams. He didn't pull away until she was halfway down the street, because she always stopped at a certain house, turned, and waved.

He waved back, even though he knew she couldn't see him any longer.

# CHAPTER TWENTY

"PETER," DUKE SAID, taking Pete's hand in a firm, dry grip. "You're looking well."

"Duke," Pete said. "You too."

Actually, Duke looked the same as he always looked: tall, bald, and pale, his eyes bright and yet somehow dark at the same time, perhaps because the light they held revealed his sarcastic, mocking character.

"Eager to revisit the asylum?" he asked.

"Alish isn't here, you said?"

"No. He's traveling to D.C. for the great maggotfest."

"Nice."

He could feel Duke looking him over.

"Are you okay, Pete?"

"I'm okay," Pete said.

"Did the Reverend call you?"

"He called me."

Duke waited him out, and Pete capitulated.

"He told me how proud he was of me and that he wants me to accomplish a few more things here before I go back. He wants photos of our enemies."

Duke clapped him on the back. "I knew you were the man for the job, Pete," he said. "I'm proud of you, too."

"Thanks."

"Ready to go see Miss Hunter?"

"Sure," Pete said, feigning enthusiasm.

Miss Hunter greeted Pete with an expansive handshake and her killer smile. Her legs, as usual, were flawless, even though her skirt went all the way below her knees. He always thought that Alish must have created her in a test tube somehow; she was so perfect and beautiful.

"Mr. Martinsburg," she said. Her hand was like Christie's, slim and smooth, but warm. "How are you?"

"I just wanted to stop in and say hello," he told her. "I'm not going to be in town much longer."

She waited.

"And, um, I wanted to thank you for all the help you gave me. I really think it's changed my perspective on the differently biotic."

"Really?" she said, smiling. "I'm so glad to hear that. I understand you're continuing your education at One Life Ministries?"

"Uh, yeah."

"One Life isn't exactly known for its enlightened view on the differently biotic," she said, and he thought he detected an extra trace of irony in the term "differently biotic."

Pete tried without success to keep his eyes on Duke as Angela sat on the edge of her uncluttered desk. Her skirt rode up past her knee, and she noticed him noticing.

"I can see why you'd say that," he said, his mouth dry. He couldn't quite read her expression.

"I'm sure you'll find your place with One Life, Pete," she said. "You have a lot to offer. Much more than you know."

He wondered if she ever took a break from being a head shrinker. "Well, thanks. Tell Alish I said hi, would you?"

"Certainly."

"I'll escort him out, Angela," Duke said. She nodded, and they both watched her walk around the desk to her seat.

"Thank you, Duke. Good-bye, Peter."

"Later."

Following Duke out into the hallway, Pete made eye contact with the girl in the admin office, and he felt his heart stutter when he realized that she was a zombie. Was his zombie radar so off that he could no longer tell the living from the dead?

"It was good that you did that," Duke said, distracting him as they continued down the corridor. "Miss Hunter's heart bleeds for everything—stray puppies, lost sheep, maggot farms. Your little talk will bother her all night."

"What is it with you and her, anyway?" Pete said. "Doesn't the Reverend own the foundation, or something?"

"It's complicated," he replied.

Pete wondered if Duke practiced being inscrutable. But

then, of course he did—if Duke ascribed to Mathers's religious views, then it was safe to assume that he also practiced the same sort of emotional mastery that he, Pete, was learning.

He realized that Duke had walked past the corridor that led to the exit. He might also have glanced at the camera mounted at the end of the hall, but it was difficult to tell because of the unreadability of his expression.

"Are we going somewhere?" Pete asked him.

"I want to show you something."

"Oh no. Not another secret lab?"

Duke laughed. "Something like that, actually. I want you to see how complicated our relationship with the foundation gets."

Pete shook his head, then he stopped in his tracks. Duke looked ready for an argument, misunderstanding the cause of Pete's hesitation.

"The girl in the office," he said. "I just realized. She was the one they were dissecting, wasn't she?"

"She was."

"Damn," Pete said, remembering things that his conscious mind attempted to suppress. Some of her organs had been removed from her body when Duke had brought him to the lab; grayish, pulpy-looking things that sat in plastic trays under glass domes like spoiled bakery confections. There was a length of intestine coiled like rope, and Pete hadn't been able to eat sausages since. He'd realized that the girl, the half that was strapped to an upright gurney, had been watching him as he peered over her insides, her wild eyes tracking him as he went from table to table like he was examining exhibits in a museum. He'd examined all the beakers containing her parts; he'd even perforated a grayish lump with the point of a pencil while she'd watched. Her attention, even more than the sight of her guts, had brought him to the point of nausea.

"You told me that the Hunters didn't know what they were doing. That Alish was crazy."

"He is," Duke said. "Even voodoo science gets lucky sometimes."

"You told me that he was just exploiting them, looking for the fountain of youth or something. 'Trying to cure death,' I think is what you said."

"He is. And exploiting them. Now will you come on? We don't really have an eternity of time ourselves here."

"She looked pretty good to me," Pete said, not moving. "I couldn't even tell that she was dead, at first."

Pete saw from Duke's sinister smile that he'd made a mistake, but he didn't know what the mistake was.

"Yeah, you've been having that problem a lot lately, haven't you? Now come on."

"What does that mean?"

Duke smiled. "What, indeed?"

They walked on.

"So you have yourself a little girlfriend now?" Duke said. He wasn't smiling, Pete realized. He was leering.

"What about it?"

"Don't you find her a little frigid?"

"What the hell are you talking about?"

"She a cold fish? A little lifeless in the sack?"

Pete wanted to kill him, but he regulated the emotion and followed Duke down the hall toward the small dormitory wing.

"She's fine," Pete said, trying to keep from sounding affronted. "She's going to go back to Arizona with me."

"Ha! Now *that* would be interesting."

Pete wanted to ask him just why he found that so interesting, but he let it lie, hoping Duke would elaborate. They walked on in silence.

Pete knew from his time working off his community service as a maintenance worker under Duke that there were six small rooms set aside for the zombies, only one of which had been inhabited at the time. The room was empty now. Pete used to sit in the monitor room and watch him on the screens when he'd take walks around the perimeter of the building. Cooper or Hooper or something like that; Pete figured that the zombie must have taken off when his dissected pal was discovered by his friends.

"Alish has had some success with his experiments," Duke said, whispering even though the cameras mounted in the dorm wing weren't microphoned. "He's like a kid playing with his first chemistry set. The walking corpse you saw is pretty much his only real success, and his failures could fill a cemetery, believe me. You don't want to spend any time digging behind the building."

The foundation was set up on a low hill, and there was a scrubby lawn, like an untended baseball field, that stretched out to the perimeter fence. Duke was right; Pete didn't want to spend any time digging there.

"I don't get it," he said. "Why does Reverend Mathers let him keep working if he's actually helping the zombies? That doesn't make sense to me."

Duke stopped in front of the last door in the hallway.

"The road to hell is paved with good intentions," he said. "Half the world's doomsday devices—nerve gases, super diseases, nuclear weapons—were all created by someone looking for something they thought would benefit mankind. On the way to finding an endlessly renewable energy source, humanity creates a weapon that can devastate a city. We reach out to explore space and as soon as we get there, point our cameras—and our missiles—inward, at our neighbors, at our enemies. We seek to cure death and instead give death dominion over the earth."

He smiled.

"The Reverend lets Alish tinker because he thinks eventually he'll discover something that can wipe out all the maggot farms in one shot."

There was a noise behind the door. Duke glanced over his shoulder, and Pete thought that maybe he looked a little nervous.

"There's something horrible behind that door, isn't there?" he said. "Another monster that you want me to see."

Duke's laugh had no humor in it.

"Oh yeah," he said. "But you still want to look, don't you? It's only human."

He stood back, motioning to Pete like a carnival barker

at the entrance of the freak show.

"Go ahead. Feast your eyes."

Pete knew he should walk away, but instead he stepped forward and looked through the window in the door.

"Oh, gross," he said.

The zombie inside the room fit the part. It was staring at the splintered ruin of what looked like a wooden bed frame and mattress. Long shreds of cloth that had been torn from the mattress lay about the otherwise empty room. Its flesh was hanging off its face in patches, and its clothing was in tattered rags that did little to hide the fact that chunks of its flesh were missing. What was left of its hair stood up in a ratty tangle.

"Alish's newest pet," Duke said. "It was the one the cops caught after we had our fun."

The fun he was referring to, Pete realized, was the night they and a few other right-thinking Americans framed some zombies for a murder that was never actually committed.

"I thought it was dead," Pete said. "Deactivated, like. The papers said it collapsed after getting Tasered."

"It was. The cops didn't know what to do with it, so they sent it here at the foundation's request. Alish got the brilliant idea of Tasering it a second time, which must have gotten it going again. Like I said, voodoo science."

The thing turned to the window in the door, as if noticing them. But there was no recognition in the unblinking eyes, not even acknowledgement. There was a hole in its face where its nose used to be.

"Gaah. It's disgusting. It looks like its arm is broken," Pete said, pointing at its left arm, which hung uselessly from the socket at an unnatural angle.

"The cops worked it over pretty good before the Taser," Duke said. "Look closely, you can see some of the bullet holes. See that black blotch on its throat?"

The zombie staggered over to the door as though each step took an enormous effort. The glass was reinforced, Pete noticed, which meant the window must have been replaced sometime after he'd stopped working there.

"The interesting thing is that Alish hasn't even told anybody outside the foundation about this."

Its lips were gone, which made its expression even harder to read than the average zombie. The eyes gazed out vacantly, as though Duke and Pete were as easy to stare through as the window itself. It leaned forward until its gray, pitted forehead pressed against the glass.

"Thanks for this, Duke," Pete said, lacing his voice with sarcasm. "To be frank, I could have gone my whole life without seeing this."

The zombie lifted its working arm and its hand fell against the glass, as though it were punctuating Pete's statement. At least two of its fingers were obviously broken, pointing from the bare knuckles at awkward angles. Each digit was peeling, in some places all the way to the bones beneath.

"Could you?" Duke said. "We weren't sure."

Pete couldn't take his eyes off the horrible monster on the other side of the door, but he knew that Duke's expression could be just as unreadable.

"What is that supposed to mean?" he said.

Duke's eyes were ticking back and forth in their sockets, scanning Pete's for data he couldn't find.

"My God," he said, finally. "You really don't know."

"Don't know what?"

"God bless America. If the Reverend knew how truly clueless you are, he'd toss you out of One Life so fast your head would spin."

"You've lost me, Duke. I've got to get out of here."

"Not so fast, sport."

"Say what you mean, then."

"Well," Duke said, tapping at the corner of the glass with his knuckle. The monster didn't react. "You've been spending an awful lot of time with maggot farms that aren't as obvious as Stinky here. A weaker man might even think that some of the maggot farms you've been fraternizing with were *attractive*. Almost like the corpse down the hall."

He paused and leaned in toward Pete until he was no farther away than the dead boy, but without the pane of glass separating them. Pete's throat was suddenly dry. The zombie's insides glistened where they were exposed to the air.

"Almost *exactly* like the corpse down the hall, in fact."

"What . . . what are you saying?"

"Your girlfriend is dead, Pete," Duke whispered, his coffee breath in Pete's ear and his nostrils. "She's a corpse."

Pete stepped back, wondering why Duke would say such a thing to him. It took him a moment to register that he wasn't speaking about Julie, because he hadn't told anyone at One

Life about Julie, not even the Reverend.

Duke smiled. "She's Karen DeSonne, and she's dead. Minus the Catholic-reform-school-girl getup, of course. She might have darker hair and blue contacts, but it's her, just as dead as ever."

Pete slumped against the wall, feeling like Duke had just knocked the wind out of him. Opposite, the lipless dead creature was pressing its face against the reinforced glass window.

"Did you kiss her, Pete? Did you give death a great big soul kiss?"

Pete's internal organs began to rebel. He knew what Duke was saying was true. It was her. *Christie.* She was the one he followed in the woods that day, the one with the crazy glass eyes. It was true. Maybe he'd always known it.

He felt his gorge rising, and swallowed it back. That morning, when Pete had gone back to his mother's car, he couldn't find his mask.

"Steady, son," Duke said, his voice almost soothing. "Everyone makes mistakes."

Pete looked at him, then at the thing against the glass. Every emotion he'd ever had was swirling around his head. How could he possibly master them all?

Duke gripped Pete's shoulder.

"The Devil is tricky, Pete. He ties some of his biggest evils inside the prettiest packages. But this is what those things are beneath the skin. Monsters cloaked in dead flesh."

Duke put his arm around his shoulder, and Pete thought he could see something, a flash, a flicker of something deep within the thing's shining eye. Something like consciousness, but then it was gone. A trick of the light, maybe.

"The Devil hides among us," Duke said. "But this is his real face, Pete. We wanted to make sure you could see it clearly."

I can see, Pete thought, staring into the creature's eyes like he would his own reflection. "I can see."

# CHAPTER TWENTY-ONE

I HAD THE MASK, AND MAYBE I should have gone straight to the authorities, to the Undead Crimes Unit, and taken my chances. But I also had a promise from Pete to leave Phoebe alone, and what I didn't have was the exact location of where his lawyer was hiding out. If I could get that, I thought, then I'd have everything I needed to take One Life down and get my friends out of the lake.

I'd also faced the blue fog and beaten it back. A couple moments late, maybe, but that was behind me now. I'd escaped the fog, my body had healed itself from wounds made from bullet and blade; I was feeling invulnerable.

But I wasn't.

I'd been squeezing my hands together so tightly the other night that my fingernails had made holes in my palms, a row of four crescents on each hand. I covered them with Band-Aids. My cover story was that I'd burnt them both gripping a hot fireplace poker, but I never got to use the excuse.

I was in the back room opening boxes with Craig when Tamara leaned her head in through the door.

"What happened to you?" she said, instantly picking up on the bandages. "Stigmata?"

Before I could even open my mouth she told me that someone was there to see me.

"Oh," I said, looking over at Craig as he rolled his eyes skyward. I stuck out my tongue at him and stepped over the open boxes to join Tamara at the door.

"Give me a minute," I said. "I'll be right out." I had the box cutter in my hand. I realized it might have usefulness beyond cutting boxes. I slipped it into the pocket of my jeans.

Pete was standing at the front of the store. He saw the look on my face, and grinned from ear to ear. Sometimes I'm less deadpan than other times. His scar was a livid red line on his face.

"Hey, Christie," he said, and Tamara looked sharply at me. She'd seen me climb into Pete's car once a few weeks ago, and to keep up the charade (or maybe to help me get into character) I'd spent more than one shift babbling on about Pete and how into him I was. She hadn't seen him up close, but it was possible that now she could add two and two and realize that *my* Pete was Pete Martinsburg, slayer of zombies. His calling me Christie probably sparked her curiosity as well. "Miss me?"

He walked over and gave me a rough, loud kiss, aiming for my mouth but getting my cheek as I turned. Tamara, a frightened look on her face, took a step backward.

"Well, did you?" he said, his face, his scar, inches from mine. He put his hand on my back as though to draw me closer, and Tamara gasped. He withdrew his hand.

"Terribly," I said, mustering up "flirty" from my bag o' many voices. "But I'm working." Sing-songy, trying not to offend.

"Oh, I know," he said, his hand going to my shoulder. "I just wanted to stop by and say hi. I went shopping."

"Oh?" I said. I glanced at Tamara, who wore a look of abject horror on her face, which I couldn't quite figure out. She always came across to me as feisty, tough. Pete was being a little scary, but I was surprised she was even picking up on that.

"Yeah. Bought a shirt."

He opened his bag and withdrew a collared dress shirt, which was creased where it had been pinned to the cardboard prior to Pete's trying it on.

"Nice," I said. Something was going on here, but I wasn't sure what.

"Hey, thanks," he said, with exaggerated enthusiasm. He looped his arms around me for a hug, and he squeezed me for a quick second, his hands patting me on the back, at my waist, and even my backside. Tamara gasped aloud as Pete stepped back.

Craig came out of his office to run a register report or something, took one look at us, and said, "What the hell?"

I'd thought Pete was acting strangely, of course. The kiss, the smile, the frequent touches. Even the shirt seemed a totally random thing.

But then he reached over and placed his hand on my

shoulder, right near my neck, and I saw what he'd been doing, because he did it again. He leaned close to me.

"I know what you are," he said, his voice a harsh, angry whisper, "I've known the whole time."

He withdrew his hand, and I saw it. Those frequent touches? The hugs and pats? Each time he touched me he'd pushed one of the pins from his shirt into my body. There were a row of them down my back, pushed in deep so that their heads were nearly flush with the surface of my skin.

"You didn't even feel it," Pete said. Something was happening to his face; some loosened veil tearing away. "You didn't feel anything!"

He shoved me into the Z display, and I went crashing to the ground. Tiny bottles of Endless broke beneath me on the floor.

"You don't feel!" he said, punctuating each word with a kick. Most were to my side, one found my face. He might have broken bones, but like he said, I don't feel.

I tried to rise and he hauled me up, spinning me and throwing me into another display. The world danced, spun, and soared. He threw me again, and I got to my feet as he was stepping over a fallen goth mannequin, something worse than murder in his eyes.

I turned to Tamara, who was looking at me like the monster that I was. My heart broke a little then; I couldn't help but think that for all of her pro-zombie talk, all the buying of Z and Kiss of Life lip gloss and all of that, that she was just as much a bioist bigot as the rest of them. Maybe—I hope—I misread her. Maybe it was the pins and my humiliation that she was reacting to. I didn't know, and I didn't have the time to fig-ure it out. She was still my only hope.

She shrieked as I moved toward her, and I stumbled against the box of product we'd been putting together. I embraced her, and she shrieked as I put my mouth against her ear, while tak-ing the box cutter out of my pocket.

"In my jacket pocket," I said. "Bring it to the Haunted House." I told her where to hide it, and I clung to her. She may have hugged me back, or she may have been so rigid with terror that she did nothing at all. I put the box cutter in my mouth, for once glad that my taste buds were only semi-functional.

"Police! Step away from her, you zombie freak!"

I stepped away, then glanced over my shoulder. One of the cops had his Taser out, and I thought briefly of George. The other cop had his gun ready. It was pointing at my head.

"Turn around! Get on the ground. Now!"

I did as they asked. Tamara was shaking, on the verge of hysteria.

"Head down! Do it!" One of the cops yelled.

"What the hell?" Craig repeated.

My hands were cuffed behind my back. I suppose the knee in my spine would have really, really hurt a living person, but I didn't have to worry about that, did I? They hauled me to my feet—easy to do, I'm just a little slip of a girl, really—and told me to walk.

I looked at the cops. The one doing all the talking I didn't recognize, but his partner, the one with the Taser, was very familiar to me. He was the one that let me escape that night at

St. Jude's. Our eyes met and I thought that he might have given a slight nod, a signal, and I decided not to resist. Beyond him, Pete Martinsburg was beaming heroically, chest heaving, protector of the living from the evil dead. Maybe there would be reward money.

"Don't look at anyone," the talkative cop said, shoving me forward. "Keep your head down."

They dragged me out, under the curious eyes of all the people with whom I'd talked and worked with the past few months, the people who I'd stop and chat with on my breaks. My only regret was that I never found out where One Life was hiding Guttridge.

No one said anything. Not even good-bye.

# CHAPTER TWENTY-TWO

I KISSED HER, PETE THOUGHT, rolling over in his bed, still not sure if what he'd just experienced was dream or nightmare. *I kissed her.* The clock read one thirteen. He hadn't been asleep that long.

He sat up. The dead girls were all jumbled up in his head. He'd been holding hands with Julie, but then her hand was frozen, and when he looked, it wasn't Julie but Karen, and her diamond eyes were filled with hate, but when he looked again it was Julie, only not Julie like he'd known her—freckled, tan, and smiling—but Julie, dead. Her freckles became purplish motes on her bluish skin. She had the dry, brittle-looking hair and the wide staring eyes that tracked a second too late. It had to be Julie, because he'd held hands with no other girl since; sentimentality had died with her, and much like the girl herself, was unlikely to ever be resurrected. Dead Julie smiled at him in that twitchy, paralytic way that the dead smile, and he cried out. The sound he made was like the sound Adam made when called to the witness stand to testify about his own murder.

Pete's heart was beating. He, at least, was alive. He wasn't sure if his dream self had cried out in horror or elation. He peered around the room, half expecting the girls to coalesce out of the shadows and step toward his bed. Julie, Karen, Julie, Karen.

He threw the covers back, climbed out of bed, and paced the floor for a few moments before taking a seat on his weight bench. Karen wouldn't survive being imprisoned. One way or another, he knew that she wouldn't walk out of that prison under her own power. He wondered if her dead friends would try to get her out, or if her dead friends even knew she was there. They'd all gone into hiding somewhere, all except for Layman and Williams, but Williams wouldn't be doing anything from D.C. Some speculated that they just gave up, that they had conceded defeat, and crawled back into their welcoming graves and pulled the dirt up over their heads, but Pete didn't think that was the case.

I should try and find them, he thought. *But then what?*

He really didn't know. Would he turn them in like he'd turned her in? Or would he step aside and let them try to free her?

Or would he help?

He lay flat on the weight bench, sliding between the struts that supported a barbell with a fifty pound plate on each end. He reached up and wrapped one hand around the cool metal.

*It's too late.* The thought came into his mind and wouldn't leave, as though whispered by a voice not his own, a voice from beyond. He was certain that the voice was speaking the truth.

There was much he regretted about what happened with Karen—everything that happened to her, not just the horrific end. He wrapped his other hand around the steel bar as he thought about the awful things he'd done to her, and the memory of those things made him confused and angry and sad all at once.

But the memory of what he'd done—what they'd done—wasn't what intensified those feelings the most. It was the look in her eyes just before the police took her away. One of her eyes had drained of all color and sparkled like a diamond, but it wasn't their otherworldly quality that haunted him so. Rather, it was the look of forgiveness that he saw deep within them.

He lifted the bar from the cradles, brought it down to his chest, and exhaled evenly as he pressed up. There was no strain; a hundred pounds was his curling weight.

I should find them anyway, he thought, returning the bar to the cradles. He closed his eyes, wondering if he could fall asleep beneath such a weight.

# CHAPTER TWENTY-THREE

**I** WAS IN A HOLDING CELL IN at the Winford police station. I was alone in the cell and I hadn't seen anyone since I'd been delivered there. I was alone in the cell and I was contemplating grave things.

It may have been midnight; it may have been another day entirely. I don't know. I don't even have a heartbeat to help me mark the time.

Sometimes my eyes would go out of focus, and the bars of the cell and the baby-vomit-yellow color of the walls would disappear and give way to blue, a harsh gray blue that blotted out the world.

I took out as many of the pins that Pete had pushed into me as I could. One or two I couldn't reach. Some were so deep I needed to pry them up with the edge of my thumbnail. A few of them were blue-black at the tips. Karen DeSonne, the human voodoo doll.

I also took out my contact lenses and placed the rubbery blue disks on the bench beside me. One of them had scrunched up under my upper eyelid when I was being beaten by Pete.

I was contemplating grave things because I'd been so, so close. One more "date" with Pete and I think I would have had everything I needed to get him and Duke arrested, get Guttridge found, and all of their evil, zombie-hating deeds brought to light. That would have given Tommy a platform to succeed in Washington.

Even more, solving the crime would have made me a better person. It would have given me the strength to tell my friends, Tak and Phoebe and Mal and Margie and everyone else, who I really was. It would have given me the strength to go back to the town where I grew up and died and find Monica and tell her how sorry I was.

I was also thinking that I wouldn't leave the prison system alive. Ha ha. But really, I was thinking about final termination—the kind that no one comes back from. The half-moons that my fingernails had made in my palms the day Pete almost caught Phoebe were still there, unhealed. Maybe they'd closed up a little, and maybe they hadn't; maybe I only had a certain amount of healing allotted me.

Maybe the next time will really be the last time, I thought.

I was thinking about this even before I had my first visitor.

I didn't recognize him until I saw his eyes, and the moment ours met he sort of recoiled, then composed himself and continued to approach my cell. It was the policeman who'd let me go on the night of St. Jude's massacre.

"Karen?" he said, looking at me. "They said at the store that your name is Karen."

I nodded. They hadn't done anything in the way of processing me as a criminal, and I'd already decided that the lack of paperwork did not bode well for my chances of survival.

"I'm Officer Pelletier, Karen. I wanted to talk to you, but I'm going to have to talk fast because I'm not supposed to be here at all."

I waited for him to continue. There were reasons I didn't want to say much.

"First," he said, "I wanted to apologize for that evening outside the church. For shooting you."

"I forgive you," I told him, through the bars and clenched teeth.

"This isn't right, what we're doing to you. What I did to you."

"It didn't hurt," I said. "Much."

"When I saw you . . . when I saw you in the street, running . . . you weren't a person to me. You were a thing."

I didn't say anything. Sometimes it's better just to let people talk.

"I was scared," he whispered, as though the admission alone was a shameful secret. "We were all scared; when they briefed us, they said you couldn't be killed and that you each had the strength of a gorilla."

I raised an eyebrow at that one. He nodded and repeated that that was what "they" said.

"But when you looked up at me . . . after I shot you . . . I could tell. I could tell by the look on your face that it wasn't true. What they told us about you wasn't true."

"So you let me go." My voice was harsh, almost like Tak's.

"I let you go," he said, and he pressed his forehead against the bars. I could have grabbed him then, grabbed him right by the throat and used my super gorilla strength to crush the life out of him. That's what would happen in a movie, I thought. Except I don't really have super gorilla strength, and I had no desire to crush the life out of him, or anybody. Even if it meant I could go free.

"I was this close to killing you," he said. "They told us a headshot might work, so most of us were shooting for your heads. But when you looked up, I didn't see a monster. I saw my daughter."

He stepped back a moment, and I was able to connect the dots. Around the eyes he looked an awful lot like Holly Pelletier, an airhead who used to date Adam. Holly is one of the most virulently anti-zombie people I know, so I thought it was pretty interesting that her father should have an epiphany while pointing his weapon at my already perforated face.

His next words made me wonder if I was projecting my thoughts.

"You'd been shot," he said, scrutinizing me. "But the wound is gone."

I didn't confirm or deny, so eventually he gave up on trying to see the unseen.

"When I looked into your eyes, all I could think is that you could be my little girl there, waiting for her brains to get blown out. Then I thought that it could be her in my shoes, and that if it was, she'd have no hesitation at all in erasing your existence. It made me think about it. It made me think about how wrong we were."

"Glad . . . to be . . . so helpful," I said, barely moving my lips and deliberately slowing and zombifying my speech.

"Why didn't you hide?" he said. "Why did you put yourself at risk?"

I shrugged, purposely lifting my shoulders out of sync.

"We can't . . . hide . . . forever."

"They're going to destroy you, Karen," he said. His voice actually broke when he said my name. A big tough policeman, and he was getting choked up about a little voodoo doll zombie. "Your parents have been here a few times already—the last time with a lawyer—but they're not letting them see you. The company line is that you aren't a legal entity, so we can do whatever we want."

"Mom . . . Did my . . . mommy . . . come, too?"

He nodded, sniffing.

"You are going to be transferred to the correctional facility in Nihantic first thing in the morning. You'll be released into gen pop. They're going to destroy you."

"Murder," I whispered. "You can say . . . murder."

"They're going to murder you. The guards will do it if the prisoners don't get you first. They were talking about it in the squad room earlier. You'll never make it."

I wondered if this was the point in our story where Officer Pelletier passed me the key, or tipped me off to his cunning plan of busting me out after causing a diversionary fire in the men's bathroom, but no such luck. Instead he was trying as hard as he could to keep the tears that were welling in his eyes from rolling down his cheeks.

"Thank you . . . for telling . . . me," I said. "About my . . . mom."

"I'm sorry," he said. "There's nothing I can do."

"There is," I told him. I reached through the bars and wiped the corner of his eye with my thumb. He didn't try to stop me. "Tell them . . . I . . . was . . . a person."

"I will," he said, standing a little straighter.

"And please," I said. "Tell my . . . family . . . I love . . . them."

He said that he would, and then he was gone.

After he left, I went back to my bench. Already my contact lenses had begun to crinkle and collapse inward as they dried out.

So that was it, I thought. I was going to die. Again.

I don't want to die. Even though the blue fog is all around me, even though I'm technically dead, and according to some people, damned, I don't want to die. Where there's life, no matter how we define it, there's hope.

I had so much hope these past few weeks. I hoped that what I was doing would make the world a better place for my kind, and I hoped that at the other side of it I could be myself. That I wouldn't have to hide or pass as something and someone I'm not.

And I hoped that I could figure out why I alone among

zombiekind was healing, because that was a gift I wanted to share.

The blue fog was all around me, but I still had hope. I was still "alive."

I opened my mouth wide. Wider, I'd guess, than any living person could, and I reached into the back of my throat with two fingers, back to where I'd hidden the box cutter. Somehow I imagined getting it out would have been easier. I probably hadn't needed to go to such extreme lengths to hide it, because they barely searched me—heck, they couldn't stand to look at me, much less touch me—once I'd arrived at the jail.

Of course, I could have used it on Pete, but I don't have the ability to hurt people that way.

Only myself.

The first thing I did once I had it was to scratch "Love Karen" in the baby-vomit paint coating the bench, just below my desiccated contacts.

Then I got to work.

I don't know where I'm going. I don't know if this will work at all, or if I'm just going to drift out into the blue fog.

But I have hope.

# CHAPTER TWENTY-FOUR

PETE, UNLIKE MANY IN Oakvale's teen population, felt no disappointment at the lack of a serious snowfall the night prior. He was, on paper at least, home-schooled, and therefore less emotionally invested in the vagaries of the usual Connecticut winter.

The roads were already cleared, so he pulled on a pair of old sneakers and a loose sweatshirt over the T-shirt he'd worn to bed, and went jogging around his neighborhood for an hour. He tried to run every day, especially now that he'd been kicked out of school and had virtually no chance of playing organized football ever again, unless someday Reverend Mathers endowed a college or something like that and let him on the team. Discipline was important, and without the loose discipline of school and the rigorous discipline of football, Pete knew he would have to generate that discipline internally.

The road was a little slippery, especially with the worn treads of his sneakers, but Pete felt like he was in total control of his mind and body. There was a period where that control wasn't there, but now it was back. He ran easily up the first hill on his street and slowed his pace slightly going down the other side. His lungs worked in a steady rhythm to match his stride. He felt alive.

He watched a snowplow rumble down the opposite side of his street, the wide rust-orange blade kicking up a rather pathetic spray that was mostly wet sand cast from the plow that had gone before. Pete liked to put everything out of his mind when he ran, all of the obsessions and compulsions of life, and just focus on the act of exercising itself. Or the scenery. The beating of his heart, the way the shaded contours of the light snow revealed the topography of his neighbors' yards. Most days, whether doing laps around the development or pressing iron in his basement, he was pretty successful in emptying his mind of thought, but this morning a concern popped like a blister in his consciousness. Something told him that the Reverend would be calling him again today.

Pete skid a little as he took the sharp corner that marked the start of the next street of Oakvale Heights, and he felt a twinge in his upper thigh. He tried to concentrate on that transient pain, but an image of the Reverend was taking shape, coalescing like a phantom of mist in his mind. Reverend Mathers had called Pete quite often over the past week, and although he suspected the Reverend had a soft spot for him, Pete had his doubts. Unlike the pain in his thigh, these doubts couldn't be forgotten by running a few more steps or doing another set of shoulder-press reps.

Pete knew where those doubts came from. Who they came from. A perfect plane of snow draping the Taylors' front yard made him think of her skin, and the thought made him clench his jaw and tighten his fists. Exercise was supposed to erase the thoughts, not encourage them.

He finished his normal workout, but instead of turning into his driveway and yelling what he wanted for breakfast to his mother, he started all over again.

Another hour later, his sweatshirt clinging to him like a second skin, he trotted to a stop at the edge of his driveway. Steam rose from his body in visible waves, but he wasn't even winded. His body did what he wanted it to even when his mind did not. He was vibrating like a struck chime, but when he held out his hand to see if it was shaking, it was steady as a rock.

Early in his workout he'd run past a school bus pulled to a stop at the top of the development. He could see the fear on the faces of the kids getting on; he had no friends in this neighborhood. He hadn't spoken to TC for a week, not since the failed attempt on Phoebe's life. The big dummy was probably sitting in class right now, a wide grin on his fat face. Pete decided he'd look up TC before he went back to Arizona on Friday.

He stood at the edge of the driveway for a moment, listening to himself breathe. He went to get the papers from the plastic boxes, which had been spared by the snowplows that pulverized them to smithereens at least once a season. The

Wimp, Pete's name for his mother's husband, subscribed to two newspapers. Pete did a quick scan of the front pages, knowing what he would find there. Duke Davidson had called him last night, about an hour after the cops had found her in her cell. Duke always knew these things first. Duke was plugged in. Pete started reading, and all the thoughts and doubts he'd tried to chase away came flooding in.

The more local *Winford Sentinel* ran her story as the headline above coverage of a car accident and a recap of a heated town meeting involving a proposed condo complex. The lead in *The Hartford Courant* was a cheerily partisan puff piece regarding a "Zombie Walk and Rally" that Oakvale's own Tommy Williams was trying to organize. A second article talked about a van full of volunteers, living and dead, who had been run off the road while on the way to join him. There was a small box with the headline "Zombie Prisoner Found Dead," but unlike in the *Sentinel*, there was no photo.

Pete read the headline out loud. "Great headline," he said, shaking his head. "Zombie Found Dead. Brilliant." He was gripping the paper so tightly he tore a section from the front page.

He started to read the article on the Zombie Walk.

While standing at the edge of his driveway, he read as much of the piece as he could stomach, scarcely noting the chill despite being soaked with sweat. When he got to the part about "the brave pilgrim, the self-sacrificing leader of the ZRM, or Zombie Rights Movement," he hawked and spit, then tossed the entire paper into the slushy mix pooling at the driveway's edge. Let the Wimp find another paper.

He turned back to the *Sentinel*. The photograph of Karen was a mug shot. She was in her prison blues, staring out at him with her unnatural eyes. She had a slight smile on her pale lips, not quite sardonic, not quite sad. *I know you, Peter Martinsburg,* she seemed to be saying. He could almost hear her voice. *I know you and I forgive you.*

> Karen DeSonne, 16, was found in her holding cell at the Winford police station, the victim of an apparent suicide. Ms. DeSonne was being held for fraud, criminal forgery, and various other crimes. It is alleged that she was also wanted for questioning in the disappearance and alleged murder of August Guttridge and his family.

"Alleged murder," Pete said aloud. "That didn't take long."

> Mr. Guttridge was the lead defense attorney in a recent court case concerning the accidental shooting of a boy who returned as a living-impaired person, and his disappearance is alleged to be in retaliation for his role in that case.

Pete glanced down at the photo. He was taken almost wholly unawares by the sudden pressure behind his eyes, and he snorted again, but not to spit. He cursed and tossed the paper to the ground, but when he went back with the intention of retrieving Karen's photo, she was already soaked through, just a clot of ink.

Pete pinched the bridge of his nose, ignoring the cold but not the dull ache in his head as he went back inside.

# CHAPTER TWENTY-FIVE

TAK'S FIST CRASHED THROUGH the glass, and when he withdrew it from the box, there was a small shard sticking out from the back of his hand.

"Tak, what the . . . hell," Popeye said. "There's a big rock . . . right over . . . there."

"And I have . . . quarters," Tayshawn added. They were at the corner of Karen's street, clustered around the newspaper box Tak had just smashed. Ignoring them, Tak reached beneath the last of the glass clinging to the frame and withdrew the newspaper from the display. His hand flexed as he read the headline a third time, and the motion forced the glass splinter out of him like toothpaste squeezed from a tube. When he hadn't heard from Karen soon after the near miss with Martinsburg, he knew something was wrong. He'd been the only one to catch sight of her driving Pete's getaway car. After catching up with Adam and Phoebe for a few minutes, feigning ignorance of the huge knife she'd found in the snow, the Sons of Romero went back into the woods and, unbeknownst to the beating heart and her man, took up their positions again in case Martinsburg made a return trip.

But then, days later, he heard her say his name as clearly as though her voice were a small stone dropped into the well of his mind, and he knew that something had happened. Something dreadful.

*I'll always know*, he'd told her.

"Zombie Prisoner Found Dead," the headline read, above a photograph of Karen in a blue prison jumpsuit. Was that some stupid breather's idea of a joke?

He could feel Popeye peering over his shoulder.

"I'm sorry . . . Tak," he said, and put his hand on Tak's shoulder. "Maybe we can get . . . that freak . . . that . . ."

"She's still . . . alive," Tak said, his voice a dry rasp.

"Look, Tak. I . . . know you . . . liked . . . her, but . . ."

Tak, still clutching the newspaper, whirled and grabbed the front of Popeye's jacket, driving him into the wall of the bus shelter behind him. There was a hollow thump as Popeye's head struck the wall. His glasses went askew on his face, his lidless eyes appearing to protrude more than usual.

"She's . . . still . . . alive," Tak said, his face inches from Popeye's.

"Okay! Okay!" Popeye said, raising his hands above his head. "No . . . worries! She's . . . still alive."

"Tak," Tayshawn said from behind him. "Ease . . . up, Tak. Come on . . . man."

Tak could see twin reflections of himself in the black lenses of Popeye's glasses, each tiny mirror image a mask of hate. His lips were curled back in a snarl over teeth that were visible all the way to the molars on the torn side of his face. Bones and leather creaked as he released his friend.

"She's . . . alive," he said. "She . . . is."

"Okay, Tak," Popeye said, straightening his glasses with his ridiculous webbed hand. "Okay."

She had to be. The bullet holes disappeared. She said she'd slashed her wrist nearly to the bone, and that had healed. She could survive whatever happened to her in jail. She had to. She couldn't be dead; really dead.

*I'll always know*, he'd said.

But he didn't.

Tayshawn waited a few moments before speaking. "What are we going . . . to do?"

Takayuki looked beyond him as a delivery truck went by. He flexed his hands until the knuckles popped. There was a thin gray line where the piece of glass had been.

"Layman," he said. "We're going to . . . talk . . . to Layman."

After a long trek, the three of them were standing at the edge of the woods behind Adam's house, this time making no real effort to hide themselves behind the big bare oaks and thin birches.

"His bedroom . . . is there," Tak said, indicating a window that faced the woods about eight feet from the ground. The

Garrity's backyard sloped sharply away from the foundations before flattening out before the woods. He and his companions did not tire, but often had trouble negotiating slick hills. Tayshawn, who wore a battered pair of high-top sneakers rather than the combat boots his companions sported, fell frequently.

"Remind me . . . why we're . . . here . . . again?" Tayshawn said.

"Layman . . . may know . . . what . . . happened," Tak answered. "He may know . . . where . . . she is."

"How will . . . we . . . get him . . . to come out?" Popeye asked.

"Ring the . . . bell. Pretend we're . . . selling . . . magazine subscriptions."

Tayshawn's sarcasm went ignored by Popeye, who tapped Tak on the elbow with his ridiculous webbed hand. The fishing line stitches were completely pulled away from his thumb now, the rubber flapping down like the fin of a dying fish.

"Hey," he said, "let's . . . wake Phoebe . . . up . . . instead." His yellow grin was full of malice.

"Aw, leave . . . her . . . alone."

Popeye turned to Tayshawn. "Oh, that's . . . right. I'd forgotten you were . . . big pals . . . with the . . . breathers."

"She's not . . . so bad."

"Not so . . . bad? She got . . . Adam . . . killed . . . didn't she? And Saint . . . Tommy . . . all messed . . . up."

"You don't . . . know . . . what . . ."

"Will you both . . . shut . . . up," Tak said.

"I vote . . . we wake . . . the beating heart," Popeye said, gripping his arm. "Let's . . . scare . . . her, and make . . ."

"You don't . . . get . . . to vote," Tak said, pulling his arm free and turning to his companions. "You don't . . . get . . . to decide."

Popeye held his ground for the first time since they'd met. "I just thought . . . I thought . . . we could show . . . the breathers . . ."

Tak took a step toward him, and Popeye flinched.

"You just thought," he said. "You just . . . *thought*. The problem is you . . . *we* . . . didn't think at all. Those . . . stupid . . . pranks . . . we pulled. What were . . . we thinking? What were we . . . thinking . . . with those . . . tricks, Popeye?"

He turned away from his friend, but not before he could see the impact his words had on Popeye's expression. The impetus to "do something" may have been from Tak, but all of the actual ideas—the graveyard posters, the installations at the mall and on the church lawn, had been Popeye's. His art was something—the only thing, maybe—that Popeye professed to care about.

"Why . . . are you . . . being like . . . this?"

It was Tayshawn, not Popeye who'd spoken.

"We were . . . trying . . . something," Tayshawn continued. "We wanted . . . people . . . living people . . . to see us . . . see us as . . . we really . . . are. I thought . . . you were . . . down with . . . that. Hell . . . it was . . . you who . . . got us . . . going."

Tak shook his head. "We got . . . George . . . killed . . . is what . . . we got. Reterminated. That is our . . . legacy."

"You don't . . . know . . . that."

Tak didn't answer right away. There weren't any lights on in Adam's house, not even in his room.

"I . . . feel . . . it," Tak said.

"What are . . . we here for . . . then? The rest of . . . zombie . . . kind?"

Tak turned toward him, glancing at Popeye, who was sitting on a snow-covered rock, with his chin on his hand, facing away.

"I don't . . . care about . . . zombiekind."

Tayshawn lifted his arms up, knocking snow from a low pine branch.

"What the . . . hell . . . *do* you . . . care . . . about, man?"

Tak stared at him.

You, Tayshawn, he thought. Popeye. Karen, George, Adam. I care about you.

He didn't vocalize these sentiments. Something had happened to him under the ice, some internal thawing that occurred while the rest of his body froze. He'd had long hours where he drifted along the lake bottom, thinking of those who had counted on him, those that he'd let down. Whatever abstract ideas he'd have of "raising consciousness" among breathers and creating "zombie pride" were forgotten when he thought about how George's dead body spasmed, then shut down, upon being hit with the Taser.

He thought about the night that he'd all but invited her to join the Sons of Romero. She'd seen right through to the heart of his words, and while she didn't accept his real invitation, she didn't close the door on it permanently, either.

They'd been talking about God, whom neither had real reason to believe in after dying and returning. Some of the zombies they knew had stories that incorporated the divine in some way, but not Tak. He'd simply been dead, and then he wasn't. Karen's return wasn't much different. But unlike Tak, she still held out a hope that He existed. She'd told him as much.

"That makes it worse," he'd told her, believing it. It wasn't enough that he lacked faith, he had needed to destroy it in her.

But that was before she'd been taken away from him. Long hours in the water, with the water in him, made him realize something.

Without death, he'd never have met her. And she was the best argument for divinity that he'd contemplated yet.

"We need . . . to talk . . . to Adam," he said. "We need to get . . . moving. The beating hearts . . . will . . . wake up . . . before long." Tayshawn had another argument ready, but he held it in.

"Popeye," Tak said, calling to the dejected lump brooding on a fallen log. "I'm . . . sorry. I'm . . . angry. And . . . worried. I don't . . . mean . . . to take it . . . out . . . on you."

Popeye turned. He looked like a man feeling rain on his face in the desert, even behind the impenetrable lenses of his sunglasses. Tak wished Popeye didn't need him so much, but forced himself to offer Popeye a hand up, anyway. He stopped short of letting Popeye hug him.

"We need to . . . get his . . . attention," Tak said, nodding at Adam's window.

"I can . . . get his . . . attention," Tayshawn said. He bent low and started pulling handfuls of snow together.

"What are you . . . planning?" Popeye asked.

"I was . . . all-state on my . . . high school baseball team my . . . freshman . . . year. Played . . . shortstop." He started fashioning the handfuls of snow into a ball.

"Didn't you . . . die . . . playing?" Popeye asked. Tak was ashamed to realize he didn't know how his friend had passed.

"Yep," Tayshawn replied. "I had an . . . acute asthma . . . attack . . . right there . . . on the field. You know they . . . say . . . 'at least you . . . died . . . doing . . . something . . . you love'? What a bunch . . . of . . . crap."

"You can . . . still . . . throw?" Popeye asked. Tayshawn packed the snow into a reasonable sphere, and they followed him out onto the smooth white landscape of Adam's back lawn. "There aren't . . . many . . . zombies . . . who could manage . . . that."

"There aren't . . . many . . . who were . . . as good . . . as me," Tayshawn said, hurling the snowball. They watched it sail perfectly toward Adam's window, where instead of splatting wetly into its component pieces, it smashed right through the glass with a jagged sound that cut through the stillness of the night.

Tak blinked.

"Nice . . . throw," he said.

When there was no answer, he turned to see his companions "running away," their stiff, inflexible limbs propelling them back down the hill toward the woods. Tayshawn's shoes failed him again halfway there, and he fell heavily onto his backside. Tak would have laughed if he'd known how.

There was commotion inside Adam's house, shouts of the living. Tak decided not to wait and see who made it to the window first, and followed his fleeing friends toward the relative safety of the woods.

Adam's dragging footsteps cut long swathes in the white blanket covering his backyard. He stopped momentarily to look at the cluster of boot prints across from his window, which were already beginning to fill up with new snow. He followed the prints, stopping just outside the tree line. Tak watched his slow progress without comment.

"You could have . . . knocked, you . . . know," Adam called. "My parents are . . . pissed."

Takayuki stepped forward through the bare branches of the trees.

"Sorry," he said. Popeye and Tayshawn, their dead faces almost comically hangdog, stepped out of the shadows as well.

"Hey, fellahs. I thought you went . . . back . . . to the life . . . aquatic," Adam said. He paused to ask a question, as if realizing that his irritation at them shouldn't affect his concern. "Is something . . . wrong? How are the rest of . . . our . . . friends?"

"Safe," Tak replied. "They're . . . safe."

"Good."

They hadn't been friends when Adam was alive, but after he'd died, Tak had tried to recruit him for the Sons of Romero;

he'd even invited Adam to hide with them in the depths of Lake Oxoboxo. Adam would have gone, too, if Phoebe hadn't risked pneumonia to stop him.

"So what . . . are you guys . . . doing . . . outside . . . the lake?"

He was aware of the boy's scrutiny, even as Popeye and Tayshawn were shuffling their feet and averting their gazes like truant school kids hauled before the principal.

Tak didn't answer. He clenched his fist, crumpling the newspaper in his hand.

"Adam," Tak said, his voice like a sigh, "I want to know . . . about . . . Karen."

Now it was Adam's turn to have difficulty maintaining eye contact.

"She's . . . in jail, Tak. Something happened with . . . Martinsburg. She was . . . passing . . . as a traditionally . . . biotic . . . person. She . . ."

"She's in . . . jail, is . . . she?"

Adam gave a slow nod. "Yeah. Phoebe . . . and I . . ."

"In . . . jail," Tak said, throwing the wadded newspaper in Adam's face.

Adam glared at him, but Tak didn't retreat. He knew Adam was used to people—living people, anyway—backing down from him, his enormous size enough of a deterrent to keep all but the most foolhardy people from starting trouble. Tak watched him smooth the newspaper, and watched his eyes as he read the headlines.

"Where . . . is . . . she?" Tak said, his voice a guttural snarl.

Adam looked up. "Tak . . ."

"Where . . . is she, Layman? Tell . . . me . . . where she . . . is?"

"Oh God," Adam said. "Oh, Karen . . . Tak, I had no idea . . ."

"You let them . . . do this," Tak said, the last word escaping as a horrible hiss through the rent in his cheek. "You stood . . . by and . . . did . . . nothing."

A reply started to form on Adam's lips, but Tak wasn't done.

"Karen!" Tak said, shouting her name. He raised a long bony finger—literally bony where the skin was missing from the knuckle—and pointed it in Adam's face. "You let them . . . do this . . . to Karen!"

Adam raised his hand from his side, in what Tak would later think was probably a gesture of sympathy, or helplessness, but at the time, Tak only saw it as one thing: an excuse. He lashed out, throwing himself at the much larger boy, actually making him stagger. Adam struck out, more to ward off the frenzy of the assault than anything else.

His blow struck Tak on the collarbone, and Tak went over backward, his body thudding on the snow-covered ground.

Tak imagined that Adam had been aiming for his face. His teeth, to be exact, the ones that were always visible. He struck out with a booted foot, hitting Adam in the ankle. Adam overcorrected, trying to keep his footing, and hit the ground, getting a face full of snow. Tak growled like a wounded animal and scrambled toward him.

Adam rolled onto his back, sweeping across with a crooked elbow as Tak closed in. Tak knew that Adam had studied martial arts, but he still considered him an inelegant fighter. He came in quick and low, but Adam's elbow thumped solidly on his head, and Tak flew away from him like a discarded doll.

Tak fell in a sprawl, his neck hideously twisted.

"Oh, man."

This was from Tayshawn, who'd stood in mute shock with Popeye, both boys obviously stunned by the savage attack. Tak lay in the snow staring at Adam, who looked both shocked and guilty. Tak knew Adam hadn't held back when he'd struck him.

Tak got to his knees and heard the dull grind of bones as he flexed his neck and shoulder muscles, twisting his head back into place. He couldn't get the alignment quite right until he placed his hands over his icy ears and gave his head a sharp jerk, eliciting a sickening crack. Adam, still sitting in the snow, watched with fascination.

"Tak," he said. "Tak, I'm . . . sorry."

"It's over . . . Tak," Tayshawn said, standing between the two boys. "It's . . . over."

Tak swiveled his neck this way and that, testing to see if his skull was settled properly. He looked past Tayshaw and favored Adam with his best smile.

"Sorry?" he said. "For me, or Karen?"

Adam looked up at Tayshawn and Popeye, who seemed as stunned as he'd been at the short but brutal fight.

"For you. Karen wasn't . . . my fault."

Tak rose to his feet, then strode over to Adam and reached down. He knew Adam thought that his motion was a peace gesture of some sort, but he ignored Adam's outstretched hand and reached lower.

He gripped the handle of the switchblade he'd stuck between Adam's lower ribs. Tak tugged, hard, and the object popped free.

"Don't be," he said, holding it up for Adam to see. A tear of viscous black fluid ran from the tip, and the moment the tear struck the hilt, Tak retracted the blade.

Adam stared at him. "You . . . *stabbed* me? You actually . . . *stabbed* me?"

"You did . . . nothing," Tak said, aiming a bony finger at him. "Stay . . . away."

"Tak . . ."

"She's still alive, Adam. No . . . thanks . . . to you." Tak started backing away into the woods. Adam made no move to stop him. Popeye kicked snow onto Adam as he shuffled past, but Tayshawn's look was almost apologetic.

"Tak . . ." Adam said.

"Stay away . . . from us, Layman. Stay with your . . . beating heart . . . friends. You aren't . . . one of us."

"She was my . . . friend, too, Tak," Adam called after him.

Tak kept walking, his companions falling in line as they put distance between them and the dead boy who sat at the edge of the forest, pressing his hand to his side.

# CHAPTER TWENTY-SIX

"IT'S SO GOOD TO HAVE YOU home, Pete," Mrs. Martinsburg said. "Would you like another glass of lemonade?"

Pete looked at his mom and smiled as he stowed the sarcastic comment that rose to his lips far back into his mind, mentally thanking Reverend Mathers as he did so. He was still feeling bruised and agitated at the memory of her pale newsprint eyes looking up at him, and part of it, he knew, was that he'd been too quick to let go of so many of Mathers's essential teachings, and so soon after leaving his company. He'd worked hard to master his emotions—he *had* mastered them.

At least until the whole business with the girl. The *zombie Karen.*

He was so confused, his thoughts a jumbled mess. The Reverend—although Pete vowed he would never confess the full story to him—would probably tell him that the incident was a necessary slip, a step in his overall development. Either way, Pete was anxious to regain his self-control. He took his restraint with his mother, the easiest and most frequent of his emotional-outburst targets—as a positive sign. In addition to being proof that he could force some control on himself, instead of a fight and tears, which would be typical of an exchange with her, he now had someone that was willing to rush off to get him refills.

"I'd love some, Mom," he said. "Thank you."

She almost blushed as she handed him the glass, so good was he at feigning a grateful, warm look.

His cell phone rang. Pete picked it up and looked at the screen, scarcely believing it when he saw that it was the Reverend himself calling, as though he could sense Pete's negative thinking from the other side of the continent.

Pete tried not to stutter as he picked up the phone. "Hello?"

"Peter," the Reverend said. "How are you, my boy?"

Peter gave an involuntary shudder. The Reverend sounded quite pleased.

"I'm very well, sir."

"Are you enjoying your break?"

"I am, sir. I'm anxious to be getting back to One Life, though."

The Reverend chuckled, a dry throaty sound that Pete would have thought sinister from anyone else. "Don't you think your ministry in your home town is more important?"

Pete smiled. "Well, I suppose it is important, sir, but . . ."

"Imprisoning the demon. Brilliant. And the press that

followed, the idea that the demons could pass among us undetected. But you know that, we've spoken often of your success. And I have spoken to my congregation of it as well."

Pete knew that happiness was an emotion that needed to be quelled as much as anger or fear, but listening to the Reverend's praise, and recalling the look on her face as the police hauled her away, it was too much to contain. He found he was holding his breath, waiting for the Reverend to say more.

"Undetected, that is, by all but the righteous! By you, Peter! By exposing the demon, the trickster, you have swayed public opinion. Those who'd begun traveling the slippery path, those who'd begun to feel a flickering flame of sympathy in their breasts for these things, these zombies, these demons that cloak themselves in the flesh of our young ones—why, you have transformed that flame of sympathy to one of suspicion! You have exposed the liars for what they are!"

Although he was still basking in the warmth of the Reverend's words, Pete wondered why the man was suddenly so effulgent with his praise. Soon, he had his answer.

"And," the Reverend said, his voice rising to pulpit pitch, "you have shown the world that demons can despair!"

"Sir?"

"Now it is back in hell, burning, burning and seething, it's attempts to lure more souls foiled for the time being."

"Sir? I'm not following you."

"The demon," the Reverend repeated. "It returned to hell."

There was a pause as Pete waited for the Reverend to continue.

"You don't know?" the Reverend said. "The demon destroyed itself rather than to continue as an example of the lying nature of its insidious kind."

"I knew," Pete said. "I knew she was dead. Destroyed, I mean." He hadn't considered her suffering in the fires of hell, however. That had not occurred to him. He felt his lemonade-rich stomach churn. But why? Hell was the first and last stop for all zombiekind, that much was clear. Not to mention suicides; self-murderers got their own special place in the fiery furnace. These facts had been internalized weeks ago, so why did they disturb his digestion now? What did he think was going to happen when he outed her, if not eventual damnation? *Redemption?*

The Reverend laughed, mistaking Pete's silence as humility. "The demon is not getting as much press as its cohort in Washington, but if you watch CNN long enough you will see a brief clip about its return to the fiery furnace."

Returned to hell, Pete thought, again having difficulty holding his emotions in check. He'd promised her that day in the woods that he would destroy her last.

But he'd also told her that they would be closer than ever, bonded by blood. The sound he made wasn't laughter.

"Stay with your mother and her husband for a few more days," the Reverend said. "We need to see if the demon's destruction brings more of the vermin out of their holes."

"Yes, sir," he replied, at once sorrowful that he wasn't going back to where the Reverend could help make the world under-standable again, but also glad he wasn't going, for fear that the

Reverend would be unable to do so. She was like sand rubbing between the folds of his brain and his skull.

"I'm sure you learned much from your encounter," the Reverend said. Pete was about to respond, but the Reverend wasn't finished. His next words seemed to freeze Pete's blood in his veins.

"But I'm more interested in what they learned from you."

So Pete told him. All of it. And when he was done, expecting the wrath of hellfire to descend upon him, there was only silence, until the Reverend spoke at last.

"I see," he said. And then he told Pete what needed to be done. The Reverend spoke very clearly and calmly. The destruction that Pete had been awaiting did not arrive; instead, a very specific set of instructions, surprising instructions, came. Instructions that the Reverend said needed to be followed to the letter. Some of what the Reverend said seemed almost ludicrous to Pete; it seemed to undo all his work in Oakvale. Still, Pete listened without comment until he got his final command.

"Go see Davidson," the Reverend said.

"I will," Pete replied, swallowing.

And then the Reverend said the words that almost brought tears to his eyes.

"Good work, Peter," he said. "This too shall pass."

And then he said good-bye.

Pete hung up the phone, and a moment later his mother scurried into the room with his lemonade. She upped the ante with a trio of cookies on a china plate.

"I didn't want to disturb you while you were on the phone," she said. "Was that the Reverend?"

"Yes," Pete said, keeping his voice flat. He found it wasn't hard to do.

"Such a nice man," she said. "What did he have to say?"

"He said that the zombie I helped put in jail destroyed herself." He took a sip of his lemonade.

His mother nodded. "I heard it on the radio. They didn't go into much detail, just said that she'd done it."

"What are they doing with the body? Did they say?"

"They mentioned something about transporting the body to the foundation," she said.

She'd put ice cubes in his drink, something she did no matter how many times Pete yelled at her not to, but he stowed this chip of anger away, too. It was utterly amazing that she had no idea whatsoever that he'd been *dating* this zombie, this dead girl. She was completely unaware. Her smile was nervous, frightened, almost, and he realized that he'd been staring at her.

"Ken called," she said, her voice quavering. "He's coming home early so he can have dinner with us. I hope you don't mind."

Pete steadied himself with a gulp of lemonade. Ken was his mother's husband, the Wimp. He tried not to shudder as one of the cubes of ice clicked into his front teeth.

"Of course not," he said, "I've wanted to talk to Ken."

His mother stiffened, reading ominous portent into her son's words.

"This is great lemonade," Pete said, smiling in what he hoped was a reassuring manner. He bit into a cookie and chewed until his mother carefully backed out of the living room.

# CHAPTER TWENTY-SEVEN

"WALK, WALK, WALK," POPEYE said. "Trudge, trudge, trudge. Then sit, sit . . . sit. Sometimes being a zombie totally . . . sucks."

Tak looked at him. He was sprawled out on the sofa, one leg on the floor, his bony arms flung out behind him. His leather jacket was open, revealing the muscles of his abdomen where he'd pared away the skin. He looked like a daddy longlegs that had been struck by a thrown slipper. Or like a dead man.

Many, many times Tak had wanted to ask him about the flesh removal. Tak had a similar patch on his torso, one that had gone all the way to his ribcage, but that was the result of the motorcycle wreck that killed him, not self-ornamentation.

Tayshawn snorted from across the room. He was flipping through some CDs they'd left behind before making their pilgrimage to the lake, but he knew better than to ask Tak if he could play one.

"What did you . . . expect?" Tayshawn said. "A big party?"

Popeye sat up, practically bouncing off the couch. "Why . . . not? We're . . . back, man. Why not . . . make . . . the most of . . . it?"

He managed to knock his sunglasses off with his wild hand-waving, and once again Tak got the full effect of his bulbous eyes. Watching him flail, Tak realized, as he often did, that he was crazy. Manic.

But then, they were all crazy.

"Yeah," Tayshawn said, tossing the CDs to the floor with disgust, or maybe disappointment. "The most."

Crazy. Manic Popeye. Mal, staring off into space, looking for God. Tommy with his messiah complex. The beating hearts, all crazy.

Tak wasn't excluding himself from the observation; he knew he was as crazy as the rest of them. Maybe crazier, because he knew that there was nothing else after this . . . *existence*, and yet he kept going. Kept trudging, as Popeye said.

"Don't be . . . depressed, Tayshawn," Popeye said, rising from the couch to retrieve his glasses. Tak wondered if he was putting on his sunglasses for Tayshawn's benefit; the other boy made no secret about how he felt about Popeye's "work," especially his eyes. "Let's . . . make something."

"Like . . . what?"

"I don't . . . know. Something. Let's . . . glue the . . . CDs . . . to the . . . ceiling. Something."

Crazy. Tak watched them argue for a moment, then turned away. He walked toward the stairs. *Trudged* toward the stairs.

The creaking of the stairs sounded like the screaming of lost souls. In the days before they went underwater, he'd heard a newlydead telling a story about a zombie he'd known who claimed he'd heard screaming and saw bodies writhing when he died, and flames, but the flames were cold. Beneath the water Tak had tried to imagine cold flames, tried to imagine a coldness more intense than the Oxoboxo during the winter—a coldness he couldn't even feel—to no avail. He had no faith in a heaven, so why would he believe in hell? He had faith in nothing. Nothing at all.

There was a photograph of her on the Wall of the Dead. She was wearing her short skirt and white blouse, and standing at the edge of the Oxoboxo woods on a sunny day. He went to it, placed his fingers upon it. It was too dark in the room for him to make out the details, but they were painted upon his memory. Autumnal light framed her against the backdrop of trees. She was amused, her chin upraised, her head tilted slightly to the left. He could almost feel the sunlight.

She was still alive. She had to be. There was nothing else.

"Tak?"

He turned. He hadn't even heard Tayshawn coming up the stairs.

"Yes?"

"Can we . . . talk . . . for a minute?"

"We're . . . talking."

Tayshaw's disgust finally came through in his expression. "What the hell . . . was that?"

"What?"

"With . . . Adam. You . . . stabbed . . . him, for God's . . . sake."

Not for God's sake, Tak thought.

"It got . . . out of . . . hand."

"Out of . . . hand? We went there . . . to get . . . his *help*, and you . . ."

"Tayshawn," Tak said, "I don't think . . . you know . . . how . . . angry . . . I am."

Tayshawn must have caught the note of warning in his voice, because he paused a moment before continuing with his questions.

"Angry? About . . . Karen?"

"Karen," Tak said. "And George. And you, and me, and . . . Popeye. I'm so . . . angry, Tayshawn. I'm so full . . . of . . . hate."

Tayshawn leaned against the wall, an awkward movement that ruffled the photographs. He folded his arms across his chest.

"Funny," he said, after a long pause. "You don't . . . look . . . full of hate."

A sly smile came to Tayshawn's face in slow increments. Tak watched the progression and couldn't help but be amused. Not that he showed his amusement.

"Funny."

"Yeah, I . . . try. We're all angry, man. But Adam's . . . one of us. Even when he was . . . alive . . . he was . . . one of . . . us."

"One of . . . us," Tak said. "You're right . . . of course. I have . . . apologies . . . to make." He didn't really believe it, but he didn't want to argue, either.

Tayshawn moved away from the wall and straightened some of the photos he'd ruffled. "Why . . . are . . . we here, Tak?"

"Honestly? I'm not . . . sure."

"If we are . . . going to . . . travel . . . back . . . to the lake . . . we should do it . . . now . . . right? While it's . . . still . . . morning?"

He saw the wisdom in what Tayshawn said. They shouldn't still be here in the daylight—there was too great a chance the building was being watched—but traveling during the day was just as dangerous.

"Not . . . yet," he said.

Tayshawn didn't argue.

"Popeye is . . . looking for . . . some paint," he said. "He's going . . . to start . . . a mural."

Tak didn't reply. He realized that he was still touching Karen's photograph, and brought his hand back to his side.

"She . . . stayed . . . with her family, didn't . . . she?"

Tak couldn't see his expression in the gloom. He wondered how Tayshawn knew that he'd been touching her photo.

"She . . . did."

"I always . . . wondered . . . about . . . that," he said. "When I was in . . . that class . . . Karen and Tommy . . . and Evan . . . lived with their . . . families. And they . . . seemed so much more . . . active . . . than the rest . . . of us."

Tak nodded.

"It seemed to make . . . sense. They all had . . . families . . .

so they . . . 'came back' more. . . . My mom . . . believed all that . . . demon nonsense . . . the news . . . was preaching. She's real . . . religious . . . my mom. She tried for . . . a few . . . days, but . . . she made me . . . leave. I never . . . heard . . . her crying . . . like when . . . I came back."

Tak heard him sigh.

"Was that . . . what it was . . . like . . . for you, Tak? With . . . your . . . parents?"

"No," he said. "My parents . . . would not . . . have . . . turned me away."

"They . . . they wouldn't?"

"No."

"What the hell . . . are you doing . . . here, then?"

Tak turned toward him.

"I . . . was ashamed. I was not a dutiful . . . or obedient . . . son," he said. "My death was . . . my own fault. My parents did not . . . deserve to live . . . with the consequences."

"You . . . you never went home?"

"No."

"Do they know you are . . . a zombie . . . at least?"

"I don't . . . know. I'm sure they . . . know . . . about the . . . motorcycle."

"Tak," Tayshawn said, "you should . . . tell them. Call them, or . . . something."

Tak shook his head. His hair had thawed some, but it still made crackling noises.

"I don't . . . think so. Better I . . . exist . . . only . . . as a memory."

"That's messed . . . up, Tak."

"Maybe." And maybe it wasn't, he thought. He had already put his parents through the pain of his death because of his poor decisions. He had no intention of torturing them further with his monstrous walking corpse of a body.

Tayshawn was silent for some moments before returning to the stairs. He might have muttered something about them all being crazy, or it might just have been Tak's own thoughts reflected back to him.

Tak remained standing in the darkness, trying to imagine that he was the sunlight on Karen's skin.

# CHAPTER TWENTY-EIGHT

PETE SAT IN HIS IDLING car for a moment, giving the defroster the chance to work on the windows. The road beyond his driveway looked slick; the sun had shone for a few hours the day before, melting just enough of the snow at the curb to make ice when the temperature dropped again at night. Pete left the heater on and the radio off as he pulled out of the driveway.

He had in his pocket a brand new digital camera, which he was supposed to use to take pictures of a bunch of beating hearts: families and friends of known Oakvale undead. Pete wondered why the Reverend seemed to be so pleased about what Williams was doing in the nation's capital; he'd assumed that any political progress the zombies made was a step backward for the aims of One Life, but the way the Reverend sounded, you'd think it was the best thing that could happen.

He drove to Layman's and Scarypants's houses. When he

approached their homes he slowed to a crawl and snapped a few pictures in quick succession. There was an old muscle car warming up in Layman's driveway, and one of Layman's stepbrothers, Jimmy or Johnny—Pete never figured out who was who—was kicking at a blackened chunk of ice beneath a rear wheel well. He looked up as Pete's car cruised by, squinting at Pete, or more likely, his car. The camera fit in the palm of Pete's hand, and he didn't think that Jimmy or Johnny or whoever could spot it.

He didn't see any sign of Scarypants or her dead buddy, but figured they weren't home from school yet. Assuming they went to school; if they'd heard about Karen's second death they may have stayed home to grieve. An image of Phoebe, crying her eyes out, came to him. He pictured them sitting on the sofa in her parents' living room, her hand in Adam's dead gray mitts. She would cry and cry, and all Adam could offer her was a cold embrace.

I could still kill her, he thought.

Pete looked in his rearview and saw that the stepbrother had walked to the edge of the driveway and was peering down the road at him. Pete didn't even bother to accelerate.

He drove over to Christie's house—her real house; the DeSonnes' address was in the yellow pages—and was somewhat surprised to find another vehicle already there, a news van. There was a reporter, an attractive young woman shivering in a purple suit, standing in front of Christie's lawn. She was arguing with the cameraman, who was wearing about eight layers of clothing and a goofy ski cap.

Karen. Not Christie. Her name was Karen.

He couldn't get her face out of his head, her blue eyes full of sparkle and life. When he'd hit her the blue disappeared and her eye was like cut glass.

A sudden anger pulsed within him, and he could see himself getting out of his car, stomping across the street, decking the cameraman, and pushing over the pretty reporter.

He went back to the time he'd stalked her in Oxoboxo woods, when he'd been about to impale her on a jagged branch. Had he really not known she was the same girl? Had he really been fooled by a change of clothes, contact lenses, hair color, and makeup? It didn't seem possible.

Or worse—had he known all along? Had something in his subconscious mind told him who she was, what she was, and still allowed him to respond to her? Because whatever he'd tried to tell Duke, he hadn't been faking. He'd liked her from the moment he saw her folding clothes in that stupid store she'd worked in. And when he was with her, he'd felt things he hadn't felt for years, and despite whatever he'd learned over the past two months at the One Life ministry, these were feelings that he had no desire to suppress.

But she was a zombie. The whole time, she was a zombie.

And he'd kissed her. He'd *liked* kissing her.

He swore loudly enough to rattle the windows, and he was fortunate that the camera in his hand didn't break when he punched the dashboard. He rested his head a moment on the steering wheel.

She'd been dead the whole time, and he'd known. Deep

down, somewhere in his mind, he had to have known.

His train of thought was broken when a man came out of Karen's house. He was carrying a little girl. The reporter tried to call him over, but the man pretended not to hear as he rushed to his car.

They can't even grieve, Pete thought. There won't be a funeral. The meat wagon would be taking her right to the foundation as soon as all the paperwork was clear.

He remembered that he was supposed to be taking pictures.

# CHAPTER TWENTY-NINE

TAK WATCHED THROUGH a crack in the boards of an upstairs window as the car made slow progress up the packed driveway of the Haunted House. He watched a teenaged girl get out of the battered brown compact car, drawing her leather jacket tighter around her shoulders. She looked up at the house and huffed thick clouds of steam into the chill morning air, as though she were trying to stoke a furnace of courage within her. She held a small flashlight in her hand.

"Who the . . . hell . . . is that?" Popeye said, drawing close to his shoulder.

"Don't . . . know," Tak said. "Get . . . Tayshawn . . . and hide."

"She has a pierced . . . nose," Popeye said, a trifle contemptuous.

"Go."

Popeye went. A moment later Tak could hear the weakened planking on the front porch creak as the girl went to the front door and opened it. Her voice filled the empty rooms as she called out a tentative hello.

Tak waited. He could hear her moving in the rooms downstairs. Tak could tell that the police had been here, but they'd left the generator, the lights, and the music equipment. Popeye, rarely the voice of reason, had suggested they spend the night in the woods and not the house, because he figured the police would troll by on occasion to see if they could pick up any stray undead.

But something told Tak that they needed to stay and wait. For what, he couldn't say, but the voice inside his head had told him to go there and to stay there. And the voice in his head sounded a lot like Karen.

He hid inside the doorway in the Wall of the Dead room, watching through the crack between the frame and the door as a pale disk of light from her flashlight tracked along the wall. Some of the papers on the Wall fluttered, and the girl shone her light into the room.

She walked in and stood in front of the wall, letting her light and her gaze linger over the faded photos. Her clothing reminded him of Phoebe's friend, the short one, except she was taller and thinner, and her hair had purple streaks instead of pink. The collar of her jacket had a fringe of fake fur.

Tak stepped toward her, dragging his injured leg as best he could.

Seeing him, she screamed and dropped her flashlight. Gray

light from outside filtered into the room enough for her to see that he was still approaching her, and she fell back. Her screams became more shrill as they rose in volume.

She's loud, Tak thought as he crouched to retrieve her light. Loud enough to wake the dead.

Still in a squat, he turned on her light, pointing it up at his face. He knew the effect wasn't as great as it would have been if it had been really dark in the room. Even so, when she saw his face the girl shrieked even louder. But not for the reason Tak thought.

"Ohmigod," she yelled.

"Not . . . quite," he said, making sure she got a good look.

"You're him!" she cried.

She was carrying a backpack, and Tak recognized it immediately. It was the one Karen had been carrying the day she'd entered the lake to find him.

He watched the girl fumbling around in Karen's bag, and wondered if she was silly enough to be going for a weapon. She withdrew a plastic bag and tossed it at his feet. Strands of black hair spilled out.

"Look at it!" she said, still loud but no longer yelling. He dumped the bag out and smoothed the hair away from the rubbery mass it was attached to, and then he saw himself. Crude, maybe, and even worse than he really looked, but it was him.

"You have . . . got . . . to be . . . kidding me."

He heard Popeye and Tayshawn come into the room behind him, and he worried that she'd start screaming again as she crab-walked to the wall behind her, but she remained silent.

"Where did you . . . get . . . this?" he said.

"From . . . from Karen," she answered.

Popeye bent down to look at the mask, and breathed a curse.

"Looks just like . . . you," he said, rubbing the edge of the mask between his fingers. "Except . . . prettier."

Tak ignored him, focusing on the girl. He held out his hand, and she handed him the backpack without speaking. Inside it was a pack of gum, a hairbrush and some twisties, a cell phone, and what looked to be a journal—a small book with a pale blue cover.

"When did you . . . see . . . her?" he asked, thumbing the pages of the journal, half of which were filled with Karen's neat, loopy script.

"Just before the cops took her away," she said, speaking rapidly. "I'm going to be late for school."

Tak and Popeye exchanged a look, and then Tak, his body creaking, focused on the girl as he rose to his full height.

"Yes," he said, "you . . . are."

# CHAPTER THIRTY

A FTER WATCHING THE watchers outside of Karen's house, Pete went home for a while and watched some television, hoping for news about her apparent suicide, but what he saw instead were stories about the Zombie Walk in D.C. An odd sort of sea change had happened to the local coverage; the media seemed very eager to lay claim to Tommy Williams as a favorite native son, and equally eager to forget that zombies were supposedly responsible for the disappearance and possible murder of a lawyer and his entire family. Were Americans really so fickle?

On the national news the pro-zombie fawning was even more apparent. There were interviews every hour with people, living and dead, who made the trek to D.C. to participate in the march. A pair of aging hippies were asked if their ancient and holey Grateful Dead T-shirts were some sort of an ironic commentary. A young zombie from Texas told a halting tale of her harrowing escape from a bioist mob, ending on a heartwarming note when she discussed the kindly trucker who veered off his route to deliver her safely to "DBHQ."

There was a noticeable lack of differing opinion, Pete noticed, whereas just a few short months ago the media was recognizably anti-zombie. The Reverend was a frequent talk show guest, one whose authority regarding the true nature of zombies was rarely, if ever, questioned.

Americans *were* fickle, Pete thought.

Photographs, photographs. He was supposed to be doing his job, getting more photographs. Of Layman and all his friends. Of the principal at Oakvale High. Of the priest that ran the zombie mission at St. Jude's. Pete assumed that he was helping the Reverend put together some sort of enemies list.

Then again, the Reverend might just be keeping him busy, trying to keep his mind off what had happened.

Pete thought about driving to the high school. He could get a few pictures for the file: Principal Kim, Phoebe's friend with the hair. Maybe snap one of his old math teacher Ms. Rodriguez for laughs; she was a zombie sympathizer, too. He could pretend to be waiting around for TC, and take care of some business.

Or he could just go kill Phoebe.

# CHAPTER THIRTY-ONE

TAK COULD SEE THAT THE girl's teeth were chattering as she huddled under the green blanket. She looked from Tayshawn to him, trying to ignore Popeye, who was staring at her from a few inches away.

"Your name . . . is . . . Tamara?" Tak asked. "You say . . . you worked . . . with Karen?"

The girl nodded. "We've gone over this already."

"Let's go . . . over . . . it again," Tak said. Popeye extended a bony finger toward the center of her face.

"Can I help you?" she asked him. Popeye grinned with filed teeth.

"Why did . . . you come . . . here?"

"I . . . ow! Do you have to touch it?" The girl said, slapping Popeye's hand away from her nose, which he'd just probed to get a better look at the stud over her left nostril.

"Yes. I . . . do. Do you have . . . other . . . art?"

Tak looked to Tayshawn, who shook his head. He'd told Tak that they should have just stayed hidden until the girl got bored and left.

"My navel is pierced and I have two tattoos," she said. "Not that it's any of your business."

"Show . . . me."

"Why?" she said, but she was already shucking her shirt from her pants.

"I want . . . to see. Please? Pretty . . . please?" He straightened his dark glasses. He'd told Tak that he'd planned on removing his nose, but Tak talked him out of it, because it would make it hard to keep his sunglasses on.

Tamara exposed her stomach, where a star on a short thin chain hung from her belly button.

"Nice," Popeye said, cupping the tiny star on the finger-tip of his webbed hand. Tak hadn't seen him so enthused since they'd emerged from the ice. His gills seemed to flare as he crouched near the girl. "What about . . . the tattoos?"

She shrugged out of her jacket and hiked up a sleeve, baring the Celtic ring around her upper arm.

"Ohh, pretty," Popeye said. Tamara didn't shudder or recoil when he grazed the line work with his fingers, Tak noticed.

"What about . . . the other one?" Popeye said.

"You can't see that one," she said, defiant. She tucked in her shirt.

He grinned with filed teeth. "Why . . . not? Tramp stamp?"

"No. You just can't."

"I'll show you mine," he said. He wasn't wearing a shirt beneath his leather jacket, and he opened it fully so she could see the patch on his abdomen where he'd pared the skin away.

"Yuck," she said, peering close.

"Check this out," he said, showing her a latticework of stitches he'd put through the skin of his upper arm. She ran her fingertips down the black threading.

"But . . . wait, there's . . . more," Popeye said. He started unbuttoning his jeans.

"That's enough," Tak said.

"But . . ."

"Enough," he said, thinking they had no reason to torture the girl, although she looked more curious than terrified at the moment. "You were . . . telling us . . . why you came."

"Karen asked me to bring the mask here."

"Here? She told you to bring it to this house?"

"She said to bring it to the Haunted House. I'd read about it when that boy was shot."

"What were you supposed to do with it once you brought it here?"

"Just leave it, I guess. She said that I should leave it upstairs, by the Wall of the Dead. That's all she had time to say."

"Did she tell you we would be here?" Tak asked.

"No," she said. "No offense, but I would have appreciated the warning. I thought you guys were all in hiding."

Tayshawn, without saying anything, managed to convey to Tak that enough was enough and that they should let her go. There was something else here, though, Tak thought, some piece of the puzzle that was eluding him, and he didn't want the girl to leave until he figured out what it was.

"Tak," Tayshawn said, impatient. It was only a matter of time before the authorities came to the house; the fresh tire tracks in the snow would make them curious.

"And you say she's . . . in prison . . . now?"

"I assume so. The cops took her."

She doesn't know, he thought.

The problem as he saw it was that the mask alone proved nothing. Maybe Karen had other evidence that she could divulge, but for him, the mask was only a reminder of how he'd been set up. If she did have information, it was unlikely that she'd have found a sympathetic ear to share it with.

Tak was regretting stabbing Adam. He regretted his loss of control for a variety of reasons, but chief among them was that Adam and Phoebe might have been able to help him sort this out. Tayshawn just wanted to get back to the lake, and all Popeye wanted to do was . . . well, it was better not to think about what Popeye wanted to do.

"Tayshawn," he said. "Come . . . with me. Popeye . . . stay here. Give me her keys."

"Aye, aye . . . Cap'n," Popeye said, leaning down so the girl could get a good look at all of the fishhooks in his ear. "But be . . . quick. We should hurry . . . back . . . to the lake."

"The lake?" she said, repeating after him.

Tak stared back at Popeye, and he heard Tayshawn curse softly. The girl turned away from Popeye's leer, pretending she hadn't said anything, but Tak could see in her eyes that she knew what Popeye's statement meant, and what it meant for her.

"Oooops," Popeye said, covering his smiling mouth with the flat of his hand as he looked back at his dead companions.

Tayshawn gripped Tak's arm as he started heading down the stairs.

"Tak, we should . . . let her . . . go," Tayshawn said, whispering so the girl couldn't hear him. "We . . ."

"Popeye just . . . decided . . . for us, didn't . . . he?"

"Screw the . . . freak, Tak. We can't . . ."

"We'll . . . have to. They are . . . counting . . . on us."

"Tak, she won't . . . say anything. She was . . . Karen's . . . friend. She . . ."

Tak could actually feel the muscles in his face contort with rage, and Tayshawn stepped back. "The . . . beating hearts . . . tried to . . . reterminate her."

Tayshawn was frightened of him, but he didn't retreat any further.

"Tak . . ." he said. "I'm not . . . going to let . . . you kill her. I . . . won't. Not even . . . to protect . . . our friends."

Tak shook his head. "Later. We'll discuss this . . . after."

"After what?"

"After we get . . . Karen's . . . body."

Tayshawn stared at him. "You aren't . . . serious."

"Deadly. And the girl upstairs . . . is going . . . to drive."

Tayshawn kept whatever it was he wanted to say to himself. He clearly thought the plan to retrieve Karen was idiotic, but realized that it would also keep the girl alive—for a little while.

Tak unlocked the trunk of the girl's car. More junk. Papers, one sandal, a jacket, some books. Tak leaned over and rooted around in the mess, throwing the detritus over his shoulder.

"Tak," a voice said from behind him. Tayshawn.

"What?" Tak flung a plastic bag of recyclables, cans and bottles, over his shoulder and onto the driveway.

"I'm sorry, Tak. I'm . . . with you. If you think . . . Karen . . . can still be . . . saved, I'm with you."

"Good."

"But . . . killing . . . the girl . . . is wrong."

"Objection noted." Tak knew it was wrong, too. But what could he do? He never really expected to become the leader of the Oakvale undead, despite all his attempts to woo them away from Williams and his philosophy of civil disobedience. Tak wanted to be uncivil. He had no illusions about which mindset was more suited for actual leadership.

But Williams wasn't here, and Karen never made it to the lake. That left him with the responsibility of his people, the nineteen—dare he even think it—"souls" under the ice.

"What are you . . . looking for?" Tayshawn asked, his words shaking Tak out of his reverie. He realized that he'd been staring into the messy trunk, no longer seeing anything at all.

"I was . . . hoping . . . for flares," he said, withdrawing a short length of metal, curved and knobby at one end.

Tayshawn looked at the truncated tire iron with disdain.

"We're going to . . . bust . . . her body out . . . of prison . . . with that?" he said. Trying to lighten the mood.

Tak looked back at him. Tayshawn was a good friend, he realized. Would he remain so if tough decisions had to be made?

"So . . . negative. Help me get this . . . junk . . . back in . . . the car," Tak said. "Then go . . . get the . . . girl."

"What am . . . I . . . your . . . porter?"

"I prefer . . . henchman."

Fast stomping on the stairs from within the house, and a muffled cry from Tayshawn, who'd just gone in to get the girl a moment ago. Tak pulled himself out of the car and was heading toward the porch just as the girl yanked open the front door. She walked out on the landing, her eyes locking on Tak's.

"You can't catch me," she said, her eyes defiant as she tried without success not to sound scared. "I've seen you limping."

He nodded, slowly. The girl was debating whether or not to hurdle the railing or try and dash past him.

"Who says . . . I have to . . . catch . . . you?" he said, showing her his teeth.

She decided not to run after all. She leaned against the rail, her breath visible in the crisp air of morning.

A minute later Tayshawn and Popeye struggled through the door, their movements Stooge-esque.

"Nice . . . job," Tak said to them.

"Wouldn't have . . . happened . . . if I had stayed . . . up there," Tayshawn said.

"Oh, yeah. You're such a . . . great . . . guardian."

"Let me . . . guess. You had to . . . show her . . . your back . . . tattoo."

"Hey, I designed it . . ."

"And she . . . just . . . took off."

"Dude, she defeated . . . you . . . with a blanket," Popeye said, and then he mimed Tayshawn's defeat, stumbling around blindly in a traditional Zombie Walk. "Help, help! She used . . . a . . . blanket!"

"Don't," Tak said, after a pause. Tayshawn wouldn't look at him. Had he encouraged the girl to run?

Popeye ceased badgering Tayshawn and drew Tak aside.

"Tak, we should . . . term her. She's a . . . flight . . . risk."

"Popeye . . ."

"We need to . . . kill . . . her, Tak. If she . . . got . . . away . . ."

"Karen sent her," he replied.

Popeye shook his head from side to side, the gills on one side of his neck opening with each twist. "Yeah, that's . . . rough. But if she leads . . . the blood bags . . . to the lake, what . . . then?"

Tak looked at him for a moment—at how eager he was—without comment. Popeye wanted to kill for killing's sake. Tak wanted to kill, too, but for what they allowed to happen to Karen. For what they *caused* to happen to Karen.

If she was really dead, he thought, they'll all pay. All of them.

"Think about this, Tak. We should . . . kill her and . . . take her into . . . the lake . . . in case . . . she comes back. That way . . ."

"Popeye," Tak said, poking a stiff finger into Popeye's sternum. "Shut . . . up."

His gills flared, but Popeye didn't say another word.

Tak reached into his pocket, withdrawing the girl's keys. There was a heavy silvered cat on the ring and a skull in the shape of a teardrop.

"You're . . . driving," he called to her, tossing her the jangling bundle.

"Where . . . where are we going?" she asked.

"Shotgun!" Popeye called.

"No," Tak said. "And put this on."

He handed Popeye a star-spangled bandana he'd found under the passenger seat.

"Cool," Popeye said, putting it over his bald head. "Disguises." He had to have the girl help him tie it. Tak put on a John Deere mesh hat he'd found in the trunk, sweeping his long hair back behind his ears. Popeye laughed and pointed.

"What are you . . . laughing . . . for?" Tayshawn said. "You look like . . . a gay . . . pirate."

"Half right," Popeye cackled, clambering into the back seat.

"I don't get . . . a disguise?" Tayshawn asked.

"You're . . . almost human," Tak responded. "Get . . . in."

"Where to?" she asked. Her car coughed repeatedly before the engine turned over. Tak tried the radio, but she told him it was broken.

"Don't . . . talk," he said. He didn't have a plan; nothing beyond finding Karen's body and taking it from them. "Just . . . drive."

# CHAPTER THIRTY-TWO

THE HOUSE REALLY DID feel haunted, Pete thought.

He wasn't sure what he'd been expecting. Jars of eyeballs? Webs stretching from the far corners of the room, giant blood-colored spiders scuttling along the threads? An untidy pile of severed limbs? Instead, there was soft, well-worn furniture that looked as though it had been culled from a decent yard sale. A futon, a couple of beanbag chairs. There were a few comic books scattered on a scratched coffee table; the blue corner of a paperback peeked out from beneath the skirt of the futon. The room felt oddly lived-in, but Pete thought there was a cloud of loneliness drifting above, along with the dust motes that became visible in the light that filtered in through the windows.

Pete went through the kitchen, then back out to the foyer, turning toward the stairs. He looked up and saw a reflection of the light on the fifth step.

He placed his fingers on it, and they came back wet. The ceiling above was free from water damage that he could see. He examined the other stairs and found them to be wet as well, as though someone had tracked snow in on their way up.

He frowned. He hadn't explored the upstairs yet.

The upstairs was considerably darker than below. He turned on his flashlight, a large, heavy-handled light that Duke had given him. It could work as a club if he needed it to. The house creaked, both with his steps and when he stood still. There could be zombies upstairs, he thought, and they probably wouldn't be very happy to see him. The weight of the flashlight was reassuring.

What he didn't expect to find were dozens of them—hundreds, maybe—in the first room that he looked in.

He shined his light across them, the faces pinned and taped to the wall. He leaned in, his eyes taking them all in at a glance.

But the more he looked, the more he saw their differences. A girl with yellow bows in her hair, clutching a tennis racquet. A boy in a doorway, slouching in a jacket two sizes too big for him. A living girl. Two boys, brothers, it looked like, standing in a junk lot beside a horribly mangled automobile. He saw one he recognized, a huge black boy that had run at him, twice, in the woods. A smiling boy with a familiar shock of red hair. A girl wearing a mask.

He stared at the photographs for a long moment, trying to figure out what was bothering him. It took a while, but then he had it.

He no longer wanted to kill Phoebe Kendall.

He should have felt a murderous rage overtaking him as he stared at the Wall of the Dead, but instead he felt . . . nothing. Nothing at all, no hatred, no loathing, no anger. He actually laughed out loud, the echoing of his voice disturbing the dusty stillness. Was this the end result of all of Reverend Mathers's training on mastering the emotions? Did mastery of emotions equal eliminating them entirely?

Alien thoughts crept into his mind as he regarded the zombies on the wall. Here was a photograph of a family, smiling parents and two boys, the smaller of them grayish-blue, grinning and dead beneath his baseball cap, his brother's hand set firmly on his shoulder. Here was another one with a girl and her kitten, its eyes perhaps a little too wide as it regarded its undead owner. Here a grainy shot of a boy leaning against a steel post with a basketball hoop set above.

He took a step back and heard something crackle beneath his sneaker. He bent down and found a photograph clinging there.

Karen.

He looked at the photograph a long moment before scanning the wall for a free pin, and finding one, he affixed Karen's image beside a picture of a somber, freckled girl that had been printed out on computer paper. The girl was standing on a beach, her brown hair trailing in the wind like the flag of a defeated nation. His eyes narrowed and then they opened wide.

His phone rang, and the blaring ringtone in the silent room was loud enough to arrest all of his biological functions.

"Hello?" he said, whispering.

"Pete. You okay? You sound strange."

"I'm . . . fine," he said, blinking, turning away from the haunting images.

"I want you to meet me. I've got something to show you."

"What?"

"You'll see. A surprise."

Pete swallowed. "I've had enough . . . surprises . . . to last a lifetime." He was having trouble getting the words out, and his voice sounded alien to him in the empty house.

"One more. It won't kill you," Duke said, telling Pete to meet him at a commuter train lot an exit up from Winford.

"Not if . . . I'm already dead," Pete said, but Duke had already hung up.

Pete clicked off his flashlight and stood in the center of the room. He could feel them, the dead, staring at him. He removed the photo of the freckled girl, put it in the pocket of his jacket, near his heart.

Then he walked out into the snow, and drove to meet Duke.

# CHAPTER THIRTY-THREE

"SO YOUR OTHER CAR . . . is a broom, huh?" Popeye said. Tayshawn told him to shut up and let her drive, and there were slapping sounds from the backseat. Tak gritted his teeth, refusing to turn around.

"No, really, I'm . . . curious," Popeye said. "That's what it said . . . on one . . . of her bumper . . . stickers. Are you, like . . . a witch . . . or something?"

"Wiccan," Tamara said, her eyes steady on the road.

"Wiccan, huh? Can you cast . . . spells . . . and stuff?"

She didn't answer him.

"Do you . . . have a black . . . cat? Wear . . . a pointy . . . hat? Have . . . unholy . . . congress . . . with . . . the Devil?"

"Give it a . . . rest," Tak said.

"You're awfully intolerant for a zombie," she said.

"Intolerant?" Popeye replied, leaning forward until his pale face was thrust between their seats. Tak never realized how much he looked like Nosferatu with sunglasses before. "Sweetheart, you have . . . no idea . . . what . . . intolerance is."

"But you do?" she said.

Popeye's voice grew loud and shrill, and his gills flared as he shouted. "I didn't even have . . . to die . . . to . . . know—"

"Enough," Tak said to him. "Seriously, Popeye. Enough."

Popeye slumped back with enough force to make the vehicle shudder.

"How long are you going to kidnap me for?" Tamara said.

"Eye . . . of . . . newt," Popeye said.

Tamara didn't respond. They continued on to the Winford police station without incident. Tak told her to park in the lot across the street. The station was on a hill that overlooked the river; Tak wondered if Karen had been able to see the water from her holding cell.

"Keep it running," he said. "And keep . . . quiet."

He got out of the car and walked to the edge of the lot, just as a pair of police cars pulled out. A woman in a suit and sensible shoes walked toward the building, pulling along a wheeled laptop case through the snow as though it were a reluctant puppy. "Tak . . . get back in the car," Tayshawn called. Tak could hear Popeye telling the girl that he would kill her if her hands moved off the steering wheel.

That's where she died, he thought. Again.

A police car cruised by. Tak hoped that his face was shaded enough by his cap as he lifted his good hand in a wave.

The cop returned the greeting and continued on. Tak went back to the car.

"Don't you . . . think . . . you should . . . get back . . . in the car?" Popeye said. Tak noticed that the gills sometimes gave his voice a buzzing quality, as if there were a hornet inside his throat.

"Wait . . . here," Tak said. "Go . . . if I'm not . . . back . . . in ten minutes."

He was going to get Karen back or die—die again—trying. If the breathers destroyed him in the attempt, so be it. Final retermination was preferable to a life without her.

He started limping toward the police station without waiting for the protests that Tayshawn would surely voice. Part of him felt like he should have given some instructions on what to do with the girl, but Popeye would just do whatever he wanted if he thought Tak was reterminated. Popeye and Tayshawn would end up fighting over the girl's life. All things equal, Tayshawn would probably win that fight, but Popeye was devious and had a vicious streak like no one else Tak knew.

All Tayshawn had to do was delay Popeye long enough to give the girl a decent head start. Popeye wouldn't have the legs or the inclination to pursue her over a long distance.

Tak was nearly at the police station. He knew that thinking about some fictitious fight between his friends was just a way of distracting himself from the fact that he was practically on the front doorstep of people who wanted nothing more than to destroy him, people who actually had the arsenal to do it.

He didn't want to kill the girl, but Popeye was probably right. Then again, Karen had sent her and it was unlikely that she would approve of her murder.

Die, or don't die. It was all the same to him. There was nothing after this world, anyway.

A woman leaving the station gave Tak a double take. He realized that with his hair swept back, there was nothing hiding his ruined cheek. He clasped his hand over the wound, as though he had a toothache. It was an inadequate disguise, but there wasn't much hope of hiding what he was from the rest of the world, anyhow.

A pair of police officers were talking by a cruiser that was parked along the street. Tak looked at them from the corner of his eye, but they didn't even give him a second glance. There would many more, a dozen at least, in the station house.

His switchblade was in his pocket. He put his hand on the metal handle of the door, seeing the dark streak of his reflection in the glass. He had no idea what was about to happen.

Karen, he thought.

There were benches and a high desk, more a podium, at which a large female police officer sat, her expression at once sympathetic and bored. She was speaking to two men, one in a gray suit and the other in khakis and a dark-green winter jacket. The more casually dressed man turned from the podium, running a hand through his white-blond hair, his facial features set in an expression of frustration.

The man glanced at Tak and froze, recognizing instantly what—maybe even *who*—he was. They'd never met, but Tak knew him right away, too. The white-blond hair, the handsome, angular face—this man was Karen DeSonne's father. Tak would stake his second life on it.

A policeman walked past in the corridor beyond, a red folder in his hand. Tak lowered his eyes to the level of his gun. The policeman did not break stride.

"What do you mean you've already transported the body?" the man in the suit said to the bored woman. "That isn't legal. You haven't even let her parents . . ."

Mr. DeSonne looked at Tak, emotion surfacing and fading on his grief-stricken face, like ripples on water, before he finally spoke.

"Please tell us where you sent her," he said, his voice quiet but still carrying over the protests of his lawyer and the murmuring responses of the cop. "At least you can tell us that."

The woman pouched out her lower lip, weighing the request. She probably wasn't supposed to tell them anything, but then again, there was a chance that if she did, this pesky shyster and his client could go bug somebody else. It was as though Tak could read her every thought.

"She just left for the Hunter Foundation," she said. "Don't tell anyone I told you."

Mr. DeSonne thanked her. Tak turned away without waiting for him to acknowledge his presence any further.

He turned and nearly bumped into another policeman coming into the building.

"Excuse me," the cop said. Tak mumbled a reply, averting his eyes as he stepped past.

He kept his pace steady as he went back to the waiting vehicle. More police seemed to be arriving with each passing moment, as though he'd caught them in the middle of a shift change, but he made it back to Tamara's car without incident, and opened the passenger door. He sat in the shotgun seat and closed the door, gently. He knew that if he were still alive, his body would be producing adrenaline at a frenetic pace, and that he'd feel it in his skin and the shaking of his hands, but instead he felt a preternatural calm.

"You are . . . crazy," Tayshawn said. "Just . . . crazy."

"That took cojones," said Popeye.

"We're too . . . late," Tak said. His dead companions were squeezed in the back, their long legs drawn up, knees nearly to their chins. "They've already . . . moved her."

"How do you . . . know?" Tayshawn asked.

"Her . . . father," he replied. "He . . . knew . . . me."

"No joke?"

"They are . . . bringing her . . . to the . . . Hunter . . . Foundation."

He fully expected Popeye to start in on all the sick experiments they would do to her there, but the gill-man must have been learning that Tak's temper was on a hair trigger over her.

"What are we going to . . . do now?" he asked instead, his voice oddly muffled. Tak turned and saw a rubbery mirror image of himself staring back. Popeye and Tayshawn burst out laughing.

"Take that off . . . you idiot," Tak said, his brief flash of optimism at Popeye's growing sensitivity dashed.

"What? I like . . . being you," Popeye said, sitting back and straightening up in what Tak assumed was an imitation of his own posture. *"I believe . . . in the sanctity of . . . death,"* he said, with melodramatic intonation.

"Idiot," Tak said. Karen was gone.

She was gone, and with each passing moment the chances of saving her grew more distant. Even if she had somehow survived whatever horror they had wreaked upon her in the jail, there was no way that she would survive being "studied" at the foundation.

There was a very good chance she was already dead. Really and truly and finally forever dead. He clenched his jaw until he thought his teeth would crack.

"Let's go," he said to Tamara.

"Where to?"

"Just drive. Do you know . . . where Fire Street . . . is?"

She nodded.

"Head . . . there."

The laughter in the backseat cut off abruptly. Popeye peeled off the mask.

"What's on Fire Street?" Tamara asked, but he could tell from her voice that she knew exactly what she'd find there.

"Here?"

"Here."

Tamara pulled over to the side of the road. Tayshawn and Popeye didn't say anything as they extricated themselves from the backseat. They shuffled off the shoulder of the road and into the woods.

Tak reached over and turned the key, cutting the ignition.

"You're going to kill me?" she said. "You don't have to kill me! I'd never tell!" Her hands were on the wheel, but her arms were shaking. He'd wondered if she would try to fight or run for the woods. She looked like a healthy girl. "I wouldn't. I'm on your side!"

"Shhhh," Tak said, but the sound was ghastly as it half escaped through the wound in his cheek. He couldn't feel the weight of the slim switchblade in his jacket pocket, but he knew it was there. It was always there. "Be quiet for . . . just a minute."

"I know you have to do it," she said, shaking her head. "I've known ever since your friend told me about the lake. I could see it in your eyes. I wouldn't tell, you know. Even if you did it and I came back, I wouldn't tell."

Tak looked out the window and into the woods where Popeye and Tayshawn had gone.

A tear escaped from Tamara's left eye. She laughed as she rubbed it away.

"Maybe I'll come back," she said. "Who knows?" Tak thought he could see Tayshawn and Popeye moving through the brush, but it may have just been the wind.

"Would you take me in?" she said, rubbing her nose with the back of her wrist. "If I came back, I mean? I could be the twentieth zombie in your little clan."

Tak looked at her.

"Yeah," she said, her breathing ragged. "They told me all about it while you were in the police station. Nineteen of you, down there in the depths. It is kind of amazing that no one has thought to look in there. I mean, where else are you going to go? There's no way that such a big group of dead people wouldn't have been spotted leaving town."

Her speaking, her breath, had already begun to fog the windows in the swiftly cooling car. The living could impact the world in a thousand subtle ways, he thought, like the beating wings of a butterfly. There was only one way he felt he still could have an impact.

"I'm babbling, aren't I?" she said, trying and failing to laugh.

He didn't answer her.

"What did you see when you died?" she asked him. "Was it beautiful?"

Ahead of him, specters of snow were called up by the wind and dispersed just as quickly, as if Nature herself were displeased with her creations.

Tak wasn't sure how he should answer her, but he felt that she deserved something, at least. The dead who came back all had different stories of what they'd experienced at the point of departure from their bodies. Like their lives, or snowflakes, no two death experiences were the same. He'd heard tales of the white light, the long tunnel, of long-gone relatives waiting with open arms. For Tak there had only been a great dark emptiness. He found himself wishing it would be different for Tamara.

"It was . . . beautiful," was what he said, his voice hollow in the cramped interior of her car.

It was a lie. God wasn't there to greet him when he died. Nothing was. He rose in the hospital morgue, six hours after he'd been pronounced dead at the scene of his accident.

He saw that her hands were white on the wheel. She began to hyperventilate, and Tak paused, fascinated by the rapid in-and-outtake of breath. He realized that she was terrified.

"Takayuki?" she said, his name a whispered aspiration. "Would you . . . would you . . . hold me?" She was crying freely now, the tears leaking from the corners of her closed eyelids.

She was so attractive, he thought, so *alive*, displaying so many biological functions at once. The streaming tears, the swift rise and fall of her chest, the clenched hands, the rose blush at the base of her throat. So beautiful, so alive, whereas his heart was like a lump of clay in his chest. Looking at her he couldn't help but think of Karen.

"Well?" she said, her voice rising, breaking.

"I'm not . . . going to kill . . . you," he said.

She opened one teary eye. "You . . . you aren't?"

"No. But I want . . . Popeye . . . to think that I did. I'm waiting until . . . he's . . . away."

She didn't look like she believed him. She also looked a little disappointed, he thought.

"Really?"

"Really. I don't want . . . to kill you. Sorry to . . . disappoint. But please . . . don't tell . . . where my . . . people are."

"Oh, I won't!" she said. "I wouldn't do that! I really sympathize with you guys, you know? Even before I knew that Karen was a . . . was one of you, I thought the way you were treated was awful. I saw a zombie arrested in the parking lot a few weeks ago, and when I told Karen she . . ."

"Please," he said. Each mention of her name was like a slap, or salt rubbed into his cuts. "Please . . . stop . . . talking."

She was silent, but only for a moment.

"Oh," she said. He wished that he could have caught that exhalation, bottled it like a butterfly. "You were in love with her, weren't you?"

He listened to the soft intake of her breath and watched the flutter of her moist eyelashes.

"Yes," he whispered. "I . . . was."

She laid her hand against his ruined cheek, and he imagined he could feel its warmth. The muscle in his cheek twitched under her touch.

"You were."

"I *am*," he said. "She's still . . . alive. Sentient."

"I'm sorry," she said.

He nodded, ashamed that he'd even considered harming her.

"I have . . . to hurry," he said. "She's . . . waiting." He reached for the handle of the door.

"Please," she said. "Before you go." She held out her arms to him.

He could see in her eyes that she was asking *for* him, because she knew he'd never ask.

She put her arms around him, and he held her. Just for a moment.

He found Popeye and Tayshawn not far off into the woods. Neither wanted to look at him.

"Well?" Tayshawn said, finally.

Tak didn't answer. He found he *couldn't* answer.

"He had to . . . do it, T," Popeye said with a practiced nonchalance. "We've got to think about . . . Mal. Jacinta . . . and the others."

"Yeah," Tayshawn said. "That's us. Always . . . thinking . . . about . . . others."

"Don't be like . . . that, T. What . . ."

Tayshawn lifted his hand.

"Don't. Just . . . don't, okay, Popeye? I've never . . . hated . . . being dead . . . this much . . . before."

Tayshawn started walking.

"Will she come . . . back, you think?" Popeye asked Tak. "If she . . . comes . . . back . . . we'll have to find her and . . . take her . . . to the lake. The bleeders . . . would . . . destroy her. Maybe we should wait."

Takayuki didn't say anything. He had the sudden sensation that the knife in his pocket was like a flaming brand against his chest. The knife that he'd actually contemplated killing Tamara with. He'd felt her breathing; felt her pulse. The knife that he'd actually stabbed Adam with. What was he thinking?

He took it out and let it fall from his hand.

Tayshawn watched the descent of the knife, which sank, point down, into the snow.

"Tak?" he said. "Will she . . ."

"We . . . need to go," Tak said, looking at the hole the knife had made. "We've got . . . a long walk."

"Where are we . . . going?"

"They are . . . bringing her . . . to the foundation."

"They are . . . probably . . . already . . ."

Tak cut Popeye off with a stare. He didn't want to hear what Popeye's theories were.

"There," Popeye said, reading the look in his eyes. "I . . . was . . . going to say . . . there."

"There's only . . . one road . . . that leads . . . to the foundation," Tak said. "If we . . . hurry . . . we can prepare . . . for . . . her arrival."

He turned, and without waiting for their response, began walking.

# CHAPTER THIRTY-FOUR

"YOU HAVE ANY TROUBLE getting out of the house?"

"Please," Pete said, climbing into the warm cab of Duke's truck. He realized that Duke meant his own house, not the one the zombies had inhabited. "Child's play. They don't care if I leave, anyhow."

Duke laughed and took a sip of his coffee before pulling away. "Starting to clear up," he said. "I think the kiddies will have school tomorrow."

"Think so." Snow was always threatening these days, but never cutting loose.

"So," Duke said, looking at Pete. "You doing okay?"

Pete gave him a sarcastic look. "What do you think?"

"I don't know, Pete. You seemed a little . . . not yourself earlier today on the phone."

"I'm always myself."

"You sure? Nothing is bothering you?"

"What could be bothering me?"

"Well," Duke said, "you spent a lot of time with that zombie before outing her. I . . ."

"I didn't spend all that much time with her."

"No?"

"No!" he said. His blood was racing, and he steadied his breath, trying to reel it in. "I got her, didn't I?"

"Yeah, you got her. I just wondered why it took you so long."

"Oh, were you spying on me or something?"

"No," Duke said. "I spy on the zombies. You, I was monitoring. There's a difference."

"You're kidding. You actually *were* spying on me."

Duke shrugged, taking another sip of coffee. "No," he said. "Well, not me, anyway. We've got to keep those vans on the road, you know."

"Yeah."

"You didn't know she was a zombie, did you?"

Pete kept his eyes steady. "I knew."

Duke nodded. "Sure you did. Hey, don't feel bad about it. She could have fooled anybody. She did things that the others don't know how to do. At least I hope they don't know."

"Do we have to talk about this?"

"Your big victory? I thought you'd want to talk about it."

"Right. So what are we doing tonight, Duke? Pet stealing? Throwing snowballs from the graveyard?"

"Funny. We're going to confirm your kill. A good hunter always confirms his kills."

Pete didn't like the sound of that.

"What do you mean?"

"You'll see."

A few minutes later they were parked in the commuter lot near the highway at the edge of Oakvale. There was a single vehicle, an ambulance, parked in the far corner of the lot, just outside the glow of the single streetlight.

"What are we doing here, Duke?" Pete said, watching as the ambulance driver came out of his vehicle, looking like he'd just seen a ghost.

"Just want you to take a look at something, that's all."

"Is she in there?"

Duke nodded at him, the smile gone from his face.

"Oh, so its 'she' now?"

Duke got out of the car, leaving his door open, letting a blast of cold air into his vehicle. Pete could hear the driver complaining about how he could lose his job, etc., etc., and Duke waved him away, saying that he'd gotten the equivalent of three weeks' pay for the two minutes that this would take. He motioned for the driver to pop the ambulance door open, and when he did, Duke called over to Pete.

"Well?" he said. "Don't you want to see? You've made the world a better place."

Pete swore he'd show Duke nothing, no shred of emotion. He exited Duke's truck and walked to the ambulance.

"Climb aboard," Duke said. "Feast your eyes."

"And hurry," the other man said. Duke told him to shut up.

Pete climbed into the back of the vehicle, which was dark, although strands of spectral illumination were cast from some of the medical equipment. There was a low gurney that was covered with a white sheet. The sheet covered a body.

Her body.

He leaned closer. There was a faint chemical smell in the vehicle, something similar to the cleaning supplies he'd used while working off his community service at the foundation.

"Go ahead," Duke said from behind him, "take a look."

Pete reached out, but hesitated when he realized that some of the shadows falling across the sheet weren't shadows at all, but dark stains.

He heard the men outside arguing, the driver urging haste, Duke warning him to shut up unless he wanted a mouthful of broken teeth. Pete tried to slow his breathing and his heart rate. There was a moment when he thought the sheet rose and fell where her mouth would be, but that was twice crazy—she was truly dead now, and zombies don't breathe.

He took the edge of the sheet, half expecting her to reach down and grab him with a grip like frozen steel. He peeled the sheet back and looked and looked. It was so awful he had to force himself to turn away, but even then it was too late— he'd go to his grave with each one of her scars etched upon his soul.

"God," he said. "What . . . what did they do to her?"

Duke laughed. "Pretty, huh?"

Pete was trying not to gag.

"What makes you think they did it to her?" Duke said,

slapping him on the back. "Self-inflicted, don't you read the paper?"

"She couldn't . . . she couldn't do *that*," Pete said, looking back.

"Turn on the light," Duke said. "Get the full effect."

Pete couldn't even answer; he just shook his head. He couldn't see clearly in the gloom, but he could tell her eyes were open—there was a brief sparkle, as though they reflected the light from the lot beyond. The driver walked to the cab and threw a switch. White light filled the cabin, startling Pete and hurting his eyes. He could have sworn that she'd blinked.

When his eyes adjusted he went back to her, leaning over, avoiding looking at anything below her chin. Her lips were parted, as though she anticipated a kiss from him, but they looked so cold and bloodless.

He looked into her eyes. Their irises were like dull glass. He looked for her in them, but saw only a diminished reflection of himself.

He lifted his hand, intending to close her eyes, but froze when Duke spoke.

"Another one off your list, Pete," he said, his voice soft. "Another victory for One Life."

*Victory*. The word echoed in Pete's head. He raised the sheet, unable to take his eyes away from hers until he'd gently pulled it past them and over her head.

He looked back at Duke, not even sure what he was feeling, but knowing that he needed to sequester it, to count and breathe and choke it back down. To crush it out. His throat was dry, and he realized that his mouth was open, and for some reason he imagined his lips were as cold and pale as hers. Instead of breathing his life into her, he'd inhaled death from her. He was going to die—this is what death was like.

Duke told the driver to kill the light, then waved Pete on with his big flashlight. A police car, its flashers off, drifted by in the street beyond. Pete took a lurching step forward, as though his legs no longer worked.

"So," Duke said. "What did you and the demon talk about?"

"Talk?" Pete said. "What do you mean, talk?"

Duke drew him up short. Pete felt slightly lightheaded from what he'd seen in the ambulance, and was having a difficult time meeting Duke's eyes.

"You spent time with her, didn't you?"

"Just a little, like I said. Enough to figure out that she was a zombie."

"Son," Duke said, gripping his arm. He wasn't gentle about it. "In most things in life, the best policy is just to keep your mouth shut."

A range of responses, some elicited by dark emotions, passed through Pete, but he was able to choke them all back. Duke didn't release the hold he had on his arm for quite some time.

Pete knew that he should have gone home, but instead he drove to the lake, almost as though he were on autopilot.

Once there, he parked his car and walked out onto the dock

where he'd been with Karen just a few short weeks ago. Dawn was breaking, although the sun wasn't yet visible in the sky. Snow covered the lake ice, and the ground and the sky were the same washed-out white, like both had been hastily spread with the same brush. The blankness threatened to swallow the bare trees ringing the lake; Pete could imagine oblivion encroaching on the horizon.

He unzipped his coat and let a little more of the cold in. He pulled the wallet from his jacket pocket and took out the Undead Studies class list. Wind pulled at the fraying edges of the paper as he unfolded it. The paper had been worn smooth, the names written in what now looked like ghost ink. Only the bold black lines Pete had drawn through some of the names with a heavy marker stood out.

*Colette Beauvoir*

~~*Karen DeSonne*~~

*Thornton J. Harrowood*

*Phoebe Kendall*

~~*Adam Layman*~~

*Sylvia Stelman*

~~*Evan Talbot*~~

*Margi Vachon*

*Tayshawn Wade*

*Tommy Williams*

*Kevin Zumbrowski*

The list fluttered in his hand like a wounded bird. He could see himself as though from far away, tearing the list into small pieces, and then tearing those small pieces into smaller pieces, and then watching the shreds drift down, like the snowflakes they would soon join, onto the icy surface of Lake Oxoboxo.

Watching them fall, a certainty as acute as the whiteness that flooded his eyes overtook him. It was so obvious he was amazed, ashamed even, that it had taken him so long to figure it out.

He knew where the Oakvale undead were.

# CHAPTER THIRTY-FIVE

"WELL," THE PARAMEDIC said, reaching across the dashboard to switch off the radio, "there goes the neighborhood."

Beside him, his partner's eyes narrowed. "That's not even funny, man." They'd been listening a report on the news about Oakvale's favorite son, Tommy Williams.

The driver looked over at him.

"Oh hey," he said. "I'm sorry, man. This is different, you know? Zombies aren't even alive, you know? Dave?"

"Uh-huh."

"Really. 'Specially the one in the back."

Grinning, the driver nudged his partner with a crooked elbow. "C'mon, Dave."

"All right."

"Don't be mad. I didn't mean anything by it."

"All right."

"That Davidson guy sure is creepy though, huh? Crazy eyes. I wouldn't want to tangle with him."

"Uh-huh."

"Pays well, though."

For a few moments they drove in silence at a reasonable speed through the dark, twining back roads of Oakvale.

"The thing is, I don't think you realize what you're telegraphing to people when you say stuff like that," Dave said. "The comments, I mean. It's stuff like that got us in trouble at that house last week in Winford."

"Oh, that again."

"You just got to think before you say things. Words matter."

"I didn't even mean it that way! How was I supposed to know? They didn't look . . ."

"That's what I'm telling you, Ike. It don't matter. What matters is that you said something ignorant. You just got to stop a moment and think about where words and phrases come from, what they really mean."

Ike was shaking his head, and he took both hands off the wheel to emphasize his point. "You are way overthinking this. They didn't even notice!"

"Keep your hands on the wheel. They absolutely noticed."

"Well, tell them they shouldn't be so damn sensitive, then."

"Jesus, Ike. It's like . . ."

"It offends me when you take the Lord's name in vain."

Ike started laughing before Dave could reply, and then Dave was chuckling along with him.

"The problem with you people is—" he said. And then he shouted, but his warning came too late.

The boy lurched from the shoulder of the road and into the glow of their headlights. Dave called a warning, and Ike hit the brakes in the same instant that he jerked the wheel. They might have avoided hitting him if there weren't patches of black ice clinging to the road. The ambulance fishtailed, and Dave cried out as he heard the solid thud of the van striking the boy. Ike wrestled with the steering wheel, but they were still turning. He tried to turn in to the skid, but then the wheels caught dry pavement, and the vehicle lurched off the road, bounding off the tail end of a metal guardrail and into the culvert beyond, where it cracked with jarring force against an outcropping of large rocks. The airbags deployed, but in the whirl Dave thought he saw Ike's head bounce off the driver's side window. The vehicle's sudden stop left the ambulance grille down at a forty-five degree angle in the culvert.

It took Dave a moment before he realized that the whirring he heard wasn't the sound of his head ringing, but the back tire of the ambulance spinning, no longer in touch with the earth. Dazed, he began fumbling at his seat belt. Ike's eyes were closed, and the cracks in the glass behind him framed his head in a starry halo, but he groaned as he leaned forward on the deflating bag. Dave's thoughts were on the boy, anyway. They hadn't been going very fast, but the noise that he'd made when the van hit him was so loud, so solid.

Dave thought the boy had to be dead.

He was right.

And the boy wasn't the only one.

He'd no sooner gotten free of the airbag and seat belt when his door was opened from the outside. He turned and found himself staring into the moon-white face of a ghoul.

"Sit . . . tight," the ghoul said. He was wearing a leather jacket that was open to the waist, revealing a gaunt body that was mostly white, except in the places it wasn't. The places where its skin had been removed.

Dave shrank back in his seat. The thing facing him had bulbous frog eyes that stared out with insane intensity. Dave realized that this was because it didn't have any eyelids. Rows of fishhooks had been pushed through its ears and the corner of one eyebrow. Some of the grinning teeth had been filed into points. It waved to him with a partially skeletonized hand, and Dave had to suppress a manic laugh that was forming in his throat.

"Good . . . boy," the ghoul said. He slipped on a pair of dark sunglasses, shark mouth widening still further at the paramedic's obvious relief.

"My friend is hurt," Dave said, keeping his voice soft.

"So's . . . mine," the monster said. "Tayshawn?"

"I'm all . . . busted . . . up, Popeye," came the call from the street. "I can't . . . feel . . . my legs."

"Could you . . . before?"

"No."

The one called Popeye laughed, a low, dark sound.

"Seriously, though . . . I can't . . . get up," Tayshawn called.

"I'm a paramedic," Dave said. "Let me help him."

The zombie thought that was even funnier. "Send more

paramedics," he said, laughing. "Sit there. You can . . . check on . . . *your* . . . friend." Dave looked back at Ike, who let loose another groggy moan. His fingertips came away from the side of Ike's head wet with blood.

"He needs a bandage."

"Lucky for . . . him . . . you're in . . . an ambulance," Popeye said. Dave heard fumbling from the back of the ambulance, then felt the vehicle rock as someone climbed onto the rear bumper and began pulling at the doors. He also heard the sound of a body being dragged along the street. "We'll be out . . . of your . . . hair . . . in just . . . a minute."

The dragging sound grew closer, and then the boy that had run out in front of the ambulance hauled himself along the road into view. One arm was bent at an awkward angle, and his left leg was broken in a way that didn't require medical training to diagnose. Part of the boy's femur was poking through his jeans toward the upper thigh.

"Jeez," Popeye said, glancing down at him, "you . . . *are* . . . all busted up. You're a . . . mess."

"Told you," the other answered. "I'm gonna . . . need a . . . hand."

He should be screaming or in shock, Dave thought.

"What do you want?" he said.

"Just . . . your . . . cargo," Popeye said, crouching to haul the other to his feet. Dave winced when he watched him drape the broken arm across his shoulders and help stand him up.

Behind them, the ambulance doors clanged open.

\* \* \*

"Karen?" Tak called, peering into the gloom.

The ambulance lights had winked out at the second impact, the one with the rocks. The gurney bearing her body had rolled back, and one milk-white arm had slipped out from under the sheet and hung down, her long nails nearly grazing the floor.

"Karen?" Slumping, he felt his heart ice over. He pressed his head against the door frame. He said her name a third time, whispering.

There was no answer.

He'd been wrong. He'd been wrong all along. The mistakes he'd made began to flash through his mind, a swift parade of recrimination and stupidity. People weren't symbols. Lives weren't allegories. He felt as though his skeleton wanted to tear itself free from his dead flesh.

"Please," he said. He prayed. He was actually praying. "Please."

Just because I didn't see You doesn't mean You aren't there, he thought. Just because it's dark doesn't mean we're alone.

"Please."

He lifted his head.

The body on the gurney sat up. He could hear a rattling, like the sound of loose bones.

"Karen?"

Her voice, when it came, was a raspy and echoing croak. "Yes."

"Karen!"

"Give . . . me . . . a . . . minute to get . . . myself . . . together."

He looked at her then, at her face, and despite her wounds, it was as though the frost were melting in his chest, as though sunlight were streaming in through the wounds on his body, making him warm again. It was like spring had come.

"I knew it," he said. "You're . . . alive."

Her eyes flashed a brilliant crystalline blue that cut through the darkness, and he knew that she was smiling.

He'd held Karen's hand and led her away from the accident. She'd wrapped the sheets from the gurney around her head and body, swathing herself like a mummy, so that only one pale arm, crisscrossed with dark bloodless scars, protruded. He wasn't exactly sure what she'd done to herself, only that she'd tried to make it as convincing as possible.

A few feet ahead of them, Popeye was half carrying, half dragging Tayshawn along, his broken leg trailing behind him. Tak wished it would snow so that the rather obvious trail they were leaving would disappear.

"Where are . . . you . . . taking . . . me?" Karen asked.

Tak frowned. She sounded awful, her voice harsh and halting. He heard something rattling in her chest when she spoke. "The lake," he said. "We'll be . . . safe . . . in the lake."

"No," she whispered, stopping her awkward progress. "We have . . . something . . . to do."

"Karen, you really aren't in any . . . shape . . . to do anything but . . . hide. We . . ."

"Tak," she said, placing her index finger against his lips. "Trust . . . me."

What an absurd request, he thought. She was the only thing on earth or beyond that he trusted.

She told Tak that Popeye and Tayshawn should leave. He didn't argue and neither did they.

"Before . . . you . . . go," Karen said, and motioned Tayshawn over. She lifted the sheet that she'd pulled over her head enough to expose her lips. Seeing her throat, Tak could see why speaking was such a difficulty for her.

"Thank . . . you," she said, kissing Tayshawn on the corner of his mouth before letting the sheet fall back into place.

"Anything for . . . a friend," Tayshawn said. He was smiling.

"Yuck," was Popeye's comment.

"Thank . . . you, too . . . Popeye."

It pained Tak to listen to her voice, which sounded nothing like her. Popeye waved to her with his webbed hand, as though he didn't want to get within range of her hugs and kisses.

"Oh, sure," he said. A stitch popped free on his thumb, and the webbing dangled by its last remaining threads.

"When can we . . . expect you?" Tayshawn asked Tak.

"Couple . . . days," he replied. He wasn't certain, but he didn't think Karen's business would keep him on the surface very long.

"Okay, then," Popeye said. "I guess . . . we'll . . . see you."

Tak nodded. Popeye expected more, but Tak had nothing more to give. He watched them lope away until they were no longer visible through the trees. Karen took his hand.

"It might be . . . faster . . . if I . . . carried you," he said.

Without a word, she looped her arms around his neck, and the sight of the scars running up and across her pale flesh made him clench his teeth. Her feet were bare, and although she couldn't feel the cold, he was determined not to let them come into contact with the snow again.

She felt weightless in his arms. He thought that he might be leaving the earth himself.

He didn't stop until he laid her down on the futon in the Haunted House. He placed her gently on the cushions, carefully tucking the sheets over her bare arms.

"They look . . . ugly . . . don't they?" she said.

"You're healing," he said. "I can . . . tell."

"Jigsaw girl," she said. "Putting myself . . . back . . . together."

"You'll be . . . fine," he said, trying not to sound as though he needed to convince himself.

"Who knows . . . if I'll . . . be able . . . to heal . . . all this. Maybe it . . . is too . . . much."

"You'll heal. Wait . . . here," he said.

He went upstairs and got her backpack and the blanket that the beating heart—Tamara—had used to "defeat" Tayshawn.

Karen was sitting up. She'd removed the sheet from her head, and now it lay bunched up on her naked body, so he could see more of what she'd done to herself.

"Karen . . ." he said, the bag slipping out of his hand.

"Not so . . . pretty . . . anymore, am . . . I?" she said with a rueful smile. "But this wasn't . . . all me. They wanted . . . to be . . . sure."

His mouth closed with a click of his teeth. It was the closest he'd come to showing emotion since his death.

"When I was . . . in my . . . cell . . . one of the . . . police . . . kicked . . . me. Used . . . the knife. Then he unholstered . . . his weapon. Pointed it . . . at my face. 'Headshot,' he told . . . his . . . partner. 'Only . . . way . . . to be . . . sure.' My eyes were . . . open. So was . . . the door . . . to the . . . cell. I could . . . have . . . tried . . . to run."

"Beating . . . heart . . . bastards," Tak said.

"Officer . . . Pelletier . . . stopped him. They fought. Argued. Had me . . . moved . . . to the . . . morgue."

"I . . . will . . . kill . . . them all," he said.

Karen looked as worried as her face was able to convey.

"Oh, don't be mad . . . Tak. They weren't . . . all bad. Before . . . I did . . . it . . . Officer . . . Pelletier . . . came and . . . apologized to me. People . . . aren't . . . all bad."

"They should . . . die. All . . . of them."

"Don't be that way," she said, touching his hand. "It isn't . . . worth it."

Was the raspy quality already fading from her voice? He spread the blanket over her, then placed the bag on her lap. A tiny scar above her lip vanished before his eyes.

"Oh, you have . . . my bag?"

"I . . . do."

"My clothes," she said, rummaging in the bag and pulling out a rumpled T-shirt. "My cell phone. Dead . . . like us.

Wish . . . I could . . . call . . . my parents. They'd . . . freak, though." She spread out her top across her lap. "Tamara . . . found you . . . ?"

"She found us," Tak said, turning as Karen pulled the T-shirt over her head.

"Is she . . . okay?"

His back was still turned as he answered. "She's . . . okay."

"Great. Here's what . . . I need . . . you to do. I need . . ."

"Whatever . . . you need," he said. "I will do."

She smiled at him, and the purity of her smile touched him, even through her mask of scars.

"Oh, Tak," she said, reaching over to him, gripping his hand with hers, "I'm so glad you . . . rescued . . . me."

He patted her hand with his, while reaching out with his scarred hand to brush the back of her neck. His fingers caught and entwined in the tangles of her hair.

"Takayuki," she whispered. "There is something you need to know about me."

# CHAPTER THIRTY-SIX

"**P**HOEBE," I SAID. "WE need . . . your . . . help."

Phoebe was looking at me as if she were seeing a ghost. Which, for the record, must be a scarier creature than a zombie.

Well, I guess she was seeing a ghost, wasn't she? The poor thing. I had a scarf covering most of my face, and a powder-blue knit cap on my head, so just about the only visible part of me was my eyes. Kind of hard to hide those without my contacts. Too bad Popeye hadn't left me a pair of his sunglasses.

Phoebe opened her door, stepped out, and hugged me. Roughly. If I'd been alive, as cut up as I was, I'm sure her embrace would have been agony, but instead it was heaven. I looked up and saw Adam looming large over her shoulder. He smiled at me.

"Karen," Phoebe said. Her lips were right against my ear. "Karen, we thought . . ."

"I know," I said. "I'm sorry. I'm really sorry."

Her hug tightened. She felt so strong, so alive.

Eventually she brought Tak and me inside. I sat down at a tiny round table opposite Phoebe. Her dog walked into the room, his nails clicking on the linoleum. He glanced up at Tak, who was leaning against the refrigerator, barked once, and took off running. I wouldn't swear to it, but it looked as if Tak were actually smiling. Again.

When I told Tak about Monica and me, I was worried that I was taking his last little spark of humanity and hope, and crushing it between my pale dead fingers. Arrogant of me, I know, to put myself on such a pedestal; Tak felt like he'd been rejected by the creator of the universe, so why would one more rejection from insignificant little Karen DeSonne have any impact? But I could see the hurt in his face when I told him. He was never one to telegraph his emotions, but I knew him well enough to know that my words hurt him.

He really loved me.

But despite loving me—because of it, actually—a strange thing happened after I told him that I, too, was in love. That I was in love with a living girl, that her name was Monica Cruz, and that I needed to see her even though I hadn't seen her since I died. Something strange and wonderful.

Slowly, Tak's expression changed. In his eyes, in his cheeks, in his ruined mouth. He was smiling—actually smiling—at me. When he moved his hand from my neck, it was only to comb out the snarls with his fingertips, not to withdraw from me.

"I'll help . . . you," he said, repeating the commitment he'd made before I told him. "In any way . . . you need me . . . I will help you."

That's love.

When someone who considers themselves rejected by God is able to not only feel but express that type of love, there's hope. Hope enough to make anything possible. His words erased my wounds.

Well, not immediately, not after the Death of a Thousand Cuts. I had to make it as convincing as possible, after all. But that's how I felt after he told me that he would be there for me. Healed. Whole.

Then again, maybe it wasn't his words that made me feel that way. Maybe it was my own.

I was watching him while we sat in Phoebe's kitchen, my wounds and my smile hidden beneath my scarf. He was looking at Adam, and I realized that something unseen was passing between them. Phoebe placed her hand on my gloved one. I could imagine the road map carved on my body disappearing, fissures healing, gray and black lines fading as though traced by an unseen eraser.

"You were . . . right," Adam said to Tak. Tak nodded at him.

Adam turned to me. "He swore that you . . . were still . . . alive. He . . . knew."

"He'll . . . always . . . know," I said, my voice muffled slightly by the scarf.

Phoebe gripped my hand.

"Karen," she said. "What happened?"

"We can . . . talk about . . . that later," Adam said. "You should . . . get to . . . the lake."

"Not . . . now," I told them. "I need . . . your help. We need . . . to go . . . to the foundation. And call . . . the Undead . . . Crimes Unit." The sound of my stilted speech, the harshness of it, really was frustrating to me.

"Our help?" Phoebe asked. I nodded.

"I need . . . a beating heart . . . with me, Phoebe. Someone . . . I . . . trust. I need . . . you."

"Why?" Adam asked. "If . . . Phoeb . . ."

"They might destroy her on sight, Adam," Phoebe said, her green eyes never leaving mine.

"They definitely would destroy Tak."

"I'd like to be . . . gone . . . soon," Tak said. "Karen . . . needs me . . . to talk to the . . . Feds, but after that . . . I will . . . leave."

I took the Tak mask out of my bag and lay it on the table. "Tak wasn't . . . responsible for the Guttridge disappearance. They will be able . . . to see . . . that. Tak . . . isn't the one in the video."

"How did you . . . get that?" Adam said.

"The other Tak!" Phoebe said, smoothing out the mask. "He was here!"

"Pete Martinsburg," I said. Phoebe looked over at the sink, beside which sat a wooden block of knives, her eyes growing wide.

"He was . . ." she began. I noticed she was wearing a

necklace, a misshapen lump of metal that hung below the hollow of her throat.

"He was," I said, quickly.

"How . . . did . . . you get . . . that mask, Karen?" Adam said.

Dead or not, he sounded furious, not that I blamed him.

Phoebe just looked confused. "Let's not worry about that right now," she said, lifting her hand from mine, waving his questions away. "We need to get Karen in front of the UCU as soon as possible. It could really help Tommy if the true story about the Guttridge murders came out. The timing is almost perfect."

I realized what the odd ornament at the end of Phoebe's chain was: a spent bullet. Whatever Phoebe didn't figure out, I'd tell her. I hoped that she'd forgive me, but from the way Adam was looking at me, I wasn't sure he would.

I looked down at the table. There was a deep, jagged slash visible across my wrist where my sleeve had ridden up; the edges of the wound gray and furled like the pages of a drowned book, the center of the fissure a greenish-black. I folded my hands in my lap.

"Okay," Adam said. "I'll get . . . Agent . . . Gray's . . . card. I don't know . . . if I trust . . . them, though."

"I trust Angela," I said. "Especially after seeing what they did for Sylvia. And she knows . . . Pete from all those . . . therapy . . . sessions. She probably . . . knows . . . what he is . . . capable of. That's why . . . we're going to do it at . . . the foundation."

Tak didn't react. He was back to his own inscrutable, emotionless ways, I guess, because when I first told him about my plan, he argued heavily against it, reminding me that my body was being sent to the very same foundation where I wanted to have the meeting.

It would only make him feel badly if I told him that I'd been *hoping* to end up at the foundation after staging my retermination. I wanted him to feel like he'd rescued me—not delayed me.

Phoebe called Angela, who apparently said all the right things and made all the right assurances. Adam's conversation with Agent Gray was terse and without any detail beyond Adam stating that he they needed to talk. Gray told Adam he would meet him at the foundation in a few hours.

"We have . . . a little . . . time," Adam said, closing Phoebe's cell.

"Good," I said. I rubbed my arm through my coat. All of a sudden it felt itchy.

I looked at him, then at Phoebe. Tak regarded the floor.

"There's something about me that I want you both to know."

I breathed deeply, and told them.

Phoebe drove us to the foundation, the boys sitting in the backseat. We listened to the local news on the radio. There was no mention of the ambulance crash or the body that had gone missing. My body. We drove past the spot where the ambulance had gone off the road; the vehicle had been cleared away, but the evidence of its abrupt impact with the guardrail was clearly visible.

I wondered if anyone had tried to follow us; with Tak leading me by the hand and Popeye half-dragging Tayshawn it wouldn't have taken Davy Crockett to follow our trail. But now the sun, at some point having broken through the gray, was high in the sky and warming the snow-covered ground, obliterating the evidence of our passing.

The Hunter Foundation rose into view, a long flat building on a hill surrounded by a high spiked fence. I hadn't realized how close the ambulance had been to its destination before they'd run it off the road.

"Why is it . . . gated?" Tak asked. "To keep . . . zombies . . . in?"

"To keep . . . beating hearts . . . out," Adam answered.

The voice from the gate was flat and vaguely hostile.

"We're here to see Angela," Phoebe said. "Phoebe Kendall, Adam Layman, and . . . guests," she said.

The gate clicked open, and Phoebe maneuvered the vehicle up the hill.

"Who was that?" Phoebe asked Adam.

"I didn't recognize . . . the voice," he said.

There was a man waiting for us at the door of the foundation; he was wearing a uniform, and his military bearing reminded me of Duke, although that was where the similarities ended. This man was broad and thick, bearded, with a mane of dark black hair that he was clearly very proud of. I thought he looked like a werewolf frozen mid-transformation.

"I've never . . . seen him . . . before," Adam said.

The man opened Phoebe's door for her, but the gesture did not appear to be an act of courtesy.

"I'm Chuck McMahon," he said. "Welcome back. I'm the new director of operations here."

McMahon regarded Tak with an expression so frank and curious it bordered on hostile. Me, he mostly ignored, maybe because I was still swaddled in layers of winter clothing. Tak made no attempt to cover his slashed cheek, and stared blankly back at the man, who didn't blink.

"Follow me," McMahon said. "They're waiting for you in the encounter room."

The encounter room, I thought. Adam was holding hands with Phoebe, and at one point she leaned into him and whispered something in his ear. Tak's boots were loud in the empty corridor.

"First room on the left," McMahon said. "Have fun." He walked down the other hallway toward the Operations room. I wondered why Duke wasn't around.

Tak led the way and came to a carpeted room that had a loose group of furniture, futons and sofas, arranged in a semicircle. Angela Hunter was sitting with Agents Gray and Alholowicz of the Undead Crimes Unit, supposedly the newest branch of the FBI. The last time I'd seen them was in this very same room, when they'd come to talk to everyone in our Undead Studies class about a rash of grave desecrations that had happened in Winford. Alholowicz was a large, unkempt man who spoke with his hands; his partner was thin in a tailored gray suit. They were both poker-faced (Alholowicz's unshaven, Gray's razor smooth) but I could see their eyes narrow slightly upon seeing Tak, who'd been the chief suspect in their desecration case.

"Miss DeSonne," Alholowicz said, hauling himself up from the sofa. "Please take a seat. Miss Kendall, Mr. Layman. And this must be Takayuki. It is Takayuki, isn't it?"

"Takayuki Niharu," his partner said. "We've wanted to talk to you for a long time."

Tak didn't answer. I realized I'd never heard his last name before.

"Please," Agent Alholowicz said. "Have a seat."

I sat down. My friends sat beside me, except for Tak.

"I'll . . . stand," he said.

"Suit yourself," Alholowicz said, shrugging as he returned to the sizable groove he'd left in the sofa. "Phoebe, here, says you have something to tell us."

I took Tak's mask out of my bag and held it up like a puppet.

"Takayuki did not kill Gus Guttridge," I heard myself say. "In fact, he isn't dead at all."

Gray said he wanted to record the conversation, and he put a digital recorder on the arm of the sofa when I nodded.

"Okay," Alholowicz said. "Go on."

I went on. I told them about how I'd nearly been reterminated after the incident at St. Jude's, and how I'd been passing as a trad at Wild Thingz! I told them about meeting Pete and tricking him into telling me the truth about Guttridge, and about stealing the mask from him. I told them everything

I knew. Angela would murmur supportive words at certain points, but the agents watched me in impassive silence, with only an occasional nod from Alholowicz to let me know they were paying attention.

I was shocked at how few questions they had for me when I was done talking.

"That's why Martinsburg attacked you, then?" Alholowicz said. "Because you'd tricked him?"

"Yes," I said. I hadn't gone into the gory details of how I'd tricked him. They weren't stupid. They could add it up.

"And he didn't tell you where in Maine Guttridge was hiding?" Agent Gray asked.

"No."

There were a few other questions, not many; mostly about where and when. I answered as best as I could, then they told me I was free to go.

"That's it?" I said.

Alholowicz scratched his fleshy chin. "Hm?"

"That's all? Aren't you going to arrest him? Are you . . ."

His partner raised his hand. "It isn't appropriate for us to discuss the details of an investigation. And frankly, I'm not so sure that the testimony of a differently biotic person would stand up in court."

Phoebe and I started protesting, as one. Alholowicz raised his hands to quiet us, and in that moment we heard the sounds of a confrontation in the hall. A raised voice, scuffling.

A voice echoed down the hallway, followed by the sound of sneakers slapping on linoleum.

"I just want to talk to her!"

I knew that voice.

Pete.

He arrived like a bad dream, his eyes locking on mine the moment he appeared in the doorway. From the corner of my eye I saw Tak reach into his jacket for something that was no longer there. I heard a strange sound, and I realized it was him, growling.

Pete opened his mouth to speak, but in that moment he was seized from behind in a rough tackle that would have knocked him down if he hadn't shifted his weight, so his attacker, McMahon, nearly went over instead. But McMahon was quick, and grabbed Pete in a choke hold.

"Please!" Pete said, his shirt riding up out of his pants as McMahon tried to haul him away. "Let me talk to her!"

"Let him go," Alholowicz called. "You might as well let him go. Stay put there, Takky."

Takayuki didn't respond, but I stood and put my hand on his shoulder, my fingers threading their way through the spikes there.

"He recognized the girl's car," McMahon said. As hale and hearty as he seemed, he was slightly winded from his tussle with Pete.

Pete's clothes were askew, and there was a red mark across his neck.

"Just listen to me, Christie," he said. He looked like he was lost. "I'm sorry. I'm sorry for what I did."

# CHAPTER THIRTY-SEVEN

H E'D STUCK PINS IN HER. The thought made it very difficult for Tak to concentrate on what Pete was actually saying.

"I'm sorry. I've got a lot to apologize for. To you two, especially. Christie. Karen, I mean. Adam. Adam, I'm so sorry for what happened, man. Things got out of hand. Really out of hand. Karen. I can't apologize enough for what happened."

Martinsburg was psychotic, Tak thought. He actually looked like he believed what he was saying—like he was sorry for what he'd done. Tak hadn't seen anyone—anyone alive, that is—who could mask their true feelings as well as Martinsburg was doing.

"No, you can't," Phoebe said.

She looked like a sleek cat about to pounce, Tak thought. She had some fire to her; some fight. Her pseudo-goth clothing might be a disguise, but there was considerably less artifice to her than to most of the breathers.

Pete nodded. "I know. I know. I can never make up for what happened. I can't even think of an excuse. I was going through some bad stuff in my life, new medication, and I just lost it. I'm sorry."

"Adam is a *zombie* because of you. Karen went to *jail* because of you. She nearly reterminated herself because of you!"

Pete's eyes affected a hurt expression. "I know. I know. That's why I'm here. Because of her, it's got me all twisted up inside. What . . . what she and I had . . . I thought it was real. When I found out it wasn't, I lost it. Again. And when I lose it, people get hurt. It's almost like I can't control myself."

"What do you mean, 'what she and I had'? What are you even talking about?" Phoebe said.

Pete pretended not to have heard her; he couldn't take his eyes from Karen. He was so good at lying, it was clearly pathological, Tak thought.

"And then when I read that she reterminated herself, I just . . . I just couldn't take it." His eyes were glassy, those of a little lost boy. "I . . . I think I was in love with you, Christie."

"Karen," she whispered.

"Karen. When I read about your re—your second death, I cried. I cried! I can't remember the last time I cried. I didn't even cry when Adam died."

"When you killed him, you mean."

"You should let him speak, Miss Kendall." This from Agent

Gray, the thin guy with the hard expression. Tak thought it was interesting that Pete didn't deny the accusation, but kept nodding his head.

"Please, Phoebe," Angela said. "Let's give him a chance."

"What do you . . . mean . . . you . . . loved Karen?" Adam said.

"She's incredible," he said, looking over at her as she stood statue-still in the middle of the room. "I thought we had something real. She listened to what I was saying, you know? And she was smart, and funny. Most of the girls I'd been with were total airheads—but Christie . . . Karen . . . she was something else. Something out of this world. Kissing her . . ."

Pete had to know that what he was saying was infuriating them. Tak was clenching his fists so tightly that the knuckles cracked. But it was Phoebe who finally snapped.

"What the *hell* are you talking about?" she said, her eyes going back and forth from Pete to Karen, who lowered her head.

Pete blinked. "She . . . she and I got close. I thought you knew."

"I have no idea what you're talking about, and I'm pretty sick of listening to your insane . . ."

"She pretended she liked me. You really didn't know about this?"

". . . lying, and I can't believe that you're listening to him, Angela, encouraging him, after all he's done to hurt us. . . ."

Pete took a hesitant step toward Karen, and Tak moved alongside Adam to bar his way.

"Or maybe you weren't pretending?" Pete said.

"And now he's literally throwing dirt on Karen's grave and you just sit there and . . ."

"Christie? Karen? Was it all a joke to you?" Softer, now.

". . . letting him run his mouth, while . . ."

"Karen?"

"He's telling . . . the truth."

Her voice, soft as it was, silenced the room. Phoebe stopped in mid-rant. One could hear a pin drop.

A pin.

Another crack, and Takayuki wondered if he'd broken his own finger.

"What?" Phoebe said, turning the full heat of her gaze on Karen.

"He's telling the . . . truth," Karen said, meeting Phoebe's eyes.

Pete affected a rueful expression.

"I'm sorry you heard it like this," he said, obsequious. Placating. "I really thought you'd all know."

"I saw the . . . Guttridge . . . tape and . . . knew it . . . was him. I wanted . . . to expose . . . the fraud."

"Expose the fraud," Phoebe said.

Karen didn't answer.

"I guess part of me always knew what she was," Pete said, going on as though he were part of their conversation. "Who she was. A zombie, I mean. I think subconsciously I knew, and that's why I let her know the things I did. I think I felt so guilty about everything . . . accidentally killing you, and then doing all those things to frame the zombies. I knew it was wrong. Deep down I knew it was wrong, and I think part of me was looking for a way out. Karen became that way out." He sighed. "I really think I loved her."

"Yeah, you loved her so much it made her dead again," Phoebe said. Tak could hear the bitterness in her voice. Certain things were adding up in her head.

Pete made bloodhound eyes at her.

"When I realized that she didn't love me . . . that I didn't lose her, because I never really had her . . . I went crazy. I did. Even though I think my subconscious mind was in on the joke, I went nuts."

Tak couldn't take it anymore. He had to speak, although he wasn't sure exactly what he wanted to say.

"Pins. You stuck . . . pins in her."

"I did. I did," Pete said, sniffling. "Like she was a human voodoo doll. It felt like I was sticking them into myself."

"Oh, please," Phoebe said.

"I don't expect you to understand," he said, rubbing at his eyes. "I don't even understand myself. But I died with her a little in that jail cell."

Tak stepped toward him. Adam placed his hand on his shoulder.

Alholowicz cleared his throat.

"Martinsburg's confessed to staging the murders with Duke Davidson, who we already have under arrest. Your story corroborated just about everything he told us. He's even told us where we could find his lawyer."

"And what . . . will happen to him?" Adam said, pointing past Tak's shoulder at Pete.

Alholowicz cocked an eyebrow. "Him? He's free to go. He's cooperated fully and answered all our questions."

Gray jumped in before even Phoebe could protest. "He gave us Guttridge. He's willing to testify against Davidson, who he says was the organizer of all the anti-zombie propaganda and incidents. We'll get Davidson on about a dozen solid charges, and hopefully he'll give up some of his coconspirators." He smiled. "And the good names and reputations of you and your dead friends will be restored."

Tak glared at him.

"Isn't that enough?" Alholowicz asked.

"No."

"Well, it is going to have to be. Because that's all you'll get."

Tak kept glaring. Maybe dropping the knife had been a mistake.

"I'd say it worked out pretty well for you, Takayuki. I'm pretty sure that the ambulance personnel would have no trouble picking *you* out of a lineup."

"So you'd charge me . . . with . . . what? Corpse theft?"

"That's a start."

"Arrest her, too," Tak said, indicating Angela. "Wasn't she . . . supposed to get Karen . . . for dissection? And her parents had . . . no recourse. Sounds like kidnapping . . . to me."

"How about reckless endangerment? Attempted murder? The driver had a broken arm and a concussion."

Tak realized that Alholowicz was enjoying the argument, but he couldn't stop himself.

"He shattered the leg of one of . . . my friends. Broke . . . his . . . arm. I have witnesses . . . the driver . . . did it . . . on purpose."

"That's crap. But if you want to bring them in, that would be great."

Tak turned from him, aware of how closely everyone was watching him. Everyone but Karen and Pete, who were looking at each other as if seeing each other for the first time.

"Let's focus on the positive," Angela said. "Right about now my father will be telling Tommy the good news. You won't have to be in hiding anymore."

"Really," Tak said.

There were conversations to be had, documents to be signed. A few hours later the agents told Tak that he and his friends could go.

Tak thought about the word "friends."

He put his arm around Karen and led her to the door.

Pete stepped in front of them, blocking their exit.

"Look," he said, speaking to Karen. Her scarf had slipped a bit, and crisscrossing lines of gray were visible on her cheek. Deep lines.

"I just want you to know, I'm sorry about everything. Everything."

"Get out of . . . our way," Tak said.

Pete turned toward him. "And I'm not angry at you anymore

for maiming me." His hand went to the scar and traced its length with his fingertip.

"Come with me, Karen," Phoebe said, holding out her hand.

Pete whispered a name that Tak couldn't catch, but it wasn't Karen. Then he said, "I love you."

Karen broke away from Tak and Pete and went to Phoebe, leaning against her as if her strength had finally given out. Phoebe took her by the hand and led her out of the encounter room. Tak was aware that Adam was standing beside him.

Pete's eyes ticked back and forth between them. He tapped his scar with the tip of his finger.

"I was angry when it happened, of course," he said. "Furious. I wanted revenge. But that's all behind me now. I just wanted you to know I'm not looking for retaliation."

Tak wasn't sure if he was speaking about the scar or about what happened with Karen. He didn't care.

He leaned in close, his voice a low whisper. He imagined that his breath, or what passed for it, would be unpleasant to Martinsburg.

"I didn't go . . . far enough," he said. "I am . . . going to kill you."

Pete straightened up, a flicker of fear in his eyes. But the flicker was soon replaced by another emotion entirely.

"You're all wet, Tak," Pete whispered. "You are so out of your depth, and you haven't even touched bottom yet."

Tak's face betrayed nothing, even as what Pete was saying registered to him.

"Be springtime soon," Pete said. "Birds. Bees. Fishing season."

"Time . . . to go," Adam said, his hand a reassuring weight on Tak's shoulder.

Tak had his friends drop him off at the edge of the woods not far from the lake. Even if Martinsburg or any of his henchmen decided to pursue him, they wouldn't have an easy time finding him in the dark icy water of the Oxoboxo.

Karen held his hand for the duration of their short ride. He didn't want to let go when Phoebe pulled onto the shoulder. He wouldn't allow himself to feel as though he'd regained her only to lose her; all that mattered was that she was still in the world.

"Tak," she said, holding him tightly once they were out of the car. "You saved me. You knew."

I'll always know, he thought. But he didn't answer. There wasn't any need.

He wished he could wipe away the hint of apology that had crept into Karen's diamond eyes. There was nothing to be sorry about, as far as he was concerned. People are who they are, and they feel what they feel. But he did lean in close and whisper something in her ear, something that Phoebe or Adam couldn't hear, and when he let her go she was smiling, but she was starting to cry, too.

"Tears," he said, amazed. He watched one trickle down her cheek.

"Just like a real girl," she said, leaning against Phoebe as she put her arms around her shoulder.

"We shouldn't stay here much longer," Adam said. "You never know."

Tak nodded. "Good luck," he said.

"You, too," Adam replied, extending his hand. "See you . . . soon?"

Tak had offered him his own hand what seemed like so long ago, on the opposite shore of this very lake. This time he took it from choice, not desperation.

"Maybe. If Tommy has some luck."

The hug from Karen had been expected, the one from Phoebe was a pleasant surprise. Since he'd returned he hadn't been hugged—or even touched—by as many girls as he had been in the past few days.

"Say hi to our friends," she said, his battered leather coat creaking in her embrace. "Tell them we love them. Take care of them."

"I will."

Walking away, he didn't look back. He never did.

But there was a moment that he clung to, a moment that he'd captured and replayed with each step toward the frozen lake. It was the moment that she'd opened her eyes in the ambulance; the moment he thought someone had answered his prayers.

It would be springtime before long, and he was endlessly patient.

# CHAPTER THIRTY-EIGHT

A LHOLOWICZ AND GRAY dropped Pete off at his house. He could see his mother through the bay window, her arms folded across her chest.

"Well, Pete," Alholowicz said, spitting his name out like someone had switched out the sugar for his coffee with salt. "I guess we should thank you."

"Yeah," Gray said. "Duke Davidson and Attorney Guttridge. Not bad."

"Best I could do," Pete said.

Gray turned around in his seat and focused his eyes, which were as gray as his suit and his name—Pete thought they were the color of a gun—on his face. "Yeah? I don't think they could have planned this all on their own. Duke and his redneck pals."

Pete looked out the window. He saw the Wimp join his mother, put his arm around her shoulder.

"Like I said, I wouldn't know anything about that."

"Yeah," Gray said. He flicked a business card at Pete, bouncing it off his chest. "We'll be in touch. Give us a call if anything else comes to mind."

Pete took his time retrieving the card from the floor. One corner was bent from where it had struck him.

Alholowicz cleared his throat, coughing. "Now get the hell out of my car," he said. "You're stinking it up to high heaven."

His mother was overly affectionate and tearful, but he could tell he'd made her happy. It wasn't something he did often, so the signs were easy to recognize. The Wimp gripped his shoulder and gave him some song-and-dance routine about how proud he was of Pete, how he'd done the right thing. The old anger rose up, but Pete fought it back. His training served him well; his mind was once again in control of his body. He could no longer summon up the energy to look contrite as his mother blubbered and the Wimp went through the motions of seeming like a father figure.

When they were done he asked for a sandwich and some lemonade, then excused himself to take a shower.

He ran the water as hot as it would go, knowing it would be some time before the furnace kicked in. He took off his clothes and then looked at himself in the mirror, his eyes involuntarily going to his scar as they always did. Then he thought of her, but not the her of illusion—the her that had seemed so full of life and energy. Instead he thought of her as she lay under the sheet in the ambulance, of the scars that marred her dead flesh, of the terrible wound at her temple. How could she have done that to herself? What could someone be carrying, what inner strength or inner weakness could a person have, to inflict that type of damage to herself?

The scar on his face seemed to lengthen and then fork as it slid beneath his jaw. Slashes appeared on his bare chest and arms, lengthening and widening slowly, as though some invisible being were carving them with an unseen knife. His temple opened up as if something beneath the skin were burrowing its way out, and a greenish black liquid began to bubble and flow glacially down the side of his face. He blinked and his left eye was gone, a dark tear falling from the socket. Air escaped from his neck with a sound that matched the hissing radiators as they worked to heat the water that flowed through the pipes and up through the showerhead.

"How could she?" he thought, watching lines open on his belly, on his cheek.

Steam began to obscure his reflected image, and when he disappeared completely he turned away with the intention of washing himself clean.

# CHAPTER THIRTY-NINE

GUTTRIDGE LOOKED LIKE A different man when they led him away from the lake house in handcuffs. He'd shaved off his thick beard and lost about twenty pounds. But Pete thought his eyes were especially different. They met the camera only once, by accident, and what they revealed was a man lost to the world. They didn't show his wife or children on camera, but she was quoted as saying, "It was wrong, what he did. I knew it was wrong, but he's still my husband."

Alholowicz made a statement to the press; his partner didn't appear. He talked about having received credible evidence regarding a conspiracy to implicate zombies in a number of crimes, but he didn't say what crimes and he didn't reveal either his sources or who the zombies suspects were. He said that they were still on the lookout for other conspirators—his word.

When asked about specific incidents, such as the grave desecrations in Winford Cemetery, he replied that they had testimony from a participant that Guttridge was involved, and that no undead Americans were thought to have participated in the crimes. He had to pause for a moment when a reporter asked him what, specifically, Guttridge and the other "conspirators" would be charged with.

"Vandalism and grave desecration can both carry a substantial punishment," he said after a moment. "As well as a number of other infractions that the courts will have to decide upon with regards to the conspiracy against the undead. Kidnapping is a possibility, too."

Pete reached for his lemonade, halting as a ragged fissure opened up on his wrist, zippering across to reveal viscous oily fluid and gray-black flesh. His whole arm was shaking as he brought the glass to his lips.

He'd missed the question, but Alholowicz was saying something about it being illegal to beat your dog or murder an illegal immigrant. He refused to comment on the follow-up question, which was about Tommy Williams and his efforts in the nation's capital to call attention to what the reporter called "the plight of differently biotic Americans."

"So are you saying that we have nothing to fear from the undead population?"

Alholowicz shook his head. "Since forming the Undead Crimes Task Force a few months ago, we have gathered no evidence that zombies have been involved in any violent crimes, except as victims."

"That being said, do you believe that zombies represent a threat to our society?"

"I believe that zombies are just like us. Just like our children," he said. "Except that they are dead."

Pete watched as another wound opened above the crook of his elbow, the skin separating to reveal a slab of muscle the color of an uncooked chicken breast.

The questions devolved from there, with Alholowicz repeatedly informing the public that he was neither a medical doctor nor a politician. There was no mention of Karen. There was no mention of the theft of her body, and there was no mention of the role Pete played in any of it.

The coverage switched to Washington, where a reporter was conducting a man-in-the-street type interview with a young girl. A young zombie girl.

"How do I . . . feel . . . about . . . his arrest?" she said. "Vindicated, I . . . guess. Vindicated. We're here in . . . Washington . . . to show . . . the nation . . . that we can be . . . productive . . . members of . . . society. We're here . . . to ask for . . . a chance."

His cell phone rang. Pete fished it out of his pocket with a hand that was now unscarred, although the skin all around was the pale, blue-tinted skin of the undead.

"Peter," the Reverend said. "How are you, my boy?"

Pete swallowed. He felt as if he couldn't breathe, as if the holes had opened up again in his lungs, the lines across his throat.

"I'm . . . I'm fine. I did what you told me . . . to do."

"Have you seen the news?"

"I was just . . . watching it now."

He heard the Reverend chuckle.

"I think the dead will soon be up from the underground, if you will forgive my pun."

"I'm sorry, sir. If I hadn't . . ."

The Reverend cut him off. "Nonsense, my boy. Don't waste time with recrimination. You may have accelerated our time-table in an unforeseen manner, but all is well." He continued after a slight pause. "When the dead are out of hiding, they're easier to find."

"But Duke . . ."

"Duke was well aware of the risks. Don't worry about Mr. Davidson. He will be well taken care of."

Pete licked his dry lips. He worked to force air through his throat. "Can I come back now, sir?" he said. "I'd really like to come back."

"Not yet, my son," was the reply. Pete's heart sank to his shoes. "We've got another plan to try, now that Mr. Davidson has been removed from the board. He sends his regards, by the way. And bears you no ill will. You did what needed doing. There was no sense in everyone going to jail."

"Sir, I'd like to come back. I'm . . . I'm really not dealing with this very well."

"Take heart, Peter," the Reverend said, soothingly. "You can't come here. But would you feel any better if I said I was coming to join you?"

Pete felt his adrenaline returning, and a flush of excitement touched his heart. He knew that he was supposed to beat back the overly positive emotions as well as the negative ones, but he didn't. He'd felt so drained over the past few weeks, the Reverend's words were like a balm on his soul.

"Really? You're really going to come to Oakvale?"

"We have work to do, my son," he said. "The Lord's work."

Pete closed his eyes, muttering a brief prayer of thanks. When he opened them, Williams was on camera, surrounded by the living and the dead. Some had signs demanding equal rights for zombies; most were smiling. Tommy wore a more serious expression, and was saying something about Prop 77. Pete turned down the volume of the set, even though Tommy's words were not touching him.

"Tell me what I should do," he whispered.

# CHAPTER FORTY

NEITHER ADAM NOR PHOEBE so much as batted an eyelash when I told them I was gay. I don't know why their acceptance surprised me so much; I'd kissed Phoebe, after all, so if anyone had a clue, it would have been her. And let's face it, Adam would have to try really, really hard to bat an eyelash.

No, it was the secret about what I was trying to do while passing as a beating heart that upset them. And who could blame them?

But my friends stood by me. They stood by me and they are with me still, even though I am going far away.

When I died the first time, I was so sick, my sky had fallen. I couldn't see any way out but the one I took. I was bad and sad for a long time even before I watched Monica walking away, hand in hand with some boy. It felt like I'd already died, so when I went ahead and took the pills and drifted away, it was easy.

What I did in the prison wasn't like that at all. I wanted to live; I wanted to be alive. I wanted to come back all the way and feel everything again—the joys, the pain. I wanted to be able to taste, really taste strawberries, and feel silk against my skin, and smell the forest after it rains.

Really, I don't think that I ever felt so alive as when I was fighting for the things I believed in, as when I could give people like Colette and Melissa and Jacinta and Kevin and Mal and all of my dead friends a little hope. As when I tried to expose the crimes of Pete Martinsburg and his One Life cronies.

As when I helped my trad friends become a little more grateful for their own lives. I think I did that. I think the second time around I made the world just a little bit of a better place. Maybe that was my purpose in coming back, if Tommy's mother is right and we really are here for a purpose. It's the life that matters, so much more so than the death.

I went to see Phoebe at her house before I left.

"Hi," I said when she opened the door. Mmmm, coffee. The warm smell permeated Phoebe's kitchen. "Still mad at me?"

"What?" she said, holding the door open for me to come in. "For risking your life, you mean? With the lunatic that killed my boyfriend?"

"Um, yeah," I said. Maybe visiting her wasn't such a great idea after all.

"You tried to warn me, I guess," she said after a long pause, "that he was going to hurt me. But I think you cut it pretty close."

I nodded.

She was wearing one of her long flowy skirts today, with a soft gray sweater. She brushed her hair out of her brilliant green eyes, and I had to turn away.

"Phoebe," I said, looking at the floor. Phoebe was back to wearing boots. "I couldn't . . . live . . . if something had happened to you."

I glanced up at her through strands of hair that were back to being ultra-light blond. Phoebe couldn't look at me, either.

"Karen . . ."

"I know," I said. "I'm sorry."

We spent a few minutes listening to the bass-heavy goth-punk music coming from the living room, until Phoebe broke the stretching silence.

"I am mad at you, Karen," she said. "But not because of the risk. I'm mad because you didn't let me know. I'm mad because you wouldn't let me help you."

"I know. But I just couldn't, Phoebe." We'd stopped inspecting the floor. "Adam never would have allowed it."

"So we wouldn't have told him. You think I tell Adam everything?"

We looked at each other, both of us realizing at the same time what she'd just said. We cracked up.

"What's so funny?" a voice said from the other room. Margi came into the room, her eyes going wide when she saw me.

"Oh hi, Karen," Normally very huggy, it was clear she didn't know how to react to me. "I thought you were Adam."

"Yeah, I get that a lot," I said. She didn't even smile as she folded her arms across her chest.

"I didn't want to come out here in case he and Pheeble were, you know, kissing."

"Margi!"

"Sorry," Margi said, clearly not.

"Doesn't Karen look great, Margi?" Phoebe said, probably trying to distract me from Margi's weirdness. "Look at her. She's healing."

"Yes, I am. Even the really nasty cuts are mostly gone now."

"It's amazing, Karen," Phoebe said. "You should go to the Hunter Foundation so they can figure it out. Imagine if all zombies could heal like that?"

I thought of Tayshawn, whose reward for helping me was a compound fracture. I thought of Melissa.

"I will, Phoebe," I told her. "But first I've got to go back home for a while. Back to Iowa. I need to talk to Monica."

"Monica," she said. "Is she . . ."

Her voice trailed off. It was kind of cute.

"She is."

"Well, hurry back. You've got a gift, you know."

"What's it like?" Margi said from the doorway. She was peering at me intently.

"What's what like? Healing?"

"No," she said. "Being gay."

Phoebe's mouth dropped open a little before she turned from Margi to look at me.

"What?" Margi said. "Did I say something wrong?"

Then we were both cracking up again.

The hardest part was saying good-bye to Kaitlyn. Tiny hands can grip really tightly if letting go might mean forever. I don't know how my parents handled my prison escapade with her, but it was clear it had made an impact.

"I'll be back, sweetie," I whispered to her. "I'll be back."

And I thought I would be. Not everything goes the way I expect it to, though—obviously!

"Take me," she said. "Take me."

My tear ducts are working again. But being able to cry makes me happy. I can taste and I can smell and I can feel my skin. It all makes me happy.

"I can't, sweetie. But I promise I won't be gone long this time."

My wounds—all of the visible ones, anyway—were gone. As worried as I was about everyone, the one I worried the most about was Tak. I was sorry that he wouldn't let me kiss him good-bye when Phoebe brought me home that day. He let me hug him, and maybe, just maybe, I felt his lips brush my cheek as we embraced. We told each other to be careful, and then he went away.

My return home was just as tearful. My mother—when my mother saw me, she shrieked. I thought the worst, but then her arms were around me, and my father's, and they both told me that they loved me and that they never wanted to lose me again. Which made it very, very hard when I told them that they needed to let me go away.

I sat down with my parents and explained to them what I wanted to do. I told them why. I told them things they didn't know before, and this time my mother didn't slap me—she sat with me and held my hand, tears in her eyes. I told them I needed to see you and apologize, because if I didn't tell you how sorry I was, I'd live out the rest of my days not as a zombie but a ghost. A ghost haunting myself. I told them that my atonement would never be complete unless I could look you in the eye and tell you how sorry I was.

They listened, and when I was finished they agreed completely. Dad even offered to go with me, but of course I told him that I needed to do this alone. I asked if I could take the car, and they did not hesitate in their answer, which was yes. I left that evening.

I wonder how you've changed. I died at sixteen and I thought that meant that I'd be sixteen forever, but the way my body is changing I can't say that for certain. The scars are all healed, even the one on my shoulder that I've had since I was a kid. A living kid. My skin is smooth and white. My eyes still look like diamonds, although Tak swears they were blue when he found me in the ambulance. Who knows what they'll look like when I see you again?

You'll be eighteen now. Probably you've applied to colleges; probably you've gone to at least one prom. Maybe you're seeing someone. Maybe you're seeing another girl.

When we were younger we used to talk about everything we would do together in the distant, far-flung future. You'd wanted to go to school somewhere on the East Coast, to Boston or New York, and I could picture you there, a wild, primal girl in khaki shorts and earth-toned tops, walking the concrete paths in your sandaled feet. I'd tell you, without thinking about what I was saying, that New York would be great. Maybe I could model there, maybe I could waitress, maybe I could act. I wanted to follow you, wherever you went, and romantic notions of a possible life together—because such things were possible in the big city, weren't they?—filled my head when we talked about life after high school. After what happened at Wild Thingz! I'll probably never be able to get a job again. I was getting sick of all the black and the icon-laden T-shirts, anyway. All snakes and skulls.

Maybe I'll open my own store, something that caters to undead Americans who don't want to look like mall goths; something upscale. "Cerements," I'll call it.

You'll still be beautiful, of course. Your skin will still be a warm amber hue, and your smile will still light up a room, or even a darkening forest.

I have butterflies in my stomach thinking about it.

Do friends often fall in love? I know it happens with girls and boys, like Phoebe and Adam. I have to wonder if there's as much pain when it happens for them, if there is as much the sense of one thing ending before another can begin.

I wasn't even out of Connecticut when I heard a clip of

Tommy Williams giving a speech, his voice clear and confident and strong. There was iron in his voice.

*"Today . . . marks the beginning . . . of a new era . . . for the differently biotic . . ."*

Smiling, I listened to his voice for a few minutes before switching the station. I wanted music, not words.

I drove the long way around the city I used to dream about, picturing us cooking together in some one-room flat. I wasn't in a rush. I had hundreds of miles to go, but I don't sleep and I don't get tired, even if I seem a little more "human" with each passing day. My reflexes and reaction times are actually pretty good, my vision twenty-twenty. And once I got out of the Northeast I could pretty much point my car west and go in a straight line, and eventually I'd get to you. You'd think that I'd already had enough time to myself to last a lifetime—several lifetimes, actually—but my thoughts were new and different as I drove across the country. Maybe it was the motion—forward progress—that fired once-dead synapses in my brain. So much of zombie "life" is stasis.

I tried to envision our reunion. I pictured it as one of warm tears and a warmer embrace, as something more than a fleeting moment in time.

Dad's car was excellent on gas, and I tried to visit a station every time the needle dipped below a third of a tank. I stopped at a highway rest stop in Maryland, and when I operated the pump no one noticed me except for boys and girls my own age and lonely truck drivers. I had a smile for everyone; I could still blend, mostly. I was dressed, for me, very plainly. Jeans, sneakers, a puffy blue coat with a matching scarf and hat. But my hair was blonder than blond again, and I didn't get my contacts replaced. Another state or so and I wouldn't need the cold weather gear any more, not even to maintain my disguise. Spring was making its way east as I traveled west.

Maybe I'd spend cherry blossom season with Tommy, I thought. If you had no forgiveness in your heart for me—and I had no right to expect that you would—then maybe I could offer penance through public service; by working to make the world a better place for my people. Or maybe I could just drive back to Oakvale, trying to pretend that I was chasing the winter away.

What if there was no embrace? What if all I found was the hatred due me?

There was only one close call in my entire journey. There was a lonely service station somewhere in the Midwest where I had to show a frisky biker just how dead I was. There were other, less risky ways to get out of the situation, I suppose, but if there is anything that my second life—and third, if you are counting! I'm like a cat!—has taught me is that I am sick of pretending to be something and someone I am not.

Either way, my tactic worked, and I guessed correctly that Mr. Hawg Wyld would not be seeking the assistance of the local authorities with regard to the willowy blond girl who'd frightened him so.

I should start a "scared straight" program, ha ha.

I arrived in the town where we'd grown up, to the light of a proverbial rosy-fingered dawn. I was close to you, very close. I realized this and I very nearly turned the car around and drove back.

The blue fog is never going to go away entirely. And now that I'm coming back, now that I've passed through death and zombiehood and started to become, well, something else entirely, maybe it will come back stronger than ever before, just like my body. That's just something that me, and whoever is around me, is going to have to deal with. I hope it's you.

The radio told me that today is Friday. I drove to the school where you'd be, and wondered how my death had changed you. Did you become sad and withdrawn? Or was there a certain feeling of relief, because now you could hide if you wanted? You could keep dating the boys you dated, and our kiss and what it represented could be a short forgotten footnote in the journal of your life. Maybe coming here was a mistake.

I could feel the edges of my consciousness growing hazy as I left the schoolyard. I drove to the lake where we'd shared our first and only kiss, but I didn't go into the woods surrounding it. We'd been through there, emerging from darkness once, and I didn't think I was ready to go back there alone. I then drove to my old house, where I died. An unfamiliar car was parked in the driveway, and there was a young sapling planted in the front yard, surrounded by last year's faded cedar mulch. I could picture my ghost looking down from the bathroom window at the sapling and smiling, waiting patiently for the new leaves to bud. Then I drove to the cemetery where I was to have been buried, and I walked along the white gravel paths searching for a stone that bore my name. Not finding one, I got back in the car. My hands were shaking, so I held tightly to the wheel. Coming back to life isn't an easy thing to do.

I drove away and thought I was heading back toward the highway, but instead the road led to your door.

I pulled into your driveway and got out of the car. Your mother wasn't home. She'd be at work, I realized, and the thought of you each coming home to an empty house made me feel sad. There was a swing on your porch, but I sat on the steps instead. I leaned against the newel and closed my eyes.

I didn't open them again until I heard the shrieking squeal of the brakes as your bus rolled to a stop at the edge of your lawn. The first thing I saw upon waking was you, stepping off the bus.

You were a little thinner than when I saw you last, and yes, maybe a little paler, too. Your dark hair was cut in a shorter, unfamiliar style, and I didn't recognize your clothes.

But you were still beautiful. Still *are* beautiful.

You looked back over your shoulder as the bus pulled away, and I thought maybe it was because you realized, too late, that you wanted it to take you away from me. You blinked, rapidly, but the mirage that I must have seemed like did not go away.

"Karen?" you said, my name a question in your mouth. I nodded and tried to speak but found that I couldn't, and I was blinking, too, because of my tears. I was frozen. It was like being in the lake; it was like being surrounded by the blue fog. I was so frightened.

"It's me," I said, my voice hitching. "Nikki, it's me."

And then you dropped your things—your coat, your

backpack, a book—all scattered, and you ran to me and put your arms around me, and I could smell your hair and feel the warmth of your cheek against mine, and I could taste my own tears. You hugged me and the fog dissipated, the ice melted, I could move again. You were laughing. You were laughing and you were crying and you kissed my cheek.

You kissed my cheek.

"Oh, Karen," you said. "I'm sorry. I'm so sorry, so sorry, so sorry." You kept saying the words, over and over.

*You* were sorry. That's what you said.

And I knew what you were saying. What you were really saying. I knew. All this time—even after what my father said, and Melissa, and Tak—all this time I never realized that others might feel like they had things to atone for, too.

"Sshhh," I said. "Ssshh." I realized that you were making the same soft sound against my ear.

And then my heart began beating anew.

**DANIEL WATERS** (www.danielwaters.com) is the author of *Generation Dead* and *Kiss of Life*. He lives with his family in Connecticut. Visit him online—and find Karen—at www.mysocalledundeath.com.

If you enjoyed *Passing Strange* then you might like
to see how it started with *Generation Dead*.

PHOEBE AND HER FRIENDS HELD THEIR
breath as the dead girl in the plaid skirt walked
past their table in the lunchroom. Her motion
kicked up a cool trailing breeze that seemed to
settle on the skin and catch in their hair. As they watched her
go by, Phoebe could almost tell what everyone was thinking.
Everyone, that is, except for the dead girl.

Across from her, Margi shook her head, her silver teardrop
earrings dancing among the bright pink spikes of her hair.
"Even I don't wear skirts that short," she said before sipping her
milk.

"Thank God for that," Adam said from two seats away.

Phoebe risked a glance back at the girl and her long, bluish-
white legs. Fluorescent lights were kind to the dead, making
them look like they had been carved from veinless blocks of
pure white marble. The girl went to the farthest table and sat

down alone, and without any food, the way the dead always did during lunch.

Sometimes Phoebe used to joke that she possessed psychic powers. Not useful ones like being able to tell when small children have fallen into wells or anything; more like being able to foresee what her mother was making for dinner or how many bangles Margi was going to wear on her arms that day. She thought her "powers," if that's what they were, were more tele*pathetic* than telepathic.

Phoebe knew as soon as she saw her that the dead girl in the short skirt would get Margi rolling on a whole host of zombie-related topics, none of which she really wanted to discuss.

"I heard that Tommy Williams's eye fell out in homeroom," Margi said, on cue. "I heard that he sneezed or something, and there it went, *splat*, on his desk."

Phoebe swallowed and placed her egg salad sandwich back atop the wax paper wrapping it came in.

"Zombies don't sneeze," Adam said around a mouthful of meatball sub. "Zombies don't breathe, so they can't sneeze."

The girls lowered their heads and looked around to see who was in earshot of Adam's booming voice. *Zombie* was a word you just didn't say in public anymore, even if you were the center on the football team.

Air hissed through Margi's teeth. "You aren't supposed to call them zombies, Adam."

He shrugged his massive shoulders. "Zombies, dead heads, corpsicles. What's the difference? They don't care. They don't have feelings to hurt."

Phoebe wondered if Tommy Williams and the girl in the plaid skirt really didn't have any feelings. The scientists weren't clear on that point yet.

She tried to imagine how she would feel losing an eye, especially losing an eye in public. And in homeroom, no less.

"You could be expelled for saying things like that, Adam," Margi was saying. "You know you're supposed to call them *living impaired*."

Adam snorted, his mouth full of milk. Ten years ago a milk snort would have been the height of biological grotesquerie at Oakvale High. Today it seemed kind of lame next to losing an eye in homeroom.

"Living impaired," Adam commented after recovering. "I think you two are living impaired. They're just dead."

He stood up, his huge body casting a long shadow over their uneaten lunches, and brought his empty tray to the conveyor system that took all of the dishes and garbage away. Phoebe just looked at her beautiful egg salad sandwich and wished that she had any desire left to eat it.

Phoebe's locker popped open on her third try. She figured that her inability to remember the three-digit combination did not bode well for her impending algebra class, which was always right after lunch. Her stomach rumbled, and she tried to tell herself that the spikes of hunger would give her mind an alert sharpness, like a lynx in winter between successful hunts.

Yeah right, she thought.

Tommy Williams was in her algebra class.

The door to her locker shook with a metallic vibrating sound. Inside were pictures of bands like the Creeps, the Killdeaths, Seraphim Shade, the Rosedales, Slipknot, and the Misfits; bands that dressed like the living dead before there were any dead actually living. There was a picture of her, Margi, and Colette in happier times, all gothed up in black fabrics, eyeliner, and boots outside the Cineplex in Winford, ready to be first in line for the premier of some vitally important horror movie she couldn't even remember. Phoebe, the tallest, was in the middle, her long black hair hiding one side of her naturally pale face, and her visible eye closed as she laughed at whatever vulgar comment Margi had just made. Colette had done her eyes like an Egyptian princess, with a single thick line of makeup at each corner. Colette and Margi were also laughing.

There was also a picture of her dog, Gargoyle. Gar was a Welsh terrier and not half as frightening as his name would suggest.

A mirror was on the door opposite the shelf where Phoebe's algebra book lay. On her mouth was a streak of smeared violet lipstick. Her long hair, normally jet-black, shiny, spiky, and tousled, now just looked dull, flat, and messy.

She thought she looked scared.

The lipstick smear was the only flaw that seemed fixable, so she rubbed it away before walking toward Mrs. Rodriguez's class down at the end of the hallway. She arrived there the same time as Tommy Williams, whose eyes, she was relieved to see, were still fixed within their sockets. He gazed at her with the blank stare of the living impaired.

Phoebe felt like cold feathers were dancing along her spine. The stare was bottomless. It made her think that she could fall forever into his eyes, or that he could see through to the very heart of her. Could he see her wondering if his eye had popped out in homeroom?

Tommy motioned for her to precede him into the room.

She held her breath as he lifted his arm, realizing it only because another one of her essential life functions had ceased, namely her heartbeat. She smiled at him. It was a reflex; courtesy was not very common in the halls of Oakvale High. She stepped into the room, and as she did, she was almost certain that Tommy was trying to smile back at her. Wasn't there a faint upturn of the lips at one corner of his mouth, or the briefest flash of light in the flat undead eyes?

She took her seat, breathing again, heart beating again. Not only beating but beating *fast*.

She didn't know much about Tommy Williams. She knew that he'd come to Oakvale High last May, just a few weeks before school had let out. Oakvale was starting to get a reputation for having a good living impaired program, good enough that families with living impaired kids were moving to Oakvale from the surrounding area. Phoebe's father had pointed out an article in the *Winford Bulletin* that said Oakvale High's living impaired population had doubled in a year. There were at least seven in her class of about a hundred and twenty.

Algebra was not a subject that Phoebe struggled with; she usually completed the next day's assignment while Mrs.

Rodriguez started to probe for answers among her slower, struggling classmates. Algebra was a class that she could drift in and out of in the way music from a car passing will drift into an open bedroom window.

She wondered how Tommy Williams had died . . .